From SUGAR to SHIFTERS

H. ELIZABETH DUNN

ISBN 978-1-956001-03-7 (paperback)
ISBN 978-1-956001-04-4 (eBook)

Printed in the United States of America

CONTENTS

ACKNOWLEDGMENTS

To Darcy, my beautiful, talented daughter; thank you for your encouragement and honesty. Victor, Elisheva and Kathy; you have had the hardest job of anybody in my life. You have possessed the dogged determination to be my friends. Through my flailing about in life and the journey of discovery that led me to accepting my worth in this world. I may have survived without you, but I couldn't have thrived.

Jeremy Spitler who said once that I made it okay to say things like, 'fuckity, fuck, fuck, fuck'. I have never forgotten that and I never fail to smile when I remember it and the circumstances. One of the best classes ever.

Wendy, for just being simply, unabashedly, wonderfully you.

Donna, Paul, Sandy, Diana of the North, Diana of the South, Michael, Jasper, Teagan, Angela, Jeren, Vincent, Kenn, Patricia, Kathy and all of the Lumen's Gaters, Sheya practitioners and Spiralers that have been privy to the bare bones work of self transformation I have done over the years, I thank you.

CHAPTER ONE

We Use DHL

I had never wanted to visit Las Vegas. I would have said "You couldn't pay me to go there," but here I was, and I was being paid.

Really well.

Regardless of how much this job was enhancing my retirement fund, the cost may have become too high.

The one thing I was happy about? Staying off of the strip.

Of course, that meant I would be in the sleaziest, most dangerous parts of the city and its outskirts. Out there, things trying to kill you were always straightforward. I appreciated that.

I could blend with the "mink and manure" crowd and had done so on many occasions. I could ride well, and hunt seat equitation was my favorite event. Taking jumps while making it look effortless was a challenge I enjoyed. And, after a long day of riding, heading to the clubhouse with the local rich and famous was my least favorite part. They could have you on the dance floor one minute taking in the strains of Mozart and stab you in the back with a shrimp fork the next.

Besides, fighting for your life in a four-thousand-dollar gown and three-inch heels is a real bitch.

On this particular job, I had, thus far, been in under lit seedy bars that I could smell a block away, dark alleys, same smell, and was currently at an abandoned house. Different smell, still unpleasant.

It was a shack at this point. I'm sure it had been a house at one time, but now what was left of the paint was peeled and chipped. The wood that lay open to the heat and sun was rotting in too many places to count.

The thin planks that served to deter unwelcome guests, covering the mostly glassless windows and ineffectual doors, hadn't really been doing its job.

I could scent the signs of occupation, and they had been recent.

Upon closer inspection, it was still boarded up, for the most part. That seemed odd.

Mold, mildew, and rot were the underlying notes to the fragrance that was this structure. The top notes included decomposition, death, human waste, urine, and stuff that would cling to my boots even after I cleaned them with disinfectant and worked magic through them for a half an hour.

Black leather trench coat firmly in place and my Kawasaki out of sight, I headed toward the side door.

Yeah, yeah. Black leather, ass-kicking boots, and a motorcycle. How much more cliché could a girl get?

Well, how about the fact that I hunt and kill vampires. Not all of them, mind you. Just the ones that the Clan Masters had deemed unstable and dangerous. There are rules and a contract and agreements and payment— payment being my favorite part.

The pay was great—if you survived. So far, so good. I hoped.

I rarely dressed in my leathers unless I was riding my bike or thought that things could go badly. Leathers protected against more than just road rash.

My partner, Marc, had disappeared three days ago, tracking a nest of unsupervised fairly young vampires that decided to stop following the rules, when all communication from him simply ended.

It scared the hell out of me. We were bound to each other through blood and sex.

It had been intentional.

Yes, that kind of shit can happen accidentally, and it rarely works out well. We cared about each other, treasured our relationship, our friendship, but we weren't mated and hadn't claim each other in a soul-deep and permanent way.

I had no illusions that as a half-vampire mutt, I would never be mated.

The upside to the binding was knowing what each other was feeling, and when we had to split up, fear was a great indicator that the other one was in trouble without having to scream. Screaming tends to attract more than help.

The sex was way more intense. Enough said.

The best part of being bound was a built-in GPS function. We could feel each others location, find each other and come running. The binding couldn't be broken except with death, and Marc wasn't dead.

I knew it; that I could feel.

The GPS function had somehow been muted. I couldn't feel his location, and that low hum of his presence in the background of my heart was gone.

I had to track his movements the old-fashioned way.

Legwork and intimidation.

At nearly six foot tall and built to kill things, I could intimidate most creatures with an impassive stare or a shift of my weight from one hip to another. Yes, I cleaned up nicely and could interact in polite society, but this was my favorite way to work.

I carried nearly twelve pounds of silver-bladed items on me at all times. A few were always placed to show. Sort of like a lowlife shifting his jacket so you can see the butt of his weapon without actually drawing it.

I was not a lowlife, but I could do a handy impression of one when necessary. This had been very necessary.

Intimidation and a silver flash or two got me to the last place Marc was before he disappeared. I left my riding gloves on as I tore the boards from the structure. Tetanus wasn't a concern, but this place was likely to be something I didn't want to put my bare hands on.

I thought it strange that the boards were in place. They had been put in place recently. The nail heads were still glistening, no signs of weathering. If I'd had any sense, I would have stopped right there.

Marc was in charge of having sense. And he negotiated the contracts and worked all of the technical stuff in the business. So, without his intelligent input, I went in anyway.

I had to find him.

The side door was still surprisingly attached at the hinges and locked.

Seemed like a waste.

I pulled power from the full moon overhead and channeled it through my body, through my hands and melted the lock. I didn't know why my gloves didn't melt in the process. I was just glad they didn't. Saved on clothing expenses.

The door swung in on rusted hinges, and the full blast of the stench that was this place hit me full in the nose.

I successfully managed to keep my dinner down and slowly entered the darkened interior of the shack.

Half-vampire that I was, the lack of light didn't create any problems for me. The scene looked like being in the shade on a cloudy day. I wasn't as strong as a full-blooded vampire or as fast. My vision and sense of smell was less as well. I could heal fairly quickly, even from a mortal wound. I found that out firsthand. It still hurt like a bitch.

I had no real problem with being in direct sunshine. My heart beat, I breathed, and I could and did eat human food. But, if I were injured, badly injured, tapping a vein could save my life. I had fangs on demand, but I had to concentrate to get them to drop into place.

As a vampire, I didn't rate; but what I lacked, I made up for in magic. Mom was a witch, and she rocked it like nobody's business.

I missed her. I missed the crazy aunts who helped raise me too.

Dad? He was a vamp. Never met him; don't care to.

So this house smelled like four dead vampires, two dead humans, three days of decay, two weres, a shifter, and Marc. All of the scents were old, except the shifter. The testosterone permeated the old Sheetrock. He had been, gone, and returned recently, very recently. I wondered if he boarded the place up.

As I made my way into the living room, I decided that it had been the dying room. The humans had likely been killed by the vamps, hence the termination order. The dead vamps were there and doing what the remains of dead, and very young vampires do best, turn to goo, and smell bad. The older ones turn to dust fairly quickly; makes cleaning up so much easier.

No Shop-Vac in the world could manage this mess.

No signs of the weres or shifter, but I spotted Marc's kit against the far wall. Lucky me, it was on the other side of the goo. My boots were getting a workout tonight.

The shack was fairly open. I came in through the side door, into the kitchen, which opened into the living room. An opening in the far wall signaled the way to a bathroom and a bedroom or two.

I spotted the front door and picture window in the front as well and a sliding glass door to the backyard. Everything was boarded up. It felt relatively secure. I could get out quickly, and anything trying to get in would make noise.

I was safe enough for now, I figured.

The floor still felt solid enough under my boots, but the squish of the carpet being more decomposing organic matter than flooring was very clear and very nasty.

Gross. Didn't even begin to cover this.

The kit usually consisted of swabs, vials, tissue sampling materials, tubes, a camera, and a prepaid, insulated, reinforced shipping box.

We used DHL.

The kit was open. Samples had been collected and were gone along with the camera. The box was still there along with the trashed remaining contents and the case it came in.

So Marc had taken out the vamps, collected the specimens, and maybe he took the photos, maybe not. Marc was nothing if not methodical.

Line up the bodies. Take the pics with identifying markers. Take and mark the samples. Photograph the vampires. Pack everything up and dispatch the vampires. Get paid.

Silver to the heart paralyzes them. Removing the head makes them forever dead. Their heads were no longer attached to the rest of the bodies. Well, actually, the skulls were well away from the lake of goo that had been the bodies.

I knew Marc's rhythms. He never varied.

He was the same in bed. That was one reason we would never claim each other as mates. We had a connection, and we had chosen to perform the binding, but we weren't each others destined mates; we knew it. We were comfortable, not passionate.

The thought made me a little sad at times.

So I knew he had been interrupted after he had collected his samples.

I stood and closed my eyes, focusing first on sound. Marc had been taken unaware. There is little that could sneak up on a vampire, so I listened and heard nothing.

I breathed in deeply and almost gagged. Marc was better at parsing scents than me. I worked on and was getting better with his direction. I scented nothing more than what I had identified when I first came in.

I moved closer to the wall. Marc's scent was attached to it. He had hit the wall at the point of the dent in the remaining plaster and cracked the two-by-four stud. He had hit hard.

It wasn't enough to kill him. I knew he wasn't dead. He couldn't be.

My heart skipped a beat. I couldn't lose him.

The scents were were-feline. The shifter, who knew? I couldn't tell. Had the were-feline taken Marc, or the shifter?

Weres and shifters were different, and those differences in scent were subtle, but I could tell.

Were-creatures were the product of a virus. They could be born, having acquired the virus through a parent or through a bite. The survivability from a bite was three in ten. The offspring's chances of surviving into adulthood was fifty-fifty if both parents were weres and much better if the breeding was mixed. Human females tended to carry a were to term, so the were community was big on breeding with human females. They had their rules and regulations around that, and they had their enforcers. I was glad for that. I didn't want to go after a law-Breaking were-anything.

Ever.

Shifters were born to shifters. Nobody knew where the first ones came from, and nobody fucked with them.

They were arrogant, obnoxious, rude, and more dangerous than not on any given day.

Would any of these guys interfere with a legitimate kill? A vampire hunter hunting his own?

It didn't make sense.

Marc was really good at hunting. I had met him after stumbling into one of his jobs and got caught up in drama of it all. He kept me alive, taught me things I hadn't known about vampires, and saw potential in me that I hadn't seen in myself.

Patience of Job. That was five years ago.

It was then I realized that I had been standing there entirely too long, lost in the scents around me and my own thoughts, trying to put things together.

Marc had always been there to bring me back to the scene when we needed to be done.

I realized that without him, I was a hazard to myself and couldn't be afforded that luxury. It could make me dead really quick.

I relied on Marc so much. Maybe too much. He had been there for years. I could count on him, and now he was gone.

No! Christ, no.

He was missing. I would find him. I had to.

A scent rose on the desert breeze that worked its way between the gaps in the boarded up windows.

It should have been a welcome relief from the death that would cling to my clothing after I left, but the wind brought to my nose a blend of man and animal.

A shifter, and the scent was familiar. He had been here. I could scent the testosterone through the death and decomposing rot around me.

My sense of smell was going to be shot for hours after this.

I could only scent one out there and couldn't place the animal. Right now, it didn't matter. I had bigger problems at hand.

I'm pretty sure that I had decided to sneak out one of the front windows to avoid the shifter when the slender tendrils of dark magic touched my senses.

It was also touching my boots.

Something else I'd have to clean off of them when I got out of here.

The magic writhed like snakes on the putrid flooring, reaching out looking for a foothold to do its worst.

I pulled power from the moon; it was bright and just past full overhead. It didn't matter that I couldn't see Her directly. I knew She was there, and She knew me. We were old and good friends.

I colored the moon's power with my will for protection. The living carpet of dark magic retreated without disappearing. I held it at bay, but barely. Whomever laid this was really talented and powerful and definitely not one of the good guys.

It was infection magic designed to go after vampires, specifically, but it would fuck with anything it could use as a host.

This magic could bend the infected persons will to the originator's.

Had that happened to Marc? Was he somebody's plaything? A vampire under the control of another was a dangerous thing, and…

Couldn't think that way.

Needed to focus on the shit around me that would love to infect me.

It needed to die.

Now was good for me.

Beneath the blatant controlling aspect of this crap was a subtle set of instructions. Specifically, where the infected needed to go after the infection set in. Beneath that was the caster's signature. I didn't recognize it, but if I found them, I'd know it. This magic had also been on sleep mode, waiting for somebody to wake it up. That would be me. Good thing I'd been paying attention, or I might have been the next victim.

If Marc had been with me, it never would have gotten this close.

Getting the location out of this mass of dark magic wasn't going to happen, not this time. It was too much and too big for me to control for the length of time it would take to get that detail out of it.

The house was going to come down during this process. Without a Shop-Vac, this was the only way to destroy the evidence of what had happened. Humans didn't need proof of unnatural or supernatural existences. They could hope and fear and pretend, but they didn't need to know.

I just hoped I wouldn't be in the structure when it came down.

The dark magic swirled, surged, and pushed at me, testing my strength and looking for a way at me.

Fuckers.

I wasn't even going to get a sample for later. Damn.

So the only way out of this mess was to burn out the magic with magic, setting the building on fire at the same time as I held it in containment and then escape before the structure collapsed on me and land right in front of a shifter.

I was not liking this one bit.

Letting the magic loose wasn't an option. I didn't want to die in here, so I would take my chances with the shifter who knew I was in here because he was in the area I had parked my bike.

If he scratched it, I'd…

Shifters were bigger, stronger, faster, and likely meaner than I could ever be. I'd get pissy and leave. That's what I'd do—teach him to tangle with a mongrel with an attitude.

A head-to-head fight with a shifter would only lead to bloodshed, and unfortunately, the blood would be mine and mine alone.

I felt the oppressive thickening of darkness against my shields. I had not really anticipated that. This magic was altering to meet the challenge. Was it actively being controlled, or was it on autopilot? I couldn't tell.

It lashed out at my shields, and I felt them quiver.

Oh, hell no!

Okay, time to quit screwing around and wreck the joint.

I pulled hard on the moon and began the burn. The tricky part was containing the snakes of magic as my power began to decimate them.

They wanted to survive, and I couldn't let them.

The containment magic encased the house and slowly pushed and herded them to my kill zone. The dark purple flames sputtered and sparked as this seemingly endless carpet of writhing darkness was slowly consumed.

The stench of death and rot was quickly replaced with the smell of burning vampire goo.

I knew my sense of smell would be shot, but I really wanted it to go now. Burning house was the next scent. The work I did was usually fire based, so that was inevitable anyway.

This was yet another joke as vampire offspring. Fire could kill vampires as well as decapitation. My magic was decidedly borne of fire.

Did somebody plan this shit, or was it just a cosmic joke?

Whatever. I was effective in ways vamps weren't. I'd get this job done and find Marc.

I pulled the containment energy in tighter and tighter, forcing the infection magic to its death. I really needed to get this done and quickly before I was buried under the flaming remnants of the roof.

I would raze this structure to its foundation, but again, a big preference for not being inside.

The snakes writhed, looking for a weak spot, tumbling over each other, searching for a way out, a body to infect. Mine was probably looking really good to it.

The containment magic had finally consolidated in the living room. It shimmered gently and glowed sky blue, pushing and dragging the last of my victims into the deep purple heat of destruction.

It really was a lovely sight. It never ceased to amaze me how beautiful the magic was. The sparkling light blues, and the deep variegated purples seemed like living art. Unfortunately, the smell really overrode the visual displays.

The structure was nearly fully involved. My one escape route would be blocked in seconds, but the magic was nearly finished. If just one of those things got out, it might multiply. I wasn't sure, but I wasn't going to take any chances.

Blowing up the place wouldn't have worked either. It would have scattered them to the winds. This was the only way, and it sucked.

The smoke thickened and burned my eyes and my throat. A few more minutes, and I would be unconscious.

I wasn't going to rely on a shifter to drag my ass out of a burning building. My vision was shot, and I had knelt down. More of my coat would need cleaning now. I could feel my knee sink into the goo. The chaps were going to need a thorough cleaning too.

Shit!

I could feel the heat beginning to close in, and the important information regarding my environment was mostly by the intensifying heat, and what my magic could feel.

The floor would hold for a couple more minutes. The roof was about to collapse. I didn't want to have to jump through the boarded window, tuck and roll, come up blind, maybe deal with a shifter all while holding on to the remnants of the dark magic in my kill zone, but that seemed to be my only plan.

Nothing too complicated.

Yeah, right.

When I found Marc, I'd kick his ass, after I kissed him and fucked him senseless.

I took a hard grip on my magic. My enhanced speed made use of the few strides I could manage before hitting the flimsy boards. They shattered like glass with the impact. I hit the backyard, rolled into a crouching position, and held on to my magic for dear life.

The dark magic was in its death throes and rallying against me. I didn't think about the shifter that was likely watching everything from my bike.

At a safe distance.

Bastard.

I could feel the heat against my face. I was way too close, but I couldn't afford to move and risk losing the infection.

The sweat was trickling down my face and my back. The leather around me was beginning to cook. I was hoping to remain rare after this was over.

It was almost done.

My body was beginning to shake with the amount of moon energy that had been running through me. It always took its toll on me. I would need to eat and sleep after this.

Marc would fix something to eat while I got cleaned up. He'd shower and then hunt for himself. He'd lay with me in the yard as I recharged in the moonlight. Holding me. We'd talk about the case, the leads, what did and didn't go right. We would find our way to bed, make plans, make love…

Not tonight. Tonight, I fought alone. Tonight, I would heal alone, and I would sleep alone.

The last of the dark magic winked out.
I had won.
It felt empty.
Marc hadn't been there.

CHAPTER TWO

"The charges are set to go off in three... two..."

I dropped my magic, letting it crash unceremoniously around me. I muttered a word of thanks to the moon and rose to meet my next challenge.

Well, that's what I thought I was going to do. Except my legs were fighting the prospect of carrying my weight.

The battle I had waged and won sapped my strength and left me crouched on the ground. That's why working with a partner had bccn important to me.

I hoped I didn't look weak, just regrouping. A badass, leather-clad chic, who had just crushed some ugly magic, brought down a house, made an awesome exit, and was looking for something else to kill.

A bubble bath to get rid of the stink would be nice too, after a long, hot shower.

I could feel him at my back. Still at my bike.

"You might want to move a little further back from that," he called out smoothly. His voice was rough, low and did things to my sense of self-preservation. Like kick it up a notch.

Running is never a good idea in the presence of a predator. It kicks their instincts into overdrive, and they like the chase just as much as they like the kill.

Shifters were all alphas. It was just a matter of who out-alpha'd who. I had a feeling this guy was undisputed. I just hoped to keep it together and see another sunrise. And to find Marc.

My heart pounded, but I remained crouched for the couple of breaths it took to convince my legs to do their damn job so I could bluff my happy ass out of this.

I turned as I stood and faced the asshole who was leaning against my bike. His was parked right next to mine, blocking it in at a tree. But he just had to be leaning against mine. He needed to show me he was in charge, and I wouldn't leave until he let me.

Again. Asshole.

"Seriously," he started, "you are way too close." His whole body relaxed against the seat of my bike. His arms were crossed over his chest, and he casually checked his watch. "The charges will go off in three... two..."

I took that hint and ran.

"One."

The explosion was sizable and effectively would finish the job I started with nothing left to indicate that a structure once stood there except for a pipe remnant. The foundation itself would be gone.

I dove and rolled. I planned to come up on my feet, but the pain that tore through my side threw me back to the ground. If I was lucky, I'd been hit with debris, and maybe a couple ribs were busted, some bruising would happen, but I could blow it off.

I didn't seem to be having a whole lot of luck tonight.

The desert breeze caught me under the coat, and I could feel the cooling of my blood, and the catch of the coat on whatever had punctured me.

Bluffing was going to get really tricky.

I made it to my feet and took a good look at the shifter still leaning against my Kawasaki. I glowered my best at the six and a half feet of prime shifter male.

The flames of the structure reflected in his blue eyes. The golden shimmer of firelight played across his features. He looked like a model for an outdoor magazine—rough and rugged. A gaze that could see right through you, lips that could make you forget what planet you are on, and a body built for killing and sex—in that order.

His spiky blonde hair was the perfect finish to a face that could make a lesser woman wet herself.

Okay, call me lesser. My body responded to his sheer male presence, but I'll call myself lucky that I was steeped in so much goo, smoke, and blood I didn't want to think about that there was no way he could scent my arousal.

Besides, he had just done something really, really stupid, which went a long way to me not really being fond of him. I was now injured, energetically drained, and getting out of here in one piece was more important than being a notch on this guy's bedpost.

He could get anyone to warm his sheets. With a look from the incendiary blue eyes and a crook of his finger, and he would have himself a little something in bed.

No argument. No negotiation.

"You, ten o'clock. You ten thirty and bring a friend," said the sheriff of Nottingham. That was this guy without the anger or frustration.

I glanced down and saw the slender shard of glass protruding from my side. It was going to difficult to get it out. The angle was bad and toward the back. It was three inches wide at the entry point and got wider the further out it went. I just didn't know how deep it was.

It didn't matter. It had to come out. I had to get my medical kit from my saddlebag and wrap this with the magically enhanced dressing and bandage I had for just such an emergency. It would stop the bleeding and draw out any debris still in there. It would also take the top off of the pain, and that would be a real bonus about now.

The true healing would take time, but I'd make it to the house Marc and I had rented for the job, get the injury and me really cleaned up, and make it to bed before I passed out.

Marc would have stayed awake while I slept. Even with the wards I'd set to keep us safe, he would watch over me. I would be helpless, unconscious, and now, alone.

"I told you. You were too close," he remarked casually. He leaned a bit and got a look at the shard glistening in the fire's light. "Wow, that's going to leave a mark."

The blood seeped from the wound and down the side of my chaps. Getting blood out of the zipper was going to be a bitch.

I was beginning to really dislike this guy. I probably had a better chance of getting what I wanted if I played beta to his alpha.

"Yeah, ya think?" I started. "Look, shit for brains. What the fuck were you thinking blowing up that place?" I couldn't stroll over to him, but I walked, trying not to favor my side. I'm pretty sure I wasn't succeeding. "Get the fuck off my bike," I growled.

I was going die. I knew it.

His eyebrow rose, but nothing else on him moved. He was sitting against my saddlebag, the one with my medical supplies. I needed a break.

He was weighing the pros and cons of killing versus not killing me. I could tell.

I hadn't given him any cons, and his eyes studied everything as I closed the distance. My survival instincts were screaming to turn and walk away, to quit poking the killing machine with a stick and hope that I can walk the six blocks back to the house without passing out.

I could always buy another bike. Right?

I stood in front of him and met his gaze, hoping the whole time I wouldn't pee on myself. This guy exuded dangerous and scary in a way that would make Jason or Freddie pee themselves.

Instead, he inclined his head with a smile I didn't trust and rose to full height.

He stood, arms still over his chest. The muscles in said chest were well defined under the T-shirt he wore. The arms matched the chest, and his torso tapered only slightly into the jeans he wore. He could snap my neck with one hand and not break a sweat.

I looked him straight in the jaw. Crap. He was going to play alpha games with me. I didn't have the strength for this.

I didn't move a muscle, except for the clenching of my jaw as I dealt with the pain and steeled myself for what I was going to have to do in front of this guy.

I could do this.

He stepped aside enough to let me reach my saddlebag. I pulled out the supplies I needed and laid them on the seat of my bike. I gingerly removed my coat and laid it over the gas tank.

"I was thinking that the crap in that house needed to be blown to hell before it got worse," he said.

I had heard that shifters, like weres, couldn't decipher magic and tended to destroy first and ask questions later. The flaming wreckage of a shack being the case in point.

I turned my back to him, showing no fear.

In reality, I just didn't want him to see the grimace that was going to take over my face when I yanked the glass shard out my body. It wouldn't be pretty.

"Well. All you would have accomplished is to spread that *crap* all over this neighborhood." I pulled a dagger from a hip sheath and cut my tank top open enough to have more room to work the dressing and bandage.

The shard had nicked the waistband of my chaps, but the low-rise jeans were in tact. Blood stained, but in one piece.

I unbuckled the one side of the chaps and now had room top and bottom to deal with this mess.

"That magic was strong and dark. Good for coffee. Bad for a magic C-4 combination." I wrapped my hand around the shard, shifted my weight to the other hip, and prayed I stayed upright.

The universe seemed to still for the moment right after I tore the projectile from my body.

I was vaguely aware of dropping the glass to the ground and then beginning to apply the dressing and wrapping the bandage around my body.

It's only a flesh wound, I thought and giggled to myself as bits and pieces of *Monty Python and the Holy Grail* filtered through my pain-wracked mind. Marc and I owned the DVD and watched it too many times to count.

My vision had tunneled, and my movements seemed far away, along with the pain that I hoped to not truly feel. Ever.

Something played along one of my senses. I couldn't tell which one. Was somebody talking to me?

I was fairly certain that I was upright and that I was tending my wound. I would need to ride my bike back to the house. I supposed I would have to get back in touch with my body and get this over with.

Words. What was being said? Who was with me? Marc? Had I found him? No. The voice was wrong. Everything was wrong.

"Are you listening to me, woman?" said the irritated voice.

"Apparently not," I whispered. Breathing hurt. My throat hurt. My eyes hurt. Fuck, everything hurt. "You were saying?"

The pain found me. I swayed and steadied myself on the bike.

I had a kick-start.

This was going to hurt. More.

"What do you know about the magic in that house? How did you know what to do?" The demand upon threat of death was clearly there in his even and steady voice.

He had almost blown me up. I had been in a building rigged to blow, and he did nothing. I guess I shouldn't have felt angry about that. He didn't know me. I didn't matter.

What I did want to know was why I was cold.

"Maybe you should have a witch on staff to advise you on all things magic before you try to blow things up," I answered. I really knew my attitude was not going to be a selling point in all of this, but I still hadn't reined in my senses enough to function. I was on default. There would be no subtlety or tact until I found the true attachment of consciousness to my body and maybe not even then.

He was going to tear my throat out. Trying to fuck with an alpha animal usually meant you ended up dead.

I had just ripped glass out of body, dressed and bandaged the wound, and he was going to kill me. Somehow that really seemed unfair, but I seemed to have no control over my mouth.

I was wearing leathers in Vegas in September, and I was cold. Had I lost that much blood? It didn't feel like it.

Shock. I was going into shock.

Peachy.

The last thing I needed was being at this guy's mercy. I really didn't think he had any.

I felt his hand on my shoulder. I didn't respond. I just started putting things in my saddlebag. The dagger went back into its sheath, and I was ready to get out of there.

If he didn't kill me first.

His hand squeezed my shoulder tighter.

It was time. I had to face him.

"You're hired," he said.

For some reason, that didn't sound like "I'm going to kill you." I blinked a couple times and tried to focus more clearly on the fact that I was having a break with reality from shock.

"What?" I had totally lost that cool, nonchalant edge that a leather-clad badass such as myself walked on a regular basis. Ha! I made myself laugh.

It was the equivalent of blinking first in a staring contest. And I had blinked.

"I obviously need a witch. You seem to know what you're doing." He gave me the once-over. I'm sure I looked my best—not. "At least where it comes to magic."

Asshole.

"I'm already on a job. Give me a number. I'll call if I'm interested in consulting for you." I shook his hand off my shoulder, grabbed my bike, and swung my leg over the seat. I stared at the seat for a very long time as my body took the time to bitch me out for moving.

I couldn't remember what I had for dinner, but I did know that I didn't want to see it again. The design stitched into the seat held my fascination for entirely too long, but I no longer wished to puck on my gas tank. Vomit did bad things to a paint job.

I eased my coat back on. It helped warm me. Funny the flaming building didn't seem to help.

"I really don't have time to wait for you to call me, honey." Arrogance. What a surprise. He'd already been rude and obnoxious, but if he thought I'd acquiesce to his command, he was wrong, and nobody called me honey.

"And I don't split my time between two jobs, *sweetheart*," I retorted. I had to kick-start this bitch. I'd have to use the side that was damaged. I wanted to cry right then and there. What I wouldn't do for an electronic ignition right now.

"If your job led you to this building, then chances are, what I want you for will be in alignment with your current employment." He rested his hand over mine. I still had a death grip on the brakes. Gods, I hurt. "You can do one job, get paid twice, and have resources here that you didn't have before."

He sounded so reasonable. I didn't trust him. Outsiders didn't get invited into the shifter community; that's why there wasn't a lot of information about them at hand.

Myself? I had hoped to avoid any involvement with shifter or were communities. Ever.

Fuck.

"Give me your number. I will call you tomorrow," I said evenly. "We can negotiate terms then."

"That won't do. You will come with me tonight." The presence, the arrogance, the self-assured commands. This fucker was royalty. Damn it!

I gave him a "go fuck yourself" look and kick-started my bike. The gas tank was lovely in the moon's light. It was painted midnight blue with metallic flake. I'd been thinking about having some detail added to it but hadn't found the time or inspiration to get that done yet.

The bodily screaming was so much louder this time. It was the last time I was going to get away with this shit, and I knew it. I would have to drive really slow and focus on every little detail to make it back to the house.

"I'll just follow you home and take you when you pass out." Arrogant and obnoxious. Lovely.

"Well, then I'll drive slow so you don't get lost." I slid my helmet in place and dropped the visor.

"Are you kidding? The way you smell, I could find you tomorrow after a rainstorm." Rude. He had covered all his bases.

I backed the bike out and took off. Really, really slow.

He followed.

I ran through everything that had happened, and it was nothing but a random jumble in my scrambled mind. I couldn't think. I didn't want to think. I just wanted a shower, clean clothing, a warm bed, and Marc to curl up with.

Marc.

A tear slid down my cheek. I'd find him. The shifter was right. He'd have resources that I didn't and that the vampire community didn't have. He might know where Marc was as well. If I had to use him to those ends, it worked for me.

He almost blew me up, got me injured, and insulted me. He owed me big, and I was going to collect.

The house Marc and I rented for the job was a small, two bedroom, cookie-cutter slice of suburbia that came furnished and was set away from any neighbors. It was ideal for our purposes.

What was left of my magic reached into the garage and flipped the automatic door opener on. I waited while the door opened. His Majesty pulled up next to me.

I removed my helmet and set it on the gas tank. He had no helmet. Of course, he didn't. That would show fear of being injured, a weakness. He couldn't do it. Fuck that, I could. I liked my brain right where it was.

"Wait here," I said and eased my bike forward. He moved with me. I stopped. "Wait here," I reiterated more slowly. He didn't need a helmet; he was already brain damaged.

I moved. So did he. Fine. He'd figure it out soon enough.

I crossed over the threshold and into the garage proper. He, on the other hand, was thoroughly zapped by the wards I had installed and found himself at the end of the drive becoming one with the pavement. His bike was in the garage with me.

The idea of closing the door and letting him sit there all night until I was ready to talk to him tickled me.

It would serve him right.

I had a feeling that there was just so much he would take from me, and I was probably reaching a personal limit on his patience.

I put my bike away as he walked up to the threshold. The look he gave me let me know that he was considering redecorating a room with my internal organs.

"I told you to wait." I echoed his attitude of me being too close to the house as it burned. Okay, so I pushed just a little more. I couldn't help myself. I'll blame shock.

I crossed the threshold, removed my gloves, and walked over to the wall.

Good boy, he followed me. But can they really be trained? I didn't think so.

I held out my hand and waited the second he took in trusting somebody he had no reason to. We had done nothing but fuck with each other from moment one. I wasn't going to take it personally.

He took my hand, and I place my other hand on the wall where I had drawn protective symbols. He was warm, and energy worked its way through me. Deep, sensual, powerful. My body flushed for a moment.

The wards lit up. The power touched me, recognized me, accepted me. It overshadowed what his touch impressed upon my body.

Asshole.

He was smirking. Pulling some fucked-up shifter crap, no doubt. Someday I'd…

Yeah, right. I'd just keep giving him shit and annoying him no end. That was my secret weapon.

I politely introduced the wards to the shifter. He was now keyed into the alarm system and could come and go as he pleased.

I had no reason to trust him. I should have keyed him in and not out. But I was going to be unconscious, and soon. I didn't need him anymore pissed with me than he already was.

"The wards recognize you as a non-threat." I chose those words special just for him. It made me giggle inside.

I turned and walked toward the door connecting the garage and the house. I released his hand. He didn't release mine. If the wards were going to throw him again, he was taking me with him.

Whatever.

Once inside, he let my hand drop.

I stopped and dropped my coat to the tile foyer. Undoing the chaps, I let them drop on top of the coat. The boots were going to be trickier.

The shifter stared at me questioningly.

"Blood is a bitch to get out of the carpet. I want my deposit back when this is over." I knelt cautiously and removed the boots. My head was swimming in exhaustion and pain. I had no doubt he would carry out his threat to take me after I passed out, but I'd be damned if I wasn't getting a shower and at least fall asleep in my own bed.

"There's leftover lasagna in the fridge, some chicken, and a couple of beers," I said over my shoulder as I grabbed my nasty leathers and moved down the hallway. "Help yourself."

As I turned the corner to the master bedroom, I glanced back. He was taking off his boots.

He was still an asshole.

The bleeding had stopped, and the bruising was a veritable kaleidoscope of color. Tonight had been a full-body experience, and the impact points all over my body showed it. I had a feeling that tomorrow I'd feel slightly worse, especially if I woke up in a strange place.

The shower removed the worst of the experience, and the scrubby had seen its last rodeo. I unlaced the french braid that was my mousey brown and thoroughly nondescript breast-length hair.

The braid kept it out of the way and relatively out of the hands of somebody who would think to use it against me. Great hand holds long hair. Great place to hide weapons, if you knew how. So there was no way I would cut it. Some people had faces that glowed with short hair. Mine was not one of them.

I was not pretty. I was not beautiful. I had been told I was exotic. I didn't try to read too much into that.

I was finally clean. But no amount of clean could hide the dark circles under my pale green eyes or the lack of any luster in the gold rings that rimmed my irises—the only telltale sign that I was a witch. Contacts could hide them, but I just didn't. Contacts could be a real liability in a fight or dirty environment.

I tended to get dirty more often than not. It wasn't worth the hassle.

I threw on sweats and a tank top to sleep in. Naked wasn't going to happen tonight.

Four nights without Marc by my side. I hadn't changed the sheets. I could still scent him. The bed was mussed. Marc wasn't here to make it, and I was just too lazy.

I swallowed hard and pushed back the tears that seemed to be waiting for a really weak moment. I was well beyond weak and into walking dead territory.

I packed two small duffle bags—one with weapons and magical paraphernalia, one with clothing. If I was going anywhere, I really wanted my stuff with me.

One last trip to the bathroom to pee and hit the eyes with Visine; they were entirely too bloodshot.

I had healing amulets on the nightstand. I'd tuck one into the bandages over the nasty gash. Another I'd lay over my right shoulder. I'm not quite sure what had happened, but it was stiff and bruised. I wouldn't even bother to bind it. I probably wouldn't move all night. Well, at least, not on my own.

I stepped into the bedroom. He was in the doorway. His eyes went from me to my bags and back to me.

"Going somewhere?"

Suspicious fuck. Probably why he was still alive and in charge.

"You seem to think I am," I quipped as the room began to darken around me and spin just enough to force me to grab something I assumed would be stable. The bathroom doorjamb did a fine job.

I held on until the ride came to a complete stop and focused on the bed. I could make it six feet. I could remain conscious enough to place the amulets. Couldn't I?

With him in the room, I had to.

"You need help?" he asked. The offer sounded sincere. No way I'd take him up on it.

I kept my eyes on the bed and willed what was left of my body to walk to the bed. It was like crossing the damn Grand Canyon, but I made it and eased myself onto the waiting softness.

"Where's your boyfriend?" There was something in his voice that let me know he was withholding information, but so was I. I had a dozen snarky remarks on my lips, but it was so much easier to welcome the encroaching fuzziness that caressed my waning consciousness.

"Probably where you have him stashed," I whispered as my body relaxed and eyes closed.

Marc's scent rose from the bedding, and for a moment, I could believe that everything was all right. Marc was by my side, and we'd be heading home once again.

We needed a vacation. We had earned it.

CHAPTER THREE

Dressed and dreading to go…

I needed to inform the Sahara that I had found the sand it had lost. It was all in my eyes.

I rubbed at the grit and tried to dislodge it the best I could. I was only partially successful.

My body wasn't doing the happy dance yet. However, the only thing that actually hurt was my side. It seemed like it was taking longer to heal than it should. Of course, it had been perforated.

Hell, I'd exhausted myself and abused my body just a bit more than usual. I also hadn't had Marc to drink from. If he'd been here…

But he wasn't, so I would hurt a while longer.

I stood. I didn't actually move for a while. I was in deep debate as to the wisdom of moving versus crawling back into bed for a day or two. Finally, my bladder joined the debate, and moving won out.

I went to the bathroom, sat, and peed, pretty much expecting to fall asleep again on the toilet. It had happened before.

I vaguely remembered a healing amulet falling to the floor during the debate. Since it hadn't said anything, I hadn't really noticed it. But now?

I hadn't remembered putting the amulet on. I touched my bandaged side and felt an amulet nestled in the wrappings.

I shook it off. I wasn't in top form. I had probably done it on autopilot last night before I passed out.

I still smelled like smoke, and I could smell the faintest traces of the goo I had slogged through last night. It wasn't terrible, but another shower needed to happen.

My leathers needed cleaning too. Not looking forward to that. I could smell them in the tub.

I also smelled bacon cooking.

I didn't have bacon in the house.

I was still in the house.

I was confused.

The glow of morning light fell around the edges of the blackout curtains as I made my way to the bedroom door and peeked down the hallway to the kitchen.

His most majestic self was puttering about, and it smelled wonderful. Unfortunately, the vast majority wasn't anything that I had bought.

He had stalked the wilds of a nearby grocery and was currently creating a feast fit for, well, a king. He wouldn't be sharing. Alphas ate what they wanted and gave the lesser beasts the scraps.

I would eat what I had on hand and be happy with my own foraging skills. The floor plan was open, so there wasn't anything separating the living room from the kitchen, so I could see that he hadn't trashed the kitchen while he cooked. I was surprised.

In the garage, I could hear the washing machine going. That quickly explained why my house guest was currently wearing Marc's robe and nothing else.

Marc's a slender, lean vampire. He's built for hit-and-run tactics in a fight, and that man can move. The only thing we really lacked in bed was mind-blowing passion, unless we had barely escaped dying. Then it was a celebration. But he knew how to move.

The shifter was built to stand and fight until there was nothing left to kill and nothing but bodies around him. Marc's robe was not prime coverage for this guy.

He was fine.

I tried to look more awake than I really was and grabbed a big mug from the cabinet, filled it with water, and set the microwave for two minutes while I got myself some tea.

Lemon zinger sounded good.

We had gotten off to a bad start last night. What with him almost blowing me up and almost infecting an entire neighborhood with dark, insidious magic, I'd been a bit testy. I'm not the most polite, politically correct person when things are going really well. So maybe I should lighten up. Clean slate. Try making nice with the guy that might know where Marc is. And hey, he did let me stay the whole night in my house. Okay, it's a rental, but it was nice to come to and know where I was.

Maybe I should try…

"You look like crap."

Never mind.

I threw some whole grain bread in the toaster, got some crunchy peanut butter, an apple, and my tea, now steeping, and sat at the breakfast bar. I hunted, and I had my kill.

The table was filled with steaks, scrambled eggs, potatoes, bacon, sausage, cantaloupe, strawberries, and half a loaf of toasted, organic, multigrain bread, a gallon of whole milk, and a pound of real butter.

I knew shifters could blow through some calories, but damn!

He sat in the corner, back to both walls. Smart guy, but that was a given. "You'll never keep your girlish figure eating like that." I warned him as I took a bite of my peanut-butter-laden toast.

In that moment, nothing had ever tasted better. My body had blown through its own fuel and was now demanding I feed it, and those steaks were really calling to me.

No way I was going to ask this guy for anything. My peanut butter was just as good. Yeah, I wasn't convinced either.

"I take it you are feeling better then, Valerie," he said smoothly as bits of rare steak began to disappear into his mouth.

I sipped my tea and glanced around the kitchen/living room and saw my saddlebag opened. He had gone through my things and found my driver's license. Hell, he was wearing Marc's robe, so he made himself at home quite nicely.

Prick.

"And what should I call you?" I asked calmly. "Your Majesty, Your Highness, or simply asshole."

There was the slightest hesitation before he started in on the third steak. I don't know what had gotten him. Either I was right about the royalty part, or he didn't like being called an asshole. Chances were he didn't get called asshole a lot to his face. At least, not more than once by any given individual.

"I am the beast master of the southwest region of North America," he said casually and ate some scrambled eggs. "You may call me master."

Asshole it is then.

"Not likely." My expression hadn't changed; neither had his. We seemed too well matched at pushing each others buttons. This was not fun. Well, not much fun, but I didn't seem to be able to stop myself.

I was doomed.

"Trey."

It took me a second to realize that he had simply given me his name. No shot, no rude remark, just his name. Trey. Simple.

I nodded and finished my toast.

"So. Tell me why you were at that house?" he asked, barely pausing in his consumption of breakfast.

"Looking for a nest of unsupervised very young vamps. I'm pretty sure the remains were in that house." I relaxed as much as I could manage and sipped my tea. "My partner—"

"Your boyfriend?" he asked.

"We multitask," I answered calmly. "He disappeared four days ago. That house was the last place I knew he had been. His scent was heavy there. So was yours."

"You don't believe he's dead?" He was so calm. He knew Marc and I were lovers. You could smell sex clinging to the sheets, not a tough deduction. And he was casually asking if I believed somebody I cared for was still alive.

I took a breath. He was looking to see how deep my emotional involvement was. Deep was not good. It meant mistakes, and he wouldn't risk that. I had to play it cool.

"No, I do not believe he's dead," I answered evenly. "So why do you think I can assist you?"

"As you pointed out, I could use a witch in all things magic, and you handled that well last night," he finished and kept eating. I was waiting for a remark. It never came.

"It's the first time I've come across it. I don't recognize the signature, but if I find the caster, I will recognize them," I explained quickly. "Do you know where my partner is?"

"If you've never encountered that magic before, how did you destroy it so quickly?" he countered. "Yes, I have him."

I wanted to slump to the floor in relief at that news. I was that much closer to getting to him, and all that stood in my way was Trey.

"I'm a quick study." I was now starting on my apple. It tasted good. "Is he safe?"

"Can you kill that crap after it's infected a person?" he asked. There was no tag on about Marc. It worried me.

"I don't know. I'd have to see the person, scan them, and…" Holy shit.

Marc was infected.

I'm sure my heart stopped as doubt crashed in on me. If I failed, it would cost Marc his life or his freedom. Forever. Looking in the shifter's eyes, I had no doubt that he would kill Marc without a thought past there being no way to save him, if it came to that.

"Run some tests. Do you have chemists and a lab?"

"Of course," Trey replied.

I rose from the stool. There was too much to think about. I had to contact the Vampire Council in LA. They needed an update. I would need more of my magical stuff from the bedroom, so I needed a third duffle bag. I needed another shower. I still smelled goo and smoke clinging to me. I had to get my leathers clean.

I sat back down.

Stars danced before my eyes. Not enough sleep, not enough to eat, and just a little too much stress. Had I sat with the moon last night and recharged? Nope. I barely made it to bed. My batteries were on low, and they were going to stay that way for a bit.

I breathed.

It's interesting how attitude affects food taste. The breakfast that had tasted incredibly good a few minutes ago now held no interest for me.

Marc had been infected. I was still weak, and the only person near me was an irritating pain in the ass named Trey, who apparently had more answers than he was sharing.

Not really a surprise, I hadn't shared everything either. We'd both held back; that was the way of things.

My vision finally cleared, and I eased my body off of the stool, and amazingly, my legs held. I washed and dried my dishes, put them away, and turned toward the beautiful shifter with a bad attitude and a long title.

"Fifteen hundred per day, plus expenses. If you have the samples and photos Mark collected, I will need them or the copies of the reports and findings." He didn't budge from his breakfast. I had a feeling that the four vamps that had died in that house would end my current job with the council, leaving me to deal with some nasty dark magic and whomever was wielding it. At least now, I had a client willing to pick up the tab.

However, since the infection was targeting vampires, the council might continue to pick up the tab for this bit as well.

"I will also need access to Marc and any pertinent information you have regarding this case."

He paused and looked at me like I was on the menu. I'd hate to be the woman he wanted in his bed. She'd never stand a chance.

"You may have copies of the photos, copies of the findings from the samples. Your access to your partner will be limited." He was still leisurely chowing down as he watched me and began his negotiations. I had a feeling that no matter what we negotiated, he'd come out better for it.

"Marc's infected. I will have access to him." That would be a nonnegotiable point. I would see my lover, I would comfort him, I would find a way to fix this.

Then I would kill the sorcerer, witch, magician, or whatever magic-using maniac who had created this shit in the first place. I had my priorities.

"I will give you any and all information that I deem relevant to this investigation. You will share any and all findings with me or

Sean, my second in command. He will be your liaison when I am unavailable."

It was at that point that I realized the Lord High Beast Master Muckity Muck had been running around unescorted, was out of his palace or cave or whatever all night, and was burning precious time playing games with a woman who looked like crap and smelled like smoke and decomp.

This was important shit. Important enough to take his personal time and attention.

Crap.

"How long have you been aware of this magic being out and about, Trey?" It felt strange to actually say his name. Asshole had been such a staple back up in my mind that I was going to have to get use to it. And, yeah my tone was accusatory. He'd been working this for a while with no success, and I was looking good for a way to get some movement on this issue.

"About a month," he said. The pile of food was dwindling rapidly. He had a huge appetite and wondered if it was limited to food.

"I will need all of your reports, dates, circumstances, times, places. All of it." He ate. I thought. Then it came to me. I'm an idiot. "Is this thing infecting shifters and weres?"

He just kept eating. I turned the information over in my head again and regrouped. "Any information gathered regarding weres or shifters that doesn't have a direct bearing on my other client and their disposition will not be passed on. If the information does affect my other client, we will discuss the necessity of passing it along and/or wording of such information before the report is forwarded."

"Yes, but the weres virus kills the infection 80 percent of the time," he explained cautiously. He really didn't like giving me the information. For that reason alone, I would make sure these tidbits made a difference in this investigation. "You cooperated! Good boy, you get a cookie."

"In the shifter population, it's fifty-fifty." HOLY SHIT!

Twenty percent of infected weres and 50 percent of infected shifters would be controlled by a crazy person. Oh, and let's not forget that this was designed specifically for vamps. That is one hell of a scary army.

This revelation was scary enough to make me want to turn tail and run. "Have your people come up with an antibody from the ones the infection didn't take over?"

He was starting to look like he'd rather kill me than talk to me at this point. "Your terms are acceptable. Is there anything else?" He rose. The robe was a waste of time. He was revealed in all his majestic glory. Not looking him over wasn't easy. He was breathtaking. The hard planes of his body were sharp enough to slice a tomato, and I struggled to keep eye contact with him, but it was hard, and so was he. Even from my peripheral vision, I could discern that the man was built in every way.

Grabbing a couple plates from the table, he walked over to the sink, set the plates down, and stood directly in front of me.

My entire body clenched at the feel of a predator being this close to me. A flick of his wrist, and I would be dead.

I don't think it would bother him much or any.

I was still leaning against the counter as his hands rested on either side of my body, caging me in.

He smelled clean and wild with a hint of the patchouli soap I had purchased.

I said a little prayer that he'd never want me in his bed. I wouldn't stand a chance, and I was too sensitive to let somebody toss me aside. Alpha predators took as many bed partners as they wanted. I couldn't be one of many for anybody.

His morning stubble grazed my jaw as he leaned in and scented me deeply.

I knew I smelled of human nothing more. Except smoke and goo.

"If you betray the were or shifter communities," he began slowly and lethally. The heat of him pressing into me, though the only place we touched was our cheeks. Fear gripped me; this didn't bode well.

I didn't flinch.

"If any of this information is used against us. If more of us die because of you. I will kill you more slowly than you believe possible."

His lips touched the shell of my ear as he withdrew and looked me in the eye.

My breakfast was trying to come back up, and I was pretty sure that I had peed myself just a little.

I knew there was a really good reason to stay away from shifters, and Trey was it.

"You can try," I said coolly.

The washing machine cycle ended. We both heard it, but neither of us made a move. Neither of us flinched. He could stay like this all day. I couldn't, but I was going to find out how long I'd last.

The seconds stretched into days. Actually, they stretched into more seconds, but it felt like days with his eyes boring into mine.

He leaned back in, his gaze dropped to my lips, then back to my eyes. His pupils were blown. I had a feeling mine were too.

His lips parted and brushed lightly over mine. I didn't budge.

However, there was nothing I could do about the pounding of my heart or the full-body explosion of goose bumps.

My sexual experiences were limited to Marc, and as much as I enjoyed him, I never knew a kiss could blot out the world around me, and I never thought I could feel the press of a mans lips through my entire body. And it wasn't even a real kiss.

I was screwed. No, wait. A bad choice of words.

Part of me wanted to cry at the thought of having any response to this guy. He was a nasty piece of work who would use me in a heartbeat, throw me away when done, and forget my name before I left his bed. The other part of me wanted to cry because I would never have this with Marc.

I eased my head back, pressed into the counter, and swallowed hard.

"I prefer to kiss men who don't threaten me with a slow, painful death." I kept my voice even and hoped it didn't sound like an invitation for more.

In his eyes, I could have sworn I saw a flicker of flame. I had to remind myself that I had no idea what this guy was. I needed to keep my own personal lust in check and remember Marc needed me.

"Your lips weren't giving me a clear no, Valerie," he whispered. He leaned back in. His lips brushed my cheek. "Tell me no."

I was trembling. I now hated myself and could hate Trey as well for doing this to me. I just hoped I didn't cry until I could get the shower going.

"Maybe, I don't think it wise to offend or insult the man who has my lover in his custody," I whispered back. Even my voice trembled.

He wouldn't kill me. I was too pathetic.

I would save Marc, do anything in my power to preserve the weres and shifters, give Trey no reason to pursue me, and get the fuck out of this place.

He leaned back. This time, I couldn't meet his gaze.

He eased away from the counter, away from me, and walked silently into the garage without looking back.

I was relieved. He didn't see the tear that had finally fallen.

I had spent the better part of an hour in my bathroom. It was the easiest way to avoid Trey and pull myself together.

I also had a good cry in the shower. It wasn't loud and involved, but I needed to relieve some stress somehow, and that was all I had.

My leathers were cleaned, I had everything packed, and I called in my report to the council. I mentioned nothing about weres or shifters and told them I believed that the nest had been destroyed and I should have evidence of that shortly. I managed to dodge questions, such as, where the hell Marc was, and why he wasn't delivering the report himself?

My hair was braided; weapons strapped on. Dressed and dreading to go, I walked into the living room and dropped the baggage.

I tucked another pain amulet into the dressing wrapped around my side. The wound was down to a dull roar. If everything went well, all I'd have to do today is look through paperwork, see what the findings told me, and see Marc.

Infected. The infection was trying to drag him to a location, and he was trapped and couldn't obey.

I wondered if there was anything left of him. Anything to talk to. Anything to connect with. I was preparing for the worst.

The front door was wide open, there was a cargo van in the driveway, and somebody was rolling my Kawasaki into the back.

From the look of the guy, I was guessing shifter. So, asshole, no, wait. Trey had called his crew, and they were doing what?

Trey came in from the garage, the door nearly hitting me. He had his sunglasses on.

Not being able to look him in the eyes was either a kindness or a true insult.

I wasn't sure which, but honestly, I didn't care. I was going to see the man I loved, and he might not know me at all. Today was going to suck.

"What are your boys doing with my bike?" I asked.

"We will drive the bikes back to the Enclave in the van. We will talk on the way." His voice was neutral, all business. The sunglasses were an insult. I didn't rate a direct gaze. I had fallen in his estimation of me. I don't know why it even mattered to me, but it did.

"I'll follow on my bike," I said calmly. I reached down and hauled my duffle bags over my shoulder, suppressing the wince of discomfort, and stepped out into the brilliant late-morning desert sun.

The last thing I was going to put up with was a long drive with somebody who was going to treat me like I was fragile. He had pushed and poked and messed with me to see what I was made of. He found a chink in my armor and wouldn't test me any further.

I was certain of it.

Well, fuck him.

"Hey! The little girlie motorcycle comes out!" I shouted at the shifter that had just pushed it in. He was built more like Marc. Long, lean, and sleek. I'd bet my savings he was a feline shifter—all grace and elegance as he dropped out of the back of the van, eyed me from head to toe and then. looked past me to Trey.

His mocha skin glistened in the sun, and his eyes looked me over much in the same way Trey had done last night. A small part of me was simply annoyed, but another part recognized that he did nothing for me.

As I rounded the other side of the van, I heard a low growl, and then the mocha shifter said, "Sorry, boss." I had no idea what had just transpired, but as long as it didn't have anything to do with me, I just didn't care.

I went to the side panel, slid it open, and tossed in the baggage. My side gave me a glare. It would be fine by the end of the day, but now it was still pissy.

Closing the side panel, I went around back and ran into Trey.

"It's a long drive, and we can use the time to get questions answered." His questions, not mine no doubt. "I had the reports brought up, so you could study them as we drove." The obnoxious asshole had disappeared, and I didn't much like what had replaced him. I didn't much like the obnoxious asshole either, but this seemed worse. "It could save valuable time."

It would be nice to have a game plan before I saw Marc. But reading while I was in a car could make me car sick if I wasn't careful.

I am badass, hear me puke.

I was going to be very, very careful. I could look up every so often and pretend I was thinking something over. Readjust my focus, settle my stomach, and dive back in.

I could ignore him the entire way.

CHAPTER FOUR

I Found It Beautiful

The house was secured.

The reports were on the passenger seat. I took off the coat and tossed it and the rest of my leathers in the back. I belted myself in and cracked open the first report before Trey climbed in and turned over the engine.

A half hour into the drive, I understood that direct contact with the dark magic was the only way it could be transmitted. It didn't seem to survive if an infected person bit an uninfected person. Good to know and good news for us.

Bad news. There was no antibody research. If a were was infected and it didn't take hold, the virus burned out the infection, leaving no trace. If a shifter was infected and it didn't take hold of their minds, they died, and the virus was burned out.

It took less than twenty-four hours.

Now I understood why he threatened me. *If any more of my people die because of you . . .* I remember him saying.

His people were succumbing to the infection one way or another. Death or mind control.

I looked out the windshield. I was nauseous. Not from the drive, but from the implications. The total and utter destruction of his people. With that information, I was surprised he wasn't murderous instead of just really unpleasant.

I read further.

There were fifteen weres missing and thirty shifters. I had death tolls, missing members, and how many were held and restrained in the Enclave, including one vampire. Marc.

Treys losses. Were they family or friends or lovers? It didn't matter. They were his people, his responsibility. If he lost one, it affected him and how others looked at him as a leader, which affected his ability to keep cohesion and order.

He had to get this thing under control and now.

They had tried to track one of their weres, but they had lost him. They had tried putting a tracking device on another. The device shorted out when placed on the person. They had tried to chain another to a vehicle, to let him lead them to the location. He stood in the same place for thirty minutes and died screaming in pain.

I had seen the name Gabrielle referenced in a number of places where there had been recommendation regarding magical defenses against this stuff. None of the recommendations were helpful. It was more like they slowed things down, unless you didn't know magic, then the ideas would seem sound enough.

Trey had a witch and had been betrayed by said witch.

I had to know more about this person and what they had done. I was going to have to ask Trey.

No. I would write down my questions and hand them off to Sean. I would get my answers that way. I wouldn't have to talk to Trey, and he wouldn't have to lower himself to speak in my general direction.

I took in the surroundings once more—flat desert with some beautiful, rocky outcroppings here and there and a mesa in the distance. The flat and the heat of the desert were very deceptive.

The swell of the mesa looked close. Close enough to walk to, but in reality, it was close enough to die trying to walk to.

It was at least an hour by car, and we were no longer on a paved road. I just hoped the shock absorbers held. It wasn't a smooth ride, and it made reading harder than it needed to be.

The clear blue sky stretched out and touched the desert here and there. It was desolate, if you didn't know what to look for. I found it beautiful. A landscape carved from wind and more wind and occasionally rain where the strong survived and thrived on the barest resources.

I leaned the seat back and stretched. My body had been folded up for entirely too long. The stretch felt good, but my side was still crankier than I thought it should be. Then again, I had never had to suffer the full length of any healing ever. Marc made sure of it.

"You're still hurt." His voice over the constant thrum of the engine was very disturbing, and I almost jumped. I had been so wrapped up in my own thoughts and assurances that it was going to be a silent drive that I had been blindsided.

"No," I replied evenly. I grabbed a report that I had, in fact, memorized at this point and pretended to go over it again as I reclined.

Something was niggling around the edges of my consciousness. Something about this Gabrielle person? The disposition of this person was important.

It could wait. I could wait and talk to Sean. He would have just as much information as Trey, and he'd probably be easier to talk to.

The niggling got worse. I focused on the report. Something was wrong, but I was missing it.

A cold chill went up my spine.

I don't know when I had gotten my favorite blades out of my bag, but I had two sixteen-inch silver dipped short swords in hand, and my heart was pounding.

It wasn't the reports that were bothering me; it was the surroundings. Something was out there and focused on the two vans, containing six shifters and one witch/vamp.

The sun was directly overhead, so I knew we didn't have to worry about vampires, but shifters and weres were a different story.

"When did you discover that Gabrielle had betrayed you?" I asked. Trey hadn't responded much to me grabbing weapons, but he was scanning the area and checking his mirrors more often.

"Last night," he said. I guessed that my informing him that blowing up the shack would have made things worse was the tip-off. "What are you seeing?" Seeing? I wasn't seeing anything unusual, and if I was scenting something, the shifters would have scented it long before me.

Setting the blades between us, I put the seat upright, closed my eyes, and let my magic crawl along the desert around us.

I felt desert, dirt, sand, rock, and malice.

I focused on the malice. It did seem somewhat out of place. I needed details and needed them fast.

"Do we want to engage or avoid?" I muttered to myself. My eyes were closed. I was still feeling for specifics. I dug into the defenses where the malice lay and found a patch of infective magic within the desert landscape. It was moving to Intercept, but I couldn't tell how it was moving. What was propelling it? I just sensed dirt, rock, and desert.

"We want to avoid," I said. I grabbed a report, flipped it over, found a pencil, and drew. One dot was us. One dot was them, and the lines showed an intercept point. "The intercept happens in five minutes."

"What is it?" He sounded calm. He was a leader. Leaders didn't panic at the first sign of perceived trouble.

"Dark magic, and it's on the move. I just don't know what's moving it," I said. I couldn't kill it at this range, but maybe I could slow it down. If I did get close enough, I could and would toast it.

"My best guess is that Gabrielle ratted you out last night after I interfered, and this is your welcome-home party."

I narrowed my scope to the dark magic and what was directly around it.

Desert. Desert and more desert.

The infection continued to move, seemingly of its own volition.

I could hear Trey speaking softly on his phone. I assumed it was to Sean. It didn't matter. I was close enough to start containing the infection and burning it away.

The containment field formed. It sparkled and glistened and looked nearly invisible against the blue of the desert sky. It wrapped and held the infection in its grasp. What I felt next was the equivalent of being hit in the head with a shovel.

Since I had been hit in the head with a shovel several years back, I was familiar with that feeling.

"Damn it!" I kept a tight hold on my magic and threw a little power into defending myself. That hit I took hurt, and I was going to make someone pay for it as soon as I found them.

I needed to exit the vehicle. I had to connect with the earth to hold on to the infection and the magic that had reached out to protect it from me.

This was some nasty shit, and I was really hoping for a long boring and uncomfortably silent ride through the desert.

"Stop and let me out," I said. I really didn't think he'd balk. Hell, he was ready to let me die last night, and he wasn't too broken up about it. So tossing me out to deal with the dark magic while he kept a safe distance, with my bike again, didn't seem like a real stretch.

"No." We were going seventy-five miles per hour. I could jump out and survive the experience, but I wouldn't be able to function after.

"I can't fight it from a moving vehicle. It's more than just the infection. Let.

Me. Out." I was getting pounded, and I needed out now.

The vehicle slowed, and I was out before he stopped, weapons in hand. I hoped it didn't come to that, but you never know. Better to have it and not need it and such.

"Go!" I yelled as I closed the door. He and his people didn't need to be anywhere around that infection magic, especially if I lost.

The vehicle pulled away, and the second one followed. Now I could focus all my attention on the fucker doing this shit.

I knelt to the desert floor, pulled earth power from it, and blasted the area with as much power as I could raise and still keep the infection contained.

It was slowing, but still moving and heading directly toward me.

Cool.

Trey would be safe. Of course, he made sure of that when he bailed. He had done what I asked. His people couldn't afford to lose him too.

The infection began to burn. I opened my eyes enough to see the dark purple in the near-distance sputter and spark within the containment field. There was a lot of it.

A wind must have been coming in because there was a dusty haze moving toward me. Had the magic been moving on the wind? No. Why not use it to disseminate the infection originally if that was the case? What would displace dust and not register? I wasn't sensing obscuring magic, so all of my senses were telling me that nothing was there.

Well, I knew that was wrong because that nothing was coming at me and fast.

I just had to hope that I could finish burning the infection before my opponent reached me. What the fuck? This was just like last night. Except last night, I would have burned to death; today I had no idea what was going to fuck with me.

I couldn't rush the burn. But maybe I could keep the forces of nature from over taking me. What the hell, I'd give it a shot.

I pulled up a secondary thread of power and pushed out. The rising dust swirled and stopped its advance.

Yes, I was liking this a lot.

I could do this.

Within a few more moments, the burn was complete. The purple fire had died, and I let the containment field go.

The dust had settled, and all was quiet. Something was really, really wrong, and I didn't like it.

I was going to start walking. I could see the rising mesa in the distance and had a feeling that it was the southwestern kingdom stronghold of his most obnoxious self.

I made it about ten feet when the desert beneath me began to tremble. A break would have been nice. I mean, I had just burned out another mass of that dark magic that had a defense system in place. My head was killing me, my side was aching more loudly, I was thirsty, and I was wearing a tank top in the middle of the desert. I was sunburned already.

The desert floor seemed to shoot up in front of me. I stumbled and rolled back, recovering quickly to find four six-foot-tall figures made from the dirt, sand, and rocks of the desert. Golems.

Golems? Really! Who uses that magic anymore. It's unwieldy and clunky, and as the first one connected its arm with my side, I went flying and saw the wisdom in using golems. The materials were available, they hit with explosive force, and you could always make more.

I needed to take out the legs. If they couldn't move, they weren't a threat.

Much.

It would take a while, but they were slow, and I could easily outmaneuver them until I was done. It would be easiest to use magic, the blades would take forever, and I was baking under the unforgiving sun.

The real downside was that I was already weakened, my side had taken a second hit, and by the time I turned these thing back into the dust they came from, I'd be finished.

I was going to have to trust that Trey was keeping an eye on me, and this time he would drag my ass out of the fire.

I started blasting the statuary, one leg at a time. I kept one golem between me and the others at all times. Becoming surrounded would result in being bashed into a bloody mess on the desert floor.

I personally liked to be recognizable.

I had taken out the legs on the third when the second one swiped my leg out from underneath me with its arm.

These things are dangerous until there is nothing resembling a being.

Whatever part is still in play will continue to do its job.

A second arm came down and landed where my head had been a moment before. I got back up and learned that lesson quickly.

By the time I had finished off the last one, I was disoriented and barely on my feet.

I looked around and saw dust being kick up in the distance. Holy freaking hell! I could not deal with anything else.

Well, whatever.

I wiped my hands on my already dust-coated jeans, gripped my weapons, and waited for whatever was going to be thrown at me this time.

The windshields glinted in the ruthless sun as it approached. I searched my memory for what form of attack included windshields. I couldn't remember. My brain was fried. All I had left was my remaining strength and the steel in my hands.

I was fucked.

The vans pulled up, and it still hadn't registered. Not until Trey had gotten out of the vehicle did I realize that I was being retrieved, not attacked.

I needed water and shade.

He opened the side panel as I walked over to him and sat my dust-coated, exhausted ass down and sipped the water from the bottle he had handed me.

It probably would have felt really good to have dumped the water over my head, but with the amount of dust I had on me, I'd be able to make my own golem out of the mud.

The A/C was low and gently washed over my back as I continued to sip and feel slightly less than death warmed over. Or microwaved on high.

The cool breeze touched my side, and lo and behold, the wound had torn open, and blood had soaked through the bandage I'd wrapped around it this morning.

I pulled the amulet from the wrapping. There was no charge. I'd likely drained it during the battle.

Scrounging around one of my duffle bags, I found another and replaced it. I really needed a clean, fully charged dressing, but I was too tired, and it could wait until we got to where ever we were going.

I leaned forward and rested my arms on my knees, occasionally sipping on my second bottle of water.

Trey knelt at my side and peeled back my tank top, revealing the blood-soaked bandage.

I kept my eyes on the bottle. I refused to react. I refused to give him any reason to further believe that I couldn't deal with a little scuffle and a pissy wound that was more annoying than anything.

"Was it this bad last night?" he asked.

I shrugged and rose slowly. He had seen the piece of glass I had ripped out my body last night. He had known how bad it was.

Prick. Or was that asshole? I was losing track.

"Can we go? I'd like a shower." My voice was rough from the dust and dirt.

Trey rose with me. I don't know what he was looking at from behind those thick sunglasses. But my reflection told me very clearly that I once again looked like crap.

I was getting tired of this already.

He stood there looking at me, probably trying to figure out the next nasty thing he could say to punch my buttons.

I would have gone around him, but it was too far to walk. Finally, he backed up and opened the door for me and didn't embarrass me by watching me struggle to get into the van.

He shut the side panel and climbed into the driver's seat.

The van pulled away, and I shifted in my seat. Everything was fuzzy, blurry. I knew there was really nothing to see except the beautiful desolation around me.

I would have liked to have taken it in, but I didn't have the energy. I reclined the seat and stared at the ceiling.

I could feel the warmth of the skin on my shoulders. I hadn't had time for any sunblock, so I knew I was crispy, and it would sting like a bitch until it healed. Once I got the magic-infused dressings in place, it would be so much better.

I whined in my head for a few more minutes about the abused state of my body.

"You need to drink more," he said evenly.

Yeah, I knew it. Sunburned, injured side, screaming headache, a half hour of intense activity in one hundred plus temperatures, and I hadn't really tanked up on fluids before we left.

I was well into dehydration.

The bottle in my lap was empty. When I had done that was eluding me. I reached and stretched behind Trey's seat to grab one out of the case. It seemed to keep moving just out of my reach. Little bastards needed a lesson in manners.

A large arm reached into view and snagged one of those elusive bottles out of the case. Easy for him.

The bottle then reappeared in front of my face wrapped in a strong hand.

The cap was off.

It had to have been magic. I sighed and reached for the bottle, hitting the arm connected to the hand that held it instead. The arm was hard and well muscled. The feel of the skin was hot and did funny things to my stomach.

There was an energy I didn't recognize seeping past my skin. Soothing and comforting, something I wanted, something I needed.

What did I need? I wasn't sure. The fuzz was getting darker around my vision. Maybe if I blinked, it would clear.

It didn't.

Maybe if I closed my eyes really hard, I could squeeze the darkening fuzz out of my eyes.

Nope.

If I closed my eyes, I wouldn't notice it, and it wouldn't bother me. That made sense.

My eyes closed. Yes. That's what I needed. Darkness and the feel of the energy I was touching.

Good.

CHAPTER FIVE

I Had Only Thought That, Right?

Something cool and wet splashed over my face.

It felt heavenly.

My body was burning up and cold all at the same time. I was shivering, and my head was still pounding though the attack had stopped with the destruction of the golems.

"Turn down the A/C," I groaned. My eyes finally opened, and Trey was letting the contents of the water bottle dribble over my face. I would now revere him as a god, at least, until he pissed me off again.

The water felt so good.

I wiped the refreshing liquid out of my eyes and looked at him.

His strong profile against the crystal blue desert sky sent a shiver through my body. It could have been the A/C, but more likely it was the sheer beauty of him.

"Come on, Valerie," he ordered. "Take the bottle and drink." Forceful and demanding, he almost sounded like he was worried.

I knew better. At a gut level, I knew he was tolerating me to his own end. That was okay. I was using him too. We'd both get what we wanted and part company.

He is just too beautiful, I thought and finally managed to grasp the plastic bottle and drag it to my lips. The water tasted like ambrosia. I sipped and savored the cool liquid as I savored the man glancing at me periodically.

Too beautiful, I thought again. A small grin lit the hardened lines of his face. *So beautiful.*

His next glance lengthened.

Wait.

I had only thought that, right?

I could feel the bottle slipping through my hand, and I didn't care to stop it. The fuzzy darkness was much more comforting than the water. I would hang out with the darkness for a while.

"Valerie!"

He was yelling, but he was too far away. He wouldn't notice if I ignored him, would he?

Well, if it was really important, he could come and get me.

I blinked my eyes open. It had only been a minute or two. I was sure of that. What had happened on the drive to the Enclave came to me along with the feeling of being hot and cold at the same time. My shoulders had been scorched, so that must be why I felt so cold.

The rest of my discomfort didn't seem too bad. I felt better.

Except my side. Too much damage in too little time. It was the kind of better that comes with rest and time. Lots of it. That would explain the darkness I was experiencing with my eyes open.

I was in a large room. French doors hung open, and the gossamer sheers drifted lazily in the desert breeze. Every surface was stone. The floors were scattered with area rugs. No, carpets, likely Persian.

The moon's still full light spilled in along with the clean breeze, lighting the night as if dawn had come. Beautiful.

That word rang through my aching head.

Something I'd seen had invoked that.

The desert? The sky? I didn't know, and once I saw the water on the table by the bed I was in, I didn't care.

I swung my legs over the edge and rolled up into a sitting position. I found that to be really unpleasant, my side burned, and I felt perspiration collect on my brow, but I could grab a bottle and start sipping.

And I did.

I was clean. I hadn't remembered showering.

My wounds had been tended. I felt magic I didn't recognize.

I was in one of my tank tops and my shorts, but I didn't remember putting them on.

I had no idea how long I had been out, but it was more than just a power nap.

A vague sense pricked around the edges of my memory. Just words really.

Heat exhaustion. Dehydration. Shock. Hypovolemia.

The last word made me nervous. Blood loss, serious blood loss. What if I lost control? Did I bite anybody? I knew I would to save myself. If I were too weak for anything else, I would draw blood so that I could live.

I sipped the water and looked around. I disregarded the idea. I'd be in a lab in a heartbeat. I was too much of freak not to be if the shifters found out about me.

I rubbed my shoulder and felt the sting of a healing sunburn.

A vampire with a sunburn—what a joke.

That's what I felt like most of the time. A joke. Less than a vampire, more than a witch, and smack in the middle of an Enclave of shifters whose witch had just betrayed them. I had a feeling I was going to be popular around here.

Sarcasm was all I had going for me most of the times. Now was one of them.

I put the robe at the foot of the bed on and walked into the moon's light. There were wrought-iron chairs on the balcony, and they were actually comfortable. I sat back, sipped from my bottle, and kicked my legs up onto the stone ledge.

I drank in the power of the full moon like the water in my hand. Slowly.

As easily as I could make myself sick by chugging the water, I could do the same with the energy. Too much of a good thing, or in this case, too much and too fast could do a lot of damage to the healing that had been done.

I didn't need that.

Marc didn't need me wasting time either.

So I let my body drink and drink. Taking in slow sips, feeling the water and energy fill me, invigorate me, flow through me, and wash over me.

I felt the energy hitch at my wounded side. The flow was off, but then again, it had taken multiple hits, so it had a right to complain.

How long had it been since I simply relaxed in Her glow, basked in Her light? Too long, and I had paid for that in spades today. I should have sat with Her last night.

I should have asked Trey to help me to the backyard.

Why didn't I ask? Pride be damned! I could have avoided a lot of grief today if I'd just asked!

"I'm not paying you $1,500 per day just to nap, Valerie." Now I remember.

He's an asshole. That's why I didn't ask.

I also remembered the touch of his lips against mine, and my body shivered. My nipples hardened at the memory. I crossed my arms over my chest and sipped nonchalantly.

"After today, you're getting off cheap," I sighed.

My body shivered again. What the hell? He wasn't *that* hot. Oh, never mind, he really was. However, the shivering was becoming constant. The desert breeze was warm. I was wrapped in a robe. The water was room temperature, so there was no reason I should feel cold. Sunburns could really screw with the body's ability to differentiate hot and cold, but this was not right.

I wrapped my hand around my side and felt heat. Not body heat, but the heat a wound throws off when it's infected.

Fuck! How in the hell could that have happened? I had that crap contained twice, burned it away. I would have felt something!

Holy crap, I did feel something. A shard of glass slicing through my body. Could that have been it?

No! There is no way. I would have known!

I wasn't showing any of the normal symptoms, like dead or zombied in twenty-four hours. If that's what's happened, I had been infected twenty-four hours ago. This thing should be full blown. What I was feeling was my body fighting an infection.

My breath hitched. My heartbeat jumped.

Antibodies. My body is fighting this! If I had, in fact, been infected. Well, I guess I was going to find out.

Lucky me. I was going to be a lab rat. Could this day have sucked any worse?

It was a statement, not a question. Don't answer that.

"What's wrong?" Christ. He had heard my heart rate rise. He knew something was up. I had to be cool.

"How sure are you that the infection can't be spread from person to person contact?" I asked. I also realized that if it was possible, he would be infected. We had been way too close to each other. Or not close enough.

Damn it.

"One hundred percent," he said. "Some of my people had been bitten by those infected, and nothing happened."

"That's really good to know. Because I don't think I can make it to the lab on my own," I said. I pulled my knees into my chest and pinned my arms there as well. I was shaking; the fever was starting to kick in big, and I was miserable.

I had heard about the effects of infections. I'd just never experienced them until now. It's an experience I really could do without.

"It's the middle of the night. Why…" He didn't finish. Bright boy that he is had figured it out all by himself.

I didn't see him move. I didn't feel the gentle, feather-light touch until I was firmly in his arms and moving down a hall.

"You shouldn't… Don't you have flunkies to do this kind of stuff?" I didn't want flunkies doing this. I could feel his heat through my fever-wrack body, easing the chills and calming the tremors that were trying desperately to warm me.

"Nobody touches you, but me." We were moving at a fair clip. It was enough to create an uncomfortable breeze and begin chilling my body again.

"That's going to make it hard on the doctor and lab techs," I whispered.

I snuggled more closely into his shoulder at the junction of his neck. He smelled intoxicating.

"I'll make some exceptions."

His blood pounded through his throat with enticing clarity. It sounded as if it were calling to me. A little bite. Who would know, right?

Probably the guy I bit. My life expectancy would be zero if I did that. Even though my bite would paralyze for a few minutes, it wore off quickly, and he was a lot faster than me. I'd never make it to the door.

And there was Marc to think about. My lover? Remember him? Guilt much?

The man who held me when I pushed too far. The man who had initiated me into sex. He trained me, he protected me, he taught me, and he loved…

He didn't. Not really. I knew it. He was fond of me in a "friends with benefits" way. We made a good team. We were compatible, comfortable.

I wouldn't risk him by losing control now. I'd never risk him. And if everything worked out, I was in the process of creating the cure within my body.

Maybe my mixed heritage would do the trick. There had been nothing in the report about humans having been infected, so there was no way to tell if that made a difference.

I really hoped his lab people were good, but then again, if they were that good, I may never see the light of day ever.

Marc was a vampire, nothing more. If he was cured, he'd be let go. I was sure of that. They would have already killed him otherwise.

I, on the other hand, might be interesting to experiment on. Even my "own kind" could be cruel to hybrids. Marc had told me enough to be wary. Marc had nearly all the contact with the council and made all of the deals for our services. I didn't even know if they knew anything about me.

This was my first negotiation. I'd probably fucked it up, and I'll be lucky if I got out of this alive. From what I'd been told about what could happen in labs, dead might be preferable.

"When?" His voice was soft, or maybe I was just that far gone.

"The shack… maybe?" I whispered. I really didn't know. The minute I'd pulled on the moon to shield myself, the infection backed off. Even before I started to actively threaten it.

Was it something about the moon's magic? It couldn't be me; it had tried to go for me initially. My head hurt too much to think.

Trey's science geeks would figure something out, and that was a worrying thought.

"How?" We had moved down I think. It was becoming brighter and louder. Yelling, screaming, roars, growls. It was deafening. I tried to curl into Trey's body, one of my arms snaking around his neck.

I wanted to scream at the assault on my senses. This was where they were holding the infected. It smelled better than the shack Trey had blown sky high. I did scent traces of disinfectant, soaps, attempts to care for those suffering.

"The glass? I don't know…" Fear was gripping me, and the man who had me in his arms would do nothing to save me unless it benefited his kind.

I could feel the panic in my heart. The noises, the smells, nothing reassured me as he continued to move, dragging me further into a nightmare.

A heavy door opened. The last barrier between me and raging, crazed, infected beings was gone. Now I truly knew what deafening was.

I began to push against Trey, trying to free myself from his grasp and run. I had to get away. Terror didn't even begin to cover what I felt, and I couldn't make any headway with a grip to equal iron bands wrapped around my fevered and sweat-soaked body.

I pulled on the moon. I had just tanked up. I could feel Her and the energy that my body was trying to use to heal and fight the infection. I was going to use it to fight Trey.

"Put me down," I gasped. By breath was for shit. Between the panic and the fact that I didn't feel like my lungs were working properly. I blasted Trey with the same power I used to burn the infection. Fire of moon and magic and fear.

He paused.

He fucking paused!

The power I could generate was sizable. The power I ran through the desert this afternoon had disrupted the golems carrying the infection. Dust rose, the ground shook, and Trey paused.

He held me tighter, but he didn't move.

Soft, warm energy began to snake under my skin wherever Trey touched me.

"Don't!" I cried. Not that it didn't feel good. It did. Blessed moon it felt wonderful. "You could become infected."

"No," he said gently. "I won't."

As sick as I was, I could still think, and I too was pretty quick. He had already done this with others. I no longer felt special, but I stopped worrying about him.

Even though I had blasted him with enough energy to kill him, it mattered that he was still safe from the infection, well, at least getting it from me.

I was feeling really messed up about now.

"Swear to me if after you have what you need from the antibodies, you'll let me go," I rasped. "You'll let me do the job you hired me for and won't keep me here. Promise me."

My face was still buried in his neck, both arms hanging on to him.

I felt him lean his head against mine. His warmth was still seeping into me though he had stilled his energy.

"I promise, Valerie."

He meant it. There was no doubt in my mind. I relaxed somewhat in his arms and nodded.

"Sorry about your shirt," I whispered. I had caught the scent of it burning when I tried to blast him. It was ruined, but he was alive, so I was going with that being a really good trade off.

I had, however, tried to kill him. He may still take exception to that at a later date.

He started moving again. The noise increasing as we got closer to the cells.

We turned a corner, and the cells came into view.

The noise increased.

As soon as the noise hit a fevered pitch. It stopped. It didn't just slow or die off. It stopped.

So did Trey.

I heard a door open, and somebody moved to Trey's side.

"What the hell happened?" It was a woman's voice. It was flat and untrusting, tinged with a slight British accent and an attitude. That may have been redundant.

"I don't know, Mila," Trey answered. "We just showed up, and they quieted.

"Is she the witch you hired?" she asked. Gods, the disdain in her voice was thick. Then again, the last witch kinda fucked them over.

"Yes, and she's infected." We were moving again. I glanced up from his shoulder to take in the scene behind us. Shifters. Some fully turned. Some half-man or woman, half-beast, and just as we entered a brightly lit clinical slice of my deepest fears, I saw Marc.

He was chained to a wall by his wrists and his neck. His shirt was gone, he was spattered with blood, emaciated, and his eyes were blackened. There were no signs of recognition, barely any signs of life, except that he was on his feet and watching as I disappeared into the exam room.

Trey set me on the exam table. At least, it was padded. Other than that, it was everything you'd expect in a medical environment. Cold, sterile, medicinal smelling and much too bright.

I had never even been to a doctor, a hospital, or any clinical office in my twenty-six years. This was everything I had come to expect, and it did nothing to relieve my anxiety.

I tried to blot out the poking and prodding and other workings and machinations that Mila performed. I recognized an IV bag. I'd need liquids, and she put an oxygen mask on me. My breathing wasn't easy or strong. I, simply put, felt awful.

Marc.

I focused on Marc. I was here for him. And now, saving him could possibly save the shifters and weres. A twofer. What a deal.

I let my energy reach out. I could find Marc. I could actually feel him again. I guess proximity allowed the binding to reconnect. It felt odd. Muffled and vague. I didn't want to think about why. I just had to believe that I could heal him, and everything would be as it was.

I'd chalk it up to both of us being a bit under the weather.

I could also feel the infection magic. I felt it in Marc and those around him.

I felt it in myself, finally. And I felt it in the room with me.

It was waiting. Like an ambush predator, it lay for the opportunity to strike.

It was within ten feet of me.

CHAPTER SIX

"If I promise to behave, would you remove the restraints?"

I reluctantly opened my eyes and blinked back the bright clinical lighting. I felt like crap before Mila had started fucking with me. Now feeling like crap was at a whole new level.

Mila and Trey needed to get out of the room. I had to tell them…

I managed to turn my head. I could see the door, an observation window, Trey sitting in a chair way too small for him in front of the window, and a cabinet to his right. It was constructed of glass and metal and held dressings, bandages, tapes, and assorted first-aid paraphernalia.

The cabinet was where the infectious magic was lying in wait. The dressings and bandages were infected. The dressings I was wearing were infected. Well, that solved that little riddle.

I now knew how I'd been infected and who had done it. Gabrielle.

If she wasn't dead, I wanted to talk to her. If she was dead, she could still be helpful. I didn't think that she was the caster, so the job was still on whether she lived or died.

First things first. I had to get the dressing off and then torch the infected dressings in the cabinet.

Well, maybe the first thing was to get up.

Easier said and all that.

Lolling my head to one side and taking an inventory of my surroundings had been a push in and of itself.

Well, maybe I didn't have to get up. I could contain and burn from a lying-down position. I would, however, have to move my hands to direct my energy. What I had left of it.

"Trey…" Goddess, I sounded worse than I felt. His head snapped up, his beautiful blue eyes focusing intently on me.

So beautiful . . . Crap, now I remembered! He had heard me muse about his beauty. The last thing he needed was an ego boost. Whatever, I'd deal with that later.

I managed to move my arm enough to reach out to him.

Amazingly, he got up and took my hand. His touch was more tender than I had expected. I expected perfunctory and, like this room, clinical. There was more. I wished I could have taken the time to sort it out, but I didn't have the luxury, and neither did Trey and Mila.

"Get out," I rasped. "Infection."

This was going to be harder than I thought. I couldn't speak much above a whisper, and stringing together a full sentence was going to be impossible.

Trey leaned in. His forearm rested above my head on the table as his fingers brushed my hair from my forehead. I was soaked. I don't think I would have touched me at this point.

Trey hadn't hesitated. His nearness did something to me, and I wasn't sure I liked it. I didn't need to be unnerved right now, not like this. The look in his eyes were a mix of tenderness and concern that I could have rested in for hours.

"I'll be fine," he said softly. "You can't infect me."

I shook my head. This brain-damaged shifter was going to get himself killed.

"No." I worked to get my breath. "Infected dressings. Cabinet."

He lifted his head and caught Mila's attention. "She said the dressing is infected."

Mila came to the other side of the table. She was not what I had expected from the accent. Her hair was black with blonde tips. It was spiky, and on her, it looked wild and sophisticated all at the same time.

Her eyes were the shade of gray, the color you see rolling in from Canada just before a wicked storm. Her skin was like porcelain, and she had a shape that only existed in magazines.

Not even the damn lab coat could hide the graceful curves and elegant posture of this woman.

"I should change her dressings," Mila said. The dressings were an obvious afterthought. There was so much to do, and that just wasn't high on the list. But right now, it needed to be off of the list.

"NO!" I wheezed and shook my head hard. It just made me dizzy. "Infected."

I was getting nowhere. I needed to act because I didn't have much to act with. If I was lucky, I could contain and burn the infection in the cabinet.

That should get my point across.

"Calm down, Valerie." Trey went for soothing. Somehow it wasn't effective. The asshole was easier. I didn't even know this guy.

I pulled on the last of my reserves, threw the containment at the cabinet, and started the burn.

Mila screamed as the colors danced and the infection showed itself. The glass crackled under the heat and magic until it fell to the floor in an unimpressive crash.

"Shit!" Trey was the master of beasts and understatements. "Draw what you need," he whispered as his hand tightened around mine.

I had no idea what he meant until I felt the vast pool of power that opened up to me through Trey's touch. It was liquid fire in my veins. Cleansing and powerful, and the burn glowed in an array of purples that I had never seen before.

His energy was intense and supported me without expectation or hesitation. It wasn't quite the sensual energy he had touched me with at the house, but a pure reservoir that was his or that of his kind whatever the hell that was.

"Cut away my bandages. Burn them," I whispered.

"Mila. Her dressings and bandages," he said strongly, shocking the doctor out of the daze she was in. "Can you remove them and get them burned without becoming infected?"

I was faintly aware of Mila nodding and moving out of my sight.

Apparently, latex was an effective protective barrier against this infection.

That's all she wore as she cut away the bandages and tossed them.

Latex. That seemed lame, but I wasn't going to complain. The crap was off of me and burning merrily ten feet away.

"Can you sense any more in the Enclave?" Trey whispered. The warmth of his breath slid across my cheek. The warmth of him filled me through his hands.

I relaxed, drawing gently of what he offered, and let my magic spread through the Enclave.

I had no idea shifters could use energy. Trey was surprising, and I was grateful for the boost. I knew I had nothing left, and I was running solely on what he let me draw.

I wondered if I would still be able to heal.

Trey's energy was so easy to wield and bend to my needs. Soft, warm energy became my own magic, and I stretched out searching the Enclave for the dark magic.

Nothing. I could feel no sign of it, and I was glad. I was just too tired to do anything more.

The burn was complete. I was really tired of this crap.

I let Trey's energy wrap around my exhaustion and injury. I could feel it taking hold and soothe my wounding. It was as peaceful as the light of the moon on my skin. The soft flutters of healing and comfort eased me into warmth and darkness.

Bright lights, confusion, fear, and violence.

That was the essence of the repeated dreams that played through my mind as my body continued to fight the infection that ravaged me.

I heard soft murmurs around me as I tried to bring my hand to my face and found I couldn't. I was restrained by my ankles, wrists, and by a strap around my waist.

He lied! Trey lied! They had found out! I was now a science project.

I thrashed and strained against the bonds.

"Let me go. Let me up!" God, my arm hurt. Why did my arm hurt? I'd deal with that later. I was screaming and loud. It was nice to know I had some of my strength back.

Trey leaned into my vision and pressed my shoulders into the exam table. "You promised me, Trey!" I screamed with all of the betrayal I felt deep in my bones. "You promised me!"

"You broke Mila's ribs, Valerie," he said calmly.

I did what? What the hell was going on? I had been unconscious for goddess knows how long. I hadn't done anything. But his statement got him the results he was looking for.

Stunned silence.

"You woke up swinging. Broke a couple of Mila's ribs," he softly explained. "Then you punched Sean in the face and broke your arm in the process of fighting them."

My heart was still pounding wildly, and I could feel sweat drenching my body.

"Couldn't you have just knocked me out?" I gasped. This was the singularly most terrifying moment in my life. It also explained why my arm hurt and told me that I hadn't been dreaming. I had been coming to, terrified.

"Mila tried that. Your body stopped fighting the infection," Trey explained.

Everything felt different, sounded different. Trey even looked different somehow. I felt too screwed up and tired to even think about it. I just wanted out of the lab and into a space that didn't trigger panic in me. The rental house worked for me. "Restraints seemed the best choice all the way around. I can't have you injuring my people, and I wasn't going to risk losing you."

Of course, he wouldn't risk losing me until this mess was cleaned up and over with. Then I'm sure I'd have an invitation to get lost.

"Is Mila all right?" I asked. Imminent danger seemed to have passed from my subconscious, and I was more relaxed. Being strapped to an exam table didn't do it for me though, and I would ask to be released and placed back into whatever room I had started in.

I would hesitate to call it "my" room. Nothing here was permanent for me. It was borrowed and would be returned, if it hadn't been destroyed in the process of this job. That's where the expenses part came in on the daily rates.

I broke it; you bought it.

"She's already healed," Trey replied as he released my shoulders and stood over me. "You're not, so I suggest you rest."

"I thought you weren't paying me to nap?" I managed a smile. Somehow Trey's presence felt more comforting, but I'm sure he wasn't done irritating the hell out of me. Not by a long shot.

"You are less mouthy when unconscious," he said. "But you have been useful."

Yup, I was right. Irritating.

The hard lines I was used to seeing in his face weren't as present, and something had changed in the way he was looking at me. It didn't really feel like he was trying to push my buttons. There was something softer in his eyes.

Maybe watching me risk my life a couple times made a difference.

I wasn't made of the hearty stuff that shifters, weres, and vampires were. When I broke, it took longer to heal. The arm on its own would take a week, maybe two. With magic, it would take two or three days. Mila had healed in a matter of an hour, maybe less.

I was sensitive to heat and cold, whereas Trey could take below freezing temperature in jeans and a T-shirt. I had suffered from heat exhaustion in under thirty minutes.

Bounty hunting supernatural beings seemed to be out of my league right now. I'd been doing this for five years, and now I couldn't go a day without some disaster or another occurring.

I could just be a mercenary witch. Hiring out for spells, wards, amulets, and the like, only taking jobs based on the risk-reward ratio.

I was going to get myself killed doing this.

Every time I turned around, something was going wrong. What the hell was going on?

Marc.

Had he been buffering me from the serious dangers we took on? Was this normal, and I just didn't know it? We had been through some serious shit together, but now I was beginning to feel that it had only been the tip of the iceberg.

Why would he do that? Why would he keep me unprepared all of this time? Once again, I was lost in my own thoughts and oblivious to my surroundings, which thankfully were not lethal at the moment.

"Are you all right, Valerie?" Trey asked. Gods, he did think me fragile. He might take a shot at me, but it didn't have the bite that was present last night, or was it the night before?

I wasn't even sure what day it was anymore.

"If I promise to behave, would you remove the restraints?" I asked, completely ignoring his query. I wasn't going to share my fears and self-doubts with him. It wouldn't do either of us any good.

"If you promised to behave, then I'd know you were lying." There was the smallest flicker in his eyes as the corner of his mouth kicked up just the slightest. "Besides, I like knowing exactly where you are."

"You've known where I was since you sat outside that house and waited for it to blow up with me in it, Trey." Yeah, I was feeling better. Sweaty, exhausted, and weak as a newborn, but the mouth was back in working order.

It didn't matter what Marc's motives were. The fact still remained that I was unprepared for this—*any of this*—and Trey was my best bet for success and survival.

I didn't know him. I didn't understand him, but I was going to have to trust him with my life. I guess I already have.

After all, I did try to fry him, and I'm still alive.

I took a deep breath.

"You made it out," he remarked casually. As if that sort of thing happens all of the time in his world.

"Whatever," I snorted. "I need a shower and food. Then I have a job to do.

You did hire me."

"Yes. And you have been a pain in the ass and worth every penny so far," he stated plainly. "You prevented me from spreading that magic through an entire neighborhood." His hands worked the buckle on one of the ankle restraints. He took his time, letting his warm hands caress my bare skin as he worked.

Awesome, I hadn't shaved in three days.

"You protected my men and myself on the way here." His voice was low, and somehow he seemed just the slightest bit pissed.

With my ankles released, he skimmed his hands up my legs, his eyes following and stopped briefly at my hip bones. The heat that radiated from his palms was sinking deeply into my body, and the lower muscle of my abdomen clenched lightly.

Damn him! It was that same energetic crap he pulled at the house. I didn't know how he could do that, but he needed to stop. I had work to do, and that was really distracting.

It made me wonder what he would be like in bed. No doubt, that was the point.

His eyes closed, and he breathed in deeply. His light brown lashes rested on his cheeks for a moment before his gaze found mine unerringly.

I couldn't read him. It was a confusing mess of anger and desire.

I was simply trying to look annoyed. I couldn't tell if I actually wanted him or if the energy he eased into my body made me feel like I wanted him. Either way, this was bad timing.

He released my broken arm, still in a splint.

"You found dark magic here in the Enclave and eradicated it though you were already infected and weakened."

The other wrist restraint was unbuckled, and he took my hand in his as he lowered his head to lay a gentle kiss to it.

I was sure my heart stopped beating all together at that point, and I suddenly understood that he did want me. He wasn't messing with me. He wanted me, and it pissed him off.

Shit!

He let my hand go and planted his elbows on either side of my hips and slowly unbuckled the waist restraint.

"And your body has given us the weapon we needed to fight this." He slid the hem of my tank top up, over my navel and kissed my stomach.

He hadn't shaved since I first saw him, and the feel of the light brown stubble against my tender flesh did very odd things to my body. Things I'd never felt with Marc. Things I didn't want to feel now… under these circumstances. Maybe later. If things were different.

My eyes had closed. I'm not really sure when that had happened, but I didn't seem to have complete control over my body's responses at this point or my vocalization as I realized a light groan escaped my lips.

I closed my eyes more tightly. I had just screwed myself. He knew I wanted him too. Chances are, he knew that when he had me caged in his arms at breakfast.

His breath caressed my belly. Full, deep breaths warmed my skin and other parts that needed to be in the damn shower!

I opened my eyes and hoped I didn't look as frightened as I felt.

The firelight that danced in his eyes wasn't reflected from any other source.

It came from him.

He wasn't canine or feline or any other common mammals that shifters normally became.

I still had no clue what he was, but his status on the "dangerous meter" just went up a few more notches.

That should have scared me. Maybe it still would, but right now, I couldn't manage it.

The hem of my tank top inched up along with the light kisses and caress of his breath.

My hands fisted in the sheet that covered the thin pad I still rested on. I wanted to touch him, and I wanted him to continue. I wanted him, but this just couldn't happen.

I had to resolve Marc.

Oh god. When had I gone from saving him to resolving him? Was Marc something I needed to manage before I could bed Trey and not feel slutty? Probably.

I sucked.

"Trey…," I started. I stammered. I could feel the burn of tears begin, and I needed them to stop. I was not going to cry!

Yes, I likely would, but later. The shower did seem like the best place. It was becoming my favorite place to cry—quiet, warm, and enough noise to cover the soft sobs that I would indulge in. I also got clean. Temporarily.

"Tell me no," he whispered against my skin. His lips brushed across the base of my ribs. The edge of my tank top had reached my breasts. The cool air of the room was a sensual contrast to the warmth of his breath tickling my flesh. "Tell me you don't want me, Valerie," he purred.

Cocky, arrogant bastard. Simply put, he was a shifter.

Intimidating, pushy, high-handed, sexy, gentle, and tender. I could do nothing except sigh at that moment.

That and put my hands on his to stop him from climbing higher and taking the shred of sense I had to myself along with the tank top.

I stared at the ceiling. His eyes would simply undo my resistance.

"I am telling you no, Trey." Wow. I sounded a lot more calm and sane than I felt, and that was good. I also felt his grip lighten under my hands, and his body stiffened almost imperceptibly, readying for rejection. I probably should reject him. That would be the smartest thing I could do right about now. "But I can't tell you that I don't want you because I do." Sometimes I'm just not all that bright. My body was telling him everything anyway. He'd know the lie the second it left my lips.

His kisses slowly trailed back down, the hem of my top following to the top of my shorts.

I expected him to have a triumphant and somewhat gloating look on his face. It wasn't there.

A flush to his skin. A soft smile. Flames that danced behind the blue of his eyes. It had been as hard for him to respond to my no as it was for me to say it.

"Mila can help you shower if you need assistance." His voice was thick, deep, and I could feel it through the path his lips had taken over my body. This was killing him, just a little. I managed to suppress the grin that threatened to flit across my face. He was hurting, and for all the shit he had given me from the moment we met, I thought a little pain could do him some good.

He was still an asshole.

I pushed up and swung my legs over the side slowly. The arm still hurt— duh, it was broken—but nothing else was bothersome. Except the utter lack of strength and energy. I needed food, I needed to sit in the moon's light, and I needed to wake up not strapped to a table.

"I'll be fine," I said and slid off the table and onto my feet. I would need to hold on to the table for the first few steps. I was sure of that. I was going to be wobbly.

"Do you have any food preferences?"

Right now, a couple bags of O positive would be great, but I didn't want to try to explain that to him—ever. It was probably a good thing that I had been restrained.

"A couple steaks, rare. Some steamed veggies. Lots of water." I gave him my order and leaned casually against the table. I would be waiting until he left the room to embarrass myself with what would be a lame attempt at walking.

"Rare." He looked at me with an incredulous grin.

"Yes. You know," I said. "Introduce the meat briefly yet politely to the flames and slap it on the plate."

He continued to stand and stare at me. He was thinking. I could see the smoke coming out of his ears.

"What?" I asked, curious to see if he was going to share the secret of what was getting him to think.

"Not many women have that healthy an appetite," he said, looking quite pleased with me. I made him happy by ordering real food. Not a salad, not the usual low-cal, low-fat crap most human women eat, but real food. God, he was easy.

"I'm not most women," I stated. It was obvious to me, but I had passed for human all my life. I had forgotten that others just assumed me to be what I appeared as. Tall, human, female, and forgettable, unless I broke you in half. People tended to remember that.

"Yes. I've noticed." His eyes roamed my body, lingering on my legs. At six foot tall, I had a lot of leg, and he seemed to appreciate it.

"Hey. Food." I snapped my fingers in front of the section of thigh he had paused on. His eyes came to mine, and I smiled. "I'm starved," I added softly.

He smiled and turned away, walking out the door.

The halls were still eerily quiet. Only the occasional rustling of chain in the silence.

CHAPTER SEVEN

I Found It Sweet Of Her To Care

There was a door on the other side of the exam room. It led to a bathroom.

My bags had been moved here, so I would have clean clothing to change into.

I was also in a different exam room than I had started out in.

The glass cabinet was in tact, and there were no marks from the burn on the floor or wall. That was how I could tell I was somewhere different, but I had no idea where I was. The observation window looked out into cells just as the other one had, but these were empty.

The quiet was almost eerie.

The bathroom itself was sparse but functional. It could have been a bare shower head in the middle of nowhere, out in the open, as long as I had hot water. Lots and lots of it.

I pulled my toiletries out of one bag and a change of clothing from another. Khaki cargo pants, a white tank top, and a black button-down shirt. It was cooler in the subsection of the Enclave, and I could remove the long-sleeve blouse later. If I made it back to the upper levels where it might be warmer. Right now, I just wanted to be clean and have a few moments to myself.

I let nirvana—that was the hot water—cascade over my body for a long, long time. It washed away the grime and sweat of my most recent brush with getting fucked by my lack of knowledge and experience.

How could I have so little experience after five years of training and actually doing the job? Marc and I had brushed up against death a couple of times, a few close calls. We had been out there! We relied on each other; we covered each other! There was no way he didn't trust me to carry my own weight!

Or, did he?

I shook it off. No matter what, I had to make sure that Marc survived this. My body still ached from the abuse it had taken. Being beaten up by an exploding building and some golems and having been infected with that truly nasty virus left me feeling exhausted and depleted. The food that I was expecting would go a long way in my recovery.

Get dressed. Eat. Tank up energetically.

I wondered if it were night. Sitting in the moonlight would be a blessing right now. Otherwise, I would draw from the earth. It wasn't as potent for me, but it worked in a pinch. Since the Enclave was built of the desert, I could do it anywhere within its confines. I just preferred the outdoors.

Trey's energy would work as well, but that was definitely a last resort. It and he were too tempting.

The way he was speaking to me, looking at me, and touching me left me feeling off guard. Around him, I needed to be on guard and ready.

I didn't know what I needed to be ready for, I just knew I needed to be ready for something, anything. Mostly, ready to say no when my body was screaming yes.

He had been upset at my fight in the desert on the way here, and he was upset at wanting me.

I let that roll around in my head as the hot water continued to pound my body.

I came up with nothing, except that it probably had nothing to do with me. Reluctantly, I shut off the water and got my prune-y self out, dried, and dressed.

I brushed my hair out and put it in a ponytail. I normally wore no jewelry. I could wear silver—it had no negative effects on my skin—but having been stabbed with a silver knife, I could verify that silver and my insides didn't get along at all. Yes, being stabbed at all is a painful experience, but silver just adds a new dimension to pain that moves into excruciating. Then the pain travels, and it take twice as long to heal.

No jewelry for me today. I'd left it all at the rental house. I didn't feel that accessorizing was necessary to do this job.

When I stepped out of the bathroom, the mocha shifter was in the chair by the door.

He stood quickly as I entered and looked me over. The keen interest I had seen in his face at the house was gone.

"The beast master will be back shortly," he announced pleasantly enough. He was taller than me, but most shifters seemed to be. Even Mila was slightly taller than six foot. He had shaved his head and was a very good look on him. His eyes were the color of deep amber, alert and aware.

His features were strong but had a fine quality that made him simply easy to look at. Feline. Panther, I thought. He moved with a fluid grace that oozed predation.

"Thank you." I paused and took a shot in the dark. "Sean." He inclined his head in acknowledgment.

"Is there anything you require until he returns?"

Polite formality. I didn't know what to make of it. I really assumed that shifters, all shifters were like Trey when I first met him. Rude.

This I hadn't expected at all.

It made me suspicious.

I made my way to the exam table and pushed myself to sit on it. I would have hopped, but I was still too weak to manage it.

"Trey said that you are his second in command and that I could come to you with questions." I crossed my ankles and swung my legs softly. I was going for nonthreatening. I wasn't sure it was working.

Sean remained standing and was doing a good job at trying to look relaxed. "Yes, of course," he responded. He wanted to pace the room. I could feel it emanating from him in waves. He was like an animal in a cage and not happy about it. "Anything I can answer for you, I will."

"Gabrielle. Tell me about her," I said plainly.

"Spy, betrayer, dead." It had been a simple and unemotional statement. I now couldn't bitch slap her myself. It would have been easier to interrogate her had she been alive. Depending on how powerful she had been, I might have been able to force some answers from her before they killed her.

Oh well. I'd just have to settle for what I could get from her stuff. Unless they destroyed her things as well.

"Tell me you still have her belongings in tact," I asked hopefully.

"We haven't gone into her quarters," he said tightly. His eyes flashed gold through the deep amber that had graced his beautiful face. "We just don't know how safe it would be."

"I'll get in and make it safe. There might be information I can get out of her room," I told him. He started to pace slowly and in a controlled manner. Did he hate being down here? Was it me? Was it the talk of Gabrielle? I just couldn't tell.

"What do you think you'll find?" he asked, barely sparing me a glance.

"I'm not thinking of anything specific. Just hoping for a clue," I said. "Beings leave residues behind, but she may have cleaned up before you got to her. I won't know until I get in there."

"Well, I do hope that you are able to unearth something helpful." Sean was trying to find his calm in the middle of the irritation. He was doing fairly well, but I could tell something was eating at him.

"I'm sure I'll find something. Thanks for the answers." I pulled the brace off of my arm and gently rubbed the broken area. The movements of lymph and other fluids felt good, and I would take the brace off every couple of hours as it healed to help speed the process along.

"I'm here to help," he replied softly.

"I appreciate that, Sean, but I don't need a sitter. You don't really need to be here," I assured him as I babied my arm some more. "I'm sure you have more important things to do."

"The beast master asked me to stay with you until he returned." The pacing continued.

I slid the brace back on and slid off of the table. That seemed to make Sean a bit more nervous.

"Is Trey angry about me in some way?" I asked and then thought about the situation for a split second. "I know you haven't had a lot of success with witches lately, but did I do something to piss him off?"

"You would have to take that up with him," the polite and, apparently, politically correct shifter replied. Damn him.

"I'd like to see Marc." I slipped my tennis shoes on and waited for a reply. I wasn't getting anywhere with this guy. Trey had even said I should go to him with questions. Apparently, I haven't asked the right ones.

"You will have to arrange that with the beast master."

"I don't need to go into his cell," I said in my most polite "I don't like that answer" tone.

"I'm sorry," he said. So stoic, so 'not sorry.' "You will have to wait." His pacing had stopped him at the door, effectively blocking it.

I was weighing the possible outcomes of just heading for the door and pushing past Sean when I heard a muffled shot. It sounded odd, almost like a silencer, but not quite right.

I looked into his eyes with a serious amount of confusion. He, however, was non-pulsed at the noise.

The scream I heard moments later was horrific, tortured, and it belonged to Marc.

My heart threatened to tear itself from my chest as I lunged toward the door and straight into Sean.

"Let me go, Sean." My teeth ground, and I was biting back the screams that wanted out. Sean's body blocked me, touching me only enough to keep me from the door. He was fucking playing with me as my lover was being tortured.

I was seriously pissed.

Marc was being tortured. I didn't care to find out why; I just wanted to stop it, and Sean was in my way.

It didn't matter that Sean wasn't as strong as Trey because I wasn't as strong as a human woman at the moment. I could push and kick and threaten all I wanted to, and I would lose. I'm pretty sure I couldn't take Sean even if I was fully healed either, but I didn't want to find out.

"You'll have to wait." Again, not a hint of emotion came from him.

"What are they doing to Marc?" I was still pushing, still trying to reach the door, and still trying to sound threatening instead of near panicked. "What the fuck is going on, Sean?"

He continued to counter my every move with annoying ease. I was tiring quickly; he wasn't going to break a sweat.

"Mila finished the serum." He delivered the news and stared at me as I stilled my movements and processed that little tidbit.

It had to have been sheer luck that the punch I threw connected with his jaw. It surprised him, but it barely fazed him.

"You're using him as a fucking guinea pig?" I screamed and screamed. "I will fucking kill you if he dies!" By this time Sean had moved so fast, I couldn't follow him. One minute, I was standing in front of him swinging and threatening. The next thing I know, my back is pressed against his chest, my arms are pinned to my sides, and my feet are no longer touching the ground.

"Settle down." His arms had me firmly banded against him, and he still hadn't broken a sweat. "Mila knows what she's doing."

"Right!" I yelled. "Marc was expendable!"

I heard metal clatter against stone just outside the door, and then the door flew open, nearly unhinging it.

Trey stepped in and took in the scene. Rage flashed across his features, and low, menacing growl left his throat.

"What did I tell you, Sean?" Trey's voice was nearly inhuman as he spoke to his second in command. Flames flashed in his eyes. Searing anger washed over both Sean and myself. "What were my orders?"

"She was going to hurt herself fighting to get to her vampire, Trey."

Her vampire, he had said. Yes, he was. Five years of working, training, healing, and taking care of each other did make him mine in some ways. He was my lover and my friend, and I was really tired of being away from him.

The pressure on my body loosened, and then he hesitantly released me. I wasted no time trying to push past Trey, who annoyingly caught me with one arm around my waist. "Forgive me," Sean continued.

Sean's words were honest, and I could feel the request for his life to continue in the subtext of that statement. Sean had done something that could cost him his life. I had no idea what that might be, but not knowing what was going on seemed par for the course for me.

"Damn it!" I cursed, unable to free myself from Trey's hold. Frustrated didn't cover my feelings at this point. Marc was screaming—wait. Marc had stopped screaming.

Shit. Was he dead? Had they killed him?

I reached out to the binding between us to find it still intact. Relief allowed me to relax just a bit, reign in my fear and anger, and take stock of my lack of energy now that the adrenaline was wearing off.

Trey's hold firmed. I was thinking he probably felt my knees begin to buckle.

"Out!" Trey growled. The tension in his body was disturbing; he was barely keeping himself together. I had no idea why he would be so pissed at Sean; he was just doing his job. Then again, apparently he hadn't followed some order I hadn't been aware of.

These shifters were pissing me off. Had I mentioned that I'd never wanted to come in contact with them—ever? Yes, I do believe I had, and my opinion hasn't changed.

Trey shook as he ordered Sean from the room. My back was still pinned against him. I tried elbowing him in the face. I connected, badly.

"Valerie," he sighed in exasperation. The blow hadn't been very effective. Hell, *I* hadn't been very effective since this whole thing started. Why should now be any different?

"Trey! You prick! Let me go!" I yelled. I was losing steam and could no longer actually scream. I hadn't eaten. The meal that Trey had gotten me was on the floor outside the room. The food was in disarray, but amazingly it was still on the tray itself. It looked really good.

He flipped me around in his arms. The blaze that had been in his eyes was now a flicker, but he still didn't look happy. Like I cared.

"He was dying, Valerie," he said angrily. "Mila didn't think he would last much longer. It was either try this on him first or watch him die." He loosened his grip and tried not to look angry. It wasn't working. "She was trying to save him."

I hadn't really calmed down much, but I was running on fumes. "You're still a prick," I muttered. "I want to see Marc, now Trey."

He looked hesitant but took my arm and led me into the dimly lit stone hallway. I could already see Marc as he hung limply from the wall from which he had been chained.

He still looked like shit.

Mila stood outside his cell with a tranquilizer gun still in her hand.

"How is he doing, Mila?" Trey asked as we stepped up behind her. She was observing from a very safe distance, but I knew that unless somebody was willing to get in there, Mila wasn't going to get the detailed information that was necessary.

"I can't tell. He's a vampire. He doesn't breathe, and his heart doesn't beat." Mila turned around and looked at Trey and glanced at me. "I don't even know if he's alive."

"He is," I said as I tried to move around her and to the door of the cage. Trey's grip tightened around my arm, halting me in place. I was so tired of being managed. So tired, period. I was going to get Marc and get the fuck out of here. Nothing else mattered. "When was the last time he fed?" I asked.

"He hasn't fed since we took him," Trey informed me. "It's been seven days. He refused the bagged blood we tried to give him."

Seven days. That meant I had been at the Enclave for three days. No wonder I was starving. And if I was starving, Marc would be downright dangerous, ravenous, and a hazard to anybody who got in the way of his fangs. He may not be infected, but he was still dying… from starvation.

I leaned against the bars, no longer trying for the door. Trey wasn't going to turn me loose anytime soon. I couldn't blame him.

"How can you tell?" Mila asked.

"We're bound." I close my eyes and reached out to Marc with the little energy I still had. I was making a choice between standing and confirming the serum had worked. My hands gripped the bars tightly. Maybe I'd be able to stop myself from falling, maybe not.

My energy touched him in our familiar way, comforting him, caressing him, and seeking the infection that had ravaged his body and mind.

It was gone.

The serum had worked, but I still had to save him.

"There's no infection," I said weakly. Mila hcard and moved fast. In seconds, I heard several people running down the hall and away from the area.

They were going to use the serum on the others.

The chains rattled as I withdrew my energy and slid to the floor.

"You will not go in there until I'm satisfied it's safe, Valerie." It was a whisper. I felt his breath brush across my cheek. Even with his quiet words, I heard the threat and felt the menace in his voice.

I didn't care. I would win Marc's life. I would do the right thing for him. When Trey had released me, I couldn't tell; but when my eyes opened, he had gone.

The blackened orbs that were Marc's eyes pierced my soul. He was in pain as only a vampire could know. Pain from depletion. The man and the beast separate. The beast takes control to survive. It will kill. Marc would kill me to live. This was going to get dicey.

"Mila. There's a tray of food around the corner. Could you get that for me?" I asked, somehow knowing that she had sent her assistants to deliver the serum.

Some part of my heart hurt that Trey had walked out. Again, I really couldn't understand why. I understood none of who he was or what he was. Then again, he didn't know me either. He never would.

Something tugged at my heart. I pushed it away and looked into Marc's bleak eyes. His skin was washed out, pulled tightly against his bones, and looked like it would rip under the pressure.

"I'm going to need four bags of blood as well."

Mila was already coming back with the tray. As I requested, she brought the blood. She set the food in front of me and remained at eye level. "He won't accept bagged blood. We've been trying every day since we've had him." There was sympathy in her eyes. She had no hope for Marc. I found it sweet of her to care.

"You just don't have the right incentive, Mila." I started digging into the cold food and relished every bite.

Mila rose.

"I'll need the keys," I said between bites of cold vegetables and cold meat. It was wonderful!

"I'm sorry…" I didn't even need to let her finish. I had heard it before.

"Yeah. Orders." I said over her. At least, she did sound sorry.

"Direct orders, Valerie." Mila sounded so serious. "You are not to be in that cell until Trey permits it."

I nodded and tried to look sincere.

Apparently, Mila was satisfied with that because she walked her gorgeous long legs and sin-on-the-move body away from me and back to her office. I heard the door close.

I'm not jealous, just appreciative. Maybe a little jealous.

Had she shared Trey's bed?

I shouldn't care. I didn't care.

I had my vampire, as Sean put it.

So I was to get only so close to Marc. There was a pole propped up against the cell. One end would hold the bag of blood; the other kept you away from the biting end of a vampire.

CHAPTER EIGHT

Great blood and a good lay.

Great. I could touch him with a ten-foot pole.

Oh well, I had other ways of getting in. I just didn't want to waste any energy doing it, but I would.

The stone floor was cold. I didn't care. I had food. I was as close to Marc as I was going to get until I had strength enough to deal with this situation and, eventually, Trey. I really didn't know what to think about him at this point.

I thought he had shown interest in me. Caressing and kissing his way up my body led me to that conclusion. I could still feel the trail his lips had taken up the soft skin of my stomach. The thought of letting him do more and go further crept up on me. Trey is a big man. He seemed to dwarf even me, but the touch of his hands on my skin was sensual, decadent, and left me feeling a need within myself that was foreign, frightening, and something I wanted sated.

Thank the goddess for the bra, my nipples were hurting.

That high-handed, arrogant shifter would wreck me if given the chance. Strange thing though. He had the chance. Several of them. He didn't push when I said no; he didn't look smug when I had said "not now."

I thought of what it might be like to have a man of his size pushing inside of me.

But would he push?

His hands had been gentle. He had been gentle in those moments he seemed to be testing the sexual waters with me.

Even when he carried me to the lab, when he prevented me from coming to Marc, he had done everything with care.

I had no doubt he could take a woman hard and fast or slow and tortuous depending on his mood, and I had a feeling that his mood would matter most.

What woman in her right mind would tell him no?

Oh wait. I told him no several times. I must be out of my mind. To even think about falling into his bed was insane. He was beautiful in an alpha predator sort of way, and I was…

I was wanting more than what Marc had given me over the years, and Trey was definitely a whole lot more.

I needed to walk away from everybody and everything when this was over. I had a hefty bank account and contacts, and I could live off Magic for Hire for the rest of my life comfortably.

So much had happened to me since Marc went missing, and I was going to walk away from him, and he had no idea. I just hoped I could explain.

Right. *I got hot for a shifter, got confused, and now I'm leaving you.*

That sounded so well thought out. Not.

I had time, not much, but I didn't have to have anything concrete right now.

Marc was going to take a while.

I had finished my dinner and was starting to draw energy from the stone around me when I heard a low and familiar growl from behind me.

Marc was coming to. Well, sort of. Scent comes first, and apparently, he scented something he liked because I usually heard that growl in bed.

The first thing that Marc's beast was thinking was sex? Sex was the last thing I needed to have on my mind because when I thought of it, I thought of Trey, not Marc.

I sucked.

I pulled the energy, slowly letting it work into me, replenishing my battered soul. The energy of earth and moon didn't judge, didn't expect, didn't try to protect me or tell me what I should or shouldn't do. It was simply there. There for me to use, and I appreciated that immensely, especially in this moment when I was judging myself harshly and expecting more of myself than I thought I could deliver.

I hadn't heard a sound in this section since Mila had dropped the bagged blood, then she left. I decided it was time to do what I needed to do.

I gathered the blood, put my hand against the lock, and melted the mechanism. The door opened easily, and Marc pulled against his chains. The beast was eager to feed or fuck. It wasn't the bags of blood in my arms its eyes followed. It was my throat.

"Soon enough, sweetheart," I said softly. "Soon enough."

I set three of the bags down on the floor and stood close enough to hear Marc's low growls vibrate through my body. He lunged; I didn't flinch. I had six inches to spare.

"We are going to make a deal, Marc." My voice was clear, my body steady, and my mind uncertain. "You are going to drink this, Marc." I held a bag up, and he peered at it with disdain. Yeah, the bagged stuff wasn't nearly as tasty as tapping a vein; but in his condition, the person he would tap would die. So he would deal with prepackaged instead of homemade until he was a lot less dangerous.

"Yes, I know. However, you want to live and I can make that happen," I explained as if Marc were truly in on the conversation. He might recall some of it later, but right now, the darkest part of him was in control.

"You will drink until you can answer some questions for me. After you answer a few questions, I will give you my throat." I trailed my fingers down the length of my neck and watched his eyes follow. I definitely had his attention. Like I told Mila, you just need the right incentive, and I was pretty sure nobody offered Marc a fresh draw to get him to feed. It was crazy.

I held the bag up to him. He didn't look happy about the deal, but it was the best he was going to get anytime soon. He would, however, make a play for me if he could. It's hard to reason with an animal.

He inched his head forward, but he kept enough of his body coiled to be able to take my wrist if I leaned in too closely. Clever beast.

"Nope. Lean all the way out, baby," I said casually.

He gave me a killing look and let his body lean all the way forward. Marc took the bag and kept his eyes on me. He was waiting for me to make a mistake, to become complacent at his compliance. Not gonna happen.

He drained the bag.

"What's my name?" I asked. I needed to connect to the part of him that had enough control not to kill me. My name would be a simple pathway there.

He looked at me as if he was thinking really hard to find the answer, but it wouldn't come. He shook his head and then tilted his chin toward me.

He wanted the cookie before he did his trick. I knew it would take some time for the blood to hit his system, so I just had to keep him engaged in the game until it did.

"No. What's my name?" I restated clearly.

Two more bags and thirty minutes later...

"Val," he croaked. Man and beast swirled behind the darkness of his eyes.

Marc was slowly emerging. Very slowly. He was in bad shape.

"Who am I to you?" I asked. This was obviously more complicated, and he would have to dig further for the answer.

He was focusing, concentrating. I could see a hint of a smile touch the corner of his mouth.

"Sex," he sighed.

Well, don't I feel special.

The beast would focus, first, on survival. Sex, mating meant continuation. I was sex for the beast. Or it was just Marc being a guy, but I wanted him to tap more closely to Marc's mind for information.

"What else?" I encouraged.

"Mission," he said, gazing past me and into space. He was finding a connection to Marc and to the information that he needed in exchange for my throat.

Mission?

What the hell did that mean?

I held up the last bag. He looked none too pleased.

"We are almost there, Marc," I said. He hesitated and started to look angry. The beast was getting tired of the game, but I still wanted to win. I dropped my fangs after some concentrated effort and nicked my thumb. The fresh red liquid flowed lightly, and I caught the droplets on the bag, letting them pool in a crevice.

I held the bag back out to him. He moved more readily and took the fresh blood as his fangs pierced the bags. For a moment, he looked happier.

"Tell me about the mission, Marc." The bag was drained. His skin had a healthier glow and no longer pulled against his skull.

"Keep you safe. Train you." His voice was smoothing out. Marc's consciousness wasn't far behind. I needed him to talk and talk fast.

"Why?" Somewhere, really deep down, I knew I wasn't going to like the answer. Part of me was going to die in the next few moments.

"My sire commanded it." Marc's eyes drifted over my throat, then to my breast, and finally took in the rest of my body. I could probably offer him my jugular and live through it.

"Who is your sire, Marc?" *Oh god, oh god, oh god.*

"Erick Olafson. Your father."

The empty bag fell from my hand as I looked into Marc's eyes. There was no hint of the betrayal he had just leveled at me. He simply answered my questions to get a fresh vein. If I had been a threat to him, he never would have answered a single question, not the simplest one. With five years behind us, we trusted each other. Apparently, I had made a mistake.

"I was a job for your sire," I stated numbly. I couldn't even begin to think about who my father was. A fucking clan master, one who was on the Los Angeles council.

Was anything about our relationship real? Did he even care about me? Had he been fucking me because he had to keep me believing in him?

My body swayed; I lost all focus. My world just came crashing down around me. All of my doubt about Marc fell in on me.

Remember how I got lost in my thoughts? How I said Marc was the one paying attention and I really needed to start doing that myself? Well, this was one of those times.

The beast saw his meal starting to move away, and it angered him. He was almost at full strength and wanted something that meant life.

He roared.

He snapped the chain around one wrist. His hand caught the back of my neck and hauled my throat to his fangs.

I felt his fangs slide in quickly, and the pull was immediate. His hand shifted from being a clamp to a caress.

I held on tightly to his shoulders as silent tears rolled down my face. I could feel Marc trying to bring his other arm around me, to embrace me as he had done so many times before.

So many nights he held me, nipping at me as he loved my body. So many times he praised and encouraged me as we came home victorious. Bloodied, but we had made it home.

Was any of our relationship real?

He moaned. Marc had always said that my blood tasted sweeter somehow, slightly intoxicating.

Great blood and a good lay. Was that who I was to him?

"Marc." My voice was thick with tears and the pain I was feeling in my heart.

The draw stopped, and Marc's body stilled for the moment before he withdrew his fangs, nicked his tongue, and sealed the wound.

"Oh shit," he whispered in my ear. He held my neck gently and pressed his cheek softly against mine. "Val, I'm so sorry."

I pulled back; desolation replaced pain. Well, it almost replaced pain. I was hurt and heartbroken.

"Sorry for lying to me for five years?" I wanted all of the stories, and I wanted it now. I felt as if I would drown in the pain I was feeling, but like removing a Band-Aid, I want to get it done with quickly. "I've been nothing more than a obligation, a job, a mission. Spell it out, Marc. Exactly what did your sire command of you? Seduce me? Keep me ignorant? Teach me just enough, but not too much?"

"No, Valerie, baby," he began, trying to soothe me. I nearly cut him off to tell him that I wasn't his baby and he no longer had any right to terms of endearment toward me, but I let it go for now.

"Listen, please." He paused. I could tell he was looking for the right words. Whether it was the right words of the whole truth or just what he could tell me, I didn't know. "Your father found you eight years ago and had me keep an eye on you. You have been my sole focus all that time. I watched you become rebellious and put yourself in danger over and over again. You would have gotten yourself killed, Val."

Yeah, he was right. I had started looking for fights early in life, and it had gotten bad in my late teens. I was heading for an early grave by the time we found each other. Or rather, he decided to take a more active role in my life. A player rather than a spectator.

I was a spectator sport for three fucking years to this guy.

"He wanted me to bring you to him then. I couldn't do it, Val. There were too many things you needed to do before taking on what your father has planned. It was my idea to train you as a bounty hunter. You needed the skills and the maturity. Vampire society would eat you alive without it."

"I want nothing to do with vampire society, Marc. You know that."

"I know, but your father is clan master, and you are his daughter. Few people know about you, but when news gets out that Erick Olafson has a daughter with witch blood, your life will never be the same. Some will see you as a threat to their power within the clan; others will see you as a pawn to use against Erick." He pulled gently against the chains that still held him to the wall and looked at me with pleading, bedroom eyes.

I thought about the binding we had performed and wondered why I had never felt the deceit that was clearly a base part of our relationship.

I felt caring, concern, fear, anger, a myriad of emotions through that connection, but never one hint of the lies that our relationship was based on.

Goddess, I was so confused.

Even now, all I felt from him was concern and pain.

"There has never been a time that I haven't cared about you and your well-being, Val." He reached out to me. Seriously? He wanted to comfort me? The pain in my heart rose to the forefront. I was going to leave Marc. My first and only adult relationship was ending. I pushed back the devastation I felt. It would keep for later.

I moved to his side to release the chains still securing him to the wall, and his arm snaked around my waist. So familiar. My body pressed against his, his nose in the crook of my neck, and his voice so soft and gentle.

"I never wanted you to get hurt, Val." Bless it, I could feel the sincerity in his words and through the binding. "You know that. You can't deny it."

I reached around him and melted the lock at his neck. I didn't respond to him. I couldn't without screaming or crying. I would go for numb until this was over. I would ensure Marc's safety and health. How he got himself back to his sire—my father—was his problem.

"I know, Marc." I pushed out of his arms half-hardheartedly. He let me go. The last lock melted just as easily. I turned away from him and headed toward the open door of the cell. I was heading toward Mila's office or at least where I thought her office was based where I heard her go last. "The doctor will check you out, and I'm sure there will be questions the alpha here wants to ask you."

I was riding a very thin edge emotionally, and I just wanted this taken care of and get out. I tried to sound dispassionate, uncaring. Marc knew better.

He took hold of my arm, and I let him turn me. He even looked like he was hurting.

"Stop, Val. Please just stop and talk to me." We rarely fought, he always seemed to have the answers, and now I couldn't trust him.

"You were infected with some really nasty shit, Marc. You need to let their doctor look you over," I said, trying to pull out of his arms and continue on my way. He wasn't going to let me slip away easily again. "Marc, don't."

"Val, I am getting out of here. I am taking you to your father." His hands gripped my upper arms, and he looked at me intently. I'd seen that look. I was weakened by his feeding on me, and we were in a shifter/were stronghold. I'm sure Marc didn't have the same warm fuzzies I did about the place. His stay had been spent in a cell chained to the wall. I'd have been leery as well.

He was barely out of being half-dead and still trying to call the shots.

I would have told him to bite me, but he already had. I would leave here under my own power and alone.

"Your mission is over, Marc. And I'm out of here, without you," I said, turning away. Well, I was partially turning away. He pulled me back to face him. My gut ached with rage and pain. What the hell do you do with somebody who cares about you but spent the last five years keeping a huge secret from you? Five years, he had been training me so I'd survive living the life my father planned for me.

I don't fucking think so.

"This place is dangerous, Val. You are coming with me." His grip tightened. Holy crap! I couldn't fight him if he chose to overpower me. We were both weakened, but he trained me. He knew every fighting weakness I had. And there were plenty.

Damn this!

Damn Marc!

"Dangerous?" Finally, something I could sink my teeth into, so to say, anger. "Do you have any idea what I went through to find you? This place, and it's the Enclave, by the way, it is safer for me than being with you!" I screamed at him. The statement wasn't completely true. Trey was a hazard to me, and the thought of throwing myself at him was looking really good. Trey would bring me to orgasm until I couldn't walk, and Marc would feel every last spasm, every bit of raw lust. And I doubted it would hurt him as much as I would have wanted it to. "I'm not going anywhere, Marc. The alpha here hired me to do a job, and I'm not leaving until it's through. You, however, are out of here." I yanked myself from his grip and continued toward Mila's office.

"You are working for these mutts?" The scorn and derision were clear in his voice as he followed me down the hall. "What happens when they find out who you are, Val? And what you are."

He was pulling out the stops on that one. I was afraid myself. I had panicked in Trey's arms as he brought me to Mila. In my fevered state, I could only remember the horrors I was told would likely await me as a hybrid if I were discovered. Now I knew it was about being some clan master's daughter. Truth within a lie. That probably sums up our relationship in a nutshell.

I spun on him and jabbed my finger into his chest. "These *mutts* saved your ass when it was just as easy to kill you, Marc! Without them, I never would have found you! I wouldn't be here!" I had never been this mad. Not for a good reason. I was angry all of the time growing up, I just didn't really know why. Marc gave me a great opportunity to be as mad as I could possibly be for a really good reason. "You will fucking be grateful you're still alive and go back to wherever it is that you started eight years ago and leave me to live a life I want and not one that you thought you were going to manipulate me into!" I turned on my heels and just prayed to the moon that I didn't get lost. That would be humiliating. *I can go live my own life . . . but I can find Mila's office.* Heaps and heaps of humiliation.

As if the goddess herself heard my fears, Mila turned the corner. One look at the blood-spattered, half-naked vampire behind me, and she half-shifted into a tiger. Of course, with all that grace and elegance, Mila would be a feline.

"It's okay, Mila." Well, I thought it was okay. Marc, on the other hand, decided she was a danger to me and roughly tucked me behind him. "Christ! Marc! This is the doctor who saved your ass and probably mine as well!"

I shoved Marc aside and went to stand by Mila, who was still wary of the vampire who was crazed less than an hour ago. Couldn't blame her; he was scary.

"He's going to need more blood and probably…" Damn it! I was getting tired of being managed. Wait, I'd said that before, and it was still true. Marc threw me behind him with more force this time, and I stumbled. He had taken a lot of blood, and I was still sub par. I hit the wall, the back of my head impacting the stone with enough force for me to black out, wake up lying on the ground, and see stars.

My head hurt, my arm hurt, and all I could hear was growling through the headache.

"Enough!" I yelled. Wow, did my head hurt doing that. "Marc, enough!" I tucked my broken arm against my side and struggled to sit up. I hadn't quite gotten into a sitting position when I found Marc kneeling next to me.

"Val, shit, baby." His hand lay gently on my back, and his voice and binding were worried. "Relax, I got you." He moved to pull me into his arms.

"No! You don't have me, Marc. You never get to have me again." I got myself to my feet and pushed him away as he tried to help me. Every touch felt bought and paid for. "Stay away from me!"

"I cannot allow you to remain here," he informed me. His voice was cool and even. "Between the infection and… them." He threw a sneer over his shoulder at Mila. Various factions of the paranormal world rarely got along, and vampires and weres or shifters were the apex predators that didn't like each the most. "The risk is too high," he finished.

"I've already been infected, Marc. How the fuck do you think Mila created the antidote to it?" I retorted. I didn't think he could have gotten any paler, but I was wrong, and it was good to see. He could freak out and know I had managed to stay alive without his help.

"I've been dealing with this shit since you disappeared." I was on a roll. I was pissed, and Marc had earned my wrath in a big way. "For a week, I managed just fine on my own, without you!" That was pretty much a lie.

Without Trey, I may not have made it past the incident in the shack. In a strange way, I had felt myself leaning on his strength to keep going. Even when I was pissing him off and disregarding him as I was doing now, I felt that he would make certain I would be whole and able to leave when the time came.

Self-doubt may have been flooding me at that point, but not so badly that I would think for a minute that Marc and my father were my only option. I would run. I would hide. I would find a life of my own. Even if I had to cut and dye my hair and wear contact lenses. I would disappear.

"You are not up to this, Val." It wasn't the words he said, but it was more of the feel of them and what vibrated through the binding. The chill I felt slithering down my spine gave me a sense of foreboding that would make the desolation I had been staving off seem like a walk in the park. "And I can't protect you adequately in these circumstances."

I felt the legs of my anger sliced out from underneath me, but I'd be damned if I couldn't kick out with the bloody stumps I had left. "For the last five years, I've been hunting and killing things right along with you, Marc. I'm sure I can do without your help now."

I turned and walked to Mila. She had shifted back to her human form, but she continued to be on edge. So was I.

"I have had your back at nearly every turn, Val," he said softly. "You're not a cold-blooded killer. You wouldn't have made it this long without somebody covering you."

I stopped, still facing Mila, but I couldn't look her in the eyes. I knew he was right. I knew my suspicions were right. Marc had managed the situations for training. I'm certain that he and my father probably handpicked the assignment for maximum training with minimum risk.

"Every kill affected you, Val." Why did he have to sound so loving? I'd never heard this in his voice before, and it hurt at a real and visceral level. Almost as badly as when I realized that Trey thought me fragile. And it seems that he was right. "When you had any doubts, you hesitated. Those hesitations would have killed you had I not been there overseeing your moves." I knew he was moving closer to me. He was too exhausted to be utterly silent, and Mila was bristling. I even heard a low growl from her. Yeah. That's how I felt too.

His hands rested lightly on my shoulders. The familiar weight seemed crushing to my soul. Even the gentle circles his thumbs made behind my neck almost pained me.

"Your heart is too tender. Your soul is too gentle." His body stepped closely behind me. I could feel his chest pressing against my back, and his lips touched the top of my head. "You battle well. You are tough and can hold your own in a fight, but there is something within you that refuses to harden." My eyes closed as I took those words in, feeling them burn me like acid in my veins. He was right.

But I was a witch. I could leverage that.

I had contacts. They were Marc's contacts. I could never use any of them if I ran.

I had money—through an account Marc had set up for me. He could make it impossible for me to access my funds the minute I tried to disappear.

My father was a fucking clan master. Nobody would go against him and live. Marc was right. Everybody would look for me, whether to return me to him or use me against him.

I was so incredibly screwed.

My gut twisted and churned as my heart broke into the smallest pieces possible. I could feel the moisture gathering on my lashes. I was expected to play the good little clan master's daughter for the rest of my life. Going to balls, playing politics, and holy shit, maybe married off to some rival master's son to keep the peace. Vampires were an old, old race, and some traditions hadn't died the death that had been too long in coming.

I felt the binding between Marc and myself. I hated it, hated him. I felt like the coffee mug I had seen in Kansas years ago.

Aunt Em,
>   *Hate you. Hate Kansas. Took the dog.*
>> *Dot*

He had won my trust and my respect. He'd had my love. I could have gone for a very long time just as it had been. I wondered how long my father had given him to get up to speed. I wondered what the expiration date on my freedom was. I was living on a time line that somebody else designed.

My fire rushed to life within me, barely contained within my rage, pain, and desolation.

Marc took several steps away from me, as did Mila. I kept my eyes closed and just focused on the lie that was that binding. Marc knew how much I had loved him, and with every breath, he let me believe lie after lie.

The force of that betrayal hit me hard. I didn't try to deflect. I didn't try to ease the devastation that wreaked havoc on my heart and soul. I channeled it.

I would manifest that power into something useful. If I didn't, it would debilitate me. I would crumble. I would acquiesce. I would become a shell.

And the target of pain fueled power? The binding. I could fry Marc. With what I felt right now, I could kill him—the fiery, really-dead-forever kind of killing. But I raged against the less animate. Marc was right. I wasn't a hardened killer, never would be. I didn't know whether to be happy or sad about that realization.

My power struck. Think lightning strike on a metal rod. Now think that the rod is actually attached to two beings. I probably should have thought this out better. But Marc had always been in charge of looking at long-term consequences of actions.

Oh well.

I just hoped Mila was out of the way.

CHAPTER NINE

Suicide by Shifter

I had just blasted myself and Marc with more power than I had felt coursing through my body—ever.

I felt my eyes open slowly and take in the ceiling of the hallway in the holding area. It was stone, what a surprise. My head felt like it had split open, and my internal organ had been put in a blender, and someone hit puree.

What was even more dramatic was that the binding was gone. Completely obliterated. That seemingly "forever" bond between two beings was a smoldering wreck, much like my heart.

The remnants of my power continued to sizzle and crackle over my body.

As I let my head loll to my right, I saw Marc.

He looked like a whole new kind of shit. I figured that I looked just about the same. Neither of us were moving. The head loll was as good as I was getting for now.

Mila looked around the corner, having taken refuge in a nearby room and looked pretty much panicked at me laid out on the floor.

The shifters had no real use for me after having gotten the antidote. So whether I lived or died at this point wouldn't matter to them. But she was kneeling at my side, checking me over and looking worried.

"Marc…" Wow. Scorched vocal cords. Lovely. "He needs blood."

He had just gotten his head back together, and now he got seriously blasted… by me. I was doing a mental high five on my success.

It wouldn't take much for him to go black-eyed vamp again, and this time he wasn't chained. Mila could probably take him, but I'd rather he not hurt anyone. Trey wouldn't hesitate to kill him if he did. And Trey might be a tad pissed at me for letting Marc loose in the first place.

"You first," she said, flashing the little penlight in my eyes. That really kinda hurt. I squinted against the harsh brightness that assaulted me and lifted my hand to block the light.

"No." I took a deep breath, rolled to my side, and pushed to my ass. The wall behind me did a fine job of supporting me this time, instead of cracking my skull, which did still ached. "He's still depleted. Pop a bag on to his fangs. He'll feed conscious or not."

She glanced over at him and decided I had a good idea. It was one of the few I had come up with in the last couple days.

I sat very still and allowed my guts to continue reorganizing themselves into something like recognizable organs.

Mila brought four bags of blood and dropped them by Marc. She looked like she was tending something unsavory as she brought a bag to Marc's lips and hooked it on to his fangs.

Good. Marc would get fed, so he wouldn't be a problem for anybody but me, and I could sit here and do absolutely nothing for a little while longer. I liked that prospect.

I closed my eyes and simply relaxed against the wall and didn't think about anything for the longest time. It felt good. I wasn't bothered by nagging worries or self-doubt or the blood I felt trickling from my nose and ears.

The air was cool, the pain in my body was down to a low roar, and it was peacefully silent.

The darkness behind my eyelids was comfortable and welcoming. I could go there for a while, maybe just a few minutes. Okay, hours.

My mom and aunts had taught me so much, I wondered what they would have thought of this.

I should probably touch base with my remaining aunts and see how things are going and see if they would let me come back home. Then again, if Marc and his master came after me, they'd probably look there first. I certainly didn't want to put my family in danger.

I needed a different topic to think about. Maybe I should just pass out.

I continued to contemplate the pros versus cons of passing out, when the decision was made for me.

"Talk to me, Valerie" was the next thing I heard. It was a soft, kind whisper. The hand cupping my face was gentle but strong and smelled like Trey.

I was still leaning against the wall of the holding area where I remembered being last as my eyes opened to find that beautiful, obnoxious shifter at my side. "There you are," he said quietly and took me in with a sweep of his eyes. There was just a hint of a smile on his lips. Lips I really wanted to kiss until nothing else mattered.

No. I really didn't need that, not now. For the last few days, I had kept my lust in check because of Marc and my own instinct for self-preservation. Now? I would be using him for solace. Hell, he wouldn't care. I would just be another in a long, long line of women he'd bedded and forgotten. It wouldn't matter, except maybe to me.

To forget for just a little while. To pretend everything was different for a couple of hours and then to run like hell until I got caught or killed.

At least it would be on my terms.

Right now, I felt like crap. I couldn't imagine how Trey had felt after I blasted him, and I was actually trying to kill him. He had looked non-pulsed at the event, but damn!

"But you always know where I am, Trey," I croaked out quietly.

"Yes, but now I know I can't leave you unsupervised." he shot back with a soft smile.

"Well, it's only for a little while longer, then you won't have to worry about that," I sighed and watched an unhappy expression cross his strong features. Could he possibly miss me when I'm gone? Yeah, right. "Did the antidote work on the others?"

"Every last person," he said with a tired and very relieved expression on his face. It made me smile a little. "The vamp had the worst time of it though."

"Lack of food…" My words halted as a few terrifying thoughts went through my mind and then out of my mouth. "If you are able to find the base of this mess, and you are able to administer the antidote to everyone infected, you may still have to deal with depleted vampires. An unknown quantity of depleted vampires. Goddess, that was brilliant."

"Brilliant? What do mean?" Trey now thought I'd lost my mind, but that was okay because I thought he was brain-damaged at times.

"A depleted vampire is dangerous on its own. You eliminate the infection, and you still have a killing machine to deal with. It can't be controlled, but that would be enough for an effective diversion in an escape. The vampires could be plan A and plan B."

"But why do this to begin with?" he asked. Holy crap! He was actually asking me my opinion. I am sure he had already had this discussion with Sean. Maybe he was looking for a different insight.

"One person could do a lot of damage with a small contingency of vampires. And it may be just that simple," I said. "Destruction for destruction's sake." I was starting to feel better. I was going to try standing soon, really. My ass was going numb from the cold of the stone floor. "Or there could be a specific target or goal in mind. Until we know who, it's really hard to figure why. Anyway you slice it, this is going to be ugly."

His beautiful blue eyes narrowed as he nodded lightly. "That's what we came up with as well." He turned his head enough to glance over at Marc still being tended by Mila. I guess I really had simply dozed off for a moment.

"Marc may have the connections to find out if vampires have been disappearing from the area, and if so, how many. It might give you a feel for the size of the opposing force," I suggested.

When he turned back to me, his lips had formed a harsh line. What ever had gone through his mind did not make him happy. And if the beast master was unhappy, then everyone was unhappy. Unfortunately, the harsh line didn't make his lips look any less kissable.

"Marc will need some more care…," I started. Honestly, I was just starting to form an exit strategy, and I was thinking out loud as much as having a discussion with Trey. Probably not the best idea.

"I'll see he's taken to your quarters when he's well." Trey spoke those words as if he smelled something really bad and had a killing look on his face that frightened me more than the first time I had seen him.

"No," I stuttered and then stumbled over my own tongue. My love life was still none of his business, but if I could put some distance between Marc and me and keep it there, I would.

"Marc and I are parting company," I responded smoothly.

"Did he hurt you?" Trey asked as he looked me over. Oh, fuck. Trey thought Marc had done this to me, and if I weren't mistaken, he looked ready to kill because of it.

"No… I-I did this." Man, I needed to stop talking to Trey and just get cleaned up. Something that I had recently done and didn't seem capable to maintain. I was also hungry—again, and Trey smelled good. He always smelled good. Damn him!

My body was starting to respond to him in a way I'm sure he was beginning to notice. Animal senses could scent arousal from a mile away, and I was sitting less than a couple of inches from him.

Of course, remembering that I had blood crusted on my face cooled my fire for anybody really quick.

I slowly pushed to my feet using as much of the wall as I could just to inch away from Trey and the heat I could feel radiating from him.

"You seriously expect me to believe you fucked yourself up this badly?" He really didn't believe me. Fine.

I took a breath and closed my eyes for just a moment to rein in my temper and try to calm my heartbeat. My self-esteem was already shaken. I didn't need Trey's shit as well. But lucky me, I was going to get it, so I needed to gear up and roll with it.

"Yes, Trey," I said as my eyes opened and jaw set. "I managed, yet again, to fuck myself up. It seems to be what I'm best at!" I raised my voice just bit.

"And your vamp. You did this to him as well?" he asked, looking at Marc with a sideways glance and then to me. He raised an eyebrow. "But he didn't hurt you." I so didn't need this.

"Let it go, Trey!" I pushed off of the wall and aimed toward the room Mila had taken refuge in when I blew the binding to hell. It was the room that contained my clothing and a shower and much-needed solitude and hot water. "Our relationship is none of your business!"

I stalked through the door. I would have slammed it, but Trey damn near ripped it off its hinges earlier, so I settled for closing it the best I could and heading directly for the bathroom, with a door that works.

He didn't follow.

I wanted to cry. I wanted to rail and rage, and I was too tired for any of that.

I showered again.

I got dressed again.

I cleaned my face and had a split lip, black eye, and very pale skin.

So I looked like shit again.

I pulled my hair back into a ponytail again and stepped through the doorway to find Trey waiting on the other side.

"So you have a cure for the infection and an inoculation, I presume." I slung my bag over my shoulder and wobbled some at the weight of it. "And you no longer have to deal with the crazed vampire. What else do you require to consider this a job well done and over?" No matter the answer, I was going to claim that I needed a quiet and undisturbed place where I could meditate, recharge, and focus. I would actually pass out, and if all went well, I'd wake up in the same place and feel better.

He stood at the lightly padded table I had been strapped to when I had awakened earlier. Where he caressed and kissed my body and made me want to tell him to keep going. But I hadn't. Because of Marc. That was over. And I still hurt like hell. Both my body and my heart.

"Help us find the base of operations," he said, propping his hip up on the table and crossing his arms over that grand expanse of chest he owned. I wondered what it would feel like to run my hands over it. "We think we have a general direction, but patrols haven't yielded any results yet."

I thought about that. I still needed to get into Gabrielle's room and try to glean something from there if I could. There was a chance I could still be useful to him. I could get a few more days worth of pay, and I'd ask for cash. I just had to hope I could get out of here under the vampire radar. I wondered if I had been followed, but I dismissed that quickly. Trey wouldn't have been able to get anywhere near me if I had been tailed by any of the clan master's personal guards. So he trusted Marc implicitly with my care and safety.

I wasn't going to make anything out of that. It didn't matter, not anymore. "I'll need any information you have gotten since the last reports. I will need to check out Gabrielle's room, and then I will likely start doing recon sweeps and try to locate the base." I was going to have to be really careful. The defensive magic that I had run into with the golems had hurt a lot. I'm sure the defenses for the base would be ramped up. I had to go in strong to get any information that would be useful to Trey.

I started toward the door of the exam room and tried to avoid Trey's eyes. His gaze had been disconcerting to say the least. The heated male interest I saw went past just screwing with me. It made me nervous, and I knew without a doubt I was going to end up in his bed. My heart was already broken, why not go for destroyed?

"I'm going to need food, water, and a room to myself with a balcony and as far away from Marc as possible." I stepped into the hall and stopped. I wasn't sure which way to go, so I looked back at Trey and his flame-touched blue eyes and waited like I had expected him to come to heel.

He slid off of the table and walked up to me, taking my bag from my shoulder and headed out.

"A binding isn't something you just walk away from, Valerie." His voice was low and serious and did things to me that I was too tired to fight. Prick.

"I didn't walk away from it, Trey," I answered more harshly than I had expected. But I felt like crap, and he seemed to want to poke in the rawest wound I've ever had. "I destroyed it and suffered the consequences all the way around. So can you just drop it?"

We had come out of the holding area, and the hallways were wide enough to allow passage of three linebackers, shoulder to shoulder. The only light was by oil lamps lining the wall, and there were random oil paintings hanging here and there. Otherwise, everything was very innocuous and nondescript. In other words, I had no idea where I was, and there was nothing outstanding for me to navigate by. I needed to get outside; then I could do some serious orienteering.

Trey stopped dead in his tracks, which stopped me. It was so sudden that he startled me, and I stepped away from him. His eyes narrowed, and he looked puzzled.

"You what?" And then I saw confusion. It was a good look on him. I would try to see that more often.

"He lied to me and broke my heart, Trey." I tried to harden just enough so I wouldn't sound as wrecked as I felt. "I destroyed the binding, and we both suffered the repercussions." I waved my hand in the general directions of the injuries I had sustained during that little incident and began walking in the direction we had been heading. "Never a good idea to piss off a witch. Worse than a woman scorned," I muttered and heard him ease to my side and pace with me.

"I've made arrangements for a meal to be sent to your room, and I will be joining you." The timber of his voice licked up spine.

"You assume I want any company, Trey," I said coolly, even as I felt my womb clench.

"We have things to talk about, Valerie." And by "talk," he sounded as if it meant to use braille to get his point across. I could feel the moisture collect between my thighs. And if I was noticing, so was he. Now that Marc was no longer in my personal picture, he thought I was fair game.

"You assume I am in any condition for a *conversation,* Trey," I responded. I would really like to be unbruised, un-bloodied, and unbroken before trying to go a few rounds with a man like Trey. I'd like to look my best, for once, in front of him instead of looking like I had lost every battle I had fought, regardless of the fact that I had won.

The last time I had dressed nicely was when Marc had taken me dancing a few months ago. We had been taking ballroom dance classes on and off during our down time, and we were pretty good. I realize now that it had been part of my "training." I would be expected to function at gatherings held by the vampire elite. Heaven forbid, I should embarrass my father by being a complete barbarian.

I spoke four languages, I could blend into most social situations, and I did clean up nicely, that is when I hadn't been taken apart by my own magic.

Daddy could be proud of his little girl. I wanted to vomit.

The door he stopped at was solid oak, banded with wrought iron, and ornately carved with an aerial battle scene between two dragons. It was amazingly detailed. I would look at it at length later. It was beautiful.

So was the room that the door opened into. Decorated in grays and blues that softened the stone that was four walls, a ceiling, and a floor. A quick tour revealed a large closet, a huge bathroom, and a door that led directly into Trey's master suite.

Subtlety was not this guy's strong suit.

I was in the "flavor of the month" suit. More likely, the "flavor of the week."

"That locks from my side, right?" I asked sternly.

"No. The lock is on my side," he announced unapologetically. "Dinner is in two hours." He strode to the door and turned, glancing back to me. "Do you think you can go that long without getting hurt?"

I turned away from him and headed toward one of the two French doors that led to the balcony.

"I doubt it," I muttered and stepped out into the warm evening desert air. The sky was perfectly clear, and the waning moon was rising right in front of me. I would forget, without Trey's help. I had Her.

The deep purples in the west were the last remnants of a day that had found my heart broken and the rest of me in doubt about everything I thought myself to be.

The balcony stretched the length of my quarters. The French doors lay on either side of the obscenely huge bed, which hadn't escaped my notice when I'd walked into the room. I sat on the comfortable pads that graced the wrought-iron furniture and promptly fell asleep in the glow of the moon's light.

Soft music worked its way into my consciousness. It was nice. Flutes, violins, a cello, and a quiet piano soothed me enough to entice me into sleeping some more.

I needed to sleep. Real sleep. Not this "passing out where I happen to collapse" thing, but real "take a shower, put on a gown, and drift off as I will" sleep.

Five years of nights falling asleep contentedly by Marc's side was over. I sat up and felt a tear slide down my cheek. I knew that the hollow feeling in my chest would recede in due course, but that didn't make it suck any less at the moment.

I rose and stepped back in "my" room just as Trey was entering from his adjoining suite.

I had slept heavily. There was a small round table set intimately for two. The silver and china glowed in the candlelight, and a service cart with covered dishes sat a few feet away.

It smelled heavenly. And I had slept through the delivery and set up of it all. My eyes drifted back to Trey who looked like his usual comfortable, unflappable self. Black jeans molded to his muscular thighs and a black T-shirt barely contained his well-developed chest.

"I don't know of anybody who gets paid as well as you do simply to sleep, Valerie." That man's voice was going to be my downfall, as well as his eyes and his body, and the heat he threw in my general direction was nearly unbearable.

As much as I hurt from Marc's betrayal, I was wanting Trey to bury himself inside of me, to make me forget. Hell, he had damn near made me forget with a single whisper of a kiss at the rental house. And what he made me feel in the exam room. Damn.

I snatched the bag Trey had dropped on the bed and headed for the bathroom. It seemed like the safest move.

I didn't have a snappy retort for his comment. I didn't even look at him. I felt crowded and raw, but I was hungry and could suffer through Trey's remarks to fill my belly.

The bathroom door was, unfortunately, located next to the door to Trey's room, so I did have to walk by him. I was trying to be hard and steely to hold in the emotions that threatened to burst from me uncontrollably. I could do this damn job, get paid, and get the hell out of this place. I just wanted people to stop fucking with me and trying to managed me.

So when Trey decided that stopping my progress by taking my arm and physically halting me by his side was a good idea, I snapped.

I had had enough a long time ago. That would be sometime before my nap. "Don't touch me!" I wrenched my arm from his grasp, and his eyes went wide and then began to burn in that way they do. A cool fire flashed through my body. Maybe I had felt that I'd nothing left to lose. My life was going to be centered on running and hiding very soon. Lashing out at somebody who could kill me and had no real reason not to if I crossed a line let me know that part of me had died, and I was willing to let it take the rest of me with it.

Suicide by shifter.

"I have had enough!" I dropped my bag and stepped back. "I have had enough of being pushed and pulled! Enough of being told how my life will play out! Enough of being lied to! Enough of having no privacy, no sense of safety!" Damn was I on a roll. I hadn't even known I was feeling half of this stuff, and I was letting it spew forth with wild abandon. I slammed my hands into his chest. *Christ, it is like slamming into a wall.* He did have the common courtesy to take a step back with the impact. "I have had enough of being fucking managed!"

Trey smiled.

Not that "holy crap, heart stopping" smile. Not that "death and dismemberment are around the corner" smile, but a smile that pissed me off to my marrow. Like he thought my outburst was cute.

I swung at his head. He ducked.

Good thing too. I'm sure impacting his skull would have broken my hand, and with one arm already broken, it could make things difficult.

So I went for a body shot, which connected and was followed up by a series of kicks, spinning and not, and a flurry of shots and combinations that had him moving and blocking, but there were no return volleys. For a while.

When he finally did start his offensive, he was fast and precise. I kept my profile narrowed and took shots that I knew had a good chance of connecting. He was doing the same. My ribs would be hurting for a while. Marc always told me to keep my elbow down, and now I knew why.

There was no way I could win a slug fest with a vampire of Trey's size, let alone a shifter. So I was going for speed, accuracy, and small successive shots. A little bit here, a little bit there until I wore him down, or he got in a shot that would drop me were I stood.

The second time I hit the bedroom wall, I noticed that he hesitated before coming after me.

He was holding back. Maybe he was toying with me. Just proving to me what I feared since this started. I couldn't hold my own. The rage bubbled up to the point that my vision darkened. I snapped in a whole new way. A way I had never experienced and couldn't control.

I felt my body kick off the wall I had impacted, and I was airborne. My hands hit Trey square in the chest, and he was thrown to his back. I rolled off to the side and was back on my feet in half a heartbeat, and Trey was gone.

There was a strange whoosh, followed by a hot blast of air, and then I was pinned under him. His hands held my wrists over my head, and his body lay on top of mine barely allowing me to breath.

I screamed, feeling myself outside my mind, no longer connected, but thoroughly enraged.

He moved, trying for a better position. He exposed his throat, and I took the opportunity to sink my fangs straight into his jugular.

His body tensed for the second it took for the paralytic agent to take effect.

"God, no" was all he managed before my bite kicked in.

The draw was sweet and warm. His body relaxed completely, and my arms embraced him, giving me a more secure hold as I drew once more. He tasted as good as he smelled. All spice, heat, and male.

CHAPTER TEN

"And you are hesitating… why?"

I moaned with the sheer ecstasy of his body covering mine and the taste of him on my tongue. I hadn't taken blood from anybody but Marc in years, and it had never been anything like this.

My vision began to clear as I drew for the third time. I had just started to think about how good Trey would have felt making love to me as I fed from him when I realized that one of two things were going to happen.

1) I was going to kill Trey, or
2) I wouldn't kill Trey, but he would likely kill me. This was the second time I had attacked him.

I couldn't kill him. I had completely lost control. The life of the beast master of the southwest region of North America was far more important than a vampire mutt who'd had a bad couple of days.

I eased my fangs from his neck and sealed the wound as I rolled him off me and sat up next to him. I tucked my legs under my body and laid my hand on his chest.

I looked at his face and into his eyes as I waited for the drug to wear off and for Trey to regain himself and kill me. The only question was if he'd kill me quickly or make me suffer.

I felt the steady rise and fall of his chest under my hand. Oh, what it might feel like to awaken curled up next to his warmth after a long night of heated, unabashed sex. To feel that rise and fall under my cheek. To feel his breath quicken and heartbeat race as we worked each other to climax.

Would he groan his pleasure or growl? Would he take me fiercely or gently? If we had enough time together, how creative could we get?

I'd never find out.

My heart hurt.

No, wait. My entire chest hurt, and I felt heat flush my body.

The cramping started low in my belly, and fire tore through my veins.

Every beat of my heart pulsed with a new pain that I wished Trey would end.

He needed to shake off the paralytic and kill me because I really wanted to die, now. I knew I was screaming, and I wished it would have done some good. It just seemed to hurt that much worse. Just a few hours ago, I had blown myself up from the inside. That was merely a skinned knee in comparison to what I felt like now. Gasoline, kerosene, and jet fuel had been poured on me, and somebody threw a match on it.

Why was I still alive? I knew I could be killed, and this level of agony should have been associated with death, a quick one. The pain began to recede. Just enough for me to hear my own pained screams and to know that Trey was mobile.

I heard shuffling, a grunt, and then glass breaking.

My body arched in response to the most recent wave of pain that washed over me, and the moan was nearly a sob. I couldn't open my eyes. I couldn't seem to move at will, just with the ebb and flow of the pain as it coursed through my body in less steady waves.

My breath was gasping, my lungs hurt, and it seemed that my internal organs would have to do that reorganizing thing again. No doubt, they were very unhappy with me.

Glass breaking?

"Fucking touch her, and there will be nothing left of you to fry at sunrise," Trey bellowed at… Marc? What the… ?

"She is my woman. My responsibility, and I will have her out of here tonight!" How did Marc find me? Well, I had been screaming like I was being slowly tortured and killed. With his senses, he would have heard; and if I died while under his care, my father would probably kill him.

There was more shuffling and crashing. The sickening thud of a fist connecting with soft tissue was next.

I was really becoming familiar with the ceilings in various areas of the Enclave because my eyes opened, and they seemed to be working.

The soft glow of candlelight had been replaced with the waning moonlight as it filtered through the French doors. Shadows danced at the insane pace of two apex predators fighting for supremacy between the doors and where I lay.

I tried to move. It didn't work.

The next crash collapsed the bed to the floor and brought down the canopy on one side.

I assumed that dinner was strewn about the room as well.

"She is a free, *unbound* woman!" Trey roared. "You're not welcome at her side!"

"You were killing her!" Marc grunted as I heard the two of them slam into another piece of innocent furniture. I don't think it survived any better than the bed. "And, until I hear differently from her…"

"Get out, Marc," I groaned. I still couldn't move, but the lips and vocal cords came around slowly.

There was utter silence in the room.

"Val? Baby…," Marc started.

"Shut up and get out," I whispered to the ceiling.

"You heard her." Trey was quick to support me, but I could hear his surprise as well as his gloating in this. "Out," he growled that low menace that he was so good at. The menace I had heard on several occasions and once connected to an order that I disobeyed.

I was in trouble on so many levels with Trey, and yet I was ejecting Marc. I'd rather take my chances with the rude, obnoxious shifter alpha who I'd given several legitimate reasons to snap my neck over the vampire who would do whatever it took to insure my survival.

I didn't even want to think about how fucked up that was.

I heard distant yelling and running, and then several bodies moved into the room.

I recognized Sean's scent, but not the other three scents that followed him into the room.

"He is to be confined to his room, until I have need of him," Trey ground out. "Insure his needs are attended to. Our fight isn't over. We may need him."

"Val!" I heard Marc half-heartedly resisting his escort. He was outnumbered and outgunned, but he was giving the sway of my wishes one last ditch effort. "Don't do this!"

"Out," I croaked, my eyes closing as if letting the visual part of my brain rest would give me more strength.

I didn't hear the door close. I assumed that it was lying on the floor somewhere or hanging on by one hinge. Doors seemed to have a shorter life expectancy around me. Too bad. I'd hoped to spend some time simply taking in the detail of two dragons in flight. Their bodies poised and tense in combat. Their wings opened, catching the wind and beating it down upon whatever lie below.

Fuck me! Trey's a dragon!

The ultimate in rare creatures and, needless to say, the deadliest. He had been playing with me. Either that, or he knew I needed to blow off the rampaging emotions within me. I'm sure me biting him came as a real surprise though. A being such as Trey was rarely surprised, so after he killed me, maybe he'd remember me for that if nothing else.

Now it made sense that he paused when I unloaded as much power into him as I could. He was made of fire, and I was about to be burned in the truest sense of the word.

I forced myself to move, rolling on to my side and pushing to my feet. I noticed fleetingly that the brace from my arm was gone, and the arm wasn't broken.

There was movement at the door, and I glanced over to find Trey pushing the door into the general position the door would have held, if it could. I also surveyed the destruction of the room, and it was absolute. The bed had taken the least amount of damage.

Trey turned and took me in with those eyes that truly burned in the shadow of the moonlight and wreckage.

I squared my shoulders and set my jaw.

"Sorry about dinner," I said calmly as he walked casually toward me. "It smelled wonderful." I met his gaze and didn't flinch as he towered over me. I took a deep scenting breath of him. Every last minute I had in my life, I wanted to fill with whatever pleasantness I could find.

Warm spices and male.

That was Trey, and I was regretting having said no to him at all.

He brushed his fingertips across my cheek and his thumb across my bottom lip. The split in the lip had healed, and my eye no longer felt of swelling. My heart fluttered at his touch, my skin flushed, and my body screamed, "Oh. My. God. YES!"

I tried to remain expressionless and composed. It wasn't going to last for long.

"You should have killed me, Valerie," he whispered his words across my cheek, and his hand slid behind my neck, cradling my skull as I gently shook my head.

"Why not?" he asked as his lips trailed down my neck. I had tried to resist touching him. My fists clenched by my side, protesting the lack of tactile involvement on my part; but I was afraid if I moved, he would stop. I didn't want him to stop. I wanted him to keep going until I couldn't stand up right, or I hadn't noticed he'd killed me for the drug-like stupor I knew he'd bring me to.

His free hand ran up my arm slowly. The callouses feeling more erotic than anything else against my bare skin. His thumb brushed against my breast through my T-shirt and bra, teasing my nipple as it passed. He nuzzled my neck and held me firmly as he did so.

I was lost. My body clenched with wanting him, and my hands found purchase at his waist as I fisted his T-shirt.

"Couldn't." Breathless. He had barely touched me, a few caresses, his body pressing against mine, and I simply couldn't breath. "Can't."

His hand twisted in my hair, and he pulled my head back as his teeth scraped against the skin of my throat.

"You tried twice, Valerie." The growl that vibrated through my body from his chest warned me, not of impending doom, but that he was clearing the air before he took me. I was going to have my question answered. And it was looking like "taking me fiercely" was on its way. That made me slightly more nervous than being executed.

"No," I panted. "Once… fever. I was afraid." He pulled my body flush against his, and the erection that I felt behind his jeans was impressive. God! He didn't have to kill me. I was going to die for the want of him inside of my body. The heat borne of the dragon was seared into my soul. I could feel it down to my core, and it wasn't enough.

I closed my eyes and simply melted into his body. His scent, the feel of his hands on me, his lips working their way back up my neck all felt completely intoxicating.

His lips pressed gentle kisses across my jaw. I could feel his breath on my face. Warm and sweet, like his blood had been. The sweeping brush of an almost kiss nearly undid me.

"You disobeyed a direct order," he whispered as his lips closed over mine, and I found a direct path to heaven. I pushed his T-shirt up and ran my hands over the bare skin of his back. Powerful, muscular, and absolute.

Our lips slid over each others, tasting and taking in perfect sync. My tongue whispered across his lips, and he opened welcoming me and caressing me.

I heard the tearing of my shirt more than felt it. His claws had made quick work of the material. Nothing else had changed. His face remained unchanged, his body hadn't altered under my hands, but he had allowed his claws on one hand to extend. A shifter who had that level of control was almost unheard of. But, of course, this was Trey. Control seemed to be his middle name. As far as I was concerned, he wasn't ripping my clothing off fast enough, and he was keeping me so tightly against him that I couldn't leverage his from him.

Well, I'd work with what I had. I ran my hands over both globes of his ass and squeezed them. "Mighty fine" doesn't even begin to describe the experience.

Unfortunately, the experience was short, and he set me back with a growl. It startled me and let me see just how far gone I had been and still was.

The remains of my shredded top and bra came off with the smallest encouragement from Trey's hand—his steady, unwavering hand. I, however, was just this side of trembling at his touch.

"Yes, Trey," I said softly. Wary. I was attempting to keep that undercover. "I disobeyed you. But I believe you said that if I promised to behave, then you'd know I was lying."

I think it was at that point he realized he'd lost ground with me. The sensual haze was all but gone, though the desire I had for him was still in full force. I was well past aroused and halfway to orgasm, and he knew that as well.

There was an amused glint in his eye as he brushed the back of his knuckles across my already aching nipples. I was immediately lost on the sharp intake of breath I took at that electrifying touch, but somehow I managed to regroup on the exhale.

He was playing me.

I was an unattached, supernatural female. There was no male to protect me nor defend me. I had made certain of that when I'd sent Marc away. I'd also not use my father as a bargaining chip.

He was toying with the one piece of myself that couldn't take another beating. My heart.

This time I created more distance and stepped back. "I do not fall under your direct command, Trey." I had caught on. He was going to wind me up and punish me using the sexual tension he was building within me.

So his full name was Trey Control Asshole.

It kinda rhymes too. I mean, what parent does that to a child?

"You are in my employ, Valerie," he started. All cool and collected on the outside, but I could feel the smallest chink in his scaly armor. He wanted me just as badly as I wanted him. Unfortunately, I sucked at the game he wanted to play.

"I am a contractor, Trey," I countered quickly.

"Same thing."

"No, it's not. Especially when it comes to taxes." He looked at me askance. I had totally taken him off guard on that one and was doing the happy dance inside my head for it. "I live in this country, so I support it by paying taxes as regularly as I can manage. Can I get a 1099 when this is over?"

"You're changing the subject, Valerie," he growled. I smiled.

"I disobeyed you, and Mila knows about it. If you didn't punish me in some way, it could make it that much harder to maintain discipline in the Enclave." I had schooled my features and gotten into a more serious mode. Of course, standing there half-naked made it more challenging, but I was rising to it. "I do understand it, Trey. However, would you consider making love to me, oh, let's say, all night, and then we can discuss a fitting punishment tomorrow? Maybe over breakfast."

He scooped me up quickly, and we headed into his suite. I noticed nothing about the appointments his room possessed. All I cared about was the bed. Obscenely huge.

Trey stripped me out of my pants and shoes as I hit the bed. He, however, stood there and devoured me with his eyes. It made me smile and feel adventurous. No games, not now anyway. Just us and what we both wanted. Sex.

I pushed up to my knees and went to the edge of the bed where Trey stood. My fingertips traced the muscle of his chest and abdomen through the T-shirt that had seen better days. Fighting a vampire or two can ruin your wardrobe. I'm sure he had plenty of form-hugging tees around. He'd never miss this one or the one I fried a couple days ago.

He let me lift it off of his body, and I leaned in and relished the feel of his soft skin under my cheek and the way my nipples felt as they drifted across his abdomen.

Trey let out a soft chuckle.

"A vampire who plays with fire," he said, removing the band that was still trying to hold my ponytail in place. My hair fell free, and Trey ran his hands through it and then buried his face in one fistful.

"Yeah," I sighed as I began releasing his jeans from his narrow hips. "My life has been one long-running joke."

"What do mean?" he asked, climbing on to the bed and out of his jeans.

Gloriously naked and hard. I knew he wasn't going to punish me tonight for my transgressions, but I would certainly hurt in the morning. A good, well-loved, all-over body ache. I may not be walking well when I got up.

"Vampire/fire witch. Sunburned and heat exhaustion. I have to think really hard to get my fangs to drop." We moved into the center of the bed, and I found his embrace comforting. I was gearing up to list a few more shortcomings when he interrupted me.

"Strong as hell. Braver than most males I've met. Beautiful." He stopped and took my lips in a gentle kiss, sweeping his tongue in for a taste. "Elegant. Tough as nails," he whispered. His hand stroked across my breast on the way down my stomach.

My fingers tunneled through his hair, and it was as silky as I had imagined it. He pulled me closer to his body, only to stop at the rock hard shaft that poked me in the hip.

Oh, yeah. Now I would be using braille to get my message across. He easily spanned my hand from pinky tip to the end of my thumb, and I could barely get my hand around him. I may not walk for days. I wondered if it was possible that when I spent the next few days limping around the Enclave, he could just let the word out that I had been punished. Probably not. He wouldn't lie to his people.

He grabbed my wrist after a moment or two of me admiring and stroking his cock. He trailed his kisses downward.

"I'd prefer not to spill myself this early in the evening," he purred softly as his tongue played with one nipple and then the other. "And when I do, it will be while I'm inside of you."

"Do they even make condoms in an extra-large-oh-my-god size?" I asked. He glance up at the smile on my face and suckled my breast hard enough to make my body arch into his and gasp with the jolt of pleasure that washed through me.

He released my wrist, and I firmly planted my hands on his head and held him to my breasts, encouraging him to carry on.

When I felt his fingers begin to play in the slick folds between my legs and make lazy circles around my clit, I made a strangled cry.

He made a murmuring noise against my breast, obviously pleased at my response.

"You are so wet," he whispered, letting his breath cool the well-loved nipple he'd been paying way too much attention to. "Let's see how tight you are." He eased a finger inside me and worked my clit at a lazy pace.

I gripped his shoulder tightly as he eased me toward the shadows in which my climax lay waiting.

I knew my body clenched tightly around his finger, and when he slid a second inside me and increased his pace, I moaned with the feeling of an orgasm approaching. His hands were masterful, and his tongue and teeth had destroyed me. I was nothing more than a wanton loving every touch and stroke that her lover was providing to find her release.

The spasms began slowly, wrapping around my body and pushing through my soul. He released my nipple, and I felt him rise over me, the weight of his body resting on me a little more, the heat of him joining with me a little more.

"Look at me, Valerie." The growl was seductive, powerful. The kiss he laid on my cheek was gentle and warm. "Open your eyes for me."

My eyes opened as the orgasm broke over me. I could feel my hands sliding to his shoulders and my nails digging in as he smiled at the pleasure he was giving me.

Within the span of hours, my body had been through hell and now heaven. I had forgotten that I had been betrayed. I had forgotten that my heart had broken. I had forgotten that the powerful creature that was currently giving me more pleasure than I had ever experienced would turn around and punish me because he had to.

It didn't matter. I didn't care. I had now. And that was amazing. I would compartmentalize this experience with him and any good experiences I have of him and keep them with me as I ran alone into a life I didn't know.

The world slowly came back into focus. The world at this point being Trey, who hovered over me with his eyes ablaze and his smile something between predatory and contented.

"I didn't think you could look any more beautiful, Valerie," he whispered across my lips and cheek as he pulled my body tightly against his.

"What?" I gasped, still trying to catch my breath and slow my racing heart. "You don't find the look of me bleeding and bruised a sexy fashion statement?" I tried to laugh, but that "whole not being able to breathe right" was working against me.

Trey's lips took mine in a hard-driving kiss. I had just gotten a couple of brain cells working again, and he has to go kiss me stupid. Somehow, I was good with that.

Somewhere in the back of my reptilian brain because that was the only part working, I became aware of Trey shifting his body between my legs. Gently nudging my thighs open with his knees as his tongue stroked mine. His weight was gentle as he propped himself up on his forearms, but his heat was like the sun after a cold, rainy day.

His hardened length eased back and forth along my opening, still slick from his earlier performance.

My hands lay on his nicely muscled ass as he rocked gently over my body. Christ! He was going to get me to come again, and he had not even penetrated me. I was doomed.

My toes ran up his calves, his thighs, and then I locked my ankles around his waist.

I could feel the restraint in his body, the holding back from plunging into me and pounding until we were both ruined. Of course, it was all I could do not to beg him to do just that.

"Trey." I was going to start begging. I had no pride and just wanted him inside me and keep the world away for a while longer. "Please, tell me you have condoms." My words were more like moans. He was rubbing along my clit, and I was near coming again. It was about then I noticed he was beginning to sweat, and his breathing was very controlled.

"Can't get you pregnant," he managed between reluctant releases of my lips.

One of my brain cells fired up enough to think about what he had just said. "Is it a dragon thing?" I asked, hoping to whatever god or goddess might be listening that it was because he was taking way too long!

Trey slowly released my lips and looked into my eyes with a sparkle I'd not seen before and a curl of a smile that made me feel as if I had just said the best thing ever.

"Yeah," he said softly. "It's a dragon thing."

The tension I had seen in his face disappeared, but he was still tense in all of the right places.

"Okay," I said with all of the inflection that gave him the go ahead, and he was still hovering above me. "And you are hesitating… why?" I asked. I really wished his body would follow the look I was seeing in his eyes because they were screaming "gimme sex!" and yet he glided over me slowly, tortuously. If that asshole was punishing me now…

"I'm afraid that once I've started," he began in that low, husky voice that I'd had problems resisting when I wasn't naked and under him, "I won't be able to stop." He nuzzled my ear, and goose bumps rippled my flesh.

"I believed I invited you to make love to me all night," I whispered and ran my nails over his back gently. "If you take that literally, then so be it."

He either chuckled or growled I really couldn't tell, and since he was reaching down to align himself to me, I didn't care.

As the crown of his cock entered me, I knew Trey was going to be a completely different experience for me. My body was used to Marc, and good as he was and as well built as he was, Trey was bigger in every respect.

He took his time working himself in using slow, short strokes. Every one reaching deeper, pushing further, stretching and filling me. Every part of my body opened to him. The whole of my awareness shrunk to sensations that careened through me.

The warmth of him didn't end where our bodies were joined nor did it where our bodies touched. His heat wrapped around my heart and soul with a whisper soft promise of something I didn't understand. It felt unbreakable yet yielding. It was "us" in this moment.

We belonged to each other for as long as this "moment" lasted. Whether it would be ten minutes or ten hours. I really doubted it would be ten minutes, but this was ours.

Our bodies twined and tangled, slicked with sweat and glowed in the moon's light. I cried out only to have it kissed from my lips.

I felt the heat rising within and between us as one orgasm blurred into another. Now I understood when he said he wasn't sure if he could stop once he started. The fact that he had orgasmed three or four times and showed no signs of slowing, I chalked up to it being a dragon thing as well.

I was really liking the dragon thing.

My skin was glowing with more than simply the light of the moon. It was his, it was mine, and I could scent the burning of the bedding we lay upon.

My magic was as open to him as my body, and it swirled between and around us in time to the movements of our bodies as we drove each other higher yet again.

When I started to come to, the first thing I noticed was Trey's body under mine. Next was the faint lightening of the skies as I spared the windows a glance. Oh, and we were on the floor.

I returned my head to the comfort of his chest just as he began to stir.

I heard the rhythmic thumping of his heart and the low contented growl as his arms wrapped around me, and he kissed the top of my head.

"Why are we on the floor?" he asked sleepily.

"Cause we set the bed on fire." I didn't move, didn't shift. I just enjoyed the feel of him under me as the night, the entire night, went through my head.

I felt him turn his head to survey the damage. His chest bounced lightly as he chuckled and kiss the crown of my head again.

"Is anything salvageable?" I asked. I smiled. Like everything else about him, his soft laughter, warmed me. I pushed the thought of the coming day away and just enjoyed every moment as they ticked by.

If I were Cinderella, dawn was my midnight. It was here, and I hurt at the sight of it.

"Maybe the dresser," he replied and relaxed back and simply held me.

Another moment ticked by.

I took a deep scenting breath and brought it and the memories of the night into my heart.

I heard a creak and a crash. I barely moved.

"Nope. Dresser's a total loss as well." I felt the muscles under me tense just the slightest. He was going to get up. I let go of my resistance and sat up, still straddling him. Trey propped himself up on his elbows and regarded me with a sly smile.

His eyes still held a flicker within them. "I guess I'll have to invest in fire-retardant furniture and asbestos linens."

I smiled and looked away. I wouldn't be here long enough to enjoy those investments, but it was a nice thought.

I rose to my feet and offered him my hand, which he took. He pulled my body into his arms as he rose and held me for a few silent moments.

Moments I stashed away within myself for future reference.

CHAPTER ELEVEN

Goddess Bless, He Was A Fine-Looking Being

I stood in Trey's shower after he had kissed me and handed me into it. I was taking my time, hoping that he would join me; and after a few minutes, he did.

We hadn't said a word to each other since getting up off the floor.

We touched.

We kissed.

We said nothing.

The bathroom door opened and closed. I could see Trey's blurred shaped through the frosted glass, and I let out the breath I'd been holding.

It wasn't over yet. There would be more moments.

The smile I gave him was one of uncertainty. I tried for warmly seductive, but I just couldn't fake anything around him. Last night, I didn't need to.

His hands cupped my face as he took my lips in a possessive kiss. I skimmed my hands around his waist and let my thumbs caress the contours of the muscles he possessed.

The tile, cool against my back, was the only indication that I had moved. One of his hands drifted to a breast and held it in a gentle caress. I moaned at his touch and felt his breath deepen, and his body moved with a sense of urgency.

My arms made their way around his neck, pulling him more tightly against me. I never wanted to let him go. I didn't want this to end. I didn't want to think about…

His hand cupped my ass and lifted it. In a flash, my legs wrapped around his waist, and his shaft pushed in, finding the very core of me.

My body arched hard against the tile and Trey as a cry tore from me. His teeth caught my nipple and nearly brought me orgasm right then and there. His breathing was harsh and mixed with growls that sounded of desperate need.

A desperation that I shared.

His mouth covered mine once more as he thrust into me without pause.

The rest of the shower ended slowly and sensually. We scrubbed every inch of each other, dried every inch of each other, as if trying to learn each other, commit every curve to memory.

He held an oversized robe out for me and draped it over my body. It was warm and smelled of Trey.

A small table had been set, and breakfast waited for us as we emerged from the bathroom.

Seeing the huge breakfast waiting for us reminded me that my time with Trey as a lover was over. We both needed to attend to things, and we had plans to make and execute.

I would find that witchy base of operations. I would get something out of Gabrielle's belongings. I would tank up on energy.

Trey's hand rested lightly on my lower back as he walked with me to the table. He seated me as a gentleman would a lady, and it was sweet, and it made my heart do a funny flip-flop kind of thing I hadn't felt in years. Oh shit.

He seated himself and offered a plate of fruit to me first. Everything inside of me got very, very quiet. As in, "Holy shit! This is important." My instincts haven't always been the best, and I'd be lying if I said I had any real knowledge as to what it meant. Right now, I couldn't even pull information I had seen on Animal Planet to really understand what I should do and how deep any response would get me.

His face was impassive as I took a large red strawberry from the plate. I barely hesitated before offering it to him. He set the plate aside and wrapped my hand in his, steadying it as he took only half of the strawberry in his bite before releasing my hand.

I ate the rest of the berry.

I was pretty sure that his proffering me the food first meant he intended to peruse me as a mate, and my giving him first bite acknowledged that. I was merely guessing.

We began digging into the sea of food and enjoying every bit of it, by the way. His expressions changed from light, almost content, and then darker. I understood. I had disobeyed a direct order in front of one of his subordinates, and he had to deal with that.

"I'm going to need access to Gabrielle's living space," I began and continued to eat. It had been entirely too long since I had, and I was going to need some serious fuel to get me through the day. "A map with the areas you've searching would be helpful as well. I'll do some recon, but I need line of sight for the best effect."

"Anything you need." His voice tripped down my spine and caressed my body nearly as thoroughly as his hands had last night. "Tell me what happened last night."

There were so many things that had happened last night, but I was going between the two standouts for me.

"Which part? Me biting you or the sex," I said. "If you have questions about the sex, then we did something terribly wrong." I peered up from my plate and gave him a hint of a smile.

"How could you possibly be a vampire?" he asked quietly. His smile was one of understanding that I wasn't quite right, and he would have to deal with that as well.

"Well. When a girl witch and a boy vampire really love each other—," I started. He cut me off with amused irritation. I loved the look on him.

"Yeah. I know that part, Valerie." He sighed and grabbed a muffin, tearing off a bite and feeding it to me. Yummy, blueberries. "You don't smell like them, you go into direct sunshine, and you eat human food."

"Yep. That's me. I'm an enigma," I said, taking on the pancakes drenched with syrup.

"Valerie." I could hear the irritation notch up just a hair. "I have been bitten by vampires exactly twice. The first one burst into flames in thirty seconds, and then there was you."

My eating slowed as I recalled just how freakin' painful the aftermath of biting him had been. I thought I would die from the heat as it coursed through my body. I remembered wishing for death over the pain I had experienced as well.

"I was probably close to going the way of the first vamp," I told him. "I've never been in that much pain in my life. But you healed me completely as well. I'm not likely to try it again though."

"I think my blood tried to destroy the part of you that is vampire," he commented.

I closed my eyes and reached out with my senses. The scent of our night together came to me first, deep and musky. And then, the patchouli soup that resided in the bag that still rested in the other room. Next, I listened and heard the skitter of a rodent through the hall outside Trey's room.

"What are you doing?" he asked. I could hear the smile in him voice, and I had no control over my answering smile. I opened my eyes and took him in. He had no right to look that happy and relaxed when looking at me.

"Accessing some of my awesome vampire powers," I said wryly. "Hearing, scenting. By the way, you smell good. My mom was a witch. Meaning magical, but human."

I saw the flames flicker in eyes. Why couldn't I just get lost in those for a while longer? Why? Because I had a job to do and an escape to plan. We both had other things to do besides each other. A virus to destroy and a crazy person to kill. And, of course, there would be an unknown number of vampires and weres and shifters under the control of said crazy person.

"So if I had done any damage to your vampire half, you'd have no 'awesome vampire powers' left to you," he said. "I'm just happy you survived."

"Yeah, I know. I've a job to complete," I said, turning my attentions back to the food and on the fact that I really needed to remember how temporary this was. "And who else is this entertaining?"

"True enough," he replied with that look that could lure me back to his bed, well, the floor with no effort. The bed was pretty well torched. "You aren't getting out of your obligations that easily."

"I wouldn't say almost dying is easy." I laughed. It was uncomfortable and forced. I had no idea if I was going to survive the day, let alone to see this case finished. I had to hope.

"And the paralysis?" he asked. "I've never even heard of that."

"Came with the package," I said, biting into another strawberry.

"Genetics. Whatcha gonna do?" The food was really good, and I could envision eating every morsel off his rock-hard body. He had been amazing last night, but I was prepared to have that be a one-night deal. A night I would never forget.

I silently wondered if the trick he did with his tongue was a dragon thing as well.

"Trey, I'm half-witch, half-vamp, and—," I started before Trey cut me off.

"All pain in the ass." His eyes lit his face and heated me in the most delicious way. Damn him!

"Your point?" I said smiling. He was right. I'd done much, but it usually included me being torn up or sick. He didn't need the aggravation, and I was aggravating. I always would be. I found it endlessly entertaining to keep him off balance.

But I could look into his eyes over every meal every day for the rest of my life. He had been tender, passionate, creative.

And temporary.

Why wouldn't my head keep that in mind? There was no way he wanted me as a long-term mate. He had probably laid claim to me in some way. Warning others from me because… what had he said? "Nobody touches you but me." I could hear the pure menace in his voice when Sean had his arms around me in the lab. Yeah. That had to be it. I was his for the duration, and when it was over, I'd get paid and get out.

"No point, just an observation," he said casually. "So what clan do you belong to?"

Politics. I hated them. The lying. The lying while trying not to lie. Marc had lied by omission for years, and I'd like to think he regretted that; but the damaged was done, and there was no taking it back.

What Trey and I had was… strange, but I wouldn't lie to him much, I hoped.

"Apparently, Clan Olafson has laid claim to me," I said, trying for relaxed, but I had hesitated before answering him. I'd never even thought about it before. Most vampires did live under the protection of a clan master. That kept them safe. Marc had told me that he worked as an enforcer for the Los Angeles Vampire Council. I'd never thought to ask if he belonged to a clan. I just thought he was under their auspices, and that was that. "I've not accepted that claim."

"Why not?" he asked. He didn't sound particularly interested, but I knew he had to be. "Erik Olafson is a powerful clan master."

"It's personal." I gave him an "I don't want to talk about it" tone and hoped he'd get the hint and go with it. I was really surprised when he did. I knew that dragons were endlessly curious creatures, and I was something of a mystery. And he was already unraveling me. I had come apart last night over and over again in his arms.

"I'll have Simon accompany you today. Sean has other duties," Trey announced as I relaxed some at the fact that he wasn't going to press for more information. "Try to get as much accomplished by 4:00 p.m. as you can. You will be joining me in the gymnasium at that time. Be prepared."

"I understand." And I did. I would be going a few rounds with him and an audience. He had seen me fight, probably already knew my weaknesses, and would take me apart to solidify his alpha standing among the Enclave. If I lost control again, I might be able to take him, but I don't know how it had happened or if I could repeat it. The last thing I wanted to do was bite him again. The searing pain was not something I'd want a repeat performance of.

The food on the table had been decimated, and our plans were laid out. It was time to go our separate ways. This was something I needed to get use to —walking away from him.

His hand touched me low on my back as he walked me to the door to my chamber and stopped me before I crossed the threshold.

He held my face in his hands and brought his lip to mine. Gentle and caressing, just for a moment, and then gone as he stepped back and held the door for me.

I heard the click of the door latch as I stepped through and marveled at the fact that the room had been put back in order. The destroyed furniture had been replaced, and it looked as if last night had never happened.

When I heard Trey throw the lock from his side, a cold chill swept over me. The fantasy we had shared was over. The beast master had things to attend to, and I was on the docket. I needed to wake up and get moving. I had Gabrielle's things to go through and a desert to search. I also needed to start ignoring the empty ache I felt in my chest. His touch, the heated look in his eyes, the sound of his voice lived there, and I just hoped when I walked away for good, it wouldn't hurt this much.

Simon had shown up at my door an hour later. He was a were-creature of the canine variety. I was dressed, comfortable, and wholly focused on the task at hand.

Gabrielle's room was booby-trapped, but it was nothing too complicated. I disarmed it and searched things thoroughly with all my senses. I felt Gabrielle's energy and the faint whisper of the person who created the virus magic. Otherwise, it was clean. Too clean.

I swept through again and found an area of the far wall that sparkled with just how clean it was and started working the layers of magic that had been hidden so well.

It took me well over two hours to shave each layer away until the elegant collections of symbols lay bare before me. Elegant and complicated, and I'd seen this before.

I grew up with my mom and her sisters. Craziest group of witches you could imagine. They were loving and caring and adventurous. They taught me control and discipline. Well, they tried for the discipline and magic. Lots and lots of magic.

Mom was gone a lot, but my aunts really made up for it in so many ways. They loved her and me. And when Mom died, Maggie lost it. The youngest of my aunts couldn't accept that it had been an accident, and she needed somebody to blame. That would be vampires. She didn't care which one; it was all of them. Mom never told anybody who my father was, but my genetics showed through early, so it wasn't a huge leap to figure out what the other half of the chromosomal contribution had been.

What I was seeing in front of me was one of Maggie's constructs, but it wasn't her energy that built it.

My energy reached into the construct slowly and carefully. I tried to ignore the thousand-pound weight that pressed in on my chest. Somebody my aunt Maggie taught magic to had lost their mind. At least it wasn't my aunt, I hoped.

I hadn't seen Maggie in six years. Her anger and rage over my mother's death drove a wedge between her and my other aunts and eventually myself. Of course, I couldn't deal with much of anything at the time. I was an angry, hormonal, young woman, but I couldn't direct my anger the way Maggie had.

So I ran, and I was going to do so again. Maybe I should just go back to my aunts in Arizona.

Or maybe I should pay attention to the energetic construct I had in front of me!

Gabrielle had been strong. Of course, she had to be just to put this thing together, not to mention the fact that she made her way into the Enclave in the first place was pretty damn amazing anyway. Lucky for me, Aunt Maggie taught me this one before I'd hit puberty. I unwound the power and felt a pang of loss for my aunts and my mom. There was always so much laughter in the house, unless I was being bitched out for something or another. I was challenging. Apparently, I still am.

Finally, the construct was disassembled, and I was looking at the spell that had created the infection in the first place. Serums were good; this was way better! Now I could create a counter-spell to destroy it instead of burning it. That would take a lot less energy, but it might mean being a lot closer to the source.

If one of Maggie's students had gone crazy, she wouldn't want them running around using her magic to destroy like this. She may have hated vampires with a passion, but she never had a problem with shifters or weres.

There were a couple of problems I was having with this discovery. First: Why keep the spell anywhere near the Enclave?

Second: The originator of this spell wasn't Gabrielle, so why did she keep this in her quarters?

I checked my watch and saw I only had three hours before I had to meet with Trey. I had lost all sense of time and needed to eat before I got my hands on a map and tried to find the base of operations. The little mysteries could wait.

Cargo pants are my favorite. Lots of places to stash things like pads of paper and pencils. I drew out the spell on the notepad and made a few notes that only I would be able to decipher and shoved it back in a pocket.

After lunch, Simon gave me the map and took me to one of the rooftop guard posts facing the direction Trey had been searching. I got the map oriented and let my energy stretch out across the landscape. I didn't rush, but I wasn't taking a leisurely pace either. The energy of this desert was pure and allowed me to draw it into myself as I searched.

An hour later, I knew why Trey hadn't found anything out in this direction. There was nothing there. It wasn't a "wiped clean of any trace" type of nothing either.

I recalled the direction the golems had come from and oriented myself. It was a ninety-degree difference. I followed my instincts and eased out cautiously.

The subtle ebbs and flows of the desert were soothing and calm. I let myself get lost in the beauty of the landscape as well as the potency that infused me during my search. This land was beyond simply beautiful. It had an innate power that put me as ease, if I wasn't too wound up to enjoy it.

I wondered for a moment if Trey needed a full-time witch here. After all, the last one didn't work out all that well, and there was a job opening. Then again, he may have decided that a resident witch was a bad idea. Couldn't blame him for that call.

The flow of the energy shifted subtly. It was something akin to the rush of water around a boulder in a river. The water still ran, but its flow adjusted for the obstacle.

I had found the edge of what was likely the base. I grabbed the map and started making marks along the border as I was feeling it. Once I had the perimeter figured out, then I could go in and determine where the wards were, how deeply embedded they were, and what it would take to bring them down.

There was also the possibility that I could cast the counter-spell through the wards. Letting the victims on the inside free from the infection could be a useful distraction.

I'm sure there were other possibilities, and Trey would take my counsel and make the decision. He is the master of the area; it's up to him.

He was also needing to reinforce his authority to those who knew he had been disobeyed. That reinforcement would be held in the gym in about half an hour.

CHAPTER TWELVE

"*I didn't hear you complaining last night.*"

I showered and changed. I went over the fight we had last night. It was difficult to remember the finer details past the makeup sex. I didn't know what else to call it, beside spectacular.

Sitting on the bed and trying to focus on how he moved, how he fought, and how easy it had been for Trey to pin me only frustrated me. There was nothing I would be able to do if he shifted into dragon form. Then again, he had me until I lost it and went vamp on him. Which I had never done before.

I finally got my ass off the bed and started warming up. It was about that time Simon had come for me. Well, so much for warming up in advance. Maybe I would have a chance when I got there. After all, I couldn't be the only one he had to deal with, could I?

Really, how many beings would be stupid enough to go against Trey? Well, besides me, that is.

He was right though. I shouldn't have gone in Marc's cell. Any number of things could have gone wrong. People could have gotten hurt. Maybe if Trey had bothered to explain why instead of ordering, I could have done as he asked. But he had ordered me to do something from a really angry place. So it didn't feel like an order, more like a pissy, arbitrary, alpha male outburst.

He didn't talk to me, didn't ask what I might do. He issued an order because he was pissed… after I told him Marc and I were bound. Ummm.

Trey had even thrown the fact that I was an unbound female in Marc's face.

We fed each other. Strawberries have never tasted so good.

"Nobody touches you but me," he had said.

How could he possibly see me as a suitable mate? That was insane! I had just ended a five-year relationship! My *only* relationship! What the hell was wrong with him? Christ, what the hell was wrong with me?

Damn it! If I got myself anymore rattled, he would pummel me without any resistance.

Fighting a shifter was never on my list of things to, and fighting Trey was going to be awful. I knew he didn't want to hurt me. I knew I couldn't hurt him unless I went vamp on him, but I didn't want to; and besides, the consequences were not really worth it. I wasn't even sure if I could survive biting him again.

I would do my best. Fight him with all of the training that I apparently lacked and let the Enclave know he was still in charge.

Too soon, we were there. A sixty-by-sixty-foot pit, twenty feet deep with raised seating on three sides. It was carved into the desert floor at the base of the structure that was the Enclave. It could seat a hundred easily, but there were only fifteen plus Trey who was warming up in the pit.

Goddess bless, he was a fine-looking being. He was shirtless, and the muscles that had participated in turning me into Jell-O last night looked more powerful in this setting. He stretched and flexed and left no doubt that if he really wanted, he could do much more than hurt me.

Last night, he had proven he could take me and do it easily even if he didn't shift. Today was for show, and how badly he chose to humiliate or hurt me was going to be his call.

I don't think I'd regret being with Trey last night. He was gentle and fierce, passionate and tender. He gave me everything I wanted and a few things that I hadn't known I needed, and now I was on my own and dealing with the consequences of my actions. This was nothing personal.

He met me in the center of the pit. Trey looked relaxed and at ease, but I could see the tension and a hint of anger in his eyes.

He didn't want this, and I was making him do it. Trey's anger wouldn't really be a factor when this started. He would do as much as he could to do as little damage to me and still get the point across to those watching.

"Ready?" he asked.

I took a deep breath. "Just for the record, Trey. You were right. I shouldn't have gone in Marc's cell. I endangered Mila and anybody else who might have come along in the holding area," I began. "Too many things could have gone wrong. So I extend my apologies to the beast master of the southwest region of North America." I inclined my head enough to show deference and took a step back. "Now, yes. I am ready."

He backed away until we had ten feet between us. I think if he hadn't possessed an iron will, he would have gaped at what I'd just said. I saw the hesitation as he moved.

"Whenever you're ready," he said.

I nodded and took another deep breath. This was it.

"Go."

Trey leapt at me. I dove and rolled to the right and was back on my feet as he turned and tried to make a tackle. I jumped high, tucked, and flipped over him. I could feel his hand brushed by my shoulder as I was airborne. My biggest problem with front flips was landing blind. He would be at my back when I landed, giving me little indication of his next maneuver.

So I landed and ran toward the wall. I could hear him behind me. I hit the wall feet first, punched off, twisted, and watched his hands barely miss my leg as I sailed out of reach.

He charged me as I regrouped. I backed up and let him catch me. As his hands came down, I grabbed his shoulders, buckled my knees, and rolled back, bringing him over me. I lodged my feet in his stomach and gave him a solid push as I released him over my body.

I had really hoped he would land on his back, but he twisted in the air, landed on his feet, and was charging me before I was fully ready.

For a big guy, Trey was amazingly swift and agile. The beautiful movements of his body could betray his dragon heritage if anybody had a clue about him.

"I could watch you all day," I whispered, knowing he could hear me. He got hold of one of my arms as I tried to duck out from his hold.

"Why's that?" he answered quietly.

I neatly twisted my body around and loosened his grip. The shove I gave him only served to push me back a couple of feet. But it was distance I needed.

"First off, you're style is elegant. Making you beautiful to simply watch," I said, taking a few more steps back and getting ready for whatever he would throw at me next. "Secondly, I could learn more by just watching you than I have learned in practice in the last five years."

That last statement, though true, hurt. I had learned a lot in the last five years with Marc, but not nearly enough. Marc rarely hurt me in practice, and if he did, he'd stop and tend my injuries. None of them were all that bad, I could have kept going, but I just didn't question him.

Young and stupid was what I was. I would have happily stayed that way for who knows how long. But fate threw me into the mix alone, and I found out the truth.

I was a better witch than I was a fighter, and Trey was fighting me at my capacity, not his. Otherwise, this would have been over at the first pass.

I wondered if I could vamp out and stay controlled just a heartbeat after Trey started moving toward me.

I had gotten distracted yet again and jumped as high as I could manage. On a good day, my vertical leap was twenty-five feet. Today was a good day. Unfortunately, Trey had a better vertical leap than I did. He grabbed my ankle and pulled.

If he had pulled hard enough, I would have impacted the stone floor with enough force to break bones. He didn't, and I landed intact but off balance.

"Thank you for the compliment," he said lighting in front of me. Trey hit the ground as I stumbled back and rolled instead of falling out of my landing.

"You're welcome," I responded as he dove for me again. I slid out of the way, jumped, planted my foot in his chest, and shoved. Trey, being the brick wall that he was, didn't move. I, however, took flight pretty effectively. I really got some good lift, and when it was all said and done, I stood on the rail at the edge of the pit and looked down at Trey who arrived at the same time I did.

"You're out of bounds," he said. Trey didn't seem at all angry or upset. He looked amused, and the fire smoldered in his eyes as he looked me over like a treat he couldn't wait to have again.

"Oh," I said with mock surprise. "There were rules, *and* you expected me to behave?" I shot him a teasing smile. He was covered with a light sheen of perspiration. I, of course, was dripping but not out of breath. He made me wet just looking at him though. Seeing that sheen coating his skin in the light of the moon as his body drifted over mine would be something I could never forget.

"Something like that." He returned the smile. I could melt in the heat of that man. Hell, we pretty much burnt the bed down.

The lightness of my heart and the smile on my face was nearly pure joy. I enjoyed this. I enjoyed him. How could this possibly be my punishment?

My hands hit my hips. "What if I don't want to come down?" I said with just the right amount of sass. "You are bigger, stronger, and faster than I am."

"You seem to be doing just fine," he replied as his eyes lit up in a way that had nothing to do with the fire he was borne of.

"Only because you are letting me." I lifted my eyebrow and just waited for him to answer that one. It was true. He knew it. I knew it. The few people watching knew it. So really, what was his game?

He regarded me for entirely too long. His eyes caressed me from my tennis shoes to my ponytail, while resting for an extended length on some of my more choice bits.

"Give me one good reason I shouldn't kill you for disobeying me, Valerie." It was a simple request, and there was no heat attached to his words. I wasn't really sure that my life was actually on the line or not. I was going to assume it was. There would be nothing more important to Trey than keeping the Enclave safe, and that meant discipline.

"I gave you the resources for the serum and vaccine," I started. "I contained the infection three times, so far. I found the spell and can create a counter-spell. I found the base of operations, and I'm pretty good in bed."

The look on Trey's face was one of pure shock.

"What?" The question came out in a roar that had our audience stepping back, even though they were a good forty feet from we were currently standing. Personally, I would have preferred to be over with them rather than this close to Trey.

"I didn't hear you complaining last night," I quipped calmly. I was fairly certain that he hadn't been talking about our sexcapades last night, but he was making me nervous. I don't think I'd ever be completely comfortable with him.

"You found the base?" His voice was a lot less human than I was comfortable with, and I had a feeling that Simon was toast once he was found. "Where's Simon?"

"He was watching me, not the other way around," I replied. Gods, my mouth was going to get me killed.

"Valerie! Are you trying to piss me off?" His face was dark. I could see the desire to cause bloodshed just below the surface of his control.

"No. I just seem to be very good at it," I replied. I was beginning to notice that the more frightened I was, the more mouthy I became. Probably not the best combination.

Trey turned toward the audience and shouted. "Find Simon, now!"

Sean and Mila moved along with three others. The remaining members of the audience, I suspect, had peed themselves and were trying to get it together enough to just get out of the area.

Trey leapt up and over the rail I was balanced on. He could have broken me in so many different ways in that pit, and he had chosen to what? Play with me? Get a feel for my strengths and weaknesses? I don't know what, but I had to admit I liked it. I enjoyed it and him.

And *if* we had a chance, he could teach me more than Marc had been willing to.

I would enjoy him while I had him, even when half of the time I was wondering if or when he would kill me.

Trey stood there, looking up at me while I distracted myself with those random thoughts. His arms were crossed, and his weight had shifted to one hip. Goddess bless, he was sexy and had me wanting him, and here and now would work for me.

"Are you finished fucking around?" he asked, shaking me from the distraction that was this sexually gifted beast of a man.

"Not really, but we had to eat breakfast and get on with our day." I was still on the rail, but I had turned to face him. Trey shook his head, clearly uncertain as to what to do with me as he stepped up to the rail. His hand lifted in invitation that I should take it and join him on the ground.

I acquiesced.

As we walked, I filled Trey in on what I had accomplished before making it to the pit. Simon was nowhere to be found, and all of the documentation I had created was gone. Including the notes I had made and stashed in my pants. I had pushed into the paper hard enough to leave and imprint. And with a little ingenuity, I was able to reconstruct most of the spell and fill in the rest from memory. Good thing I could remember everything I had done.

There were plenty of landmarks on the map to allow me to recreate where the boundary of the base was, and the counter-spell was a no brainer.

Trey had decided that the counter-spell needed to be woven into a number of fun objects, including but not limited to hand grenades, RPGs, and mortar rounds.

Shifters have the best toys!

I also recommended some nonlethal delivery systems.

"Snow globes?" Trey responded, almost horrified at my recommendation. "Seriously?"

"Yes. Snow globes," I said. "Glass ones, not the cheap plastic ones. Plastic screws with magic. The glass will break on impact, and the filling is enchanted, so the splash will disseminate the counter-spell."

He just looked at me for a long moment. Clearly, he was trying to figure out just how crazy I was.

"If there are any number of vampires being held, and they are depleted, the last thing you need are bleeding bodies to set them off into a frenzy." I really liked the confused look on his face. It did wonders for me. However, my logic was sound, and I thought he would see it my way.

"Has Marc been any help as far as the number of missing vampires?" I asked. I hadn't seen Marc since last night. I assumed he was sleeping since it was broad daylight. I didn't even know if Trey had spoken to Marc, except to threaten him.

"Not yet," Trey replied as we stepped into, what I assumed was, the war room. "I will speak to him tonight about the situation, and as you had suggested, he may be useful in getting information regarding how many vamps are likely to be involved."

Sean stepped into the room right behind Trey and myself. "Simon is gone," he reported calmly. "There's no trace of him."

Trey punched the stonewall, leaving an impression of his knuckles behind. "Damn it!" he muttered as he rounded on me. My heart rate shot up. I hated the fact that part of me didn't trust Trey in a very basic and elemental way. Maybe my heart was looking for somebody else to love, and I wanted it to be Trey. He wanted me sexually, but I was coming to believe that was all we would share, and I wanted more.

"Is there anyway he could have been infected and you missed it?" Trey asked as he loomed over me.

"Is there any way that he wasn't in the Enclave when I swept it?" I responded, looking annoyed though I just wanted to cry. "Why don't you check with Mila and find out if he had been inoculated. I have to actively search for it. He could have been infected, and I might not have known."

Trey glanced over to Sean and nodded. With that, Sean left the room.

"He's checking with Mila?" I asked.

Trey blew out a breath and nodded. "Scan the Enclave," he ordered, having gotten some of his temper under control.

"What's the magic word?" I asked innocently. He had scared me; therefore, I must screw with him just a little.

He closed his eyes and took a deep breath in. I could see the muscles in his jaw working.

"Valerie…" He was grinding his teeth as he said my name. I thought it best to stop messing with him for the time being.

"Okay. Jeesh! Don't get your panties in a bunch," I said and began to reach through the Enclave.

It took about thirty seconds before I found two small patches of the dark magic. Searching the Enclave had been easier using Trey's energy. It was warmth and strength and comfort, but that could have been because I was half-dead at the time I used it. Oh well, just one more thing to miss when I left.

On the wall of the room were aerial drawings of the Enclave. Each level was drawn in detail. I held the location of the magic in my head as I went to the wall and tried to match the physical location with what I was feeling.

There were five floors above ground and six under. Wow! This place was a fucking fortress. There were also a number of tunnels, emergency exits that came out a half mile from the Enclave itself. Impressive to say the very least.

The infection was located on the third sub-level.

"I found some," I informed the cranky beast master as I continued to scan the layout. "It feels like two people, and they are in your armory."

I was on Trey's heels as he hauled ass out of the war room and toward the armory. He was also on the phone giving instructions to Sean.

Trey and I arrived first and therefore were the first targets the two infected shifters were firing at.

Trey shoved me to the side and pressed himself against me, nearly crushing me between himself and the wall of an alcove. We were pinned. Me more than Trey.

I tried wiggling out from in between him and the wall, but he was having none of it.

"Trey! Get off me!" I yelled. I may not have any weapons, but I wasn't helpless. "Give me some room to work here!"

"With your track record? No way am I taking that chance," he growled as rounds continued to come in our general direction.

"And when they blow the armory, what's going to protect either of us?" I yelled. Trey paused. "They already have their weapons, Trey."

Sean and Mila turned the corner and immediately ducked back behind the wall. Live fire was a great deterrent from moving forward.

"Get those two under control, Mila!" Trey yelled.

I managed to get a look at Mila who was armed with the tranquilizer gun I'd seen earlier.

I remained crushed between a stonewall and Trey's body, which did feel like a stonewall as Sean and Mila contained the situation, and the gunfire finally stopped.

Trey, however, did not let up as Sean dashed to the armory.

"Trey!" I yelled into his neck. "Get the fuck off me!"

He stopped crushing me against the wall, but he gathered me into him as he bowed his back and looked around the wall to check on Sean's status. Once that was done and my level of pissed off had increased tenfold, Trey looked into my very angry eyes and blew out a very annoyed breath.

"Boss," Sean called out from the armory. "We got a problem." "How much time before the explosives go off, Sean?" I yelled. "One minute, twenty seconds," he yelled back. I pushed against Trey.

"Get out of her, Valerie," he growled, releasing me with light shove in the direction of the way out.

I was here to do a job. Maybe getting blown up wasn't in the job description, but I could contain a lot in my magic and was pretty sure I could contain the explosion. That is, if I knew how much explosives were involved. Trey was going to need the armory intact if he and his people were going to survive the upcoming battle. He was also going to need to increase his inventory of snow globes.

"No, Trey!" I said moving toward the armory. "Don't argue, just let me work my magic and get out of my way!"

"One minute, ten seconds," Sean yelled.

We headed into the armory, and I saw a good five pounds of C-4 explosives. Definitely enough to set off the armory and collapse a good chunk of the Enclave.

"Let's move the bomb into the nearest tunnel. From there, I should be able to contain it well enough to lessen the damage," I suggested.

Sean didn't argue. He didn't ask. He didn't even look to Trey at all. He simply grabbed the device and ran with it. I followed with Trey right by my side. He had ordered Mila to leave and to evacuate certain sections of the Enclave. She was on the phone and on her way in seconds, which was what our timing was boiling down to.

"Forty-five seconds," Sean yelled. He had made it into the tunnel and was lost in the darkness of it. Trey prevented me from going in after him.

"You'll do whatever you need to do from here, Valerie," he growled and held me in place.

"Thirty seconds." His voice seemed too far away.

"Tell him to drop it and get back here, Trey," I ordered. Part of me giggled and part of me knew I was going to pay for having taken control of the situation as I did. Sean would as well. He had taken my orders without question.

"Far enough, Sean!" he yelled. "Get back here!"

"Twenty!" Sean started counting down as he hauled his ass back to the door. "Nineteen… eighteen… seventeen."

I reached out energetically and found the device. I was pretty sure the tunnel was going to collapse no matter what I did, but I hoped that it would only be a small section, and it wouldn't affect any other part of the Enclave.

"Nine… eight… seven." Sean made it through the door and headed down the hall and around the corner. Trey picked me up and headed out with Sean.

Okay, I could ignore the fact that I was slung over his shoulder and still keep my focus, but he needed to stop manhandling me like this. It was getting old, and I was getting annoyed.

I diverted all of my resources to the containment and held on tightly as Trey slowed, moved around the corner with Sean, and brought me into his arms. That was much more comfortable than bouncing around and getting my breath knocked out of me.

"One," Sean announced.

I felt Trey curl his body around mine, shielding me from anything that might come from the direction of the blast. It was strangely comforting.

The explosion hit my shields and sent a shock through my body. I'd never dealt with anything that big before, but I felt the containment field absorb the kinetic energy of the explosion, and I knew that the amount of damage had been greatly reduced as I had expected. What I hadn't expected was blacking out afterward.

CHAPTER THIRTEEN

I'm an Idiot!

I've blacked out before. I've been knocked unconscious before. I had never dreamed during those times. Normally, I simply wake up and feel, more or less, awful until the reason I'd been knocked out or blacked out had been dealt with.

The dream was less visually graphic and more of a feeling. Warmth and comfort surrounded me. Soothing sounds caressed me. I felt rested. Peaceful.

I took a deep breath in and scented warm spice and male.

My body stretched and felt no pain.

I rolled into the warm spice I had scented and felt arms encircle me gently. "You could have warned me that you were going to pass out, Valerie," Trey whispered.

"Had I known, I would have told you," I replied in the middle of another stretch. I felt wonderfully boneless in Trey's embrace. "So what's the damage?" I snuggled more deeply into his warmth. Why my brain was trying to be all professional on me was beyond my comprehension.

"Small section of tunnel collapsed," he replied softly. "It will take three or four days to dig out, shore up, and be put back into use."

"What's the status on inoculated versus non-inoculated denizens of the Enclave?" I asked. I was still completely relaxed and warmed in Trey's arms. Part of me just wanted to feel secure in his embrace, and the other part of me had a job to do.

"We believe that all current occupants are infection free," he said as his lips whispered across my forehead.

I let my magic loose to scan the Enclave to make sure he was right. In doing so, I found the reason for my having passed out. I had no energy left to do anything but cuddle and fire up a couple of brain cells.

"Crap," I whispered. There was no heat, no energy behind my words. I couldn't be anything but slightly annoyed at the discovery. "Is the moon up?" I asked.

"Yes. What's wrong?" I was beginning to love the sound of his voice so close to my ear and the feel of his body next to mine. I tried to ignore the fact that this was temporary.

"I'm beyond depleted. I need to sit in the moonlight for a bit," I told him. "Then I might be able to function again."

He wrapped one of his hands around mine and opened up that vast pool of energy as he had before and let me draw from it.

Fire dragon energy coursed through me, easing into every corner of my being. I could just let it curl around me and lull me back into sleep. Powerful as it was, it couldn't re energize me.

But since he made it available to me, I swept the Enclave.

"There's nothing." I sighed and relaxed into his embrace. "Moonlight, please," I said, slipping into sleep once again.

Once again, I began to stir to yelling. At least, this time the furniture wasn't being destroyed. Well, not yet. The moon was hanging over me in her waning glory, and I could feel that my energy was back up to speed. Well, not entirely back up to speed. I had just woken up and was still groggy.

I was curled up on a padded wrought-iron love seat, and Trey stood in front of me, facing indoors.

"I don't care if the pope's here!" Trey bellowed. "Put them in VIP quarters. They can see both of us tomorrow night!"

"Clan masters aren't known for their patience, Trey." Sean's voice sounded more than just a little irritated. At the mention of "clan masters," I woke up really fast.

I pushed to my feet. "What's going on, Trey?" I had an idea, but I really wanted to hear it from him. *So yeah. Go ahead, Trey. Bring my worst fears to light.*

"Nothing that can't wait until morning," Trey said calmly as his arm slid around my shoulders. "Or much later. Are you feeling better?"

"What clan master is here and why, Sean?" I asked, allowing my body to ease to Trey's side. I could feel the tension in him, pulling him to the breaking point. I wondered how much of the conversation I had missed.

Sean looked like he was about to answer when his eyes went to Trey, and he suddenly swallowed his words.

"It's nothing that needs to bother us tonight, Valerie." Trey turned toward me and pulled me into his arms. Goddess bless, I wanted this man under me, over me, anyway I could get him. But I knew which clan master was here and the trouble that could stem from his presence might be more than the amount of help he could give would be worth. Trey needed to know. Maybe he could help me get a head start. I had no illusions that he wouldn't fight for me, but I could hope that he would help me just a little.

"Just an unexpected guest. I assume Marc has solicited some aid from the local vampire population." Trey was so dismissive it worried me.

"Clan masters are not local, Trey. Not to this area," I said sternly. I didn't want to be stern. I wanted to be in Trey's bed quietly ruining a good night's sleep with some more incredibly scorching sex. But I didn't want Trey to get blindsided or put on the wrong end of a clan master's ire because of me. "Tell me what's going on." I searched his eyes and found nicely contained rage hiding behind desire. The rage had little to do with me at this point, though that would likely change soon.

"Olafson is here with a small contingency of guards," Trey explained easily enough. Right now he hated somebody for something, but he was keeping it together fairly well. "He wishes to meet with myself and my resident witch to discuss strategy. However, it is late, and you need your rest. It can wait until tomorrow."

Olafson knew exactly who the "resident witch" was, and the bastard was playing games, well, more games. He had better be here to help if he was going to be here at all.

"Had Marc told you anything, Trey?" I asked. The faintest sneer crossed over his features. The one other man who had shared my bed was definitely on his shit list. A smile tugged at my lips. He had claimed me for the duration of my stay, and those possessive instincts had kicked in just a bit. I guess it didn't matter whether what was his was long or short term, but I definitely was his for now.

"Only that we would be receiving help from Los Angeles with the problem out here," he answered.

I took a deep breath, steeling myself against what needed to be said, but I'd rather do it in private. I looked at Sean who seemed cool and collected, but he had raised his voice to Trey, which meant he wasn't.

"Sean, give me fifteen minutes, alone with Trey." Sean didn't hesitate. He simply nodded curtly and left the room.

I turned to Trey. I couldn't decipher the look on his face, but I really didn't have time.

"You might want to sit for this, Trey," I said. Goddess, my heart was pounding in my chest, and I would probably break out in a cold sweat any minute. I fully expected Trey to distance himself after I told him what was going on.

My never-before-seen father would stake a claim on me the minute he walked into the room, and there was no way Trey would risk conflict with a clan master over the convenient, hot monkey sex we could be having.

I would never see his eyes blaze in want or lust, at least not in my direction again. However, I had been trying to get it through my thick skull that he was temporary no matter what I had come to want.

So I pulled on my big girl panties and readied myself to stand in front of the beast master of the southwest region of North America.

Except that when Trey sat down, he pulled me into his lap and wrapped his arms loosely around my body.

He was not going to make this easy for me, and I don't believe he understood that.

"Trey." I was trying for professional and detached. He started nuzzling my neck. It's really hard to be professional when your insides are curling in anticipation of having a powerful, beautiful creature, such as Trey, do things to your body that could never be copied by anybody else, ever.

It's a dragon thing.

I love the dragon thing, especially his.

My arms went around his shoulders as he licked and kissed my neck and shoulder.

"You taste so good, Valerie," he whispered. "Thanks for getting rid of Sean," he added as he nipped the juncture of my shoulder and neck.

"We only have fifteen minutes, Trey," I moaned. This was so unfair. He was making it impossible for me to think, let alone to speak.

"I can do a lot to you in fifteen minutes." I could feel his smile ghost across my skin as he kissed me again.

"But we need to talk…" I lost my breath as his hands skimmed up, went under my shirt, and caressed me lightly.

"I'm listening," he whispered. Warm lips traced the shell of my ear. Warm hands kneaded the muscles of my back.

"What? Oh right. Talking." What little plan I had as to how this tale should unfold left me as the clasp of my bra let go. I was going to make a mess of this and would probably end up naked and sweating before Sean returned. "Clan Master Olafson is my father." That was probably not the best lead in for this conversation, but I was sure it would get his attention.

Trey paused. He didn't shove me off his lap, horrified at my pronouncement. He didn't let go at all. He paused.

"Go on," he said as he returned to the gentle caresses and soft kisses he was bestowing upon my thoroughly aroused body.

"Never met him," I panted. Oh gods, he started caressing my breast and playing tenderly with the nipple. I was dying here. "Never knew he was my father. My mom and aunts raised me."

He lifted my shirt and bra out of his way and wrapped his lips around my already sensitive nipple.

"Um… he found me… I was eighteen." I had only the thinnest grip on my higher brain functions at this point, but I was fairly sure I could get the important information out in the allotted time. "He sent Marc to watch over me. When I was twenty-one… he… um, oh, that feels good." My fingers tunneled through his hair as he held me tightly and began to suckle with more force. I was gone, and there was nothing I really wanted to do about it except moan and encourage Trey to continue.

I could feel my body warming quickly. Light perspiration had covered me, and desire washed all thought of clan masters and hidden agendas from my mind. All I wanted was Trey's arms to hold me, his lips to taste me, and the rest of his body to love me until we torched every flat surface available, and that included the walls.

"Marc told you?" Trey whispered softly as his lips found their way to my neck once more.

All I could do was nod and make a vague noise of affirmation. All I wanted to do was be naked with Trey. Trey being naked as well. He pulled me tightly against his body. There was no doubt in my mind that the hardness pushing against my hip was evidence that Trey wanted us naked as well.

I pulled at his shirt, almost desperate to feel his bare skin against mine.

Forget "almost." By the time I had gotten it off of his body, it was in pieces.

His shirts had a short shelf life around me, as well as the doors.

Trey, being so much more reserved, had my shirt and bra off, and they were intact.

"Is that why you destroyed the binding?" he asked as he lifted me from his lap, turned, and laid me on the love seat.

Again, there was nodding and unintelligible noises involved in my reply. He stripped me of my pants and underwear and unfastened his jeans. In his eyes, I saw rage seething underneath the desperation to sink himself into my body. He pushed his jeans down just enough to free his hardened length.

Trey pulled my hips over to the edge of the loveseat and ran his fingers between my thighs. I was wet and more than ready for him to take me.

"You want me?" A playful smile cross his features as two fingers sank inside of me.

My body arched hard with the sensations that ran through it. He knew how to touch me, and I wanted his touch and more.

"More than I should," I moaned. His fingers pumped slowly as his thumb played with my clit. "God! Please, Trey…"

His fingers left me. I tried to catch my breath, but he gave me no time before he was deep inside of me and thrusting with a wicked coordination of manipulating my hips in time with his.

"I have never lied to you, Valerie," he said as his pace quickened. "I will never lie to you." His breathing became labored; mine was more like one long moan. I ran my hands up his arms. I could feel the muscles as they worked my body with ease. My nails dug into his biceps as I began to climax. My eyes were closed, and there was nothing but the feeling of Trey and the pleasure he was giving me.

I cried out as the wash of bliss crested and broke. "Trey." His name spilled from my lips as his orgasm took shape and he held himself tightly to my body. He leaned forward, his forehead touching my chest as his body shook with each spasm.

There was nothing but the sound of our breathing for a long, peaceful moment. I caught the scent of scorched pad under me, and I wondered if we could melt the furniture. In the back of my mind, I thought it would be fun to try.

Trey began to stir. He kissed the center of my chest where his forehead had lain. He kissed each breast almost reverently. His weight shifted back as he slid from my body and kissed my navel.

"I will never tire of you, Valerie," he said quietly.

I smiled and looked into his eyes. I must have been high on the endorphins and sex because it looked to me like he meant it. I could see it, I could feel it, but my mind refused to believe it.

He picked up my panties and slipped them up my legs. My pants followed and then the rest of my clothing slowly and carefully until he had dressed me and I was on my feet.

When he had finished with me, he tucked his still hard cock into his jeans.

It looked uncomfortable. I was looking forward to seeing to his comfort later.

"Do you understand that, Valerie?" he asked softly. His hands went to my shoulders, and his eyes were riveted to mine.

I guess something about what he was saying and how my head was interpreting what he was saying triggered a fear response in me because my mouth was about to get me in some hot water.

"I'm just new, Trey," I began. "The novelty will wear off, and then somebody else will have the privilege of occupying the adjacent room to the beast master."

"Do you honestly believe that?" As he asked that question, I saw a mask of distance cover his face. He was once again getting ready for me to reject him.

Now if I was smart…

I could feel the burn of tears behind my eyes. I was going to do it. I was going to hang what was left of my broken and battered heart out there for somebody else to destroy. I'm an idiot!

"I don't want to," I whispered. "But you are the beast master and a rare breed of shifter, and I am a mutt with more baggage than you should have to deal with." My voice was breaking, I was so screwed, and I so didn't want to start crying again.

"Every single person in the Enclave is of two natures, Valerie," he said softly, the distance having left his face. "You fit in perfectly in more ways than you understand."

He pulled me into his embrace and kissed me lightly on the lips. "The adjacent room is reserved for my mate, Valerie."

My heart stopped as I took in a ragged breath. "It has never been occupied. I am nine hundred years old and have never taken a mate. I have never found a female who could turn me on, piss me off, stand up to me, lay down with me, and make me want her more and more with each passing moment."

I was utterly confused and couldn't rally any cohesive thoughts regarding being mated to him. I assumed that I would never have a mate, ever. At least not one of my own choosing. A mate who loved me for who I was, in spite of what I considered serious flaws within myself just didn't seem possible.

"Olafson intends to bring me into vampire society," I told him. He needed to understand that I was not worth the trouble. You don't buck a clan master. Then again, I was planning my own escape from his clutches myself. "Marc's been 'training' me." Yes, I even did the air quotes. "We took a lot of cases that involved having to mix within high society. I learned to blend." I had eased out of his arms and away from the safety that I felt there. I'm sure that the distance I saw in his face earlier would return as soon as he understood what was going on. "I was actually hoping that you'd pay me in cash, then I was going to disappear."

I walked to the balcony rail and looked out over the moonlight-drenched desert. It was so deceptively peaceful, but the beauty of it was a truth that I felt all the way down to my soul.

It was hard to believe that somewhere out in that stark beauty was a crazy person with a very scary army.

When Trey walked up behind me and wrapped himself around me, his lips caressing my neck, his arms holding me in a loving embrace, I had never felt anything so right, so perfect.

"The only way you are leaving here is if you want to leave, Valerie." He gave me a gentle squeeze. "You are an independent contractor, currently working under the auspices of the Enclave. You have our backing in any decision you make in this." He nuzzled my neck, scenting me. It never failed to inflame my body and make my mind forget everything happening around me that isn't Trey. "And I am officially offering you employment here. You are good at what you do, and your loyalty is more than admirable."

"How so?" I asked softly. I had found heaven in his arms and was currently basking in its glow.

"You risk yourself when you could run. You place yourself between danger and those who are vulnerable." His teeth grazed the side of my neck sending shards of desire through my body, settling between my thighs. Maybe we should stick to having sex in the shower or tub. Things didn't tend to burn there.

"Are you talking about the attack on the way here?" I asked.

He nodded and licked the tiny scrapes on my neck.

"You could have been killed," he whispered as his tongue traced the shell of my ear. I wanted nothing more than to strip our clothes back off and do things to him. Lascivious things to him. "The hardest thing I've done was to let you out of that van. But if I couldn't trust you to know what you were doing and know how to do your job, then you weren't the woman I believed you to be."

"And who do you believe me to be?" I asked. Honestly I was just peripherally engaged in the conversation. Most of my attention was on Trey's arms holding me gently and his lips nipping and kissing me. If I had the capacity to purr, I would have been all over it.

"My mate," he whispered against my neck.

Now he had all of my attention. I mean, hell, I got the part about me sleeping in the room reserved for his "mate," but me? Seriously?

"I just find that really hard to believe, Trey." My head leaned back against his shoulder as I looked into the night sky filled with the heavenly bodies that kept watch over me, or at least I liked to believe that. How could I not be watched over by something bigger than myself.

I had been raised with love, though I was just now beginning to understand that. Marc had been a kind and gentle lover. My life had been a grand adventure over the last five years and now, I was learning just how powerful I was as a witch, I had an amazing lover, and he wanted me as his mate.

It boggles the mind.

I turned in his arms and watched his beautiful blue eyes flame softly.

"You need somebody who can command in your absence and is strong enough to handle challenges from your people," I stated calmly. "Your last witch fucked you and your people over. It's not going to be easy to be accepted simply as your resident witch, but as your mate?" I shook my head.

"You're already being accepted, Valerie." The grin on his face made him look impish. I liked the look of confusion on him slightly better, but impish was good. "How did you get Sean to leave?"

"I told him to give us fifteen minutes. What's the big deal?" I asked.

"Yes. And he obeyed you without hesitation," Trey explained softly. "He didn't even look to me for confirmation. And it's not the first time either."

There was a knock on the door.

"I may have to kick his ass for that," Trey finished as the knocking continued.

Our fifteen minutes were up, and Trey was right. He could do a lot to me in fifteen minutes, and I was impressed and appreciative of his skills.

I closed my eyes for a moment and took a deep breath. Warm spices and male flowed to me. Soothing and relaxing.

I was going to meet my father. I had no idea how this was going to go, but I was sure it wasn't going to be fun.

"Nervous?" Trey asked quietly.

I didn't open my eyes. I didn't speak. I leaned into his warm and well-muscled chest and nodded.

"Let's do this," I whispered.

We made our way to Trey's office and stepped in. Trey took his place at the large mahogany desk that was incredibly beautiful. It had been carved and polished with care and attention to detail.

Sean stood to his left and I to Trey's right. There were six vampires in the room. I didn't like the odds, but I was sure Trey had backup of some sort, just in case.

I recognized Clan Master Olafson immediately. He was the only one seated, though there were four chairs available. He was also the only one dressed in business casual who didn't look like a bodyguard, and then, there was Marc.

I glanced at Marc and tried not to feel anything, but his betrayal still hurt, and I would have to get the hell over it. I looked the bodyguards over very carefully until at last, I had no choice but to see the man who physically sired me. The individual who I owed my existence to.

When my head put it that way, I wasn't sure what I was supposed to think or feel about him. I had grown up indifferent to the thought of him for the most part. And after the conversation I'd had with Marc, I was simply outraged at the betrayal. But now? If it hadn't been for him, I simply wouldn't be.

If nothing else, I had to give him that, but I didn't owe him anything.

He was an inch or two taller than myself since Mom barely topped out at five feet two, I'd say I got my height from him and the hair. The color was the same, and if he let his grow out, it would curl slightly, just as mine did. I saw myself in the person who sat before me and knew without a doubt that he was my father.

CHAPTER FOURTEEN

Magic Was A Gift

I felt his mind reach out to mine. It was an ability all vampires had to control their prey, to wipe their memory of being fed from, if the feeding wasn't meant to kill. I couldn't do it, but I couldn't be controlled either. He could also pry into my thoughts if I let him, and that just wasn't going to happen.

Sorry, Dad.

I gave the clan master a nearly imperceptible shake of my head. I felt his attempt stop as he smiled and shrugged just the slightest. Something in me relaxed a bit. He didn't seem at all upset that he didn't get his way.

"I'm not usually kept waiting like this," the clan master began. "Especially when I'm here to assist." He sounded only slightly put out and all professional and businesslike. He was slick, and from the feel of him, he'd had centuries to work on the persona I saw before me. Classic and elegant without being pretentious. Even the blood red ruby cuff links and tie tack were simply elegant against the classic cut of the Armani suit he was wearing.

Understated power. I had no doubt he could kill all three of us without his guard if he had wanted to.

I felt his mind brush over mine again in an attempt to ease into my thoughts. His eyes met mine, and I just had to smile.

I had learned many years ago how to shut my mind off to that type of intrusion. I thought it was simply to focus myself, but now I knew that my mom and aunts were preparing me to deal with vampires, along with an assortment of other creatures.

Again, I shook my head slightly. He shrugged again.

I still wondered how differently I might have been treated if my human nature had been more dominate than it already was.

"My apologies," Trey said casually. "I had pressing matters that couldn't wait." Trey didn't even flinch. I was nearly dying inside trying not to bust up laughing. *Sorry to keep you waiting. I was busy banging your daughter on the balcony.*

I managed to keep it together somehow.

"Well, let's get to this, shall we?" Erick began. The facts were laid out, and the clan master was willing to commit fifteen of his men to the task should they be needed. Seeing as all of his men would be inoculated, their risks were greatly reduced.

Marc had contacted Erick several days ago, and apparently, the combined reports cited twenty-seven missing among their numbers.

"We should be able to overwhelm their base if our numbers are accurate," Erick commented. "How much information do you have on their base?"

Erick and Marc both glanced my way. I had said nothing to this point and had been going over the information I had gotten and Simon had taken off with in my head. I was certain that I could pull the location from memory. There was no way they could move their base any time soon, but shifting their defenses wouldn't be a problem, so what I had on that was now worthless.

I had hoped to get through this meeting without having to contribute, but that hope died as Trey spoke.

"Valeric, please tell us what you know about the base."

I took a deep breath and looked at the map Sean had produced. I pointed out the area I knew the base to be and explained the basic dimensions that we were working with, along with the fact that it extended approximately two hundred feet under ground.

I had a feeling that there were several entry/exit points, but I would need to go out there, get closer, so that I could be as accurate as possible.

There were several high spots surrounding the base that I wanted to hit to survey the area and hopefully get the specifics necessary to see this thing through with less casualties.

Trey nodded knowingly and was completely collected throughout my briefing.

"I have no doubt I will be able to extract more information once I get out there and take a look around in the actual territory."

"What about offensive or defensive magic?" Erick asked. I could tell that he was truly engaged in the discussion. He was on his feet, leaning over the desk, looking at the map, and listening intently. He was here to work, but I was sure it wasn't his only reason for being present.

"I've run into some of their defenses, and they are good," I reported factually. I could definitely combat the golems with portable spells, but the defense used that felt like my skull was being caved in was going to be difficult. I hadn't had the time to explore the weaving of that spell, defend against it, and handle the golems all at the same time, so that was going to be just a tad more challenging. "I will be able to create portable spells to help combat their defenses when we actually go in, but, again, until I go out there, get close, I won't have specifics. Give me a day or two."

I glanced at Trey and saw the light burn in his eyes, but it didn't feel sexual.

He was not a happy beast master.

Nothing else betrayed his feelings, and if I hadn't been paying attention, I never would have noticed. Obviously, we were gonna chat later.

"Is it really necessary that Valerie get closer to the base?" Erick's eyes went to Trey's. His face was impassive and unreadable. It made me nervous. "I don't want my daughter any closer to this than is absolutely called for."

I felt a bit blindsided by his admission of our relationship, but I didn't feel anger. I was taking that as a very good sign.

"I have been hired to do a job, Erick," I said carefully. "I will pursue the safest course of action possible, but safe may not be possible." He seriously played the relationship card? Well, at least he wasn't belligerent about it. I just didn't know what to make of him yet. I was really prepared to have a knockdown, drag-out fight and have to flee for my own sense of freedom. Now? I just wasn't sure.

"Just how close do you need to be in order to get the detailed information we need?" Trey asked.

"The base is approximately five kilometers from here. I was able to detect their boundary, some dimensions, and where the warding might be." I pointed out the possible locations the wards on the map. Of course, I knew they wouldn't be in the same places now. "But I'm too far away to get details on the type of wards and any other defenses that are implemented at this time. I would like to cut the distance in half for my next pass for information. "I'd also like to ward the Enclave."

"That would be huge job, Val," Marc chimed in. It was true. It would be huge, and I would likely have to sleep off the after effects for ten to twelve hours, but it needed to be done. There had been an attempt to blow the armory, and the fact that Simon came and went with no problem let me know it was imperative. "If you need me to help in your recovery, I'm here for you."

The tension that I felt race through Trey was palpable. I didn't give him anytime to respond. He had already had at Marc once before, and I really didn't want a repeat performance. No more furniture should die needlessly.

"I appreciate the offer, but I will decline," I said politely. I no more than glanced at him as well. I wanted an end to that thread of the conversation quickly, like now.

"I know how much setting wards takes out of you, Val," he continued. Was he oblivious to the fact that continuing to open his mouth endangered his life? Or was he trying to bait me or Trey?

"And covering a place this size is going to fry you. Let me help."

"No. Again, I appreciate your concern, but it's not going to happen." I was keeping my voice level and my affect calm. Erick seemed mildly interested in the byplay, and Trey was going to rip Marc's head off any minute if he didn't shut the hell up.

Marc took a breath. I held up my hand to stop him. Damn it! We needed the clan master and what he had to offer. His vampires could handle those we would find infected at the base better than a were or a shifter. Bloodshed would not be helpful at this point.

"We will discuss this privately, Marc," I said quickly. I gave him a killing glance. His eyes showed surprise for the barest second, and he nodded, keeping his expression closed.

There was nothing I wanted more than to get the hell out of this office and take a shower. Preferably with Trey. Unfortunately, I had the feeling that this meeting was going to be a long one.

I could plan out the wards tonight. I'd seen the blueprints for the Enclave. I knew the layout and figuring out where the wards should go would take an hour at most. I still felt good, awake. Trey's earlier attentions on the balcony came to mind and relaxed me somewhat.

I could let go of the irritation I had felt with Marc, and I would get the warding planned out tonight and out of the way.

"I hope to have more detailed information to you by tomorrow night so strategies can be formed," I continued. "If I'm not needed any further, I have things I need to get done." I looked at Trey to see if he had anything further. The slightest shake of his head was all I needed. I was so out of there. The vampire contingent could catch up with me tomorrow at the next meeting.

I made my way out of the office and headed back toward my room. My gear was in there, and I was going to need some of it. Then I'd need to make my way back to Trey's war room.

I could get this done with in short order if nothing interfered.

"Wait up, Val." Marc's voice was soft but irritated. It made me smile, and I kept on walking. He could be as irritated as he wanted. I didn't care, but I wasn't in the mood to deal with any overtures he had planned. You know, things to do, places to go, wards to plan.

"Not tonight, Marc. I'm busy." I threw it over my shoulder and didn't pause.

"Val." Marc touched my shoulder. Yeah, I didn't figure I'd get off that easily, but I had hoped. "Come on, please. Just one minute."

I turned toward Marc and looked at the wrist that would have a watch if I wore one. Arms crossed over my chest, my hip kicked out, and the look of annoyance on my face. "One minute."

His dark hair fell around his face as his eyes looked at the ground, uncertain as to how to proceed. Something had happened. He had never approached me with anything less than absolute confidence and self-assurance. Now he looked uncertain.

"We have spent five years together, Val," he began. "I know what happens, I know what to expect, and I can care for you after you work the wards. Don't throw what we had away."

"I'm not throwing anything away, Marc." I searched myself for anger, hurt of some kind, betrayal. I could feel the edges of it, but letting any of that get the better of me wouldn't help the situation. "I'm simply walking away from that path and you."

Marc reached out for my shoulders, his expression soft, almost cajoling as his eyes met mine in a new way. I let him touch me, why? I couldn't say.

"Val, I've talked to your father about the situation. He is willing to let you continue working. He knows how much it means to you." Marc continued talking of the kindness and generosity of the clan master and how he chooses to allow me freedoms in my life.

My. Life.

I breathed deeply, letting my eyes drift shut as I wrestled the anger that his words brought to me.

"If you can forgive the subterfuge, he is willing to allow me to stay with you." Marc's smile was more than endearing; it was hopeful. We had spent five years together, and I knew the look. He was sure, beyond a doubt, that he and I would work things out and be together.

I thought of the many nights we worked together and spent together. I would mourn them, but I wouldn't repeat them. It was over, and my decisions would either be accepted or fought.

"Of course, he would assign more guards, but he will set up an office in Los Angeles for you. Your own base of operations and a staff to support it."

I held up my hand for Marc to stop. His hands dropped from my shoulders as I took a step back.

"No," I said firmly. "As generous as the clan master seems to be with my life, I choose to live it by my desires, not his. Your minute is up, and I have things to do, Marc. Good night." I turned and walked off. I had made it to the end of the hall and was about to hit the stairs. We were two floors down and one section over from Trey's office. I was learning my way around slowly but surely.

"He'll even forgive you for sleeping with that shifter trash." Marc had moved with vamp stealth and was right behind me, breathing those words into my ear like a curse.

I stopped without turning.

"There was very little sleep involved in what Trey and I have done together," I managed the response without heat or anger. I amazed myself in that moment. "And I think you should be grateful that the 'shifter trash' kept you safe and let you live." I paused long enough to take a breath. I felt sadness rise in me. Marc was going to start lashing out at me if he didn't get his way. Oh well, shit happens. "Return to your master, Marc. I have things to do." I pushed into motion and headed up the stairs. This time Marc didn't follow.

I had made it back to the room Trey had me in. Yeah, his mate's room. I was still having a problem with that. Trey was sure, confident, and powerful. There was no way I could ever live up to what an alpha shifter's mate should be.

My gut clenched in rebellion to my thoughts. I wanted to be that woman. *The* woman. The one who could stand at the side of a badass and support and defend him and his people.

I thought about the job offer and what he had said about me already being accepted in the Enclave. I just didn't know.

How much did the Enclave really need a full-time witch anyway? Did they really have that much trouble? This kind of crazy shit couldn't happen all that frequently. And once word got out that the Enclave witch was Clan Master Olafson's daughter, it might bring a new kind of grief to Trey and his people that he definitely didn't need.

I made it to the bedroom and my stuff. The small cauldron, herbs, and charcoal came out on to the balcony with me as I fired it up and let it burn. I left it on the metal table and headed to the war room.

I studied the layout of the Enclave, seeing each floor and the orientation. Stepping back, I put it together and saw it in my mind's eyes. I moved it around and found the best configuration to lay the wards for maximum effect.

The wards should stop anybody infected with the virus and alert security as to the attempted breach and its location. I was going to have to set thirty-two wards. This was gonna hurt.

Maybe if I set a few tonight, just the ones in the tunnels, it would knock the number down and make it easier on me at the same time.

It was after 11:00 p.m. I could get those wards done, have the prep work for the rest finished, recover sufficiently, and still be able to head out tomorrow and scout around. I was gonna be a busy, busy girl.

Getting naked with Trey again would be a bonus. But chances were that he would be tied up with the clan master until very late. I just hoped Marc had returned to the office so I didn't need to run into him again.

I wondered what other attempts the clan master would throw my way before the threats started. Maybe blackmail. Violence? I wouldn't be hard to take down. Marc knew all of my moves. Damn him!

The hurt and anger washed over me for a moment. I knew it was going to be like this for a while. I'd hurt, and then it would ease up only to blindside me again. Then the pain and sorrow would fade.

I wondered if it would be the same when I walked away from Trey.

No. I don't think I'd ever stop hurting. He had made his way into my heart where nobody had ever touched. Trey was nine hundred years old. He had been there and done that so many times I couldn't believe he would honestly be happy with me for the remainder of my life.

I made my way back to my balcony and continued to feed herbs to the heated coal as I let the moon's light soak in. I could still identify the scents of Trey, myself, and us combined. The faint odor of melted cushion had wafted away, but the wrinkling of the pad was evidence of its exposure to heat.

My insides curled with the memories of his touch. His lips tasting me. The nips and licks that drove me to distraction.

Trey was good. Too good for me.

I remembered this morning and the breakfast we had shared. It was soothing and calm. As if we had done it a hundred times and would do it a hundred more.

I shook my head and drove the pleasant thought from my mind. I had other things that needed to be done, besides breaking my heart earlier than necessary.

More herbs fell upon the coal, snapping and burning, the smoke reaching skyward as it drifted and curled, lifting a silent prayer to facilitate the work I would be doing this night.

The power swirled around me and through me, giving the herbs and coal purpose and direction. I had always liked the idea of singing the magic as it worked its way through and around me, but I just didn't have a voice that wouldn't rear my inner critic. So rather than fight my feelings of self-worth on yet another point, I simply watched and knew the power I wielded was strong.

The magic was mine. I earned it. I worked for it. I practiced for hours every day for it. But though it was mine, I respected it and the divine from which it flowed. Magic was a gift. I didn't abuse it, but my aunt Maggie might have.

I could feel her in the spell on that wall. What if she had started this? What if she had taught others this magic and together they were seeking the destruction of the vampire race? It didn't make sense. The darkness didn't feel like something Maggie could have sunken to, no matter how hurt she was. Besides, it wasn't simply affecting vampires.

I pulled my mind back to the work before me.

An hour later, I was ready to get some of the warding out of the way.

I began in the lowest sections of the Enclave. The tunnels are a great secondary escape, but a nice way to get in under the radar. Of course, I knew that the tunnels were wired with video feed, but warding would be a good backup for that.

I had called to the Enclave security office before I began and told them I had the go ahead from Trey and that I would be up later to install the panels that would light up if the ward was breached.

The panels were small planks of ash with pentagrams drawn on them with the remains of the burnt herbs and charcoal. Each pentagram corresponded with the section designation of the ward location. The section designations were already a part of the Enclave layout. I was piggybacking on their established system. Their system was logical, and I liked it.

The first panel came with me to each location. As the ward was set, the corresponding pentagram signature was embedded, and the whole thing would be activated when I lit the wards.

Granted I was going to do this in two stages—the underground entrances and then the Enclave proper. Tomorrow was going to be a bitch of a day to get through, but some of the work would be out of the way.

It was three in the morning. The last underground ward had been set, the panel was in place in the security office, and I was headed back to the third sub level to light it up.

There had been extra security in the armory level as well as those directly above it. They were leery of my presence, but let me do what I needed to do without a problem.

I also didn't need to go into the armory, so that made it easier all the way around. I did, however, go as far into the collapsed tunnel as I could to set the ward. I didn't really think that would be used as a possible breech point. It was still unstable, but you never know.

So from the middle of the third sub-level, I felt for all of the wards. I was in the intersection of six hallways. From here, I could see the armory doors and the guards who continued to keep an eye on me. The wards felt solid and stable as I gathered the power within me and set off the chain reaction that would fire the wards up and let them glow with a soft green glow. The panel would reflect it in the security office.

If a ward was tripped, it would glow red. I like to keep things simple.

The power spiraled from me and gently worked its way to the wards. I felt them pop into being, from an idea to something more concrete and viable.

The guards at the end of the hall looked to their right toward the tunnel that had been collapsed. The door hadn't been reattached, so they could see the ward in all its glory.

However, the fact that I could see a faint glow of red being cast from that direction didn't make me feel all that good.

"Call security!" I yelled as I closed the distance between me and the two werewolves pulling guard duty. As I hit that intersection and turned to assess the problem, the guards were already standing at the ready to face an oncoming threat. Luckily, it wasn't me, but something was coming down the tunnel.

They shifted, both wolves, big and loud, as they bound down the hallway to intercept the three vampires who had breached the wards.

Tranquilizer guns had been issued to all security personnel. Why the guards hadn't picked it up and started firing was beyond me. Hopefully, they would survive to answer that question.

I picked up the unfamiliar weapon and moved toward the fray. Both were-wolves were engaged, and the third came at me with vamp speed. I got a shot off, and it connected. My relief was short lived as he kept coming. I didn't know how long the serum would take, but the effect was obviously not immediate.

He tackled me, and we were both airborne. His arms had wrapped around my middle, shoulder firmly impacting my solar plexus, knocking the breath out of me.

My head spun as we hit the floor, and the weapon slid another twenty feet down the hall.

I felt his claws dig into my back and tear through skin and muscle. The coppery tang of blood hit the air along with my scream.

As I rallied myself enough to fight back, the vamp let go. He screamed as if dying and curled into a tight ball, rolling off me. So I was willing to call it a thirty-second delay before the serum took effect. Since the vamp was out cold, I'd be willing to bet the serum was laced with an actual tranquilizer. Go, Mila! I liked her more and more.

My back burned from the rending it had received, and I knew I wasn't going to get much done tomorrow. I was pissed. I had a schedule, and these fuckers screwed it up.

I got to my feet, not with a lot of grace, but I was up and retrieving the lost weapon as the sounds of continued fighting rang through the hallway.

Within a few minutes, the other vamps had been tagged, the were-wolves were a bit torn up but still breathing, the ward glowed green, and a half dozen reinforcements were in the hallway.

It was about time!

The Ambush Took Fifteen Seconds To Happen

My orders were quick and clear. The three vamps went to holding cells near the med labs, the two guards were replaced, and then they headed to the med labs for a thorough going-over and treatment. They both got magically enhanced dressings before they left, and I snagged one myself. I handed the tranquilizer gun to somebody and told them to get it reloaded and to fucking use it as a first line of defense.

Things got a bit hazy after that. I recalled heading toward the stairs, remembering that I was bleeding when the pain reasserted its presence, and I faltered, finding a wall to steady myself on. The dressings were going just so far.

The doors to the stairwell opened, and Trey stepped out, my father and Marc hot on his heels.

Fuck!

I pushed from the wall and tried to look steadier than I felt. Trey took me in and looked relieved and unhappy all at the same time. How he managed that was a mystery to me.

"Three vamps came in through the collapsed tunnel. Nobody dead. Vamps are headed to the med lab holding cells." I was running through the information as I tried to keep my mind off the fact that I needed to see Mila myself. "The vamps were well fed. I am now worried that there are either humans being held as food or they are snatching and killing to feed them. The wards…"

"I will get the report from Sean," Trey said calmly. "What about you?" His blue eyes barely contained the fire of anger within them. His muscles bunched and relaxed minutely. He was trying to keep it together and doing a fine job. But at this point, the guy has got to be used to me getting banged up by now. Dude needs to chill.

"I'm fine." Yeah. I wasn't, but I didn't need Daddy and my ex getting their undies in a knot because I got scratched up some. Trey could fume and fuss all he wanted, but in the end, he would let me do my damn job.

"You've been injured." Erick circumvented Trey and stepped up to me. If he was going to start in with me, it would not be pretty.

"A couple of scratches," I insisted and moved between Trey and my father. I actually pushed past them. Both of them. "I'm getting it looked at, and then I'm going to bed. Good night, gentlemen." I was past them and heading up the stairs, leaving the men in my wake.

I was just really glad that the med lab was only up one flight and over two sections. There was no way I would have made it much farther.

I was halfway up the flight of stairs when I overheard the clan master talking to Trey.

"If you are not capable of safeguarding my daughter," he began. *Oh no, he didn't!*

"Don't start, Erick!" I said loudly enough to be heard over him. "You don't get a vote. This is my life, and how I proceed as the contracted witch of the Enclave is not your decision. So back off!"

I had hit the landing and was starting to feel my injury through the dressing.

So maybe I was hurt a bit more than I had originally thought.

I was lying on my stomach as Mila stitched up my back. I was tired and really just wanted to sleep. I had also bitten the bullet and asked her for a bag of blood. Yeah, she raised an eyebrow, but other than that she didn't say a word.

I was really starting to like Mila.

"Okay. That's it," she said as I heard the snap of the vinyl gloves coming off of her well-manicured hands. "How are you feeling?"

"Like I got lightly mauled by a vampire," I replied. The blood helped, and yes, if I took Marc's blood or any vampire's blood, the injury would heal immediately, but I would rather take the night to recover and deal with things as they stood. I was going to have to do this sometime anyway, why not start getting used to it now?

"Well, the wounds were deep in a few places, but nothing important was punctured," she said. I was slowly working my ass off the table as she spoke. "You heal fairly fast, so just take it easy." Mila rose and started cleaning up. "You need a pain amulet?" she asked.

"Nah. I have some upstairs," I replied. "They are tuned to me and will work better than the generic ones you've got."

Mila's movements slowed. Her attention had split between what she was doing and something else that was important to her. Good thing I couldn't move all that fast. It gave her time to organize her thoughts and get on with it.

"Could you make some for the Enclave?" She had stopped the cleaning of the area I'd bloodied and waited.

"Of course." I looked into her eyes and saw hesitancy. "It's a small thing to ask since you've saved my ass and stitched me up. Did you think I'd turn you down?" I leaned against the table, more to ease the stress on my back than for anything else.

Her lips curled into a knowing smile. It was gorgeous, just like the rest of her. "No, but I'm asking it as a personal favor and not as part of the contract you have with Trey," she said. "I can pay you—"

I put my hand up to stop her from continuing. She had cared for me when I couldn't do anything for myself. I owed her and appreciated the fact that she didn't look at me like she had looked at Marc. Then again, Marc was being a dick before hand.

"I'll give you a list of ingredients. I'll put them together. Easy." I eased away from the table.

"Thanks, Valerie." Mila went back to cleaning, and I headed for the door. I was not terribly surprised to find Trey and Erick in the hallway.

At least a) They hadn't barge in. b) They hadn't bloodied each other. c) They didn't immediately ambush me in the hallway.

The ambush took fifteen seconds to happen.

"Marc will drive you to a private airfield," my father began. "You will be in Los Angeles in a couple hours."

I looked at him with a very unpleasantly surprised expression for just a moment. I didn't even look at Trey to know Erick's announcement didn't make him happy either.

"Yeah, Erick. The thing is… no." I pushed past the men once again and headed up the hall. I would be in my room in ten minutes and asleep in fifteen. "Good night." They could just stew. I didn't want to be rude to Trey. Well, at least, not this time. But I didn't want to lean on him in front of Erick. I just couldn't show weakness in front of him. Marc probably had him convinced that I couldn't hack it, hence the offer of work staffed by Daddy's handpicked boys.

"Valerie!" The power of my name from Erick's lips ran through me. It curled through my gut and squeezed me. The energy of his voice was like a hand grabbing a kitten by the neck and lifting. Unfortunately, with the injuries I had, Erick's power play gave my back spasms and buckled my knees. Gravity did the rest as I hit the ground and held back the cry of pain that really wanted out. I didn't take a pain amulet from Mila. Why? Because I had my own. Upstairs. I could wait.

That might have been a mistake. Ya think?

I had to get up and shake this off. Fuck Erick for pulling this! Before I could get my knees under me, Erick was there next to me.

"Feed her and then take her home, Marc." Erick's voice was smooth and mellow, like fine brandy. I could hear victory in his voice. Not gloating, no smugness. He had no doubt his wishes would be granted, no questions asked. He needed to learn to live with disappointment.

"Touch me, and I rip off your man bits, Marc," I bit out angrily as I struggled to my knees. Marc actually flinched at the mention of bits removal, and I was glad for it. But I'm sure on the one-to-ten scale of scary, next to my father, I didn't rate.

"You need to learn some manners, young lady," Erick chastised me as if I were a child. Well, in comparison to him, I was, but it didn't stop me from being seriously pissed off.

"You first, old man," I groaned and finally made it to my feet. Trey was standing a few feet back and looked ready to kill with extreme prejudice. I knew why he was holding it together, and in that moment, as I looked into his eyes, I fell in love with an obnoxious shifter with a long title and a bad attitude. Alphas did their own dirty work. He couldn't step in. Erick wasn't an encroacher. He was my father, and this was my fight.

"I will not approve of you remaining here, the situation isn't stable," he blustered and asserted his authoritarian air, but he didn't try to push with his preternatural powers again. "It's too dangerous. I want you out. Now, Valerie." He really tried to regain his calm, self-controlled air. His dark hair seemed a little less than perfectly coiffed.

The suit had a wrinkle that wasn't there before. There was a stress in his voice that the attempted smoothness couldn't cover.

He was a frightened father with no clue. This I could work with.

"Then prepare to remain disappointed." I took a breath and stood firmly in front of a vampire who was old when dirt was rocks and dinosaurs roamed the earth. He scared the shit out of me. "I have given my word to the beast master. I have made an agreement between myself and the Enclave to resolve this problem."

I steeled myself and took a step toward the clan master and just hoped the trembling was only on the inside.

"Does your word mean so little that you would have mine mean nothing?" I asked, letting my anger gently bubble to the surface. I was going for righteous indignation. The one thing I did know about most of the "big bads" in the supernatural world was that their word was their bond. If they said it, it happened. Good or bad, the deed was done. The daughter of Clan Master Olafson had made an agreement with the beast master, long title, and was being asked to go back on it. Yeah, I don't think so.

Erick turned to Trey. I had no idea what that was about, but I didn't like it. "Release her from the agreement." Erick's words were a soft demand. All I could think of was "fuck." I didn't want to put Trey in the middle of this, but damned if that wasn't what happened anyway.

"It is her decision. She's invaluable, and her continued presence will only serve to find a quicker resolution to the current situation."

There wasn't a flicker of emotion on Trey's beautiful face as he tossed the ball back into my court. Yup, I loved him.

"As I said, I have a job to do," I said smoothly as Erick turned toward me again. "I need to rest, and I have a full day tomorrow. I'll have more information for you in the evening."

I began to walk away. My back was freaking killing me, but I had to get this done. Once in bed, I didn't care about anything or anyone… well, maybe Trey. He needed to crawl into bed with me and keep me warm and comfortable while I healed. I hated doing that alone. Waking up with him this afternoon had been amazing. I wanted more.

"I could force you, Valerie," he said casually.

I stopped and turned to face him. I regarded his features, his posture, and the air about him before I spoke.

"Yes. You could. And I would hate you instead of simply dislike you." Silence hung in the air as I turned and walked away.

Every step closer to being horizontal and resting with that damn pain amulet tucked in against my wounds was hard won. I didn't flinch, I didn't grimace, and I didn't pause until I was on the other side of my bedroom door, and it was locked in place.

Part of me wanted to slide down the carved surface and rest my aching body on the cool stone floor. The other part of me knew that a pain amulet and a soft surface would be much, much better, and I made my way to my bag.

I pawed through the various bits of magical stuff until I found the amulet and then crammed it in the bandages on my back. The sense of relief was immediate and nearly dropped me where I stood.

I reminded myself that the bed looked infinitely more comfortable than the floor. Everything but my bra and underwear came off. The bag was tossed onto the floor, and my weary, beaten-up body crawled into the softest sheets I'd ever experienced. The only thing missing was Trey.

I was in his mate's room. For the moment, this was where I belonged, and I wouldn't expect to share his suite unless he wanted to have sex with me. Right now, sex was out of the question… probably.

No! It really was out of the question. Besides, I'm sure Trey was still dealing with the clan master in some capacity or another.

I drifted off wondering how the vampires got through the warding. It did go off as expected, but it should have stopped them from actually breaching the Enclave.

I'd check out the area tomorrow. Tomorrow, with all of that copious amounts of free time I was going to have before the next meeting with Erick.

Right.

Before my eyes opened, I knew it was barely light out, and my back was doing much better. It didn't bitch loudly, just whined a little.

I wasn't really sure why I had woken up. I really needed a couple more hours of uninterrupted unconsciousness.

It could have been the cool morning breeze lending a slight chill to the air or the fact that my body was wrapped around something warm, sturdy, and Trey-shaped.

I'm going with Trey-shaped.

"Hey, beautiful." His arms held me to him. I was thoroughly sprawled across him and pretty darned comfortable. He sounded as if he hadn't gotten much sleep either though. His voice was gravelly and coarse. It slid over me like silk and made me have to choose between really waking up for a morning romp and staying semiconscious and drifting back to sleep for more much-needed rest.

I made a small movement in the direction of early morning activity when my back explained that it hadn't hurt because I wasn't moving. So more sleep it is. Damn.

It was the first time I'd heard Trey use an endearment. My heart fluttered the tiniest bit.

He'd only used my name in the long form before now. Had something changed?

I barely cracked my eyes open enough to see the wall directly across from the bed and noticed that something had changed. My location. Trey had moved me to his suite as I slept. Some tough-ass warrior I was. I bet I never even stirred as he lifted me from a bed in a strange place and moved me.

Whatever.

God! What time was it? When had he moved me? What happened after I left?

All valid questions, all deserving of answers. There were things we needed to do today, important things!

"Back atcha." My voice wasn't any better, but his warmth and scent just made everything okay. My eyes had drifted closed once more, and I listened to the rhythmic thumping of his heart under my ear.

"Any reason you weren't in our bed when I came up?" I think I managed to raise an eyebrow, but not much else. What the hell did he mean "our" bed? This was his suite. I had the one reserved for his mate.

"Your suite, your bed," I croaked out still too tired to really have any conversation. I loosely gestured to the door that led to my suite and continued. "My suite, my bed." I didn't bother dragging my hand back to its original position. Though my fingers definitely missed the feel of his chest under them. My tired arm just dropped over his waist like a dead fish, but less nasty.

"Separate suites is a dragon thing," he began with his voice going smokey and husky as he picked up my hand and brought it to his lips. "I decided I don't really like it." He kissed the knuckles of my hand and laid it on his chest still wrapped in his.

I, apparently had no say in the matter? Obnoxious, pushy, arrogant, warm, sexy… damn. All I could do was sigh and mutter a barely audible okay and let darkness envelope me again.

It was full light out the next time I opened my eyes, and I heard the faint muttering of male voices across the room. What? No yelling? They're slacking off.

Without moving, I tuned into the quiet conversation going on.

"And he's pissed," Sean reported. "Olafson has every right to be worried about her. She's a damn disaster magnet!"

"She caused none of this, Sean. Remember that," Trey sounded much more calm than I'd heard him in a while. "But she has busted her ass trying to figure this out, keep the Enclave safe, and deal with an ex-boyfriend and a father she never knew she had. So back off and support our resident witch. I'll be in the security office in… an hour or so. She's going to need transportation and an escort when she heads out, and she will go out there, Sean. It's her job."

"I'll go with her." Sean sounded defeated and unhappy about it, but what was he going to do? Challenge Trey? "I'll take Adams, Richardson, and Petty as well. We will keep her safe."

"I know you will," Trey finished, and I heard the door snick shut gently. I didn't hear him move across the room. The only signal of his having moved was feeling his weight ease on to the bed.

I slowly tried to stretch, making sure that my back was going to put up with it before attempting to enjoy the full-body experience of that particular activity. There was another activity that I was hoping to enjoy before breakfast.

His hand splayed across my stomach, warm and caressing as my stretching eased and my eyes found his.

"Breakfast will be up in thirty minutes." His beautiful blues expressing a softness that needed to be there more often. I'd say content if I'd ever seen that on him. It made me smile.

"Good, then we a have a few minutes to work up an appetite." My fingers traced the lines of muscle down the center of his chest and brushed across the cords that defined his abdomen. I was headed much, much lower as his hand caught my wrist.

"I like the way you think." His voice rumbled in his chest, and his smile deepened into something that left no doubt he was on board with where my mind was at. "But I want to see your back first."

I shrugged and rolled away from him. I knew the wound would look much better today. The stitches should have fallen out, and I'd expect there to be what would looked like angry red welts in its place. I hadn't felt anything significant when I'd stretched.

Trey gently peeled away the covering. I could feel the tension in his touch as he traced the marks still remaining on my body.

"Well?"

"How does it feel?" He asked as his hand left the injury and brushed against my waist. I felt his body shift just before his lips touched my shoulder.

Damn. My entire body responded without a single hesitation. Gooseflesh covered me from head to toe, and my nipples hardened almost painfully.

Of course, the loose pants he was wearing hadn't done anything to hide the fact that he was hard before he made it back to the bed.

I rolled back to the man who could set me alight with a single kiss. "It feels a little stiff, but then again so do you."

Last night, Trey had said he could do a lot to me in fifteen minutes, and he was right. Trey had rocked my world and removed any and all traces of intelligent life as he touched and tasted my body.

This morning, there was a wickedness in his eyes that I'd never seen before. My heart skipped a beat as his eyes never left mine while removing what little clothing remained between the two of us.

He soothed and caressed me with great attention. Slowly, working my body to the heights from which I would fall into ecstasy.

He kept my hands from playing with his body as he played with mine. He said he didn't want me to be distracted.

I couldn't think of a bigger distraction than having all of the strength and power that was this gorgeous dragon shifter focused on nothing but bringing pleasure to my body. Intense, nearly fatal pleasure. Okay, maybe not fatal, but he had held me at the edge of orgasm for what seemed to be hours while he nuzzled, nipped, and stroked by body higher and higher.

When I fell, it was utter destruction. I came apart so completely in his arms that I felt as if there was no way I would remain intact as my mind, body, and soul came apart and then tried to reform into a singular cohesive entity.

He finally came as pieces of me began to recognize the whole of what they should be. It was my turn to hold him. The one thing he allowed from me in this. Did he trust me to hold him together? Or was he in fewer pieces as he came?

The warmth of his body infused me as his release took him. I felt his teeth graze my shoulder with the slightest sting. His arms pulling me to him as if we could fuse into one being in that moment. Maybe we could. I was still interested in trying to melt the balcony furniture at some point.

His body stilled as he pressed deeply into mine. Our breaths and heartbeats came faster and then eased as the strength of the orgasm slowly ebbed.

We were done. Well, at least I was.

His embrace relaxed as his teeth eased from my shoulder, only to be replaced by the gentle touch of his lips and tongue. A languid warmth infused me from that place, and I was barely able to recognize his body slipping from mine, still semi-hard.

Physically, he could go a couple more rounds. Me, not so much.

I am a lucky, lucky girl, I thought as my sigh came out as a low, contented moan.

"I'd be happy to get nothing done today," Trey whispered as he trailed kisses up my neck and across my jaw and brushed a few across my lips.

The scent, taste, and feel of this man would be burned into my soul forever.

A part of me clenched in an unpleasant way. I had fallen in love with Trey.

I didn't feel that there was any way I could be what he needed or what the Enclave needed. A clan master would be a terrible enemy to have, and right now the Enclave was vulnerable.

I couldn't doubt that the dark magic and the person, or persons, behind it would fall, but there would be the dead and injured to care for. There may be humans to deal with. Trey would be taxed in coping with his people, and the clan master had a contingency of vampires with him and more than a dozen that may be at his command when this was over.

Erick would have enough of a force to do some serious damage if he wanted to. If Erick wanted to do that, I would walk away from Trey and the Enclave to spare them.

That act would crush me. I could feel the faintest tearing at my heart with the simple thought of leaving him and this place.

I would guarantee Erick a daily fight for my cooperation in most any matter. Just out of spite.

I closed my eyes and tried my best to let go of what may never happen. There were too many things that were real and concrete and had a potential to inflict a world of hurt on Trey, the Enclave, and myself, to lose myself in those morbid musings.

My eyes flickered open, meeting his as I realized that he could tell that I had gone someplace dark in my own thoughts.

CHAPTER SIXTEEN

"Nobody will notice if I kill her!"

After the heart-pounding, soul-wrenching sex that he poured every ounce of his being into for me, for my pleasure, I immediately feared losing it.

Well, that's one way to ruin a great morning, and if I didn't knock that shit off, I would.

I saw the concern in his eyes, along with questions. But before he had a chance to voice any of it, I smiled wryly and reached up, running my fingers through the silk of his blonde hair and reveled in this moment in his presence.

I drew him down. His lips found mine in a gentle touch and then deepened for a heartbeat.

He broke the kiss first. I hadn't been trying to seduce him away from his concerns or questions. I just wanted to find a bit of balance before I spoke, or he did. I hoped I had.

"That's not what you were thinking, Valerie," he whispered and pulled back a little more. I knew he thought I was trying to distract him. Emotions have scents to them, and he must have caught my scent changing with my feelings. I wasn't going to lie to him anymore than he would lie to me.

He promised he would never lie to me, and I believe him.

"A few insecurities is all," I said. Truth enough.

I released him and let my hands slide down his neck and across his shoulders. The smooth, soft skin that layered over hard-won muscle warmed under my touch.

The look on his face clearly stated he didn't believe me. I mean, really, how could I possibly be insecure? A big chunk of my life has been a sham, thanks to a father I'd never known and a lover I had trusted with everything I had. How could I have never even had the slightest inkling that Marc wasn't being honest with me? Obviously, my judgment is suspect.

And Trey? He could have any woman, sight unseen. He was the fucking beast master, blah, blah, blah! He wields some serious power in that position, and the woman who would stand by his side would share in that. Along with coup attempts, assassination attempts, and of course, lest we forget, being the target of a nut job with more magic than morals.

Maybe I should rethink staying here.

Then I look in Trey's eyes, and maybe life-threatening events are worth having that smoldering gaze aimed at me and me alone.

He was still propped up on his elbows, keeping his weight off me but resting over my body, trying to figure out what was going on in my head.

"Yes, Mr. Incredulous," I said lightly. "Insecurities. And they are mine, mine, all mine. But you make a convincing argument."

Now he looked somewhere between confused and suspicious. Again, a good look on him in my eyes.

"Argument for what?" The confusion faded, and suspicion was in full force.

He was sure I was going to screw with him.

I might.

Maybe.

Probably. It's fun.

"For just about anything you want." I smiled. He could distract me from just about anything at any time. I might have to work on that. But damn it! When he makes love to me, nothing else matters. Nothing else exists.

A wicked smile crossed his lips as he whispered a kiss across my cheek and nestled his body more closely between my thighs. "So accept the position I offered." He reached down and pulled my thigh up against his hip. My body opened to him without hesitation, and he eased himself back inside of me.

"And that would be the missionary position?" I asked with a glint in my eyes and a low moan as he filled me again.

"For starters," he growled low in his throat, his hips taking up a slow rhythm that promised a very late start for both of us. "I will get around to many other positions, and I hope we can make a few up as we go along."

I wrapped my legs around his body as he again proved that his dragon thing was tireless.

Have I mentioned that I love his dragon thing?

"Your witch, huh?" I moaned as my hands gripped his shoulders.

"No." He kissed me hard as he pushed a hard-driving rhythm, sliding across sensitive nerves that had my body writhing for release. "The Enclave's witch. My mate."

How could he be this good? Nine hundred years of practice, that's how. And I would like to thank those women who came (literally) before me so that I may know this pleasure.

"I'm gonna need a job description for the position of mate before I make any commitments," I managed as my body arched into his, and our bodies found a rhythm with each other. I could feel the sweat pooling between my breasts, both his and my sweat.

My hips rushed to meet his thrust for thrust. Our moans mingled, and the world around us simply vanished. Trey's arms wrapped around me, burrowing between my flesh and the sheets. Our strains were more frantic as we pulled and shifted in time with each other. The warmth of our energies tangled and glided within and around each other. Searing pleasure infused the moment my orgasm began to crest.

I pulled Trey to me more ferociously. My nose buried in his neck; the scent of him overwhelmed me. The pulse in his throat tantalizing me.

There was nothing but the weight and movement of his body wringing pleasures from me. Nothing, but the scent of warm spice and dragon musk. Nothing, but the orgasm that was breaking over me, obliterating my senses.

For the briefest moment, his rhythms hitched and then recovered in earnest with a roar that echoed around us.

Warm, sweet liquid touched my tongue as my orgasm crested and broke again and again. The heat, the searing pleasure of Trey burned away every doubt that I belonged with him.

Our combined releases eased, and our bodies relaxed somewhat. The only sound came from our breathing and the beating of our hearts.

We were still wrapped around each other, clinging to each other, buried within each other for long moments after. His arms moved so that he rested on his elbows at my shoulders, his face resting in the crook of my neck, and his warm breath heating my skin as it caressed me.

"Gods, Valerie," he panted roughly. "Tell me you're all right." He kissed my cheek and pulled away enough to look me in the eye. Trey's hands framed my face, and his worried expression roved over me. "Please, tell me you're all right."

I felt my brows furrow with the question in my mind. I wondered if confusion looked as good on me as it did on him. I doubted it.

"I'm fine, Trey," I began. My hands skimmed his back gently. Something had worried him. I wanted nothing more than to reassure him. "I maybe worthless for the rest of the day, but I'm fine."

He blew out a shaky breath and pressed his forehead to mine as some wicked tension left his body.

"When you bit me," he started.

"Whoa. What?" I interrupted. Holy crap. I had bitten him? No freaking way! He had never stopped moving, and I hadn't felt as if I were burning to death from the inside out.

"I could feel you coming. You pulled me to you." He lifted his gaze, and I could see the barely banked desire in his eyes. He could go again, I was sure of it. Especially since he was still hard and still in me. "I felt you nick my skin… your tongue… your lips… I was afraid you'd be hurt, but you were coming hard, and it felt so damn good. I couldn't stop."

I ran my hand over his neck, finding the small nick, which was already closed. I tasted his blood in my mouth, and my fangs ached to drop and take more.

"You shouldn't have been able to keep moving." Yeah, I was thoroughly confused. I remembered his rhythm faltering for less than a heartbeat, but other than that? Nothing to indicate I had bitten him. Well, except the mind-blowing orgasm.

I thought a bit harder, and yes, it hurt to do much else but lay there, but the series of orgasms was something I had only heard about. The mind-blowing, holy-mother-of-all-the-gods succession of orgasms claimed mates enjoyed. His blood hadn't nearly killed me, and my bite hadn't paralyzed him.

Had our bodies made adjustments? Accommodating our differences to each other?

I shared my theory with him and talked for a few moments, finally falling into playful banter and tender, loving touches when the pounding on the door heralded our breakfast's arrival.

I headed for the bathroom as Trey answered the door.

I was Trey's mate.

That thought roamed around in my head looking for a place to make sense. I just couldn't reconcile what had just happened with anything else except me being Trey's mate.

I had met mated couples of varying species over the years and found the new ones to be wildly insatiable and the older ones reservedly insatiable. Mostly, they were content and in accord with each other. They balanced each others strengths and weaknesses. It was beautiful to see the causal touches, the knowing glances, the barely there smiles in passing as they moved together and apart in social settings.

I'd done my best not to show the sense of envy I had for those or the sadness in my heart that it would never be mine.

Now Trey was as much mine as I was his.

Daddy dearest wouldn't be pleased.

Daddy dearest could kiss my witchy white ass.

Breakfast came and went too quickly. We talked, shared our plans for the day, which sadly didn't include each other until I was finished with the warding. It would be just in time for the evening meeting with Olafson and crew.

I would get the report regarding the target bases warding and defenses put together and in Sean's hands before I completed the Enclaves wards, just in case I was too spent to get it done after the wards.

Maybe since Sean would be with me, I wouldn't have to write a report at all. Even better? I wouldn't have to attend the meeting at all. I could just get some rest and wait for Trey to ruin a good night's sleep. I was good with that.

I was wearing light khaki cargo pants, a long-sleeve sand-colored shirt, hiking boots, and a floppy hat for my foray into the desert. The course was set, and Sean and his men loaded us into a well-worn but serviceable jeep.

My senses were on alert as we headed across the terrain and into the area I believed would best suit our purposes.

It took longer to climb to the overlook than it did to drive into our target area, but once we were in position, it was well worth it just for the view.

Rough, rugged, unforgiving, and deadly were some of the adjectives that would accurately describe this landscape. But the planes and angles among the weather-smoothed gullies were breathtaking. The variety of colors and formations could easily distract me for hours. What I wouldn't give for a camera.

Sean handed me the camera with a telephoto lens. Unfortunately, I couldn't take pretty landscape shots this time out. It was for planning and recon, blah, blah, blah. I would come back out here when this was over.

My vision followed my senses to where my energies touched the boundaries of the base still a bit more than a mile off. We moved to the far side of the ridge and slowly worked our way closer.

When we finally stopped, we were only twenty feet away from the boundary that magic protected. I could see the vague rippling in the air and the greenish cast along the rocks and sand.

This was bad. Really, really bad.

I'd seen something like this years ago. The barrier wasn't simply a shield to keep people out; it killed on contact, and it was a painful death.

In the heat of the desert, with the sun pounding down on my body, I felt an icy chill run down my spine.

The kind of chill that is a clear indicator for leaving the area. Preferably, now.

I had gotten plenty of shots to be able to give a cohesive presentation with visual aides when we returned. I'd also run my energy out to get a bead on the location of the wards. I made some notes and shoved them into a pocket on my thigh.

So with that done, I turned to Sean to tell him that we needed to start backing up when Adams tapped me on the shoulder and pointed out the company we had closing in.

So enemy to the front and painful death shield to the rear. Luckily, we were armed, and between the four of us, we should be able to take out all the shifters or weres that had been reported missing, if they had all been sent out.

I thought that unlikely.

There wasn't much of a breeze, so we could start firing with greater accuracy and a farther distance. Those tranquilizer darts didn't act like bullets. My favorite part, of course, being the actual tranquilizer that had been mixed in the serum.

"Andy," I heard Richardson whisper. There was pain in his voice, and I was quick to understand that these were their friends and family. My heart clenched hard, and I just prayed to any divine presence that the men who were out here with me didn't end up killing their friends or family.

My hand wrapped around the grip of the gun as I moved to a better location. I didn't like having any of my guys in a direct line of fire. There were only four of us, and losing one to friendly fire would suck beyond all measure.

The speed with which the shifters and weres attacked was frightening. I had barely gotten a shot off before a full-grown male Bengal tiger was bearing down on me.

My second shot nailed a wolf as the tiger dug his claws into my thigh before the sedative took affect.

I went down hard on the uneven, rock-laden ridge, and it was going to hurt like a bitch once the adrenaline wore off.

Sean and his men were moving fast and effectively. I, on the other hand, was pinned under a whole lot of tiger and couldn't move for shit.

I kept firing from where I was, not that I had a choice, and reached into the earth for the molten core of fire that had better give us a leg up on the situation. No pun intended.

The numbers we had suggested approximately forty-five shifters and/or were-creatures were missing. We had downed fifteen so far, but we were beginning to lose ground and had nowhere to retreat to.

What really sucked was knowing that we wouldn't be able to get them all out of here with us. I had no idea if they could be reinfected, if they would be killed after we left, or if they would come to and head back to the Enclave before they were retrieved.

I pulled on the power the earth had to offer and let it reach toward the continuing onslaught of infected beings still coming at us. I hoped this was going to work, but I also knew without a doubt that when the tunnel collapsed —and yes, there had to be one around here somewhere—somebody was going to die.

I thought of Trey's words not so long ago. *If any more of us die because of you . . .* Shit.

I needed a controlled collapse. Slow enough to block the stream and give those coming in time to retreat.

Fuckity, fuck, fuck, fuck!

I had to stop firing and concentrate on what I was doing. I yelled to Sean and let him know what was up.

"Are you fucking serious?" was his reply, yelling as he continued to move and fire with grace and precision.

"Yes!" I yelled back. "If I don't, we are seriously fucked!"

"I really hate this magic crap!" he shouted, leaping out of the way of a panther whose claws grazed him before he tranquilized it.

I dropped the attention I'd had on the weapon and slowly began shaking down the tunnel. The edge of the ridge started collapsing. Petty was the closest but managed to keep himself from dropping into the rock slide as the tunnel became less and less stable.

As the collapse continued, I watched the terrain shift as the depression revealed the tunnel's path past the wards and well within the boundary of the base we needed to breach at some point. I also noticed that the tiger, whose claws were still deeply embedded in my thigh, was beginning to come to.

This did make me a bit nervous.

I let go of the energy and knew the collapse was complete enough to make the tunnel useless. Now I had the six infected, mobile shifters or Were-creatures that my crew was still dealing with and a really big Bengal tiger that had moved enough to tear my thigh open instead of just perforated it.

Christ on a crutch! Yeah, I screamed. Loud. Part of me thought how lucky I was that he'd caught muscle and was nowhere near an artery. The other part was in charge of screaming, and it took the job seriously.

"Stop fucking moving!" My hand pressed into the paw, trying to hold it in place. Like that would make a difference. The paw was the size of a freaking dinner plate!

If the big cat decided that I was going to be lunch when its head cleared, then lunch I was going to be.

The cat's eyes opened and were glazed. Its huge body shifted just the slightest as if it was going to make a move.

No! My pants were now soaked with my blood, and I was going to lose a bit more before this day was over. I hope Mila stocked up 'cause I was gonna be a quart low.

"Don't fucking move!" I shouted. "Just lay still and get your shit together! Then get your fucking claws out of my damn leg!" Fear, pain, and my mouth are such a lovely combination. Next thing would probably be something along the lines of "nice kitty"."

I was really hoping that whoever this was would come out of this with the infection cleared and the ability to function. We could really use the help.

Sean and his men had dropped the last ones, and Richardson closed in on me. But not too close. Eh, I couldn't blame him. I felt entirely too close to this as it was.

"Andy?" Richardson's voice was soothing and gentle. The tiger eased his gaze from me to the wolf shifter sitting a few feet away. "It's okay. We're here to take you home. Just try not to hurt our witch, will ya?"

The smile on his face made me want to slap him. I knew he was trying to resolve the situation without any more bloodshed and for that he was the best ever wolf shifter ever! But damn!

"Let's not talk 'try' here. How about succeeding," I inserted.

The pain I felt as Andy shifted back to his human form was just bad enough to have me utter a few select words to help manage it without passing out.

Good. Now we could get the few…

There was a sudden hand around my throat and the full-body weight of a 250-pound man pinning me.

"Another fucking witch?" he growled. "I'm going to more than hurt her." Richardson moved fast, goddess bless him, and tackled the shifter trying to strangle me, dragging him off of me and into rocks just the other side of the ridge.

I listened to the two of them tangle. Rocks sliding from their purchase interspersed with the pros and cons of killing the witch. Being said witch, I was going with the cons of killing.

I also managed to tear up my shirt and wrap it around my leg to slow the bleeding.

Sean made his way over to me. He didn't look pleased. Sean was going to have to answer to Trey for my injuries. Trey was going to have to get over it. Shit happens, and occasionally I bleed. I'm not at all happy with it, but it happens.

"I'll make it out. If the others come to as quickly as the tiger, we may all get out of here."

"Nobody will notice if I kill her!" I heard from the other side of the ridge.

Obviously, the argument was still raging.

"I'd notice!" That was my latest offering to the pro/con list.

"You don't count!" the tiger yelled.

"Don't be an ass, Andy!" Richardson yelled. "She's probably the reason you're alive."

"How many others are coming to, Sean?" I asked, still half-listening to the argument that continued to be punctuated by the occasion punch or kick.

"About half," he reported. "They're weak, but I'm sure they make it."

"Weak?" I asked. "Like Andy weak?"

"Everybody will make it down under their own power," Sean said. Then there was a look. A look that then came out his mouth. A look that reflected the dislike he had for me. I was an asset and a liability for the Enclave. "Everybody but you."

We all have our weaknesses. We all have a self-doubt of some sort. Not being able to hack an ugly situation on my own was one of mine, and he just had to go there, didn't he?

"Can't I just maim her a little?" Andy countered loudly as his argument continued with Richardson.

"No!" Richardson, Sean, Petty, and myself replied all at the same time. I felt pretty good that not maiming me was unanimous even by Sean.

I struggled to my feet, even batting Sean's hands away as he reached to help me.

I thought about punching him in the face. I had done so twice thus far, though I only remembered one, and that was terribly satisfying. However, I was fairly sure he couldn't fight back without incurring the wrath of Trey. Damn it. How was I going to prove myself to him?

Fuck it. I would or wouldn't in due time. Right now, I had bigger worries than Sean accepting me.

"Get everybody ready to go," I ordered Sean. Yeah, I didn't suggest or ask. It was an order. "I assume you called this in, and we'll have additional transportation waiting at our vehicle."

He nodded. The look on his face was unpleasant in the fact that I was issuing orders, and he was obeying them. I didn't want to fuck with Sean, but I was going to have to provoke him into a fight at some point. Now would not be a good time for it though.

Sean headed over to Petty, and the two of them continued to organize those who had regained consciousness.

Richardson and Andy were still on the other side of the ridge.

"Hey!" I made my way to the top of the ridge and looked down at the two shifters still arguing. "If you two are finished playing grab ass, we need to get the fuck out of here."

I got a few more photos and did a last light sweep of the area. I was surprised that there had been no energetic attack, just a face-to-face brawl.

We were also getting seventeen shifters and weres back. All in all, a good day.

CHAPTER SEVENTEEN

It Just Felt Like The Right Thing To Do

"This was just supposed to be reconnaissance, Valerie." Trey wasn't nearly as happy about the outcome of today's mission as I was.

I was seriously stoked about returning so many of Trey's people to him, and yet one little tiger clawing my thigh seemed to put him off.

Mila had done her usual unparalleled job of patching me up, and this time I accepted the pain amulet. I still had the remaining warding to put up in the Enclave to call my day finished.

"Yes, well, it went from sugar to shifters pretty quickly." I kept my eyes on Mila's handiwork. The stitches would fall out by the end of the day, and the wound itself would be down to an irritation by the end of tomorrow. "But now we have pretty decent sources for intelligence. Better than I could have gotten on my own."

The vampires we had captured last night had no useful memories of their time in captivity. The were-creature and shifters memories were much clearer and would prove to be very useful.

My pants were blood soaked and shredded. I didn't even try to form an argument regarding the relative safety of the operation. I knew that Trey had some of the same instincts as the clan master regarding my safety. But Trey wouldn't try to lock me away for safe keeping. I looked up at Trey as I eased off of the exam table.

"It could have been much worse, Trey," I said. "Everybody came out in one piece." He stepped closer and pushed some wayward strands of hair over my ear.

It had started.

That simple act let me know that Trey and I were an official couple in his mind. The intimate touches, the warning glares to other males, the protectiveness and possessiveness that would make itself more and more known and obvious to those around us.

"Your pieces are my main concern, Valerie." His arms came around me, pulling me close. I melted into his body as his chin rested on top of my head.

Can I say it?

Wow. Just wow.

I could just curl up in his arms all day and be at peace.

After I go get the rest of the wards up.

"Everything in me wants to keep you protected in the Enclave," he whispered. My hands drifted up and down his back as I enjoyed his scent and warmth and the feel of his body hardening against mine. If we lock the doors and pull the curtain across the window, we could… "I know I can't. You haven't done anything completely reckless, and you haven't taken any risks that I wouldn't have given your skills, so I can't even make recommendations."

I pulled away from him, just enough to look into his eyes. "You can always make recommendations, Trey," I interrupted softly. "If they are valid, they're valid. It doesn't matter that it's not your skill set. I will listen to what you have to say."

His lips covered mine. I could feel the tension leave his body. I could get use to his honesty. And the way he made my body feel with a touch. And the way he kissed me.

"I'd like to talk to your father about officially declaring you my mate." He had broken our kiss for the barest second. Just enough to drop that little piece of news. I guess I shouldn't have felt blindsided, but I did. I hadn't been taking him seriously on the whole mating thing, not really. Part of me had wanted to though, and here it was, plain as day.

"Hey, you all right?" he asked. I had left the conversation and zoned out on him. I brought my focus back to his strong features, his beautiful eyes, and the lips I could kiss for hours on end.

"I'm still trying to get use to the idea of 'father' in connection to me, that's all." I gave him a quick kiss and eased away from him. I needed to change my clothes and get on with the warding.

He let me out of his arms, though I could feel his hesitancy, and followed me to the door and into the hallway.

"And I don't care what Erick has to say," I began as we made our way out of the subsections and into the living area. "My answer is yes." I had officially accepted him as my mate.

I couldn't decide whether to giggle or throw up. Everything felt so right being with him. Just talking or making love, sharing a meal or dealing with the latest incident I'd found myself in felt like we had been doing this forever. "I still want a job description though."

We had only passed a few people on our way. Mostly nothing was said outside of a polite, in-passing greeting, but I did get a few longer looks. Nothing threatening, just interest. I suppose the possibility of me staying had been in the rumor mill for a while. I'm pretty sure Trey didn't spend this much time with Gabrielle. If he had, we were going to have a conversation.

Oh, and I was fucking him. That was likely a piece of information that had made the rounds before my first orgasm.

I wondered when the challenges would start.

It took a good twenty minutes to get Trey out of my room. Okay, it took sex in the shower to get him out, but I was finally dressed and had gotten my gear together to set the wards. And I had only popped one stitch.

The sun was just beginning to go down. The colors that streaked across the sky were beautiful, like a watercolor painting on a really huge canvas.

I watched long enough to see the lighter oranges and reds shift to purples. I was going to stay here.

I was going to see this beautiful sunset every day. I would wake up with Trey every morning. I would learn to deal with Enclave issues and the weirdness that could be found in the desert.

I would learn Trey and what it meant to be his mate. Trey would learn what it meant to be mine.

Within two hours, I had the wards in place and ready to power up. This time I had an audience of fifty waiting on the roof to watch. Including Andy.

The were-tiger stood in the middle of the group and tried to look as if he wasn't there. Since he had introduced himself to me claws first, I would always know when he was nearby. My thigh itched at his proximity.

Andy was built like a swimmer with broad shoulders and a narrow waist. Sandy blonde hair that reached to his shoulders, and blue gray eyes that took in everything and everyone around him. He looked to be about six foot and probably weighed in at 250. I wasn't sure how a 250-pound man could become a 600-pound tiger, but I didn't need to know anything past the knowledge that a 600-pound tiger could do a lot of damage fast.

I pulled power from the waning moon. Having Her soft glow directly on my face felt soothing, and if I did this right, I wouldn't be depleted when I was done, and Trey and I could pick up where we left off in the shower.

Energies wound down from the sky and up from the earth. Their colors mingling and swirling, mixing and shifting in tone and hue. I was amazed at how beautiful and vibrant the colors became as they shimmered, glowed, and encased the Enclave.

I was warding a fucking fortress. This place was huge and housed nearly 250 individuals. Males, females, and children lived here and loved here, and a few had died here very recently.

I would protect them the best I could just as Trey had been doing, just differently.

I could feel the energies moving through me as well as encasing the structure, and it felt as good as it looked. It was definitely worth basking in if I hadn't had a job to finish.

I could hear the crowd muttering in the distance of my conscious mind. It was a mix of trepidation and appreciation.

I let it go. I would focus on the energy filling the wards I had set, bringing them to life, giving them purpose.

The sliver of the moon continued to give me strength as the energy followed my will, and in a flash of conscious thought, it was done. I took a moment to check the work, test the resilience, run a diagnostic. All was well.

I reached into the wards I had set yesterday and found an energetic anomaly running though the tunnel where the ward hadn't worked properly.

There was a interesting bit of nature in there that I hadn't caught. Then again, the attack had happened too fast, and I hadn't had the chance to check the work. Honestly, I had forgotten until this moment.

It felt like a vein of metal. Silver to be exact. There was a small fortune in raw silver running within the boarders of the Enclave.

Best day ever! I wondered if I could get a finder's fee. I'd love a vacation in Europe. I'm sure I could find older and scarier things over there to kick my ass. Mostly, my mom's family. Grandma, grandpa, and a great-grandmother still lived in Ireland. I hadn't seen them since mom's funeral. Hadn't kept in touch as I should have either. I should go and let them chew me out in person; then they would spoil me rotten for as long as I hung out there.

Anyway, a few tweeks of energy, and the issue with the silver was fixed.

Now if anything infected came up on the ward, they couldn't get in.

Yea, me! Mission complete, and I'm not bleeding. What more could I possibly ask for?

"You're going to be late for the meeting." You know if it had been Trey, I would have told him about the silver as I picked up my belongings and walked off with him to the meeting.

But it wasn't Trey.

It was Marc.

"I'm not really necessary. Sean has all of the pertinent data to be presented." My tone was uninterested, and I picked up the small cauldron that still smoldered with the last of the herbs I'd used. I would have to see if Gabrielle had a stash around here.

Shit! I should have asked earlier. I had searched her quarters but hadn't thought that she might had a work space.

I saw Mila milling in the crowd. She glanced over to me and smiled, until she saw Marc. Her smiled dimmed; mine didn't. Marc hadn't won any points with Mila, and the rude remarks he threw around didn't go unnoticed.

Now *he* got to be the prick or asshole, depending on my mood.

I headed over toward her to ask about the possible stash when Marc slipped up behind me and took hold of my arm.

The low buzz of conversation stopped in a way that was disconcerting to say the least.

"Your father wants you there, Val." Oh, the imperiousness of his tone. I had a feeling that Marc was no longer Daddy's favorite boy. I wondered if it had anything to do with Trey and the whole mate thing. Probably. Sucked to be Marc.

I stopped and turned toward him. My face registered slightly annoyed as I looked at the strong pale hand that was wrapped around my bicep, and then up to the familiar face of the man I'd spent five years with. Every time I saw him, something changed. I felt a little more distant. He felt a little less tied to me and more to my past.

As I met his gaze, his grip became a drift of his hand over my arm before he dropped his hand from me completely.

"Clan masters expect to be obeyed, Val." Marc was trying to come off as stern and commanding, but he was having to work for it. Something was definitely up, and Marc was in the middle of it.

"He'll just have to learn to live with disappointment, Marc." I turned back around and continued on toward Mila. I could see her and a few others smiling faces as I gave Marc grief. If I knew I'd make friends giving that vampire shit, I would have started earlier.

"Do you think what he did to you on those stairs was bad, Valerie?" Marc was right behind me, and the faces in front of me were expectant. Why? Beats me. "That was nothing. And if you push him, he will push back. Next time, you won't get up and walk away."

I stopped walking and took a deep cleansing breath. I could go to the meeting. I would give some input and listen to what was being said, but Sean could give them more information than I since I hadn't been in on any of the questioning of the people we had brought back.

Besides, I'd rather have Trey brief me when he got to bed. He would get to the point, not waste time with unimportant details, and then we could get down to some serious sweating.

I wondered if he'd had the opportunity to look into asbestos linens and fire-retardant furniture.

"I don't have any more information to add to the meeting, Marc," I said as slowly as possible but tried not to sound patronizing. Well, not too patronizing. "I'm still getting things organized from my end and don't have time for this."

I wasn't sure how much of a lie that was. I still did need to work up the counter spell for the infection, and I was sure I could enchant a few snow globes to take out the wards as well. That shielding was seriously ugly, but I had seen it before.

The thought that my aunt Maggie might be involved in this made my stomach ache. I needed to tell Trey what my suspicions were regarding my aunt. Talking about it would help me prepare for the possibility that somebody I loved might end up dead by the time this was over.

Shit! The next time I contact my other aunts might be to let them know Maggie was dead and then have to tell them what she had done. Christ on a bike!

I couldn't let myself get worked up over something that may not be. There were other possibilities for what I was sensing besides my aunt having become a crazed murdering psycho.

"That can wait. The clan master cannot." Oh, the attitude was coming out, and Marc was pissing me off again. "I've been ordered to collect you."

I dropped the crucible. It was heavy duty and could take the impact with ease. So could Marc's jaw, but it didn't stop me from throwing a jab/cross combination.

He stumbled back a few feet, and I stepped back as well. I reached down inside of myself and searched for that part of me that came out and went after Trey two nights ago.

Not the part that enjoyed sex all night long in the shower, and on the balcony, and in the shower again. Sigh. Where was I? Oh, that part that was more deeply connected to my vampire genetics than I'd thought.

If I was going to take on Marc, then I needed all of the ammunition I could get my hands on.

Since I'd thrown a couple of solid connecting punches, it did look like I was taking him on.

Marc came at me swinging. I was vaguely aware of the people who were watching. I thought I heard somebody calling for odds and taking bets.

I never would have said that Marc and I were evenly matched, but I'd never fought him for anything but practice until today. I wasn't afraid to hurt him, and I knew he wouldn't hesitate to hurt me. He was going to drag me to that meeting and my father one way or another.

Somehow I was managing to hold my own. He had connected a couple times, and my ribs were going to be sore until morning. I'd probably have a black eye as well. But the best part? I was still moving, and Marc was getting pissed off and sloppy.

His usual speed wasn't helping him. I could sense his movements just before he executed them, letting me be just a hair ahead of him.

So he resorted to taunting.

"Been practicing?" he asked smoothly. "With all the time you've spent fucking that guy, I'd figure your skills would have slacked off."

He leapt at me.

I rolled under him, tangling his legs and forcing him to roll out of the landing. I was hoping for a face plant.

"Well, it looks like kissing Olafson's ass hasn't done anything for your skills." I heard a few snickers from those who stood by and watched. And then the collective "ow" and wincing as Marc hit me hard enough to throw me back a good thirty feet where I landed on my back.

Andy came into my vision as I lay there on the hard, hard roof.

"You might not want to do that too many times," he said as he looked down at me.

"What? Taunt him?" I asked casually.

"No. Get hit," he replied as if this were a quiet, friendly conversation and not the middle of a brawl between me and my ex. Right then I decided that, even though he mauled my leg, I liked Andy. "Need any help?"

I looked around and saw Marc getting geared up to come at me again. There were also more people coming up on to the roof. Maybe we should have negotiated for pay-per-view. "Nah. I got this," I replied and rolled onto my feet.

There was very little moon tonight, and the last traces of daylight were gone. The stars shone brightly overhead. I knew this because I had landed on my back again, close to the edge of the roof and was currently taking inventory of the injuries, which were surprisingly few.

I had never done this well against Marc, and I was gaining strength and confidence. I reached out to the stars. Those little bit of fire in the very distant sky and felt the trickle of power find its way to me.

It was foreign and odd, but it found its way into my system.

On my feet again and just to be clear, Marc had spent just as much time getting up as I had. I rushed him.

He readied for the frontal assault.

What he wasn't ready for was my sliding into his legs, twisting him, and pinning him face down.

I grabbed his hair and bashed his face into stone. It just felt like the right thing to do.

The crowd loved it too.

I hadn't quite made it out of range when he grabbed me by the ankle and tossed me into the side of the guard tower. Hard. Really, really hard.

I guess I finally pissed him off.

I was again seeing stars. Unfortunately, they weren't the ones in the clear desert sky. But I could feel the faint energy from them.

When I had vamped out on Trey, I had been angry. Righteously angry with everything that had been going on. Right now I wasn't angry. I didn't even want to fight with Marc. I just wanted this to be over. We didn't have time for petty politics while lives were at stake.

My father was flexing his muscle at the worst possible time, and that muscle was Marc at the moment. He was good muscle. He had taken care of me. He had treated me well while we were together for my father and his agenda. This was also a part of my father's agenda.

I hadn't quite regained my sensibilities when Marc lifted me up and pinned me against the wall I had slid down. He didn't hesitate with the right cross to the side of my face.

White hot pain exploded inside my skull, and everything went black for the amount of time it took for Marc to right my body and stop it from hitting the ground again.

He was also pulling back for another punch.

Then, it dawned on me. I had to win this fight. I didn't quite know why, but it was important that I did. My brains were just too scrambled to get the specifics.

I felt my vision darken, and my fist shot out, catching Marc in the chest.

He stumbled back, his eyes wide in surprise as I closed the distance and threw several successive punches, two of which connected. It kept him too busy to do anything except defend.

Part of me had a plan as I continued to assault Marc and back him toward the edge of the Enclave. I didn't know what the plan was, but my conscious mind just stayed the fuck out of it and went with the flow.

Marc ducked my left hook and came up quickly, shoving his shoulder into my ribs and wrapping his arms around me. He lifted me off my feet and slammed me onto the stone, his body following.

Having the breath knocked out of you is unpleasant. It's one of the downsides to having to breathe in the first place. A solid strike to the solar plexus is enough to disable an opponent, if they need to breathe. If they don't need to breathe, it's much harder to win without doing a lot of damage.

If I was going to win this fight, I was going to have to hurt Marc and hurt him badly. Hell, I could break every bone in his body and rupture most of his internal organs, and he would be good as new in twenty-four hours.

I had to start fighting him as if he were the enemy. In a way he was.

We grappled. Neither of us could get the upper hand, but we were covered in dust, and our clothing might be good for cleaning rags at this point.

Marc finally got some leverage and threw me off him. I recovered quickly and got to my feet. But his foot connected with my chest before I'd truly gotten my shit together. When I'd stopped rolling from the force of his kick, I was less than ten feet from the edge of the roof and, I decided, in a good position.

I moved slowly and tried to look more injured than I was. If this was going to work, Marc was going to try to kick me while I was down. Part of me hoped like hell he didn't though. It would mean that he hated me. I could live with it, but somehow the thought hurt.

"You couldn't just go with it, could you, Val?" I was on my hands and knees, parallel to the edge as Marc advanced on me. I had one arm wrapped around my ribs. I really was nursing them. Marc had kicked me damn hard, but it made me look even more vulnerable. "Your life could be an absolute dream if you just stop fighting it." I saw him move into position and lift his leg. The sole of his shoe rested against my shoulder for the moment before he gave me shove.

My plan would still work, and I was also very relieved that he hadn't kicked me while I was down. He wasn't a complete bastard, and maybe someday I could like him again. Maybe. If I really wanted to. But right now?

"The man your father has chosen for you to be mated to will be good to you." Marc knelt by my side and pulled a strand of hair out of the blood that was drying on my cheek. "You'll need to brush up on your ballroom skills." He sounded almost sad.

I didn't say a word as I grabbed his shoulders, pulled his body down, jammed my knee in his stomach, twisted and dumped him off of the edge of the roof.

Some of the very old vampires can defy gravity. Not just hover, but actually fly. Marc is not one of them.

CHAPTER EIGHTEEN

Come to the dark side, I thought. We have cookies.

"**Y**ou bitch!" echoed into the night, and then, there was silence. I looked over the edge and saw his motionless form laid out on the ground nearly one hundred feet below me. Two guards rushed over to check him out and then stepped back.

One looked up and saw me observing the scene. He waved.

"Don't stake the vamp," I called out to the guards on the ground. "He's a guest and is to be treated with respect."

I got the thumbs-up, and they moved away, but not before one gave Marc a swift kick in the ribs.

The guards *were* complete bastards, but they were shifters, and that explained it all.

Marc probably shouldn't have been trash talking the residents of the Enclave so much either.

I rolled on to my back. Mila stood over me, arms crossed her chest, her weight shifted to one hip. She raised an eyebrow and looked me up and down. Or left to right since I was down.

"Make sure he gets to the med lab. Throw a couple bags at him," I told Mila. "Try not to let anybody do any more damage to him. I don't want the clan master to be able to go after anyone else."

"No problem, since you made me a couple hundred bucks tonight." Her hands went to her hips, and she tilted her head some. "Need a pain amulet?"

"Oh yeah." I stuck out my hand, and she produced one from her pocket. "Around you, I'm learning to be prepared." She slapped the amulet into my palm, and I tucked it into my bra. "Your thigh's bleeding again." She tacked on sourly.

I bent my knee and lift my head enough to see the blood seeping through my pants. It really wasn't that bad, but a couple more stitches had torn.

"It's only flesh wound," I said with a light British accent. God, I loved *Monty Python*.

"Would you say that if your leg had gone off?" Mila asked. I snickered and decided Mila was my best friend. She was a *Holy Grail* fan too.

I smiled and laughed as much as I could without something aching. "So what were the odds tonight?" I still hadn't tried to get up. I would when I was ready. I'm sure the sunrise would look lovely from up here.

"You were not the favorite. But the odds were closer to even, if you had used your magic," she told me. "Why didn't you?"

I stretched.

My body ached like I hadn't worked out in months, and I could feel the blood cool in the evening breeze, mostly on my face and thigh.

I flexed my fingers; two were broken. The ribs felt well and truly bruised, but I didn't think any of those were broken.

"My magic is fire based," I told her. "I really didn't want to kill him. Not in a permanent way."

"You made me fifty," Andy chimed in happily. "Sorry about the leg."

"You're only sorry because I made you fifty bucks," I said. "Now you just feel guilty."

"Probably."

"How much did you win Sean?" I asked.

He hesitated.

"You bet against me?" I remember part of the conversation he had had with Trey. "Because I'm an accident magnet." I couldn't be mad; he had a valid point.

"Pretty much," he said.

Most of the spectators had filed out leaving me with Andy, Mila, and Sean.

"Now what?" Andy asked. I wondered why they were waiting.

"I don't know." I yawned. "Hot shower, cold beer?"

"You drink beer?" Sean asked. Why was he surprised? I did occasionally drink. It would take me a month to go through a six pack, but sometimes a good beer just hit the spot. Now actually felt like one of those times.

"Not often," I said with a sigh. Andy moved and put his hand out for me. "Once in a while though." He hefted my tired ass off of the ground and got me to my feet.

We began moving to one of the roof accesses. "You like micro-brews?" he asked. "We make some small batch beers here. It's a hobby, but they are pretty good."

"Sounds good." It really did, and I would join them another time because as the access door opened and Erick and Trey walked out, I knew playtime was over. "But we will have to make it another time." I leaned into Mila; she looked nervous. I couldn't blame her. I was too. "Make sure Marc's taken care of."

Mila nodded and made her way past the two men who did not look pleased. "Where's Marc?" Erick asked firmly. He looked me over and scanned the roof, and then he brought his gaze back to me.

"He's getting a better look at the landscaping around the Enclave," I replied. Andy snickered, but he quickly stifled it.

"There is no landscaping around the Enclave." Trey looked even less happy than my father, but I knew he was pissed because I had been injured. He was showing a huge amount of restraint in continuing to let Marc live.

"Then he's going to be disappointed," I remarked casually.

"Sean, what happened?" Trey asked. Well, I hadn't been forthcoming, and Trey had lost his patience. His second in command wouldn't hesitate to brief him on the situation.

I have one word for him.

Tattletale.

"After the wards had been set, Mr. Brighton accosted Ms. Hannigan," he reported quickly. "She then kicked his ass."

Sean was now one of my most favorite people ever.

"Her name is Olafson," Erick said fuming.

"Not according to her birth certificate." Sean was smooth, cool, and completely unflustered. I turned to him.

"You checked my birth records?" I asked quietly.

He shrugged and returned his attentions back to the clan and beast masters. Behind the impassive stare of the regional beast master, I could see his need to smile. He wasn't going to let it happen, but I could see it.

I was going to give him many reasons to smile later.

"Mr. Brighton should be in the med lab any minute," Sean tossed out.

"How did she do against him?" Trey asked. Okay, now it was me trying to hide the smile.

"Actually, better than I thought she would." Sean was still in reporting mode. No emotion.

"You bet against me," I remarked.

"Hence you having done better than I thought you would." He glanced at me with a slight imperiousness that pushed me harder to keep from smiling. Sean was fucking with the clan master, and Trey had joined in. I could get used to this place and these people.

"I won fifty bucks," Andy tossed in.

"That's because you had faith in me." I smiled sweetly to Andy and could feel Erick getting more and more pissed.

"Nah," he said. "I've got a thing for long shots."

"Enough!" Yup, dad finally lost it. "Enough of this!" He grabbed hold of my wrist, and I could feel the power of this ancient vampire take hold of me. Anyone he sired, he could indirectly control if they were not cooperative. It could be a pain worse than death, it could pleasure bordering on the obscene, and it could be a neutral display more frightening than anything I'd seen so far.

This was his neutral display. I could feel the fear pouring off me in waves. "You will attend me in this meeting. You will do as you are told, and you will embrace the life waiting for you in Los Angeles."

His hold on me was absolute. I felt like I was being dangled off the edge of a cliff, and the wrong word would get me dropped. I loved wrong words.

"Fuck you," I gasped. I heard the low growls of two big cats just behind me.

"I will ask you to take your hands off my mate Clan Master Olafson." Trey's voice was that low menace I had heard in my ear before. "And you will embrace the life she has chosen here." As Erick's grip loosened, I was finally able to see something besides his soul-searing blackened eyes.

Marc had been more than right in stating that the clan master's earlier display had been nothing in comparison to what he could do.

Surprisingly, as his hand slid from my wrist, his power unwound itself from me. Not just my body or my heart, but my very soul. I was his daughter. He had sired me in the most primitive and forever way. His power had wound around my soul.

It was kind of nice to know I had one, but damn. Not really the way I'd wanted to find out that a soul resided within me.

Though Erick no longer had physical contact with me, I was still unable to move. I wasn't even sure if I could speak anymore.

But I was happy to have gotten in a "fuck you" before most of my basic abilities locked up on me.

Erick slowly reached out and shifted my shirt, exposing one shoulder and then the other.

"She's not marked," he said. "She's not claimed and therefore, not anybody's mate." My heart raced. Trey had used my unbound status to back up my demand that Marc leave me a few nights ago, and now Erick was using the same argument to impose his will on me.

The frightening part was, Erick actually had a claim on me. By blood and by vampiric law.

I was now understanding why Mom may have wanted to ditch this guy and keep me in hiding. Now it looked like I had blown her hope for me all to hell.

"I asked. She agreed," Trey argued. "The rest is a formality. I thought it respectful to talk to you of your daughter's status before we completed the task.

Task? The boy was all hearts and flowers. But this was the professional distance he needed in order to eliminate, or at least reduce, the amount of bloodshed that was on the line if things went badly.

I'd let it go for now, but in the future when he spoke of me, there had better be love in his voice, and his heart had damn well better skip a beat!

I still hadn't moved and wasn't really able to feel my body much at all since Erick took hold of me. I reached out to the energy of the moon and the stars and came up with a blank wall.

I could feel the panic beginning to set in. Erick didn't need to be touching me.

Again. Fuckity, fuck, fuck, fuck!

My energy began searching for a chink, a weakness, a rough spot, a ledge, something within the smooth and seamless enclosure Erick had me in.

My flow pushed and swirled. I felt my feet and the balance of my body over them. There were the smallest shifts and adjustments of weight keeping upright. Those shifts that we no longer feel because it's automatic. I was aware of them. I was hoping this was a good sign.

Erick's hold began to waver slightly, and then I felt the smallest of fractures as my thoughts continued to process what my energy was experiencing.

"Formality or no, she isn't mated." Erick was done arguing, and as far as he was concerned, he'd won. "Come, Valerie."

I felt my balance shift to my toes. I didn't want to. I really, really didn't want to. I wanted to stay with the obnoxious shifter with the long title and bad attitude. I wanted to stay with the mocha shifter who'd bet against me and the were-tiger with the micro-brew hobby!

I fought to counterbalance, but my body continued to move. I pushed hard against Erick's hold, and the fractures broke. The structure collapsed like broken glass at my feet. The shards raining down on me, following the path of my energy, and finally falling away.

My weight shifted back to my heels. Erick's eyes went wide and then narrowed to slits. The grim line of his mouth spoke of rage. I had hoped for more of pride or impressed. I'm sure nobody had ever done that before.

I took a deep breath in. That breath felt like fresh water after a week in the desert or the first day of spring after a long cold winter. I do suspect that I'd not really been breathing since Erick grabbed me.

"What part of 'fuck you' was difficult to understand?" My words came out in a rasp, harsh, and with difficulty. "He's my mate. Get over it." Stalking out of there would have been great, but I didn't think I could walk, so I glowered. That used a lot less energy.

"You are my daughter!" Erick bellowed, his voice echoing in through the desert. I heard a covey of birds take flight from atop the northern most guard tower. "There are plans in motion, and I will not change them! I never should have given you the freedom Marc had requested."

There was something in his voice that chilled me with fear. It wasn't fear for myself, but for Marc.

The clan master wasn't getting his way, and he wanted to blame somebody.

Marc was looking really goat-like right now.

"Your daughter is mated to the beast master of the southwest region of the North America," I said calmly. "Strategically, that will have its advantages. Especially if you and I are on good terms, Father."

Wow. That sounded so strange. Father. One word. A word I'd never said in reference to actually having one beyond the abstract concept. Erick had a very detailed plan regarding who his daughter was supposed to be. I was not that person. I could never authentically be that person. I might be able to fake it for a while, but for the rest of my life? No way in hell.

Erick seemed to still for a moment. Maybe he was considering what I had said. Maybe he was gearing up to argue or fight some more. Don't know. Don't care. We needed to get moving. I hoped I could move when the time came.

"I'm not going anywhere, Erick." I had interrupted his train of thought, but he looked even more unhappy in that moment. "Neither are you." Okay, he figured out that I wasn't continuing to buck him. I was simply stating facts.

"We have more pressing matters to deal with. This issue will keep until we resolve what is happening in that desert and to your and Trey's people."

My voice was beginning to flow more readily. I needed water, and a shower, and a nap, and something to eat. I was starting to mentally whine and squashed it quickly.

"So take time to think about a different set of possibilities, and I'll be at the meeting." I could see that his mind was already turning ideas over regarding what I'd said. I would convince him that having the regional beast master as a son-in-law was a much better thing that mating me off to some stuffy, undead aristocrat who I would have to kill out of sheer boredom in a year or two. Maybe a month or two. "Give me an hour to get cleaned up."

His mind still churned.

Come to the dark side, I thought. *We have cookies.*

Erick laced his fingers as he brought his hands up. Steepled forefingers touched his lips as his eyes narrowed in a thoughtful gaze.

He took a breath in and dropped his hands. "I have the perfected gift to present you for your union." With that said, he turned elegantly on his heels and walked through the access. The vampires that had accompanied him blocked my view of him as he descended into the Enclave.

I had never seen the vampires standing there in the first place. Maybe that would be because I had been terrified.

Sounded reasonable to me.

I simply stood a dozen feet from the darkness of the roof access doorway, unmoving.

"I don't know if I'm more worried or less," Trey said. "But I'm impressed with how you cleared the way with Erick." He stepped close enough for me to feel the heat that emanated from him. That warmth that soothed and caressed me. He reached up and touched my shoulder lightly. "Not that I completely trust it."

"Me neither."

The weight of his hand on my body let me get my bearings around have full control of my body again.

I looked up at him. His eyes, beautiful, blue with just a touch of flame behind them.

"I need to get cleaned up," I sighed. "Again."

My Thigh Still Tingled

Showering was beginning to be my favorite activity. Especially since Trey tended to shower with me. I asked about the capacity of the hot water tank only to find out that he had a flash heater, and the hot water wouldn't run out, ever.

We barely made the meeting in the hour I had asked for.

Marc didn't make the meeting. Having broken most of the bones in his body, he wouldn't heal for twenty-four hours give or take an hour or two.

Should I feel badly? Maybe.

Did I? Nope.

Somebody would fill him in of the details of the meeting later.

The meeting was productive and mercifully short. The information Sean had gotten from the were-creatures and shifters we had brought in was interesting, and the logistics were detailed. A rough drawing of the base had been created along with where the holding areas were.

As I had feared, humans were being held. Many had been killed in the course of feeding the infected, but some still lived. I momentarily hoped we would be able to get them out, but then wondered if it wouldn't be a kindness of sorts to kill them.

I could only imagine what they were going through, and if their memories couldn't be wiped, they couldn't be let back into the general population.

Even if nobody would believe them, they would have been traumatized with no way to get help working through it. Their lives would be over.

I stood at the beast master's right and shook those thoughts away as Sean continued with his briefing.

"They were able to identify four witches working together," Sean said. He gave descriptions, and none of them sounded like my aunt. I breathed in and sighed in relief. It was short lived. "There is a fifth that is being kept isolated in the same holding area as the humans, and apparently, a few weres who after initially succumbing to the infecting threw it off. They are being kept alive and experimented on. The infection is being reworked, refined."

There was silence in the office. We were going to have to move fast. The information I had to go on to create the counter spell had an expiration date, and it was coming up.

"They also said that things had stopped over the last few days because their leader had been injured. She still hadn't recovered as of their liberation," Sean continued. "Her injury was due to a magical attack the day Ms. Hannigan was brought to the Enclave."

I thought about that for a moment. The only thing I could tie that to was the golem attack in the desert.

I must have kicked her ass pretty good. Then again, it took me some time to recover as well. But she was still down or was as of a few hours ago. That would definitely work to our advantage.

Powerful witches do not work and play with others. They do not want other powerful witches around them to steal the power they, themselves, want and are using others to get. Nobody would have the power to step in and take her place.

This was getting better and better.

"Valerie, how long will it take to work up the counter spells for the infection and the wards to their base?" Trey asked. "We got the shipment of snow globes in today."

I smiled. He was still incredulous about the snow globes, and I could hear it in his voice. but they would work. And honestly, breaking things could be just as much fun and blowing things up.

"Have them taken to the roof. I'll work them up tonight." I saw the worry flash across Trey's features. Did he think I couldn't do it after how the night had gone so far? Possibly. I was sporting a black eye, a cut on my cheek, my fingers were still knitting, and what had been deep-purple-and-black bruises were down to a noticeable yellow and green. Not my favorite color combination.

"There's no moon," Erick said. "How are you going to get it done?"

"The moon is still there," I explained. "And the absence of the reflected light is perfect for what I need to do. Destroy, take away, interfere." It didn't really matter what phase the moon was in. It was all about the wording and intent. I could make this work on a full moon, but dark moon would make it much easier.

Easy was sounding really good about now.

My eyes shifted to Trey with a reassuring smile in them. He wouldn't question me; he wouldn't stop me. He would trust me to know that I could do this and ask for what I needed.

"I think you should wait." Erick, on the other hand, was an ass. "At least until you're healed." He was sitting in one Trey's comfy wing-back chairs. Legs clad in tailored black silk, stretched out and crossed at the ankles. His hands were folded over his stomach as he leaned negligently into the butter soft leather.

Power would ripple off him if he didn't have it on a tight leash. I was quickly learning to buffer what power he allowed to slip through, just so I could function. Bastard was still fucking with me.

"I appreciate your concern," I began and then stopped. He let more power slip his leash. I could get mad. I should get mad. Trey hadn't noticed anything beyond my sudden pause. I turned my head to look at him.

"Trey?" I focused on those eyes to keep me balanced as Erick's energy pushed at me lightly, but it was distracting nonetheless. "How many of yours have died since this began?"

"Twenty-three," he answered. He was confused, but hiding it well.

My gaze returned to Erick as his met mine. The power eased up.

"Then let's not waste anymore time," I said, my stare level and unwavering. The clan master conceded with an inclination of his head. "I'll need two men from security and the were-tiger, Andy. Tell him to bring a six pack."

"A six pack of what?" Erick asked.

"Beer."

Within the hour, I was on the roof still wallowing in delight over the look on Erick's face at the pronouncement that I wanted beer. I told him that *Cristal* and *Dom* had their places, but a good hand-crafted brew could not be beat. I didn't tell him that the beer would be needed for the work I was going to do tonight. It was too much fun to see if he could stroke out.

Trey hadn't asked what was going on. But he would. I was Trey's mate regardless of the fact that the dragon had yet to sink him fangs into my body and mark me as his. Literally, marking my body as a sign that I belonged to him.

I would do the same to him, but I'm sure that my bite would be a whole lot smaller.

I felt butterflies in my stomach at the thought of being marked. It would scar. A forever sign that I was a mated female. It wasn't a mark of ownership, but of having been paired, accepted by another. Forever entwined.

I smiled to myself as I continued to set things up. My body momentarily remembering the feel of Trey's hands as they had palmed my breasts in the shower. His body pressed against my back as his lips touched my shoulder and neck tenderly just before I turned in his arms, and I found my back against the cool tiled wall.

"Get your mind out of the gutter and back on your work," Andy growled.

Animal senses could be a real nuisance.

"What's the matter, Andy?" I said, focusing back on the task at hand. "Not getting any?"

He mumbled or rather growled something and stalked up wind from me. Then my security laughed quietly and simply kept their distance. Tinkerman, aka Tink, I knew there was a story behind that. It was more than just a shortening of his name, and I would find out; but right now, he wasn't willing to share, and I didn't have the time to pry it out of him. I had a feeling it would take a lot of beer and relentless questioning to get him to spill. Or I'd find somebody to spill for him.

The other guy was a werewolf nicknamed Cujo. Honestly, he didn't look like much beyond what I'd expect. Tall, well built, handsome, but quiet. I had a feeling the quiet part was there until things went wrong. Cujo.

Andy had given me the six pack. It contained six different beers, and he explained each one.

Aunt Maggie loved beer, and she did have her favorites. I chose a summer wheat with raspberry notes. My aunt would have loved it.

I held the picture of her in my head. Not the last time I'd seen her—angry, pale, and wan from the grief that had overwhelmed her— but the fun aunt who taught me how to pick locks. Even though I could melt them, it taught me patience and gave me an alternative to permanent damage to a structure.

Aunt Maggie was still young and filled with life and the love of her family. The small wrinkles around her eyes were just beginning to show when she smiled, which was often. Her eyes were more turquoise than green, and her hair blonde and short framed her oval face.

I could hear her laughter in the early summer mornings as she tended her greenhouse gardens and marveled at the life around her.

That was the Aunt Maggie I held in my mind. This was her magic. At least, hers had been the basis of it. I tasted the beer she would have loved, held her face in my mind's eye, felt her energy in the echo of my memory, and went for it.

The circle had been set, candles were placed and lit in protective holders, and the herbs and resins were burning.

I rarely used the trappings anymore, but this was life or death, and I wouldn't take any chances by being lazy.

The larger amount of snow globes were encompassed by the circle. I empowered the cardinal points and lit it up like a Christmas tree. From there, the rest was slow going. I had to maintain a connection with the feel of the infection magic as I wove the counter spell into the glass spheres. All three hundred of them. Luckily, I didn't have to do them individually.

My eyes were closed as I held the vision of the dark magic in my head and watched as the counter-magic slowly formed and congealed in my mind's eye. It overtook the infection, smothered it, killed it.

I felt a tendril of energy brush against me. Soft, soothing, familiar, and supportive. Maggie.

Shit! Maggie really was there. In that base. She was the witch they had locked up. I couldn't put off telling Trey any longer. I wouldn't be holing up in the Enclave when the time came either.

I would have unhappily stayed behind for Trey. He hadn't asked, but he didn't need any more worries than any commander leading his people into battle.

There was no way I was staying behind now.

I sent a reassuring vibe back to my aunt. I was coming for her.

With the first set of globes charged and ready, I had Tink and Cujo call down and have the globes moved to the armory.

My shirt was soaked by the time I'd finished with the first working. This was not easy, and it took its toll in so many ways. I didn't mind waking up with Trey, but I'd really rather have some memory of actually getting into bed with him.

The next circle was smaller, and I only had a small box of seventy-five snow globes to do this time. I tapped in as I had done before, this time finding Maggie's slim connection and weaving the energy that would negate the protective warding around their base.

I'm not saying that this was going to be easy, but it just got a whole lot easier now that I had inside help.

As I began to unwind the energy, I took another swig of the summer wheat beer and thought hard on my aunt. If energy could laugh, hers did.

I broke the connection, gently easing out and letting go. Goddess knows I didn't want to. I had no idea how long she had been there. Or how they were treating her. She was a prisoner, but a useful one to be sure. I had to believe she would be fine, and I would have her safe soon.

Andy stood next to me and downed one of his beers as I polished off the one I had used earlier. We watched the boxes of globes disappear one by one into the roof access doorway in companionable silence until the last box was gone and Tink and Cujo waited for further instruction.

I handed them the box with the last remaining beers. Two were chosen, and the rest set down. The caps were popped with a satisfying hiss, and the four of us drank.

"So you're our alpha's mate," Cujo commented softly.

The desert breeze was soft and cool. Clean scents came to us and mixed with the yeasts, hops, and other smells of the variety of beers we were enjoying.

"Looks that way." I placed my empty bottle in the box and pick up a second beer, a honey wheat, and cracked it open. It wasn't as cold as the first, but it didn't affect the subtle flavors of my drink.

"You did well against that vamp earlier," Tink said. "You planning on training with us?" He took a long draw off his beer. He never took his eyes off me. I didn't know whether training with Trey's men was a good idea or not, but he was waiting for an answer.

"Likely," I said casually.

"Good," Tink said, a slow grin spreading across his face.

"Am I going to regret it?" I asked.

"Likely," he replied, his grin never wavering.

"Will there be beer?"

"Likely," they said in unison.

I paused and sipped my beer in contemplation. "Worth it," I said as I saluted the men with my bottle and headed to the door. "Good night, gentlemen." I threw over my shoulder and made my way to another shower, a warm bed, and a warm shape-shifting dragon named Trey.

"Are you sure it's your aunt?" Trey asked.

"I have no doubt." I burrowed in more closely to his body. He had made love to me like he hadn't gotten any bedtime in months. I had been tired before we began, but that gave me a second wind. Right now, though, I think he was giving me some recovery time before we went for round two. "I felt her."

"Why didn't you say anything earlier?" He held me close and felt his lips press gently into my head.

"You didn't let me get two words out before I was naked and you were in me," I reminded him. He shrugged as I continued, "And I wasn't about to stop you."

My fingertips drifted lazily down his chest, following the contours of his muscles and admiring the smoothness of his skin.

"You could have mentioned something." Now he was just teasing me, and I have to admit it, I loved it.

"You have a tendency to render me utterly senseless," I told him simply. "So in effect, it's your fault."

I looked up to catch his smile just before he laughed quietly. Relaxed and content. I did that. The very simple fact that I was in his arms sated and playful made him happy and put him at ease.

I returned his smile, and something serious flickered across his features.

He didn't give me a chance to ask or ponder before his lips touched mine and then deepened into a kiss that signaled round two.

Our breakfasts were starting later and later. That was explained by the fact that our nights were ending later and later. I had spent many years on a late night schedule, but it hadn't taken much to push me into a normal human schedule. Now that the clan master was here, we were on his sleep patterns.

So we had breakfast at eleven in the morning.

Trey would be spending most of the day working up an attack plan that would be implemented tomorrow. We needed to work fast before they were able to make any drastic changes to the infection or defenses.

I had told him that I was going in to find my aunt. I wasn't going to hold back, and I even suggested that I be allowed to go in as an advance party with four or five others. I was sure that I could keep us hidden from detection and do some damage from the inside as the main attacked began outside.

I had grabbed a slice of toast and rested my elbows on the table as we talked about it.

"I just don't like the idea of you being in the middle of it," Trey said. "It's not that you aren't capable, but it doesn't look to me as if you've been trained to do that type of work."

I said nothing. I simply stared at him and casually bit into my toast.

"I understand she's family," he asserted.

I stared and chewed.

"This can't be easy for you, I know that." He took a deep breath and sighed as he put down his fork. "Valerie…" He scrubbed a hand through that silky short blonde hair. The thought of touching him made me tingle, but I sat, unmoving. Staring and taking another bite of my toast.

"Would you consider staying back if I dedicated a team just to her rescue?" he asked. "Maybe you could do something for them remotely?"

I stared and took the last bite of my toast.

"Okay." He blew out a harsh breath and leaned back into his chair. "I'll give you three men, but you listen to Terrence and follow his orders. Communicate with him. Get some practice with maneuvers and hand signals. He'll pick the other two for your team."

I swallowed my toast and leaned over to him. He met me halfway, and I kissed him tenderly.

I loved him in a way that I could feel all the way to my bones.

If I could get my way by saying nothing and staring him down, I was all for it.

Oh my god, I stared down Trey. I didn't let it show, but I tucked that away in my fledgling arsenal of how to deal with an alpha shifter.

I didn't have much to do until the nightly meeting with Erick, so I caught up with Mila and found Gabrielle's work space. It hadn't been warded past some basic protection. I found it clean, neat, orderly, and well stocked.

In other words, score!

I whipped up pain amulets for both were-creatures and shifters and a dozen or so protective charms that would help deflect a direct assault. Instead of a bullet hitting you square in the chest, it might hit your shoulder. For things with less velocity, it worked even better.

I couldn't do much more than fifteen though. It involved having to bend the space around a person. That took a lot of energy to create and attach to a small wooden disk. Energy I'd used last night—in bed.

See? It is all Trey's fault. And the sooner he got used to that idea, the better. I had gotten the space cleaned up and the remaining ingredients put away. I had put my head down on the table and had lulled myself into a nap with the thoughts of how I fell asleep last night and finding Trey's head between my thighs this morning as a wake-up call.

He said it was a dragon thing.

That was an out-and-out lie, but I really couldn't complain because I really enjoyed it.

I could feel the warmth of those memories suffusing my body. I may have broken out into a light sweat as well. A smile eased over my lips, and I may have groaned.

"Are you always horny?" I managed not to jump. I hadn't even heard Andy come down the hall, let alone open the door. My thoughts of Trey were as distracting as the man himself. I could live with that.

I smiled.

"Yup," I answered, lifting my head from the table and turning to face the were-tiger. My thigh still tingled. "Whatcha need?"

"I heard you were making pain amulets for Mila." He hesitated as if suddenly unsure of himself. A fortifying breath later, he continued, "Could you do a locator spell for me?"

He wasn't comfortable asking, but again the last witch made a lasting impression, and I would have to get through their distrust.

"Who do you need to find?" I fully pushed my body off the table and sat upright in the chair.

"My brother," he replied as he seated himself on the table my head had just vacated. "He's been missing for three months. He was last seen in Northern California. Redding."

"Sure." I could do that for him. It was a small thing, and I got the ingredients together in fifteen minutes. Andy retrieved a brush that his brother had used. It still had his hair on it. Very personal, very connected and a great focus object for location, and many other spells.

Within thirty minutes, I had a map of the United States out along with individual maps of all fifty states, plus Canada and Mexico. Oh yes. Gabrielle's supplies were very nice.

The pendulum I had was rutilated quartz. It was a rough two-inch single terminated point and hung from a twelve-inch silver chain with a silver ring on the end. I threaded my finger though the ring, laced my fingers together, set my elbows on either coast of the big map, and waited.

I waited for my breath to find its pace, my heart to slow down, and my mind to relax. It took less than thirty seconds.

My hands hovered over the Midwest, but the tug of the spell on the pendulum brought the point down to Northern Oregon. It was in the middle of nothing. Between towns and in the mountains.

"That's where he is." I sat up and pointed to the area on the map as Andy leaned in and looked hard enough to burn a hole through the paper.

"Is he okay?" Andy asked. I heard the hesitance in his voice. He was seriously frightened for his brother's safety.

"All I can tell you is that he is alive," I said. "Otherwise, I wouldn't have been able to get anything from him this easily."

"Is there anyway to be more exact? Maybe find out what's going on with him?" Now Andy's eyes were burning a hole through me. I have to tell you, it was really uncomfortable.

"Yes. But there's no way I could do this until after the current issues are resolved," I told him, and he understood that dealing with the threat took precedence. It would also knock me on my ass to do it. The amount of energy I'd have to run through me would leave me in recovery for a day or two.

I would have to make arrangements with Trey.

The thought of still needing somebody rankled just the slightest.

Shouldn't I just be able to dip into the energy of earth or fire and use it?

Why did it always leave me weakened?

Maybe it was a vampire thing? If it was, I didn't like it.

I was going to start a notepad of commitments and projects soon if the requests kept up. Some I could do on the spot, like the locator spell. Others would take more time and preparation, so I was going to have to stay organized.

The thought lightened my heart. I was going to help the Enclave long after the situation with the infectious magic was resolved.

This was mine. I would negotiate. I would receive compensation. My magic. My knowledge. My intelligence. My place here with these people and Trey.

I think I needed another job description though. What were my responsibilities? What I had done for Mila and Andy, did that fall into the job description? Or was it on me?

Andy had left with the answer he came in for, but he was no less worried for his brother. I wouldn't be terribly surprised if he took off tonight and headed out toward Oregon. I hoped he didn't. There were still too many questions. Which left too much room for error. I liked Andy and didn't want to see him hurt, and going off half-cocked could get him worse than hurt.

I hadn't realized that I'd returned to napping until somebody knocked…on the table, my head rested on.

I don't think I'm getting enough sleep.

CHAPTER TWENTY

"People are going to die."

What struck me first were his eyes. Large dark chocolate brown orbs. Sinfully deep and soulful. He stood slightly shorter than I and probably outweighed me by seventy-five pounds of pure muscle. His skin had a golden sheen, and his T-shirt strained around his mass. It had become obvious to me that shifters didn't know how to order the correct size shirts for themselves. They were always just a tad too tight. Always outlining every curve and ripple of their magnificent physiques.

Never mind. Tight was good.

"Is this your idea of alert?" he rumbled in a low, gravelly voice. It was sexy as hell, and so was he. Standing in a classic defensive stance with his arms crossed over his chest, legs slightly spread, and his weight evenly balanced between his feet.

"Nope," I said as I sat upright and glanced at the clock just beyond his body mass. I had been asleep for thirty minutes, give or take. "It's my idea of a nap." And it hadn't been long enough.

"You're suppose to train with me today." He sounded annoyed, but he was a shifter, so that was par for the course. I couldn't wait to see rude, obnoxious, and arrogant. I was sure Trey could do those much better, but it's nice to be able to compare and contrast. "You're late."

"You're early," I countered. There had been no set time. I hadn't even had a chance to contact him. What with my napping and such. "But since you're here, I guess I could tear myself away from my work."

He looked at me as if I'd lost my mind.

His arms dropped to his side, and he backed up a step as I rose from the seat.

"You were asleep," he commented.

"That, and I was checking my eyelids for light leaks." I strode by him and headed for the door leaving the shifter glowering at me. "You coming?" I asked as I waited in the hallway for him.

He met me in the hallway, and we both simply stared at each other for a long moment. He was sizing me up. His gaze drifted up and then down and then up very slowly.

The look on his face told me he wasn't sure he liked what he saw. The bulge in his pants said differently.

"I take it you're Terrence," I said neutrally.

He nodded and headed down the hall. I shook my head and followed behind him.

He introduced me to the team. Cynthia and Lance both had the same basic look as Terrence, so whatever type of shifter he was, they all were. I was betting on mountain lion. Shorter than most feline shifters, but still powerful and deadly.

He ran us through drills after a tutorial on hand signals, and I came out of it no worse for wear. A few bruises, but I gave as good as I got and stood my ground at every turn.

By the end of the session, I knew that I had won points for not putting up with their shit, but still respecting them for the knowledge and training they had that I didn't.

Trey would have killed them if they had outright attacked me, but I knew that they were testing me. I could deal with that, and I wondered if I would be outright challenged. I stopped to think and wondered if being his mate equated being the female alpha or if that was a different position.

I hadn't heard about any other alphas in the Enclave, but I was hoping that Trey would be filling in the blanks for me soon.

I made my way back to Trey's suite. Our suite? Everything just happened so fast. Marc seemed like a lifetime ago. My uncertainty and fears were fading fast. Even my worries about Erick were dimming. He had seemed taken with the idea of Trey and me. Hell, for him it could open up a lot of possibilities. Especially if he could see his way clear to not be an ass toward me.

I took a shower. It was short because I was alone. I sighed and threw on shorts and a T-shirt and climbed on top of the bed. I could smell Trey on the pillow as I curled my body around it and let myself drift off.

We were gearing up for the attack on the base tonight, well early morning at least, and there were still several hours before our last meeting. Being well rested seemed like a good idea.

I was roused as I felt warmth curled around my back and somebody fiddling with the zipper on my shorts.

"I was hoping to get a bit further before you woke." Trey nuzzled my neck and became much less cautious with the zipper. "I liked the way I woke you earlier."

I rolled over and helped him remove what little clothing I had on. His came off just as quickly.

"Yes. Well, being naked and exhausted made me an easier target this morning," I replied lazily.

"You met with Terrence?" Trey asked quietly. I could hear the anxiety in his voice as his breath slid across my cheek just before his kiss.

"Yeah," I sighed. "We'll be fine for this. I've got a good feeling about it." Also, knowing that my aunt would do what she could from the inside gave me that much more confidence.

"The regular patrols will go out as if nothing is different. The attack troops will filter out over the course of two hours and find their positions." His arms tightened around my body and pulled me on top of his. "You'll go in first." The words seemed to stick on his throat. He was hating this. Me going in first with three others and trying to negotiate our way into the holding area without being seen, caught, or killed wasn't a popular thought in Trey's mind.

"You will have thirty minutes, unless it's obvious that you and the team have started some shit before then."

"Okay," I said softly. The steady beat of his heart was as soothing as was the warmth of his body underneath me. "If I somehow manage to sabotage the wards before you use the first batch of globes, then they can be used on any other static magic in place to varying degrees of success."

I felt him nod slightly. I straddled his waist and propped myself on my elbows. His hands glided down my back and caressed my ass. He tried to soften his expression, but he met with limited success. I'd almost say he was scared, but I rather doubted anything truly frightened Trey.

"We'll be fine, Trey." I ran my fingers through his hair. He took in a deep scenting breath and stretched himself underneath me. His arms encircled me in a firm embrace.

"I would like to complete the claiming," he announced quietly as his lips covered mine. I loved the way Trey kissed. Not just the soft, gentle touches he gives me often, but the hard claiming and possessing of my lips with his. The kisses that leave my lips slightly swollen, bruised with passion, and in this case, meant to insure I don't have a chance to ask questions or shoot him down.

Normally, it would work. This wasn't normal.

I broke the kiss and immediately missed his taste.

"After." That was all I said before I dove in and tasted him some more. Our tongues met and danced. Our heat rose a few more degrees.

"Now," he managed. I could feel the hard length of him pushing at me. His hands were maneuvering me into a favorable position.

"No," I breathed the word rather than said it. My injuries had faded a bit more since last night. The light bruises were gone, the black eye was my least favorite shading of bruise, and my formerly broken fingers simply ached. "After."

My body ached for him, and the flexing and releasing of my lower muscles let me know how ready I was to take him inside of me. He nipped my lips and my chin and traced kisses across my jaw as he began to press inside of me. His hips rose and fell gently as his hands softly pushed and pulled my body over him.

It was exquisite. He was exquisite.

This was a slow, methodical game of inches; and with him, that could take a while.

He held me fast, preventing me from sitting back and driving myself down his length. I think I actually whimpered.

"You're my mate." His voice thick with wanting was barely discernible over our breathing.

"Yes," I breathed and then lost my breath as he drove himself to the hilt.

My back arched. My head thrown back, and I felt fangs graze my throat.

That delicious warmth begin its journey through my body. Every thrust pushed me closer to the edge. Dragon claws pierced the flesh of my hips. The pain quickly faded as the endorphins and the need to climax took hold.

"I am yours." The growl was low and almost inhuman. Trey had partially shifted. I'd figured it out a couple minutes ago. I didn't care. This was Trey. This was the man I loved, and he was getting ready to claim me as his mate.

I wanted this. I had accepted this. But I'd wanted to go into this fight without any disabilities. Like an injured shoulder. I wouldn't be healed until tomorrow or the next day.

"Yes." I wasn't sure I'd said that out loud. There was nothing but the feel of slick heat, desperate movements, and the bone-deep need for completion.

"Claim me," he growled as his thrusts grew faster and more fierce.

I was beyond speech, but I still had a spark of self-preservation and shook my head. I wanted him. I wanted this. I needed to be able to function fully when the time came. I also didn't want to think about how much more it would hurt if something happened to Trey in the battle to come. My heart would be ripped from my chest instead of simply being crushed where it rested.

The room spun for just a moment, and it took a heartbeat to realize that I was now on my back. Trey paused long enough to scoop my legs up, so that they rested in the crook of his elbows. My hips shifted up, and everything that Trey and I were separately, merged. This was the perfect time to claim each other. We were on the edge, holding on by a thread and at the same time trying to break it so we could fall.

His arms kept my body open wide to his relentless rhythm. I looked into his eyes. His face wore an expression of desire and agony. The need to come kept his body taut, hard, and pushing me to orgasm. He needed to feel my body pulsing around him, milking him. He needed to watch me let go in the throes of release.

Trey too knew the perfection of this moment, but he could feel my holding back from taking this from incredible lovemaking to a claiming.

When we claimed each other, there could be no holding back, no reservations, and no hesitation.

His features were shifting back to fully human as his head dipped to catch my breast with his lips. His tongue teased, his teeth nipped and pulled, and he pushed me over the edge and into invoking a divine presence.

"Oh God!"

I'm not really sure how articulate I was, but I was making noise as Trey held my body tightly under his and wrung every last moment of heaven from me before his release took him over.

He dropped my legs, and my body bore his weight as he shuddered and roared and buried his face into the pillow and my hair next to me.

Heavy breathing was all that existed for a long moment after.

Trey eased up to his elbows, creating a shadow of the climax we had experienced. We both flinched with the pleasure. His eyes were closed for a few moments until our breathing returned to normal. I watched his face as he worked to regain control of himself. The only thing that bothered me was the deep working of the muscles in his jaw. I only saw that when he was angry or really frustrated.

Since I had effectively stopped him from claiming me in the middle of making love to me, I figured that was the reason. Then again, I seemed to be a regular reason for his jaw to get a daily workout.

The full weight of his body kept me effectively pinned. I could have thrown him off, but honestly, I loved the warmth and closeness of him.

I ran my fingers through his sandy blonde hair and let the recent memories wash over me. My lower muscles clenched in response. Since Trey was still in me and still hard, he was aware of my state of mind and body. He growled low in his throat and opened his eyes.

They burned hot.

"Wrap your legs around me, woman," he growled. His body gave mine just enough quarter to be able to do so. There was too much in his eyes and his voice to truly know what he was thinking or feeling, but I was slightly wary. "Why do you resist the claiming?"

Trey took up a gentle rhythm, rocking over me as he spoke.

"Why do you do this and then try to engage me in a conversation?" My breathing was already off. The slow languid dragging of his body over mine had me halfway to another orgasm in seconds.

He laid a gentle kiss to the corner of my mouth. "Answer me." I turned and tried to kiss him, but he moved just out of range. "Answer me," he repeated in a soft, low growl that vibrated throughout my entire body.

"I don't want to hurt," I whispered. Goddess mother of us all, I was going to black out. He had pinned my hands over my head and was gently nipping at my jaw and throat as he slowly pushed me to the edge.

"You are not squeamish, mate," he said with a disbelieving growl as he nipped my neck tenderly. I arched into him hard. I was so close. A few more strokes…

He shifted his weight, keeping me just out of reach of my release. He was a cruel, cruel beast! But he was a talented beast, and I just couldn't work up a good mad over the fact that he was using my body as a weapon against me to get information.

He could have just asked. He didn't have to go to these lengths. Trey shifted his body again, and I was edging toward release once more.

"Do you want the claiming?" he whispered in my ear just before tugging on my earlobe with his teeth.

That was it. My legs pulled hard on his body. I tried to wrestle my hands from grip so that I could hold him as I came. His grip tightened, so the answer to my silent desire was no.

His pace increased, and I felt his fangs graze my throat once more. My body writhed beneath him as I worked to get closer, but at the same time to get away. It was intense, almost too intense to bear.

I felt tears tracking from my eyes into my hairline.

"Tomorrow!" I screamed. "God. Yes, Trey! Please, tomorrow." I was nearly sobbing as Trey unleashed his own desires and tumbled into release right after me.

When I came to—and yes, I think I did black out for a moment—Trey had rolled off me and pulled my body tightly against his side.

My leg was thrown over his hips, and he had one of my hands wrapped in his. His other hand rested on my shoulder as his arm circled my back. When he felt me stir, he brought my fingertips to his lips and kissed them gently.

"Trey?" I mumbled, having barely opened one eye at that point. "Ummm."

"If you ever use that as an interrogation technique on anybody but me, I will kill you in your sleep."

A deep rumbling laugh shook me as I lay on his chest.

"I'm not kidding." I was trying to sound serious. I would have given him state secrets if he hadn't pushed me into orgasm soon. It was both amazing and torturous. His cruelty knows no bounds as far as I'm concerned.

He laughed harder, kissed my fingertips again, and hugged me tightly against him for a moment before relaxing into a familiar ease.

"I still didn't get the information I was looking for," he reminded me. "Why do you want to wait?"

I managed to lift my head and roll back enough to look into his eye and take in his face. The hard planes and angles I'd thought he wore were so much softer now.

He could be hard and harsh. His position in the Enclave, the immense responsibilities would make it difficult to live a life that didn't require making life and death decisions. It showed.

Right now, we were in an oasis smack in the middle of life-or-death decisions. I was lucky to see him at ease, relaxed, and contented, and I was soaking it up for all it was worth.

I took a deep breath and steadied myself to speak a truth that I just didn't want to deal with, but his question required an answer, and an honest one was what he deserved.

"In the next few hours, a lot is going to happen," I started. "People are going to die," I hesitated. I just didn't want to give my fears a voice. This made it all too real of a possibility, and my heart couldn't take that kind of loss. "If anything happened to you…" I felt like a coward, but I just couldn't bring myself to say it out loud. At least I wasn't tearing up. "I just want to wait until tomorrow. It will be an all-round celebration. The dark magic will be destroyed, I'll have my aunt back, the clan master can drag his happy ass back to Los Angeles, and we can spend several days going at each other with wild abandon and no battles in the near future."

Trey looked thoughtful and pensive even before he nodded. "Okay," he said. He didn't look angry, disappointed, frustrated, or upset. He understood probably more than I could guess. I shifted my body enough to reach his lips and discovered three things.

First, my hips were sticking to the sheets, both top and bottom. Second, my hips stung, and third, Trey was still hard.

I flinched. Not only because I remembered that Trey had dug his claws into my hips to hold me still and had probably bled, but there was no way I could go a third round with Trey and be able to function for my mission. As it was, I was pushing it.

I peeled the sheet down and found that I was, indeed, bloodied and drying to the sheets.

"Don't move," Trey said calmly. It almost sounded like an order, but I'm pretty sure he was stunned. He had barely held on by the skin of his teeth, so I wasn't surprised that his partial shifts had left a mark or two or three holes on each hip.

Trey came out from the bathroom with a bowl of hot water, several cloths, and a towel. He was also still hard. I had to gawk. It was magnificent and seemed to utterly defy gravity. The man had sexed me up for over a half hour and came twice himself, and he was showing no signs of tiring. Well, at least, his dragon thing was showing no signs.

"Aren't you supposed to call a doctor if an erection last more than four hours?" I said as Trey set his supplies down and sat down next to me.

He gave me an unhappy look and went to work cleaning the hip he could get to since I was still laying on my side.

"Why didn't you tell me?" he asked as the hot water cleaned and soothed the injury.

"I sort of figured you'd notice that you have been sporting wood for the last thirty minutes or so." I threw a smile over my shoulder, but there was something more serious in his features.

He kept working on my hip as he spoke. "You are my mate. I know that. The dragon that I am knows that." I simply nodded. "As far as the dragon is concerned, there is no reason to delay. And in order to claim you properly and completely, we must be having sex." I nodded again, waiting for him to give information I didn't have so that this would make sense. "The dragon is waiting and not patiently, I might add."

I cocked my head, and I knew I looked slightly puzzled until the answer hit me.

"Oh my god. You mean you are perpetually hard waiting…" Trey cut me off as he dabbed some ointment on the puncture marks. They weren't large or deep, but they were effective.

"Yes. I am holding back every bit of the base instinct to claim my mate, to mark her, and to let everybody know she is mine." He motioned for me to roll over. I did so very carefully. The sheet was sticking to the injury, and we were trying not to make it worse. I was also trying not to laugh. I couldn't imagine how uncomfortable Trey was. Even after back-to-back orgasms, the man was still carrying lead.

"I'm so sorry, Trey." With all my heart, I felt for him, but not enough to give in.

"Just know that the longer we wait, the harder it will be." He focused on the injury and washed it clean. The water was cooling, but I hadn't really noticed much.

"You couldn't get any harder than you already are, Trey." It was an observation. Plain and simple.

"That's not what I mean." Trey's eyes burned behind the blue, and I saw tension creeping into his shoulders. I was beginning to realize the strain he was under, and now here he was tending me as I lay naked in front of him.

It had to be killing him.

"Valerie, I've never claimed a mate successfully, but I've seen it, and I've heard stories." He dried my hip and spread the ointment. He got his supplies off the bed, and I rose. Together we stripped the bed. "It can be a brutal act and bloody."

"What do you mean?" I asked. Bloody and brutal did not sound like my idea of a good time.

"When two dragons mate, the female is usually fighting back. The male has to subdue her or die trying to mate with her." We tossed the sheets into a corner and pulled out a fresh set. "I am at the end of my control."

"But I'm not a dragon, and I have no intention of fighting you or trying to kill you." We began making the bed. "Again," I added.

Trey smiled and shook his head as we finished the bed.

"I don't know if it will matter. I don't have any information about human/dragon mating." Trey called to the kitchen and arranged for food to be sent up.

"Don't you have anybody you can ask?" I threw his robe on and sat in the plush chair in the sitting area of the suite. "This can't be the first time this has happened."

The hesitation and the tension in his body screamed that there was something wrong, and he was not sure he wanted to share it with me. I knew how he felt, and I hadn't come out and told him.

"Trey," I said as he threw on some shorts and wrestled mentally with himself. "If I had let you claim me tonight and you were killed, I don't think I'd could survive that kind of loss after having established a connection like this." I took a deep breath and tried to relax into the chair as Trey expression softened. "I also don't know what kind of damage you are likely to do to my shoulder, and I have to function."

There it was. I put it all out there for him. I was open, honest, and hoping that it would encourage him to do the same.

"I haven't had any interactions with my kind in several hundred years. I don't have anybody I can turn to and ask questions of." He walked to the sitting area and knelt in front of me. I reached out and brushed the back of hand across his cheek and smiled.

Trey is certainly the strongest being I've met, and right now, he was vulnerable and uncertain. I didn't think I could have love him any more than I had a minute ago. I was wrong.

"The few stories I'd heard about human/dragon matings weren't matings." He caught my hand and kissed my palm as something painful crossed his features. "Male dragons are fertile for about two weeks, twice a year. It is nearly unbearable to have no mate during this time. I tried to mate once. It was unsuccessful, and I barely escaped with my life." He swallowed hard and laid his head in my lap and kept my hand pressed to his cheek.

"Some of my kind find it impossible to make it through those times, and they will hunt for easier prey to mate with. They will shift into human form and rape..." He faltered.

My free hand stroked his hair tenderly, and his brushed against my hip.

"I don't want to hurt you, Valerie." He sighed. "I become fertile next month. Making love to you these past few days has eased me a great deal until now." He glanced up and kissed my palm once more.

"Now," I began for him as I looked into his pained eyes and continued to stroke his hair. "You're feeling the onset of becoming fertile, you have a mate in your grasp, and she won't let you claim her, and you have nowhere to turn for advice. A perfect storm."

He snorted softly as a rueful grin crossed his lips.

CHAPTER TWENTY-ONE

"Breathing can be a serious handicap."

We managed to make it through dinner together, but we decided that I wouldn't attend the briefing. It would be unseemly for Trey to strip off my clothing, throw me across his desk, and claim me with an audience that would include my father.

Of course the idea of being bent over his desk was an attractive one, and we would explore that at length at a later date.

Instead we went over the plans as we ate.

All of the teams would be set at 2:00 am. There were eight wards; a two-man team was assigned to each ward. Each team would carry four globes to the ward. One or two globes should be enough to destroy the wards, and the teams would head into the base from the nearest access tunnel. Of those, there were four, and one had been collapsed.

Three-man teams would go in from the tunnels and make their ways into the labs, the holding areas and personal quarters. Everyone had tranquilizer guns and counter spell globes.

Even though we were sure there wouldn't be more than thirty or forty captives opposing us, we wanted to outnumber them as steeply as possible.

The fewer dead, the better.

I met up with Terrence and the rest of the team, and we were in position within twenty minutes. We all had pouches that contained globes for the various jobs. On the one hand, I hoped we had enough; and on the other, I hoped we didn't need what we did have.

With a deep breath, I encased us in the energy I had infused some of the globes with, and we walked through the ward tripping nothing as we went.

I knew it had been successful because we were alive, and I felt the deep pull of the death that should have been ours tug on my chest.

Once we were well away from the green haze that marked the base's protective warding, I stopped and dropped to my knees, trying desperately not to cough up a lung.

By the time I had it under control, Terrence was looking concerned, Lance looked annoyed, and Cynthia, well, I don't think she liked me to begin with, so this didn't help.

"We need to get going," Lance commented. "The noise isn't going to help us here."

I pushed to my feet and leaned momentarily against the tunnel wall.

"I got us through alive, asshole." My voice was still rough, but I was ready to go. "Next time you go in first."

Terrence brought up the rear, my rear to be exact. I was the least experienced in the group and therefore the most vulnerable, and the most dangerous for the team. Cynthia was in the lead scouting ahead, and Lance was ten feet behind her and fifteen feet in front of me.

So far, we hadn't run into anything as we made our way into the roughly carved out base. So either we were good to go, or it was an ambush.

The tunnels were rough cut through desert rock and angled at a gentle slope. A small sphere glowed blue every fifty feet or so for lighting. There wasn't much that could see in absolute darkness, so the little light that was cast was more than enough for vamps, weres, and shifters that inhabited the base. I wondered what the witches did for their lighting when they were traveling in the tunnels. They were likely full human, and the little lighting wouldn't be enough for them, but it was lovely.

The lighting was a soft, beautiful magic that took little energy and would continue even after the caster died. Something like this would burn itself out in a decade or so.

At every cross tunnel, the signal came back to stop and take a knee. Getting low to the ground, but ready to move quickly. Terrence kept a eye on our rear, and I kept my magic reined in. We had a map, we had a plan, and I didn't want to trip an alarm by being too outgoing with the energy.

Fifteen minutes inside was when we found what looked like a roving patrol. An interesting note in the difference between darting and the counter spell globe was, with the globe there was no unconsciousness, no pain, no down time.

The dark magic simply ceased to be, and the victims were now operational and on our side.

Our new team members led us to the security office where I could eliminate the wards, and our team grew by three more.

I wasn't going to get over enthusiastic about how our odds just shot up, but this was feeling better and better.

Lance stayed back at the security office with a ward destroying globe and two of the newly converted. The rest headed to the edge of the warded area in the tunnel to wait, and Terrence, Cynthia, and myself found our way into the holding cells and my aunt.

As Terrence and Cynthia released the captives, I knelt beside my aunt. She was wan and gaunt. Her skin was sallow, her eyes held no sparkle, and the gold rings were almost imperceptible.

She was being drained and had been used nearly to the point of death.

She looked like a great-grandmother, not the youngest aunt. I wondered if she would survive once we got her out of here. I wondered if she could survive being moved at all.

"You are an amazing woman, my niece," she rasped.

"I had amazing teachers," I whispered so my voice wouldn't crack. I took her hand in mine. She was so fragile I feared the lightest touch would turn her bones to dust.

I closed my eyes for a moment. I needed to know if she still held any energetic connection to those who had done this to her. I found none.

There was barely enough energy to keep her alive. I was surprised they hadn't drained her completely.

"My beautiful niece." Her dull eyes took me as much as she could. I saw regret. "What I've done, the lives I've cost… for nothing."

"Shh." I tried to soothe her. I could feel Terrence behind me. We needed to get out, and now wasn't the time for a family reunion. I knew that, but I didn't trust that she would survive the trip out. I might never have another chance to talk to her again. But I had to risk it. "We are getting out of here. We'll talk later." I paused for just a breath. "I love you, Aunt Maggie," I whispered just before I slipped her one of my pain amulets and left her side.

Terrence moved in and scooped up my aunt, blankets and all. It looked as if she weighed nothing in his arms. When my eyes moved from her to him, the look he gave was grave. She was wasting away.

I needed to keep my cool. I truly wanted to do some damage to whomever had used and hurt my aunt. I thought about splitting off and searching on my own. We had less than ten minutes before the globes hit the main security panel and things got way more dicey than they already were.

I caught up with Terrence who looked almost terrified to be carrying such a fragile package. I don't think he had expected to find her, let alone be responsible for her transportation. I thought he was holding up well.

I couldn't have managed it. Every step would have reminded me of how close to death my aunt was. I just had to hope that Mila could help her.

I stopped at the security office as Terrence went on. I was counting down until I knew that my aunt was safely away before I went after the security board.

"You found her?" Lance looked relieved when I crept back into the office and told him where we were in our mission.

He was pleased, but I think he had been secretly wishing he could have mixed it up a bit more. All in all, this whole thing couldn't have gone better. More of Trey's people were getting out. The few full humans Terrence and Cynthia had found were in halfway descent shape and could move on their own; the vampires were healthy and not depleted. Who could ask for more?

As the time came to smash the globes against the panel, my heart lightened. The only real problem would be dealing with the four witches who were in the base and had yet to be seen.

The darts would take them out as quickly as anything else, but the tranquilizing effects were short lived. I had a feeling that Trey's orders were "kill first." I couldn't blame him after what they had done.

It was time, and I had a smile on my face. I had found my aunt, the wards were going to come down in a minute, there were few troops left in the control of the witches to get in the way, and soon

Trey and I would be in throes of claiming each other and probably not seeing light for several days.

I never asked myself "what could go wrong?" It is always the kiss of death, a raspberry to Murphy's laws and a finger to the fates. That's why I just don't ask. Ever.

That doesn't mean I don't let myself relax when I shouldn't. It doesn't mean that I don't get careless. It doesn't mean I shouldn't have thoroughly searched the office and the panel before I hit the panel with a globe.

As I smashed the globe against the panel and the sickly green of the fatal wards began to shimmer light blue and white as the bite began to drain out of them, I smelled something burning. It was faint, it was small, and it just wasn't right.

I dropped to my knees and looked under the desk in time to see a small charge of C-4 explosive set to blow.

I didn't know I could outrun a were-mountain lion, but I pulled ahead just as the charge went off.

Half of the tunnel collapsed, and Lance was caught in the tumble of rocks. I managed to extricate him fairly quickly, and he was lucky that nothing big landed on him.

We began to move again as another charge on the other side of an intersection blew, cutting us off from our original escape route.

That was okay. We had several, and we quickly chose the next closest and headed out.

As we made our way, we could hear back-to-back explosions and could feel the base shake and rumble as we continued to make our way through the tunnels and if we had good intelligence, toward freedom.

Dust and small rocks rained intermittently down as we continued at a pace that I would describe as seriously motivated.

I tried to reach out with my other senses to get a feel for any pattern in the explosions, but moving like we were and trying to direct my magic had never been compatible. I'm thinking that practicing and making that happen would give me a huge advantage in a running battle.

I just never thought I'd be having a running battle with a fortress that was collapsing around me.

The air became thicker and heavier with dust. I was pretty sure that our current way out was no longer viable. The dust was my first clue; the fall of rocks was my second.

We turned tail and headed back to the last intersection and turned left.

"Is there any way to do a witchy thing and feel if the tunnels are open or not?" Lance asked. It was valid and a really good idea that could save us time. I explained that the tunnels have an intention, and that intention will still be present whether it's collapsed or not. It would still feel like a tunnel until enough time passed that the energy dissipated.

Lance snorted. It was either because he had dust up his nose, or he found me useless. I think it was the latter. Fuck him, let's see him do any better.

I stayed a few paces behind him and followed his lead. Lance had spent more time with the maps than me, and I trusted him to lead us into more options, not fewer. As we passed through a rather large intersection, another explosion rocked us. This time it took out the intersection we were crossing.

I backpedaled as Lance tumbled forward, and the rockfall effectively separated us. I couldn't be sure he hadn't been buried anymore than he could know what may have happened to me. But what I suspected was that I was on my own.

I yelled to Lance in hopes that maybe the fall wasn't as bad as it looked and heard nothing but the continued gentle rainfall of dust and stone as the collapse settled in front of me.

I coughed some of the dust from my lungs as I climbed the few feet up the slope of rock and dirt to see if I could dig through.

Before I could make any headway, something grabbed me and tossed back into the hallway, just as another significant segment of ceiling collapsed where I had been standing.

"How is it that you walk into an unstable area without thinking?" Marc was standing over me, arms crossed looking entirely too self-important. "I've kept you alive for five years and tried to teach you some things about self-preservation, and you completely ignore them."

I got to my feet and dusted myself off, never taking my eyes off him. I was pretty sure he hadn't forgotten our last encounter, and I didn't think he would take it all that well.

"I don't completely ignore them," I said calmly. "And thanks for yanking my ass out of there." See I can be gracious. Even to Marc. "Any idea which way is out?" I asked.

Marc rolled his eyes and reached for me. It wasn't an attack, just a "let me take you by the arm and lead your stupid ass out of here" move. I don't think so. I pulled just out of reach.

"A simple yes or no would suffice, Marc."

He pointed to the tunnel opposite from which Lance and I tried and headed out.

"Do you know if Lance can make it out from where he is?" I asked as we picked up the pace.

Marc glanced over at me as a sneer crossed his lips. I had no idea why Marc personally had issues with the shifters and weres, but vamps and the two-natured community didn't get along for reasons that were steeped in history that existed before recorded times.

I didn't have a problem with them, besides not knowing many and knowing that they could be brutal, ruthless, and violent. Now that I put it that way, I guess they aren't much different than vampires. They just scare me more.

"Don't know. Don't care," Marc said calmly as he sped up some more. "Keep up."

The thing about running with a vampire is that he doesn't actually need to breathe. Me? Breathing is necessary, and the vast majority of the air down here was filled with particulate matter that didn't mesh well with my lung tissue.

I started coughing.

"Breathing can be a serious handicap," Marc said over his shoulder as he sped up a little more.

"So is being an asshole, and it doesn't stop you any," I replied and kept his pace. "What are you doing down here anyway?" I asked as we made our way through what I thought was the other side of the base from where we started, and I think we had drifted up some.

"Erick sent me. Once he found out your weren't in the Enclave, he was royally pissed." The tunnel had opened into a cavern. Like the rest of the base, it was a large hole roughly cut from the rock. Chains were fixed to the walls and floor. As I looked up, I took in the chains that dangled twenty feet overhead.

A decomposing corpse was the only resident present, and it sat still chained in the corner. The empty sockets stared at us as bits of flesh tried to hold on to a skull that had been caved in on one side.

Marc barely glanced at it as we passed through the expanse. I would never forget it and would hope to find out who it had been. It hadn't been a vampire; there was too much to it. But it didn't look human, so it was likely were or shifter. The identifying scent was too degraded, and I couldn't parse it out from the smell of death and decay.

I did a short energetic survey of the area for infection, and finding none, I caught up with Marc.

"You will always be too soft when it counts, Val," Marc commented truthfully. I would be sensitive to things like death and destruction. Nobody should suffer needlessly, and yes, I did believe that sometimes suffering was appropriate. But I doubted that whoever that was had deserved it. So I flipped Marc the bird and kept going.

I could tell we were getting close to the surface. It's a vampire thing. One of the many vampire things I had going for me. As we rounded a bend in the tunnel, I saw the glimmer of a fine piece of obscuring magic clinging to the wall.

I slowed and called to Marc as I stood to the far edge of it and looked at the seamlessness of the work. It was beautifully done, and it wasn't my aunt's work. It ran floor to ceiling and spanned fifteen feet across.

My magic pressed against it for only a moment before Marc grabbed and dragged me bodily from the wall.

"Damn it, Valerie!" he hissed. "Self-preservation! Work on it!"

He didn't have to pull hard to get me to move because he was right. It was likely that the witches were behind the magic I'd seen. I mean, literally.

"This place is coming down around us, and you want to check out the scenery," Marc said as he continued working his way through the tunnel.

"No, it's not," I said quietly. "This area is stable. The witches are back there. Safe." I slowed my pace as my brain churned the last half hour or so. "Have the labs been destroyed? Have the origins of the infection been destroyed? Do we know how many shifters, weres, or vamps are still missing?"

I stopped, and Marc, pissed as all hell, stopped and rounded on me. "I will knock your dumb ass out and drag you out unconscious if you don't move!"

"We didn't run into many vampires patrolling the area, Marc. We found some, but not enough as far as I can tell." I started moving because Marc really looked like he would knock me out and enjoy doing it too. "This was too easy. I will bet you anything that those witches will simply set up somewhere else. We have to end this here, Marc."

"Then you work this from up top," he remarked. "Not down here."

We were coming around a bend when he slid to a halt. I stopped right behind him, but before I could see what the problem was, he shoved me roughly back the way we came and yelled.

"Run!"

I listened and ran—for about ten steps.

Now it was my turn to slide to a halt.

Marc grabbed hold of me and shoved my body behind his and against the tunnel wall.

I wanted to be incensed, but it drove home the reason I would never let myself fall under my father's control. I was safely tucked away. Okay, not really safe, but pulled back, not treated as an equal. I might be allowed to skate the edge of danger, but not really be allowed any closer.

There were at least six vampires, three on each side of us, and one of them was old. As young as he looked, the power he kept locked down was immense. This guy could give my father a run for his money.

He resembled a young Norse god in his strength and beauty. He had been a warrior for hundreds of years, and the cloak of humanity that vampires developed to remain secreted even when right in front of mortals was thin and unraveling fast.

It was then I realized that he was a clan master who had been enslaved to witches, and it hadn't been fun and games, I'm sure. I saw the hate in his eyes as he looked at the rings in mine and sneered. He was hoping to kill me just because I was a witch. I was guilty by association.

"Bring them to me," a woman's voice called out from behind the obscuring magic, and I couldn't see her, but I assumed she was in charge. "Alive!" she amended quickly. That did not bode well.

"Give me time," I whispered to Marc as I focused my efforts on weaving the counter spell. If I could free them all simultaneously, then we'd have a chance. Then again, with the hate I saw in the clan master's eyes, we might have only a slightly better chance.

Marc pressed me harder into the wall. He could only give me seconds. I didn't know if it would be enough.

I found and held the images I needed as I brought the energies up as quickly as I could.

"Stop her!" the unseen witch screamed.

Shit.

I pushed to finish, but the next thing I knew, Marc was gone from in front of me, and I couldn't breathe for the force that was crushing me.

My eyes flew open, and I caught sight of the ancient vampire whose power was killing me slowly. He looked entirely too pleased as I struggled to do something as simple as breathe.

"Jeremy!" the witch yelled. "Don't kill her! And bring her to me!"

His murderous eyes left mine as he half-glanced back and then succumbed to the infection and did as he was commanded.

I fell to the ground when he released me and dragged in breath after breath. He was fighting the compulsion with everything he had, and if I could break a globe, he'd be an ally, a strong one and the only one we would need in order to finish this. He was strong enough to detain every vampire and the witches. Although I figured once free, the witches were toast, and I wasn't sure that wouldn't include me as well.

He stood before me. "Get up, bitch," he growled. Yeah. Not feeling the love here, but I had to take a chance. I got to my knees and twisted my body just enough to conceal the pouch and slide my hand in. The globe fit in my palm, and I grasped it firmly.

As I came up, I brought my arm around and aimed for his chest.

When he caught my hand in his own, my heart pounded. Again, his eyes were telling me of death and painful destruction, at his hands, in the near future, if he had his way.

"She didn't say I couldn't hurt you," he hissed as he crushed the globe. And hurt me he did. Most of my fingers broke in more than one place, along with several bones in my hand, plus shards of broken globe were embedded in my palm. The up side? He was hit with counter spell as the globes contents spilled from my broken hand.

So I had been successful in a very painful way.

Jeremy's grip loosened. Unfortunately, that did nothing for my pain, and I really hated screaming, but it seemed necessary for the moment.

His hand around my throat stopped that pretty quickly though. My good hand went to his wrist. He didn't squeeze; he just stared into my eyes. I felt his energy roll through me and immobilize me at the same time.

He wasn't going to kill me. Whatever he had done had given him information that had just saved my life. But he didn't look happy about it.

The energy stopped. He gave me enough space to breathe, and without removing his gaze, he reached around me to the pouch. His hand slipped in. He grabbed several globes and flung them at the ceiling over the three men who had held Marc. A fine mist rained down on them, and they shook off the infection.

Jeremy did the same with the remaining men. They all looked at each other silently. At least I thought it was silent, but they moved together without a word.

Marc was still restrained, but not fighting. I was now in front of Jeremy. His hand wrapped around the back of my neck, guiding me back down the tunnel and toward the obscuring magic I had sensed earlier.

My shredded hand throbbed as I cradled it in my good one. I didn't look. I didn't want to see how bad it was, so I kept my eyes forward and went where I was directed.

We passed through the opening in the tunnel wall that had been hidden, and Jeremy pushed me forward. I fell to my knees and looked up at the witch who had nearly killed my aunt.

"So. You recovered," I said. The witch was in her fifties and looked a bit worse for wear. I recognized the signs of somebody who been magically attacked. I'd seen it a few times in the mirror. She was tall for a human, maybe five feet ten, and was slender. Her hair was short and a pretty mixture of black liberally streaked with gray. Deep blue eyes with a gold ring were undeniably stunning, but it wasn't going to save her life.

The other three were young, too young to die, and they looked sensibly frightened. I felt badly for them. At some point, they realized the mistake they had made, and it was too late. They could not control these beings that now surrounded them, and if they stood up to the elder witch, she could simply have them killed, or worse, they'd end up like my aunt.

"The golems were a nice bit of magic, so were your defenses." I was silently wondering why the vamps weren't moving in or doing anything, but appearing to be obedient. "Hurt like hell, but it was good practice."

She stood a solid ten feet in front of me and smiled as she cast a negligent glance at Marc and then back to me.

"You are much like your aunt, Valerie," she said smoothly.

"In some ways, yes," I said casually. "But I'd never be stupid enough to teach a sociopath magic, like she did you."

The smile fell from her face. It made her decidedly more frightening.

"Hurt her, Jeremy," she commanded with a controlled anger that came from somebody who was about to snap. "But not too much."

Before I was able to flinch, Jeremy had pulled me to my feet and held me fast all without touching me.

I knew this was the level of ancient that my father was, and he could snap me in half slowly and leave me alive, but not wanting to live at the same time.

The pressure around my abused hand increased until I felt a light sweat break out on my face. I breathed deeply through the increasing pain. The witch's smile returned to her face as the energy clamped down, and I screamed. I imagined that the glass shards had been shoved further into my hand.

I heard the quiet struggle of Marc trying to free himself from his position, but he was outnumbered. There was nothing he could do until these vampires decided to tip their hand and end this.

The energy released my hand, and the searing pain reduced to simply pain. I caught my breath and looked at the witch in charge. She was pleased with herself. I knew her breaths were limited, and I smiled.

"Knowing who should be on the top of the food chain and being willing to do something about it is strength of character," she explained carefully to me as if I were a retarded child. "Your aunt was short in her visions. She only wanted to eradicate the vampire influence from her dearest niece." She came closer to me and looked me over with an appraising eye. "She was sure that the vampire in you was limiting your magical potential."

I was stunned, but I tried not to let it show. I had no doubt that what my aunt had started was out of her love for me, but her grief and anger twisted it into something I couldn't imagine. How many had my aunt killed in her quest before her protégé took over and took it further?

If my aunt survived she would be executed for her crimes regardless of her motivations. But for now, I really wanted this part over. And Jeremy was waiting for… what?

"You were infected," she said absently as she circled me. "I can feel it. Why didn't it take?" she mumbled to herself. "The infection was developed specifically for you and yet… ?" Her thoughts and words drifted off as she lost herself for a moment.

"Probably because you fucked with it too much," I said as the pain evened out. I was still immobile, still unable to physically protect myself, and this woman could feel it if I raised any energy at all and stop me before I could get anything done.

"I have the old formulas," she mused. "We could back track and see if those work. I'm sure we would find one that would achieve the proper goals." As she came to face me once more, she gently took my chin and looked into my eyes. "You would be so much more powerful without that lower influence muddying you."

"Kicked your ass well enough," I said, breaking her from her musings.

She dropped my chin from her grip and backhanded me. With everything I had been through since this started—being nearly blown up, perforated, ill, depleted, and currently dealing with the state of my hand—the gesture was laughable.

And laugh I did.

"How dare you!" she hissed as she turned and took her place with the other witches who looked like they wanted to be anywhere but near her.

"Oh, I dare, lady," I said through my soft laughter. "I would no more wish to change the basis of who I am than you would want to go on meds and deal with that nasty little personality disorder you have going there."

"Destroy her mind, Jeremy!" the witch bellowed. "Do it slowly and painfully!" Her arms crossed and body relaxed as a smug grin lit her face. She was utterly certain that she was in control. "Your power will add to our strength with or without your consent."

Oh shit.

Jeremy stepped in front of me, blocking the witches' view and looked deeply in my eyes.

I had no idea what he would do to me. But it wouldn't be because he was compelled by any means other than self-motivation.

"Can you destroy the rest of that magic?" he whispered.

I nodded slightly and waited.

Faster than my eyes could follow, the four witches were dead.

CHAPTER TWENTY-TWO

"*I will eviscerate you!*"

They never even had the chance to scream. It was quick and, knowing what vampires are capable of, merciful.

Jeremy had also released me, and Marc was now standing by my side. Marc gently cradled my mangled hand. I still choose not to look at it. "Your body will eject the glass, but it will take time," he said quietly. "I could pull the shards out. It will hurt."

I thought back to the night at the shack and the shard of glass that had perforated my side. I had pulled it out and nearly vomited on my motorcycle. I didn't know if this was going to be worse, but I was probably going to find out. And then, I would take blood from Marc and speed the healing because this whole thing had pushed me to a new limit.

A clan master I didn't know held my life in his hands. I had gotten him out of the hell that witches had created for him and his men. It was over for him and he had been able to exact revenge on those who had done this to him and his people.

I hoped he remembered that as he saw the gold rings around the green of my eyes and knew me to be the witch I was, I had saved his ass.

Marc slipped an arm around my shoulder as I finally looked at my bloodied and disfigured hand. I didn't want to look at the carnage around me, so I focused on the carnage that was my body part.

I sighed as Marc spoke softly to me and reassured me. It seemed strange and comforting all at the same time. Marc had never let me hurt for any longer than it took to feed me his blood and move along. We were over. We had fought. I threw him off the roof of the Enclave, and we stood in an uncertain situation. My hand was mangled, and we were surrounded by six unknown vampires.

This was not a comfortable situation, but Marc's presence was helpful simply by its familiarity.

"You're going to be okay," he said softly.

I let a soft snort of laughter and looked into his dark eyes. I saw the want and regret in them. He knew it was over as well, that he had lost me, and he may see me only on the rare occasion when my path would cross with his master, and it would cross. "I've had worse, Marc."

I pulled another pain amulet out of my back pocket and gripped it tightly as the magic began to weave itself around the injury and take the top off the pain.

"I guess I knew you were tougher than I wanted to admit," he whispered as I tucked the pain amulet in my bra.

"I wish you had trained me harder than you did," I said. "It would have been less of a shock these past few days."

"I'm sorry, Val."

"Yeah, I know."

I barely registered the approach of the clan master.

"If you're finished with the touchy feely shit, the witch has a job to do," he said tersely.

"Yes, well. The witch has a name," I started.

"Like I care." He cut me off and continued, "Get to work." Marc started to say something, but I cut him off.

"Look. The job is going to take everything I've got, and the injury will interfere with my ability to make sure it is done right." I felt Marc tense as the vampires preternatural power eased from him. I buffered against it the best I could and just got a bit pissed. I could understand why he wasn't in the best of humors, really I did, but I was going to get this done, and he had contributed to this not being the best night I'd ever had. So he needed to back off and help out. "I'd appreciate it if you would help…" My knees buckled, and Marc caught me before I hit the ground. The clan master had used his power to pull the glass from my hand, and it happened too fast for my mind to completely process anything, but the spike of pain that punched through the amulet that rested against my skin.

"Fuck…," I breathed out harshly and rested in Marc's arms. "Thanks for the warning."

Marc held me tightly. "Just breathe."

I smiled at how easily Marc just fell into the way we had been. I couldn't, not really. Even though we knew each others rhythms and how we flowed in certain situations, we weren't the same and never would be again.

I straightened and stood in front of Jeremy. I took a deep breath and presented him with my still mangled hand, which was bleeding more profusely than before.

"You going to finish it, or is causing me pain the only thing you're interested in?" He was roughly my height, and I looked him squarely in the eye as his men tensed. Like I was going to attack their master. I might be foolish, but I'm not stupid.

He grabbed my wrist with one hand and nicked the thumb of his other and let a few drops of blood fall to the wreckage of my hand.

"There's always time to hurt you again later," he said.

"Take a number," I replied as the potency of this ancient vampires blood hit my system and worked its way through the injury.

I would have pulled away, but his grip remained tight, and his gaze remained on mine.

The bones knit quickly, and the deformity in my hand righted itself in seconds. I ground my teeth and breathed through the spikes of pain, breathed and never let my gaze stray from Jeremy's.

The whole process took less than thirty seconds, and it felt like eons.

"Now if you are finished whining," he said as he dropped my wrist. "Get on with it," he ordered.

I couldn't help the smirk. Marc had told me that clan masters expected to be obeyed, and this guy was no different. I assumed he knew my father, but I had no idea what terms they may be on.

"The local Enclave of the beast master is five kilometers from here. Marc can point you in the right direction," I started. Dawn was still a couple hours away, but Jeremy and his men needed to know that they would be taken care of and given a safe place to rest and make arrangements to return themselves to where ever they belonged. "Clan Master Olafson is also waiting to assist with whatever you may need."

Jeremy's eyebrow raised at the mention of the other clan master, and he looked thoughtful.

"What is the clan master to you?" he asked. The question was loaded, and I didn't know which way the gun was pointing.

"A pain in my ass," I said. "So you and your men can head out, and I'll start working on this thing," I finished and turned to Marc.

"I'm going to have to do a complete burn, not just the infection, but anything that can burn," I told him. We were huddled together, and I was talking softly. "I'll get the energetic recon done and put together a plan while you get the beast master out here." I was sure that Trey wasn't too far away, not with me inside the base and half of the place collapsing. "It will be light before I even start this." Even though the other vampires in the room could hear everything said, I just didn't feel the need to specifically share my plans with everybody. "Get them headed in the right direction, and I'll scan the area and see what I'm up against."

Marc stiffened as the clan master approached us. His power leeched softly from him. Icy blue eyes looked us over as a superior would appraise underlings. He wasn't happy with what he was seeing or rather, hearing.

"I will stay with the witch." The vampire was in master mode and issuing commands. I wasn't feeling very good about this. "You, take my men to safety." He nodded imperiously as he indicated Marc and dismissed him with no doubt that the order would be obeyed.

At this point, I realized that so far, both clan masters were the same. They were much like the rude, arrogant, obnoxious shifter I met a week ago. But he wasn't connected to me through blood and had no vested interest in my survival. I was pretty sure he didn't like me one little bit.

"There is no way in hell I'm going to trust you with my safety," I said long before my brain kicked in with the self-preservation that Marc was sure I didn't posses, and in this moment, I knew it wasn't my strong point, and I should work on it… if I survived. "And the magic I work is fire based, and you are highly flammable. You would have to trust me with your safety as well, and I'm not really feeling that between us. And as I said, it will take time to work up a plan and implement it. You will need to be in the Enclave."

"Valerie…," Marc growled a low warning.

"What?" I said, turning my attentions away from the shocked-looking clan master and to the ex-boyfriend. He looked nervous. Maybe I should have taken that as a clue. I'd likely gotten away with more shit than a clan master would tolerate from anybody in my interactions with Erick. I didn't even know who this guy was, and

I was bucking his will, authority, and demands with impunity. "He has no idea what's involved, and it's not his call, it's Trey's. This is his region."

"No." The clan master's word were soft, but the power that surged forth was not. I was in danger of losing my dinner. Marc took a shaky step in front of me. "You are right. I have no reason to trust you. I want that magic eradicated—now. And you promised to insure that."

"Clan Master." My voice cracked. I found it disconcerting, but I swallowed hard and continued. "I will destroy the magic. On my word, I will." I paused and breathed. I could feel a trembling beginning to form throughout my body.

"I have no idea what I will run into. I will assume that this place is rigged magically in ways that will endanger me and anybody with me. The beast master is better suited to deal with the situation than you are."

The energy relaxed some, but not nearly enough for my comfort. "We don't even know if everybody is out yet."

"You seem to have some authority in this place," the clan master said smoothly. "You issue orders and expect them to be obeyed." Jeremy nodded in Marc's direction, and I realized he was right. I did feel I had the right to order Marc around in this case. I had the knowledge and experience; he didn't. Crap.

"I'm not in charge of anything," I told him. "I'm just pushy." That was plausible, and I was pushy, so it was the truth.

He nodded to his men, and they gathered Marc between them and headed out.

Marc resisted and glanced in my direction. I gave him a slight shake of my head, and he made no further effort to stop the progress. Marc would find Trey or Erick, and they would be here in a matter of minutes.

Well, shit.

The clan master pulled his power in, and I found a nice place to sit. I dropped like a stone in water.

I didn't try to get up. I just found a nice comfortable sitting position so he could interrogate me at his leisure. Or torture me or whatever.

Trey will be here soon was my mantra to quell the rising panic in me. It was surprisingly effective.

"Do it," the clan master ordered.

I pulled my knees into my chest and wrapped my arms around them. I closed my eyes and took a deep breath. When my eyes opened, I flexed and clenched my hand and watched as I did so. There was no indication that my hand had ever been injured at all. Except the blood that had soaked into my shirt sleeve.

How could I get my point across to him? More importantly, get my point across without pissing him off.

I stared across the small cavern. It was roughly twenty by thirty feet, a domed ceiling approximately twenty-five feet high at the center. On the other side of the cavern, I spied another piece of obscuring magic. I filed that away for a later time. I tried not to take in the four corpses along the far wall, but there's just so much I can ignore.

Jeremy stood in front of me, and I stared at the tops of his boots. A much better view than the dead. I heard the leather creek and stretch as he knelt down.

When I saw his face, I knew he wasn't happy with me, but who really is when they first meet me? Had Trey been? Nope. Marc? I had thought not, but now? Who knows? My father? When I stop laughing, I'll answer that. So why should Jeremy be any different?

"When the beast master brought me to the Enclave, I ran into the witches defenses," I started before he could get his clan master mad in gear. "I don't know how long I was incapacitated after. Twelve hours? A day and a half? I just don't know." I took another fortifying breath and took heart in the fact that Jeremy was letting me speak.

I related a few more recent incidences and their consequences and simply looked into his eyes for a breath or two before I finished.

"If I don't go in slow and have as many resources available to me as is possible, I could get myself or you killed." I dropped my gaze and shook my head slowly. "I'm not going in half-cocked for anybody. Not even a clan master whose mercy I am at."

He was so completely still he could be mistaken for a statue, and it wasn't until the silence was almost uncomfortable that he spoke.

"I understand." His voice was much less threatening, his physical presence less intimidating. I'm glad he wasn't going to push me to do anything right now. Of course, I wasn't particularly thrilled with the prospect of dealing with this at all—ever.

"So. Tell me who Erick Olafson is to you." He was still relaxed, but the question was still loaded. I skirted the question before without lying to him, but I didn't think I'd get away with it this time.

"He's my father." I waited for some sort of negative response. I wasn't sure what type, but knowing Erick as little as I did, I was certain there were a lot of people who didn't like him. He was an ass. So I waited.

Jeremy's expression didn't change. It was as if he was trying to decipher the words that had just come out of my mouth. English may not have been his first language, though he spoke it without accent. Finally, he looked confused, and I felt we were making progress.

"You mean he's your sire. He made you." Obviously, the concept of Erick fathering offspring was escaping Jeremy completely. I quietly found that amusing.

I didn't know him well enough to really fuck with him, so I went for quick clarification.

"No. I mean he had sex with my mom, and I happened nine months later."

"How is this possible?" he started. I thought about the girl witch and boy vampires remark I'd made to Trey a while back, but nixed it in favor of shutting the hell up. "I find it hard to believe I had no knowledge of this." Jeremy narrowed his eyes and looked me over in a whole new light. As I had looked for myself in my father when we first met, Jeremy was looking for the family resemblance between myself and Erick. It didn't take long for his expression to change from incredulous to belief.

"I didn't know about him until a few days ago," I volunteered softly. "I think he found me eight years ago, but I haven't had that conversation with him, so I don't know."

Jeremy sat in front of me and took my formerly injured hand in his and held it gently. He looked so relaxed, so nonthreatening that it was easy to forget he was a predator who could move faster than I could follow.

How many centuries had it taken him to perfect the look of ease?

"Why did your mother leave him?" he said, caressing my hand tenderly.

"The only thing she ever said," I told him, "was that 'being with him had never been a mistake, but staying with him would have been.' I never asked anything else."

He nodded thoughtfully. I expected that he was thinking on how he may be able to use this information to his advantage at a later date. But all in all, I thought Jeremy to be somebody I'd probably trust before my father.

"Where is your mother now?" The question was tentatively probing, and now I knew he was interrogating me. If he had tried Trey techniques, I'd have killed him, but I respected this approach.

"Dead." I felt the length of the day, the weight of the conversation, and the up and down spikes of pain and adrenaline had taken its toll on me. "Jeremy, I need to get out of here, regroup, plot, plan, scheme, and get some rest." He released my hand as I shifted my body to rise. "I'm sure you and your men need blood and rest as well. You will be safe in the Enclave."

Jeremy rose with me, but before I could organize myself to head out, there was a horrible noise. It echoed through the tunnel. An inhuman bellow of rage and pain, and frighteningly enough, it was calling out my name.

I had barely taken a breath to call out to my mate and felt the lifting of my heart knowing that he was all right and had come for me, when Jeremy's hand clamped over my mouth and his arm banded my body to his, keeping me immobile.

He hadn't used his energy to do so, but he was physically restraining me. It was nice to know he still a hands on kind of guy regardless of how powerful he was.

I struggled for the second before I realized that Trey hadn't made a sound normally associated with feeling safe. Jeremy had no idea what the hell was out there, but it was big, bad, and too close for comfort.

I relaxed. I breathed. I let my body lean in to Jeremy's and tried to achieve "bored."

"Valerie!" Trey bellowed again. "Where the fuck is she, bloodsucker?"

I snickered. Not that I doubted Trey's dislike for Marc, but they were trying to work together to find me; and though Trey was afraid for me, it was somewhat fun listening to the interactions.

"These goddamn tunnels all look alike!" Marc replied. "She's around here somewhere. I can smell her."

They passed before the obscured opening. Trey was dirt smeared and looked exhausted, but he was alive and well.

"I smell her blood!" Trey was really good at bellowing. I could tell he practiced a lot. "She's injured. So I'd advise you to find her, fang!"

I turned my head enough to catch Jeremy's eye and looked at him as if he were an idiot.

"Who's the blonde?" he whispered as he loosened his hand from my mouth just enough to let me answer him.

"Beast master of the Enclave. Trey," I whispered.

"You abandoned my mate!" Trey raged at Marc. I was concerned that he was going to bring down a section of ceiling if he didn't tone it down. However, he was a horny dragon on the edge. Nobody who got between him and his mate was his friend. Especially his mate's ex-boyfriend.

Jeremy looked at me questioningly. Yeah, that little piece of information would make a difference. Now he knew. I shrugged as if to say, "What? Not like it came up," and I waited.

"I was outnumbered! And if you haven't noticed, Valerie is quite capable of fending for herself," Marc retorted as he continued to try to find something that looked familiar.

I made a token move to free myself from Jeremy, but he tightened his grip. "Informative and entertaining at the same time," he whispered. "It's been weeks since I've been entertained."

I sighed and relaxed the best I could. I wanted Trey. I wanted to relieve his worry. I wanted to be alone and tearing up the sheets with him.

"I will eviscerate you!" Trey yelled as he paced the tunnel. "If anything has happened to her..."

They were moving down the tunnel away from us. The pace slow, but tension was ratcheting up between them.

"She was mine long before you!" Marc yelled. Jeremy looked at me and raised an eyebrow. I rolled my eyes and waited for this little piece of hell to be over. Yes, Jeremy was getting more information than I really wanted him to have, but there was little I felt I could do without causing undue problems. Like Trey trying to kill a clan master.

"She's mine now!" Trey's voice bounce off the stone, and a minute after, a fall of dust and stone trickled from the sidewall in the cavern.

"You haven't even managed to claim her!" Marc yelled back. Things were going too ugly really fast if Jeremy didn't let me go.

"Shit." I heard him hiss as he released me.

Yeah, that's right. There was a big shifter searching the tunnels for his mate so that he could claim her. I think the entertainment Jeremy had been enjoying just went south.

As I took a step toward the concealed opening, I grasped Jeremy's hand and called out to Trey.

"I'm fine, Trey. Jeremy and I had some things to discuss." I stepped through the opening with a vampire in tow. Trey turned and came to stand in front of me. He looked into my eyes with relief while glowering at Jeremy at the same time.

He reached out and caressed my cheek, making sure I really was there, safe and whole.

"Trey." I smiled. I knew there was work to do. The cleanup was going to take time and drain me, but it wasn't going to happen until the claiming was done, and I managed to crawl from our bed because Trey was too exhausted to drag me back. "This is Jeremy. Jeremy…"

The clan master stepped slowly around me and extended his hand to Trey. "I am Clan Master Jeremy MacLauren. I am honored to meet the beast master of the southwest region of North America."

The two men shook, but Trey was strained in his civility and stretched in his political correctness. In other words, the boy was ready to snap.

"It is I who is, of course, honored Clan Master MacLauren." As their grip broke, Trey slowly pulled me closer to him. His hands caressed my shoulders, and his body warmed with my nearness. "I do not wish to appear rude, but if you wouldn't mind, Marc will lead you to the Enclave and help you find your men."

Trey began to hustle me up the tunnel. Marc and Jeremy were close on his heels.

"The witches are dead," I said.

"That's nice," Trey replied.

Trey had warned me that the longer we waited, the worse it would be. He wasn't listening to anything but the pounding of the blood flowing through his nether regions. All the blood was going to help the little brain.

"Trey, is my aunt okay?"

"What? Oh. Apparently, she drained the energy out of all the pain amulets that you had made for Mila." Trey kept one hand wrapped around mine and an arm around my shoulders. As if he didn't hold me close, I would disappear. "She's stable."

I let out the breath I was holding, and my heart felt lighter. I wouldn't think about her future or the possibilities that it held for her. Right now, she was okay.

"How about Lance?"

"He's fine."

Every answer became more strained and clipped. I knew I was going to pay for this, but making him try to think with the big brain was amusing; and after what I'd been through, I needed a good laugh.

"I'm sure the infection is contained, but I'm going to need to do a thorough burn of the complex."

"Whatever you need."

"How many globes and what type are left?"

"Globes?" He was slowly starting to lose it. "I-I don't know. Sean, I'll ask him after."

"After?" I asked innocently. "After what? I have to get the logistics down as quickly as possible." I was going for the jugular.

We had finally broken ground, and the scent of fresh desert air hit me. He pulled on me and dragged me to his body.

"Quit pushing me, woman!" Trey raged with exasperation. Okay, maybe I went a bit too far, but it was fun to see the unflappable beast master at loose ends. "You will be lucky to see anything but the ceiling of our suite, let alone inventories or schematics for the next three days, and that's a conservative estimate!"

He threw me over his shoulder and picked up speed.

"I need a shower, Trey." I put just enough whining in it to make certain he knew I was messing with him.

"There are four broken tiles and two scorch marks in the shower stall, we proved we can multitask in there," he growled as he slapped my ass playfully.

"We are going to need to eat," I reminded him.

"You straddle my lap. I will feed you and fuck you at the same time." He came up on a vehicle and ordered everybody out. Well, that wasn't accurate. He more like growled loudly, scaring the shit out of the occupants to the point of abandoning the vehicle.

True to his word, Trey got me to the shower first. It felt good to be clean, and we added another broken tile to the collection.

There was no getting into our bed, but we did make it to the bed, so Trey got high marks for his continued restraint. Once there, however, all bets were off. He pinned my hands by my head and wedged his body between my thighs while lips and fangs kissed and nipped at my body.

I tilted my hips to invite him in and wrapped my legs around his waist. He refused to release my hands, but within a few seconds and shifting of his hips, he found the perfect angle and seated himself inside of me in two strokes.

His rhythm was hard, deep, and relentless. The shower had been the warm-up, a very good one I might add. I was ready. My body was warm, slick, and supple, taking everything he was giving me.

I lifted my head, reaching to kiss his lips, his jaw, his throat, but he pulled back and out of my reach with a growl and snarl.

I thrashed enough to test the strength of his grip on my wrists. It was solid, though he tightened even more and issued a low warning growl.

I remembered what he had said about female dragons trying to kill those who would try to mate with her. I'd told him I wouldn't fight him or try to kill him.

I lay my head back and moved my hips in time with his. My legs pulled at him, trying to drive him deeper still. I watched as his body tightened and tensed, waiting for the attack. I felt his claw lengthen as they scraped my wrists. I saw his fangs lengthen and knew this was it. No more nipping and scraping. This meant holding, pinning, and a bite that meant business.

His eyes held nothing but flame, his face a mask of want, lust, and animal instinct, and he was mine.

The only sounds were flesh sliding against flesh, the grunts and groans of desire, the need to climax, and the rasps and pants of our breathing.

Trey's body pushed me over the precipice first. I could feel my body latching tightly to his, milking him as he continued to pound into my body looking for his own release.

I felt Trey tighten his grip and adjust his position, readying to claim me. As the first true pulse of my orgasm hit, I stuck at him first. My fangs dug in at his collarbone, nicking the artery behind it and biting down hard. If he resisted, the bone would snap before I'd let go.

Trey snarled loudly and angrily. I could feel his fear, but at the same time, his rhythm didn't stop, and his struggles were token.

After one long draw from my mate's body, I bloodied myself to seal his wound as his body spun into release, and the dragon roared at the beginning of his climax.

I released Trey, turned my head, offering myself to his claiming. I moaned in the pleasure of my own release and the taste of his blood, warm and spiced on my tongue. His warmth, Trey's warmth. My mate.

I felt his lips touch my shoulder the moment before his fangs took it his claiming grip and pierced my flesh.

My waning orgasm spiraled up, washing over me in new, more powerful waves of ecstasy that drowned the pain into a distant memory.

In the span of a heartbeat or a breath, there was nothing. The silent beauty of two souls touching, each coming away with the knowing of the other so intimately neither would be the same.

Trey's scent became clearer, stronger. I knew it well, but now it was different. I was now a part of it, a part of him. Would my scent change as well?

My skin as his body slid over me felt caressed at a cellular level. He was not just my mate, but a part of me that lived within, not just by my side.

With all of the things I had yet to accomplish, I couldn't imagine leaving this bed. Ever.

I don't know when his hands had released my wrists, but my hand gripped his hair, and I held him tightly to my shoulder as our rhythms slowed.

His fangs shortened and released my shoulder. His body moved slowly, a caress of lovemaking. The frantic need to claim a mate, to stake a territory had been sated. Now it was us without the primitive need or aggressive instinct. It was the feel of how our bodies fit together, moved together, belonged together.

The only coherent sound for the next few hours was the contented hum of satiety. The occasional growl. A giggle. A moan.

Who needed words?

CHAPTER TWENTY-THREE

I Think I Heard Him Whimper

When Trey and I finally emerged from our suite, I learned something about the occupants of the Enclave.

They will bet on anything.

How long will the claiming last? Eighty-seven hours, twenty-three minutes, and thirty-seven seconds from the time the door closed to the time one of us stepped out for something besides retrieving the food set outside the door.

Three people got the time down to the minute. The seconds would only count if more than one person hit the trifecta.

Seriously, a trifecta.

How many meals would be brought to the suite?

Six. Didn't matter how much or little we ate, the meals went inside.

Seven people got that one.

How many tiles, total, would be broken in the shower?

Eleven.

Four got that one.

So twenty-one betting slots had been hit.

Four people hit two out of three slots.

Nobody got them all, but I was both impressed and a bit disturbed by the whole thing. I mean, how did anybody know how many tiles we had broken in the shower in the first place? What the hell?

There had even been a side bet regarding whether or not either of us would require outside medical attention at any point during the claiming.

We didn't. Okay, there wasn't anything I could handle at the time.

What surprised me most was that Clan Master MacLauren was one who hit two out of three. He had made introductions and connections quickly within the Enclave and was much favored over my father.

I supposed that had something to do with the fact that he and his men had been the ones to dispatch the witches.

All but my aunt.

There had been a call for her blood, but Sean maintained her safety personally. I owed him. Since he won two out of three betting slots and had recouped all his losses from betting against me the last time, maybe I didn't.

Yeah, I did.

Mila had cared for my aunt, and by the time I saw her resting comfortably in a guest suite, she looked much better. Older than her years, but more like the woman I remembered. Color flushed her face, the golden rings in her eye shown more brightly, and shame covered her face as I strode toward her.

I had called my aunts in Arizona and brought them up to speed. By the end of the call, they chastised me mercilessly for having not stayed in touch and were already packing.

The Enclave is a powerful fortress with a powerful witch protecting them. Yeah, I was feeling better about my myself and my abilities at this point. It might not survive the arrival of my other three aunts. They are a force of nature.

Aunt Maggie was sitting in an overstuffed chair that had been dragged to the balcony. No direct sunshine hit this side of the Enclave, but her skin hadn't seen daylight in months and simply being above ground was enough for now.

I pulled a chair up and sat at her side as she put the book she'd been reading aside. Historical romance. Where the hell she had gotten it was beyond me, and I would ask later.

I took her hand. She still felt fragile and breakable. It would take her months to recover, if she could recover fully. That witch had nearly killed my aunt, drained her of her knowledge, power, and nearly, her life.

For the first time in a very long time, my aunt smiled. There was an ease about her that had been gone long before she fled Arizona and the pain and grief that she had held there. Of course, when she left, she took it with her, and it had cost her dearly.

Sean had interviewed Maggie a couple days after she'd been brought in. I wouldn't call it an interrogation because my aunt referred to it as a "nice long talk with that hot shifter cat, and oh, by the way, is he single."

I read the interview before I'd gone in allowing me to be prepared for anything my aunt might say. I wanted to be a rock for her and for myself.

Before she'd made the acquaintance of the woman who subsequently tried to kill her, Maggie had been trying to work up a spell that would free me from my vampire genetics.

"Veronica had so many good ideas," my aunt said grimly. "Most of them involved using young vampires as test subjects." She looked out over the desert and sighed as her thoughts collected and her feeling coalesced. "I hated their kind. I believed they had been responsible for your mother's death, still do. But I just couldn't bring myself to do that. I figured it would make me as bad as them."

She squeezed my hand gently and looked into my eyes searchingly. "I convinced myself that you would be happier and more powerful if I could take those influences from you."

The smile I found was a sad one at best.

We sat for hours, had lunch together, and talked. I told her everything about the years she had missed with me. She wasn't pleased that my first love had been a vampire, but she looked oddly satisfied when I told her he had broken my heart. "Of course he had, he was vampire, and nothing good could come of them," she had said. "They don't know how to love."

I didn't know if I believed that. I didn't know enough to make that decision for myself. I thought them capable. Marc had been caring and kind. I didn't think all of his actions toward me were simply a reaction to keep his master happy.

When Maggie began to lag a bit, I realized that she had been pushed too far and needed to rest.

I felt better having talked to her and spent thirty minutes on the phone with my eldest aunt, Molly, telling her everything that Maggie and I had talked about.

All of my aunts were packed and would be hitting the road in the morning. I almost felt sorry for Trey.

As I stepped out of her room, I found a note pinned to the door. "Call me."

I had no doubt who it was from, and from the strained writing, I knew what it was about.

I hit speed dial as I headed back to our suite.

"Our suite. Now" was all he said and then disconnected. I felt heat rise through my body and the anticipation of making love to Trey settle between my thighs.

I was more than ready for him when I opened the door.

I didn't really have an idea what I would be in for. Eighty-seven-plus hours apparently took the top off for Trey, but satiety was a transient state, and he was back to horny.

I had barely stepped foot inside the suite before I was in his arms, and the door was kicked shut.

He was already starkers.

Gloriously, beautifully naked as the day he was born or, um, hatched. We hadn't gotten around to all the conversations we needed to have to know each other more properly.

I still hadn't gotten a job description.

We needed to talk.

"So how has your day gone?" I asked as he tossed me to middle of the bed.

He followed me down and began undressing me with a sense of urgency.

"Badly," he mumbled as my shirt and bra disappeared. "And you're not naked."

"Problems?" He tried to pull my chinos off, but they were caught on my boots, which were still on. He sliced through the shoelaces with his claws and pulled the boots off along with the socks.

"Yes," he said, barely sparing me a glance and solely focusing on the task at hand. "You still have clothes on."

The pants came off, and my panties weren't far behind.

"Not anymore. Problem solved." I laughed softly. "Now that your day is problem free, I need inventories and schematics." I just couldn't hide my smile. Trey was less volatile, but still edgy. I couldn't blame him. I missed the feel of him, the scent, the growling, and the curling up with him all warm and sated.

Trey eased me down to the bed by nuzzling my neck and kissing the mark he had left on me. Once down, he straddled my hips and reached for my wrists.

I suppose that since his first and only other attempt at mating before me resulted in the female nearly killing him, the dragon had some trust issues. Right now, the dragon was much closer to the surface and wary, even though I'd had him at a disadvantage more than a few times over the days we spent claiming each other.

We'd work it out. We had time.

Now seemed as good a time to start as any.

I grabbed his wrists, lifted my hips, and twisted. I got him flipped over and with a minimum of effort straddled his waist.

He snarled, but he didn't fight me too much.

"Trust me," I said softly as I found the dragon behind the soft blue eyes of the man under me.

"You have fangs," he growled like a put-out child. It was all I could do not to laugh, but I didn't think it would do any good in this situation.

"So do you," I reminded him. "And yours are bigger." A slow smile curled on his lips as his gaze fell to my shoulder where he had marked me repeatedly. I knew the marks would fade some over time, but they would never disappear. Right now, the angry-looking red wounds were still healing.

I leaned forward as he looked like he was going to speak.

"Ssh," I breathed out. My breasts grazed his chest before I settled my weight on him. "Trust me," I whispered. My breath caressed his lips, and then my lips brushed over his. Gently, softly, barely there.

I remembered the rental house, and the "barely there" kiss he brushed across my lips and how it nearly undid me in spite of the fact I'd been bound to another.

I wondered if it was the same for him.

A low growl was the answer to my unspoken question. He lifted his head to kiss me, but I pulled back, just out of reach. Trey looked almost hurt at my evading him, but he relaxed back and let my lips softly explore contours of his face and neck.

I let my fangs graze his throat as I shifted my body down and found that his cock was now firmly between my ass cheeks.

He groaned and brought in a sharp breath as I nicked him with my fangs and then soothed the sting with my lips and tongue.

The small taste of him lingered, and for a moment, I wondered if I would last long enough to do what I wished to him instead of slamming my body down his length and riding both of us to exhaustion.

I kissed the marks I had left on him. They were much smaller than mine and had finished healing as well as they ever would.

I knew better than to linger there. We found out pretty quickly that those marks were directly linked to arousal, and right now, I didn't need any help getting the beast master aroused.

He squirmed a bit beneath me as my kisses trailed to his chest. His skin was warm and smooth as my lips brushed across a flat dark nipple.

Trey's hips lifted slightly accompanied by a low and deliciously abandoned moan. He was beginning to lose himself under me. I smiled as my lips and tongue worked one and then the other nipple.

His breathing became more and more strained while his hips picked up a regular, slow thrust. He was going to come, if I didn't do something about that. I didn't want him to come. Not just yet.

I had a plan, and I was going to stick to it, damn it!

Of course, the length of him caressed the opening to my core and just touched my clit at its apex. If I didn't move, I'd climax before him.

I had to move. Okay, no, I didn't have to per se. But I really wanted to finish what I started.

I shifted my body lower and let my hands drift from his wrists to his chest. I nipped at his hip bones. Trey bent his knees and let them fall to the side, giving me all the access I would need to his body.

At this point, if I had been successfully attacked from above, I would have been impaled by Trey's cock and not in the fun way. I'm talking staked through the heart. The boy could drive a nail through concrete with that thing. I was hoping for a slow drag, my body skimming along its length as I dropped lower and lower, but no, I actually had to lift a bit to continue my journey.

Trey moaned and growled, but he didn't try to take over as I freed his wrists. His hands rested gently on mine as I let my nails skim and tease the hard buds of his nipples.

I made out the words "gods," "heaven," "Valerie," and "interrogation." His voice was barely human, and I could tell he was barely restraining himself to let me proceed unhindered. Not because he didn't trust me, but because he wasn't going to last much longer.

I was more than willing to give him this. A long, slow, full-body exploration and an orgasm that was his and his alone. He could focus on nothing else, but the sensations coursing through his body and not have to think about holding out for me.

Though I do appreciate his "ladies first, second, and sometimes third before finding his own release" way of doing things in bed. Or the shower, balcony, random piece of bedroom furniture, and at some point in the future, various pieces of office furniture.

I had goals.

By the time my lips brushed over the satin-like skin of his erection, his body was drawn tighter than a bowstring, and he was holding my hands tightly against his hips. His breathing came out in harsh rasps, and his moans sounded pained.

I was taking that as a sign that I was doing my job very well.

I smiled to myself as my tongue ran over the flared head to find a drop of precum awaiting me. Salty with a bite and a warmth that had me wanting more. Luckily, I was well on my way to getting it if Trey's reactions were any indicator.

I eased one of my hands out from under Trey's and wrapped it around his base as I took him into my mouth and stroked slowly up and down his length.

I think I heard him whimper.

It's not easy to smile with something that large in your mouth.

I let my tongue swirl and caress as my lips kept him encased in the slick warmth of my mouth.

His other hand left mine as I realized he was now fisting the comforter and straining desperately to hold back.

On my most recent upstroke, I brought my head up to catch his gaze as he had been watching me.

"Come" was all I whispered, and I took him back into my mouth as he let go. His body released, not simply in orgasm, but the stress and tension of old fears and uncertainty.

I was his mate.

Not because he subdued me and I hadn't managed to kill him, but because I wanted to be with him.

We had a lot to learn about each other. If it was all like this, then I would thoroughly enjoy each and every discovery. I was sure that it wouldn't all be this amazing, but I believed in balance, and this experience could balance out a whole mess of unpleasantness.

At Trey's last shudder—and yes, I had heard him whimper—I released him and slowly crawled back up his body, pausing here and there for a kiss, lick, or nip as he lay more still in our bed than I'd ever seen him outside of being asleep.

What amazed me most was that fact that he was now flaccid. I'd never seen that before on him. Semi-erect, yes. Unable to go again after one orgasm? No.

I suppressed the urge to do a victory lap and simply looked into his eyes.

Flames burned deep behind the blue, and his body had a fine trembling to it.

His breathing slowed, and he still said nothing but held my eyes with his.

Finally, his arms wrapped around me. He delivered a gentle kiss to my lips and rolled me to my back.

And then, the unexpected happened.

He rolled to his side, threw a leg over my hips, an arm across my chest, snuggled into the crook of my neck, and began to snore softly.

He was out like a freshman at a frat party.

It was still light out as I dozed on and off, letting my thoughts take me here and there.

Trey hadn't budged, and I was feeling awfully smug about it too.

From the angle of the sun, I knew that we had a few hours before we would have to meet with Erick.

My thoughts drifted to the things I still needed to do, and clearing the witches' base was top on the list.

I knew it was going to take a lot of energy to get the job done, and I wasn't looking forward to it.

Looking at Trey's still-sleeping form, I wondered if I could access his energy to get it done instead of using mine and losing a day. He did seem to have a vast reserve.

So the first thing I would do when he woke and was ready for grown-up conversation would be to ask him.

Then, of course, I'd need those damn schematics of the base and the inventories of the globes. If there were any beings still in the base,

I'd want them out before the burn for obvious reasons. Some of the globes may be useful in case I ran into any defensive magic that had survived Veronica's death.

I sighed, and Trey nuzzled my neck, took a deep scenting breath of me, and tightened his hold on my body for just a second before he relaxed and began snoring again.

I also remembered that I had three aunts who were on their way. I needed to call Sean and let him know to have arrangements made for their visit. I had no idea how long that would be, but I'm sure it would involve Maggie and her fate. So let's just call that an indeterminate length of time.

The phone was just out of reach, but if I could inch over…

The low warning growl rumbled in his chest, and the clenching of his body effectively stopped any progress I'd made toward the phone. Which was none.

"Come on, Trey," I said softly, hoping to rouse him. "Things to do. The bed will still be here later."

"It can wait," he rumbled against my neck.

"What can?"

"Whatever it is."

I had suspected as much. No real coherent thought was present as of yet. "But my aunts are coming." He rolled on top of me and pulled my legs around his waist so fast I was impressed as hell.

"Not before you do," was all he said as he slid into me in one smooth stroke.

....

By the time dinner had arrived, we had both worked up an appetite.

I had let Trey know about my aunts, what I'd needed from him in order to burn out the base, and I finally remembered to tell him about the silver vein running through the Enclave.

With that, I had just paid my own salary for the rest of my life.

Trey made sure that arrangements were made for my family and looked entirely too calm at the prospect. I tried to warn him that these women were all just a bit off-center and could be difficult to deal with in their own way.

I think I used the word "crazy" and the phrase "psychotic but not dangerous, well, not really dangerous" at least once.

My biggest concern was my aunts and father being in the same place at the same time. I wasn't sure I really wanted that, and I just hoped that Erick would be leaving with his people tonight.

The schematics and inventories were delivered along with dinner. I quickly figured out where I wanted to be when I did the sweep and the burn, and it all involved being topside. I did not need to nor did I want to be back inside that base.

With Trey's help, I hoped we could get it done tonight and still have time to sex each other up some more and get a full night's rest.

We had showered and were getting dressed when Trey circled my towel-clad body with his arms and kissed me.

"Wear a dress to the meeting," Trey half-stated, half-hoped.

I gave him a sideways glance. Not that I didn't want to christen his office, but sex before the meeting would be rude. Vamps, shifters, and weres had a sense of smell that would tell a story out loud that I just didn't feel like sharing. Especially, not with my father.

After the meeting would be fine, but it would likely put us behind in getting the base burned out. Not as much a problem, but I didn't want to get distracted.

That left during, and I didn't know if I could trust Trey not to go there if he got aroused and I was readily accessible.

I silently promised myself to give Trey a day that I would wear a dress, heels, and nothing else and not tell him until we were in a public setting where he couldn't do anything about it. I would pay dearly, and we'd probably have the best sex to date because of it.

I smiled at my own thoughts and then told him no. I pulled out of his arms with a kiss on the cheek and went in search of my clothing.

"A skirt?"

I shook my head and threw on the chinos I'd been wearing earlier.

"You better not like those pants," he mumbled as he dressed and followed me out the door.

Trey's office was crowded. Between those we had expected and Jeremy's contingent, it was packed. The two clan masters took seats as well as Trey. Marc took an empty seat next to Erick, and the rest stood behind their respective masters.

Sean joined us as well and briefed the room regarding the outcome of assault of the base. It was less an assault and more of a neutralization. Tonight, we would burn it and, hopefully, seal it from further use.

The surviving humans were well enough to have their memories wiped and reasonable memories installed to explain their disappearances. There were eight more vampires found than had been reported missing, because Clan Master MacLauren and his guards' disappearance hadn't been reported. There was another, but he hadn't belonged to a clan, so nobody missed him. Every were and shifter from the Enclave had been accounted for, though nine had been killed during their time in the base. The corpse I had found was Antonio. A werewolf. I didn't ask for details regarding who this person had been in life. There would be time for that later.

Trey lost one shifter from a team as a ceiling collapsed during the initial explosions.

It could have been so much worse.

I hated it that we lost anybody, but it was over. Now there would be celebrations for those returned and grieving for those lost. I still didn't know many of the inhabitants here, but I still felt a sense of loss as the names of the dead were read, and Trey made notes to send messages, gifts, and support to those left behind.

This had to be the worst part of his job here. I could see lines of stress bracketing Trey's mouth as he spoke to Sean and jotted things down on the tablet before him.

Both clan masters made notes and offered their own support to the families left behind. The gesture warmed me more to both of them. Even though it would be easy to believe it a political maneuver on my father's part, I couldn't see that for Jeremy.

I was already condemning my father for no other reason than I didn't like him. He and I were going to have to talk at some point, or we would have more problems.

The vampires had taken the least amount of damage in all of this, and they were being generous no matter what their motivation and, I think, grateful that their losses hadn't been higher.

I caught Jeremy casting me an appreciative glance more than once, and Erick looked proud.

Funny that it mattered to me. I guess it was because he approved of me. Not who he had wanted me to be, but who I was and what I had accomplished.

So hopefully Marc was off his shit list, and he'd be more than supportive and less of an ass.

The meeting wrapped up with tonight's plan for scanning the base and then burning it out.

"I'd like to stay for that," Jeremy said, "if you would extend your hospitality another day for myself and my men."

Jeremy was smooth and polished. His long blonde hair had been pulled back neatly at the nape of his neck, and he oozed a comfortable confidence that my father lacked.

Erick was confidence from power. Jeremy's came from centuries of experiences that had yielded him good fortune.

My father wished me the best in the endeavor, but he declined to be present for tonight's performance. As Trey and I followed the two vampire contingents into the hallway, my father stopped and kissed me lightly on the cheek.

I was surprised but not displeased at the display. Maybe he wasn't such an ass after all.

I mean, people have good days and bad. A lot had gone wrong with me as far as he was concerned, and he had to change plans and restructure his thoughts around me and my future. Right?

"I haven't yet given you a gift in celebration of your union," he announced pleasantly. This was the kindest I heard him speak since he had arrived, and my hopes sprung toward something thoughtful and meaningful.

"Marc." That was all he said.

CHAPTER TWENTY-FOUR

"No. We have religious experiences."

I was waiting for something else, like Marc presenting Trey and myself with a gift, a card, a song and dance number, something.

Marc, however, went even more pale than I'd ever seen him, and a side glance at Jeremy said he knew what was coming and didn't like it.

The other vampires in the hallway looked equally uncomfortable. Finally, Erick continued.

"Mr. Brighton has been a grave disappointment to me and has done you a great disservice as well as hurting you." Now I wished he'd shut the hell up. "He is no longer recognized as a clan member, and his current existence as well as his final death are yours to do with as you see fit."

Holy mother of all the gods!

Everything in me completely locked up. My expression was impassively blank as I groped around mentally for what this meant. I couldn't even look around to the other vampires for a clue, and Marc simply stood there mute, terrified, and angry all at the same time.

"I accept your gift Clan Master Olafson," I said smoothly. I had not one clue as to what I'd just done or what it meant, but Marc was now mine in a whole new way, and he and I were going to talk about this in short order.

"Well, then," Erick said happily as he clapped his hands together and then rubbed them vigorously. It reminded me of somebody whose plan was coming together. "I'm off, my daughter. The plane is waiting, and I have a meeting in four hours." He leaned in and kissed my cheek again and then offered his hand to Trey, who shook in amenably.

"It was a pleasure to have made your acquaintance, Clan Master Olafson," Trey said formally.

"No need for formalities. You are my son-in-law," Erick said, releasing Trey's hand. "Call me Erick." My father turned and walked down the hall. "I'll be in touch, my dear." He cast over his shoulder and disappeared.

The rest of us stood in stunned silence for a good minute before Trey finally spoke.

"What in the hell just happened?"

"I have no idea," I said as my gaze went from the empty hall to Marc's look of utter betrayal. "Marc?"

He glanced at Jeremy and then back to me. Anger and hurt shown clearly in his face as he searched for the words that would explain this, but he didn't want to have to say it.

"This is a private conversation, Valerie," Jeremy began. "I can meet you at the base."

"No," Marc cut him off with all the indignation he could muster. "You might as well stay. You know what happened, just not why."

Marc cast his eyes around to the faces that surrounded him. His ex-girlfriend and assignment, his ex-girlfriend's mate, the Enclave's second in command, a clan master other than his own, and five strange vampires. Marc was alone.

"I am cut off from the protection of my clan and clan master," he began. "He has given you my final blood. You may kill me, torture me, give me away, use me for your own entertainment or the entertainment of others." He took a step toward me. I could feel Trey bristle, readying to defend me if necessary. "I am yours to command, Mistress Hannigan." He dropped to his knees before me and looked up into my face.

I waited for an expletive to explode in my head. Marc had been abandoned, thrown away as if his usefulness had ended.

Instead of getting angry, my heart broke for him.

I closed my eyes, hoping to form some thoughts. When they opened, Marc still waited at my feet expectantly.

"Please, Marc," I whispered. "Get up." This pained me. I couldn't even imagined what Marc was going through.

"Yes, mistress." His voice resigned and movements precise as he rose before me and kept his gaze off mine. Submissive. Subservient. I didn't like it one bit.

"Don't do that, Marc," I said.

"Of course, mistress," he said and gave me a small inclination of his head in deference to my status over him.

I was going to have to throw him off the roof again.

"Okay. So Erick is the asshole he appears to be. Fine," I said. "You're free to do whatever you want then. You're a good rogue hunter, could you still work for the council?"

Marc shook his head, but Jeremy filled in the blanks.

"A vampire without a clan is an unprotected target. If he continues to hunt rogues, he does so without the backing of a clan master and the clan resources." Jeremy took a breath so he could keep on talking. I really needed him to keep talking because I still didn't have a clue as to what I was going to do with Marc. "Ex-rogue hunters are dead ex-rogue hunters very quickly if they have been turned out by their master. Erick will protect him as his gift to you, but if you declare him free of any ties to you, he will be permanently dead within a week."

I let that sink in. Marc had to remain attached to me in order to stay alive. Fuckity, fuck, fuck, fuck!

Ah, that was the expletive I'd been searching for earlier. It worked just as well now.

"Marc," I sighed. This was just too much for me right now. Even though my brain clicked into the guilty pleasure Marc and I had shared during our years together, this was not going to be easy. "The Enclave is your home now, so you can go anywhere you'd like." I smiled just a little, and I saw his mind take the same turn. "Except the west wing."

"What's in the west wing?" he said with a small return smile.

"It is forbidden!" I replied, and our *Beauty and the Beast* moment was concluded. I think something in him felt better for the moment. I know I felt better. Watching the Disney flick repeatedly was one of the simple joys we had shared. That and *The Princess Bride* and *Monty Python and the Holy Grail*. It was going to be weird, but we'd be okay. Marc would be okay. I hoped he'd be okay.

We had a history; it was still there. Now it looked like our futures were intertwined as well.

Trey and Jeremy looked at us as if we had lost our minds, but that was okay. We probably had.

"Catch up with me tomorrow night," I told Marc. "We'll figure this out."

"Of course, mistress," he said with the same inclination of his head to me. I now decided that he would do this just to annoy me.

"Marc, don't call me that."

"Um, Valerie?" Trey interrupted. I stopped and looked at my mate. My mate. It would take a while for that to sink in.

"Yes?"

"That's your title," he said quietly as if not to startle me. "You are the mate of the beast master of the southwest region of North

America." He paused waiting for me to connect the dots. I took too long. "You are the beast mistress."

Marc stifled a laugh. Bastard was going to milk that for all it's worth. I'd let him, but I'd give him shit as well. Marc had been made by Erick nearly 250 years ago and had been in service to him ever since. This depth of betrayal wouldn't heal without a lot of time and compassion.

Of course, there was always the possibility that my father still had a spy in my life and in the Enclave.

Peachy.

I took a fortifying breath and tried to glower at Marc.

"Tomorrow night."

This time, there was a bow with a flourish, and he was gone.

Now I had a clan master and company, all who looked endless entertained.

"I think we will leave in an hour?" I looked to Trey for confirmation, and he nodded.

The clan master, his men, and Sean all made their departures, leaving Trey and me in the hallway.

"Do I have anything to worry about?" Trey asked as he drew me into his arms.

"No. Of course not," I said and kissed the mark on his neck.

He moaned low. "But you two have a history." His fingers went to my shoulder with a gentle caress that did things to me that should be outlawed, but we were in Nevada, so it was licensed.

"Yes. We have five years together." I breathed and was now sorry I'd worn pants. "Five years of working together, playing together, hanging out, watching movies."

"Having sex." Trey sounded uber unhappy about that, but it was a fact that couldn't be changed.

"Yes, having sex." I nuzzled Trey's neck and kissed it lightly. "But you and I don't have sex, Trey," I whispered.

I could hear his eyebrow go up. "We don't." It wasn't a question.

"No. We have religious experiences." I pulled back enough to see his eyes and gave him a wicked grin. "How many time have I said, 'Oh! Gods! Yes, Trey!'?" And I managed it with a great deal of orgasmic enthusiasm, which may have been a mistake.

Trey's smile turned predatory, and I ran for our suite hoping to get in and get my clothes off before he shredded a perfectly good pair of pants.

An hour later, we were heading out to the base, and my wardrobe was short one pair of pants. I decided that my salary would now include a clothing allowance.

When we arrived at the site, all of the tunnels were under constant surveillance against both incoming and outgoing persons. Apparently, Jeremy and Sean had gotten together and put Jeremy's extensive knowledge of the base to work since he and his men had been the personal guard to Veronica and her crew.

I consulted the schematics and found a spot dead center of the base.

Trey and I found a rocky outcropping that we made ourselves comfortable on as he pulled me into his arms and entwined our fingers.

He held me comfortably. I was ensconced between his legs. His and my arms wrapped loosely across my body. I leaned back and relaxed as Trey opened that pool of energy to me.

I slowly scanned the base for infection, magic, and life. I found all three. The schematics of the base lay by my side along with a pencil. I started making notes as to what I was finding and where.

Sean, a half-dozen people from the Enclave's security force, Jeremy, and his men had circled around us, waiting.

As soon as I had dismantled the traps that had been set, Sean loaded his men with counter spell globes and sent them in after the few beings that I sensed still in the base.

The whole thing took less than two hours including the burn. I was beyond ecstatic with the results. It was over. Though I was sure there were probably pockets of infection here and there in Nevada, I couldn't scan the whole state. My range was roughly five miles under the best conditions, which was impressive but not practical to use in a statewide search.

Maybe I could use a locator spell. I still had the original spell that I could use as a focal object. I'd think about that later. Right now, I was happily in Trey's arms, in the middle of the desert with a sliver of a moon overhead and an erection pressed against my back.

We also had six vampires watching us with unnerving stillness. Jeremy moved closer to us, and I addressed the clan master.

"Satisfied?" I asked as he stood over us and eyed me from head to toe. I felt Trey tense behind me, but he didn't move at Jeremy's approach.

"Witches are a confusing bunch, to say the least," he began smoothly. "I am glad that things worked out as they did. You certainly have shown yourself to be terribly useful."

"Well, thank you so much," I said with a little too much enthusiasm and thinly veiled sarcasm. I knew full well that he was happy to have let me live. It could easily have gone badly for me. I did like Jeremy, though I hadn't gotten to know him all that well.

Jeremy smiled in a way that I'm sure he'd practiced all of his undead life. It was relaxed and beautiful and hid the lethal predator almost completely.

"My main home is in the Cascade Mountains in southern Washington State," he said. Trey and I rose slowly from the desert floor and faced a vampire that equaled my father in levels of scary covered by a seamless veneer of sophisticated polish, tact, diplomacy, ease, and self-confidence.

I think it made him slightly more dangerous than my father.

"I cordially invite either or both of you to join me there any time you wish." He extended his hand, and I offered mine. His grip was cool and firm, and I could feel him trying to ease into my mind.

It was gentle, like a whisper.

I gave him a crooked smile and took my hand back.

"All you have to do is ask," I said graciously.

"I don't know what I'm looking for," he said quietly, almost uncertainly. Trey stepped up next to me, and though he didn't touch me, the action was almost possessive and protective. Jeremy took a wise half-step back. "Do you have any siblings?"

I thought that was a very odd question.

"No. Only child," I told him with a smile. "Can you imagine more than one of me?"

"I suspect that you are one of a kind," Jeremy said sweetly. Just how dangerous Jeremy MacLauren was, I hoped to never find out. He could put the most paranoid of person at ease with his easy charm, grace, and beatific smile. And still he did nothing for me.

"We're honored to have been of service to you and your people Clan Master MacLauren," Trey said evenly. The big guy certainly had a way of bringing things back to the here and now.

"No, certainly, we are in your debt, Beast Master." Jeremy stepped back, and without any signal I could discern, he and his men moved together as a unit just before they disappeared. With as fast as they moved, it's a disappearing act that no magician could hope to duplicate.

But that left me and my mate alone.

"What was that about, Valeric?" he asked, drawing me into his arms.

"Honestly, I'm not sure." I rested my head on his shoulder and soaked up the heat of his body.

"You're going to tell me what happened when you were alone with him in the base." His voice had just the right amount of growl in it to let me know that he'd more than willingly go after the clan master with a bowie knife if he didn't like the answer.

"I'm lucky to be alive, but for the most part, he was gentlemanly enough under the circumstances."

"What does that mean?" I felt his teeth graze the side of my neck, and I knew where we would be headed soon. It worked for me.

"It means that I've no complaints regarding the clan master and his treatment of me." I breathed as my head fell back, and Trey kissed my throat and ran his hands over the marks on my shoulder.

With the base burnt out, the infection well neutralized, Aunt Maggie recovering, my family on the way, my father gone, and Marc on pause, our work tonight was done.

But with my mate's not-so-subtle maneuvers to get me naked again, I knew my night was just beginning.